F. MA..

QUEEN
OF THE
PHANTOM WARRIORS

Romar Press

Romar Press

3157 CR 518, Stephenville, Texas 76401
publisher@romarpress.com
www.romarpress.com

Text and Illustrations Copyright © 2024 by Romar Press
Cover Model: Aspyn F. Dent

Any resemblance to actual persons, living or dead, or actual events is purely coincidental.

Hardover: ISBN 9798985360950
eBook: 9798985360943

All rights reserved.
This publication may not be reproduced in whole or part in any form.

Table of Contents

1 A Soldier's Funeral 1
2 A Grave Moved 13
3 Broken Sabre Ranch Gathering 21
4 Bernadette and Sonia 31
5 Taking a Story 41
6 The Ludwig Estate 49
7 Saying Goodbye 55
8 The Interviews 57
9 Anna Meier 59
10 African Royal 63
11 General Scott Interview 71
12 Retrieving Three People 77
13 Indifference Toward the Enemy 81
14 Interview with General Scott Columbia 83
15 Akita and FRBs were the Target 87
16 Insane 89
17 President's Orders 93
18 The Hunted Becomes the Hunter 97
19 Anna's Second Interview 101
20 Domplatz 105
21 Julia 109
22 Nikita Wolf 113
23 Mom 117
24 Kirsten 121
25 Betrayed Friendship 125
26 Lady Savannah 127
27 Petra 129
28 The Dance 131
29 Wedding Plans 135
30 The Death of the Last FRB 139
31 Shots Fired 141
32 Cover Up 143
33 Eliminating Evidence 147

34	A Hand Found	151
35	Morgan	153
36	Setting the Trap	157
37	Robin in Control	161
38	Unwanted Guests	167
39	Texas Ranger	171
40	Helping a Friend	175
41	Jo	179
42	State Trooper	183
43	Lessons Learned	189
44	Arranging Transport	195
45	The Hand Over	199
46	First Date	205
47	Unsolved	209
48	Leadership Meeting	213
49	Warrior Queen	225
50	Mom's Way	231
51	Dining with the Boss	235
52	Capture Worldwide	239
53	A Head Taken	247
54	Skinner's Orders	257
55	Face to Face with Skinner	263
56	The Gift	271
57	Three Years Later	275
58	The Trip to Wetzlar	277
59	Urbarra	281
60	Clandestine Meeting	285
61	Mahthildis	289
62	Memories	293
63	Lazy Ass	297
64	Lady Savannah Arrives	301
65	Cunning	307
66	Cursed Savage Queen	311

F. MAYS

QUEEN
OF THE
PHANTOM WARRIORS

CHAPTER 1
A SOLDIER'S FUNERAL

Lee Ann works for a network news company in New York City, but we will not divulge the name. She remembers well when she received the assignment that would change everything: her, the world, the way she understood it. Her boss Mike Makary called her into his office. Mike sat behind his desk and talked on the phone. He motioned her in and then told her to sit. The top of Mike's desk was clear in the center except for his nameplate. It read "Editor and Chief." Stacks of books, folders, and papers more than a foot high covered both ends of the desk and had spilled over onto the floor.

As she sat there waiting for him to finish his call, she thought, *how did he work this way*? He finished his call, leaned back in his chair, and said, "I am sending you to Peacock, Texas. You will be covering a soldier's funeral."

She compliantly said, "Yes, sir." However, questions were already starting to form. A lot of them.

Her assignment seemed straightforward enough on the surface, but she felt an intuitive uneasiness. The soldier's name was Clint Haddox.

Mike asked, "Are you familiar with a Four-Star General named Robert Scott?"

Lee Ann hesitated, thinking through the list of generals she'd heard of. "No, I can't say that I am," she said decidedly.

Mike explained, "Well, he has enough power and influence to request you by name. He contacted the owners and upper management and specifically asked that you be assigned to this story. I don't know General Scott. I've only heard of him in rumors."

She patiently waited to hear more.

"To tell you the truth, this is a waste of your time and talent to cover a story about a funeral of some soldier no one's ever heard of, but I don't really have a choice. I need you to interview Scott. I gave Kim all the information on this, and she's booking your travel to Texas."

Then he turned around and picked up the phone to make a call. To Lee Ann, it seemed that she was being dismissed. Mike glanced sideways at her, heaved a sigh, and said, "If you have any problems, let me know."

A Soldier's Funeral

"Ok," she said as she stood up. There was nothing more to say. Mike had already moved on to the next thing on his lengthy list for the day. She showed herself out.

Lee Ann stopped at Kim's desk. As her assistant, Kim sometimes knows what Lee Ann needs before Lee Ann herself knows it. Kim is middle-aged, small in stature, and speaks with an English accent. Her trademark is her no-nonsense demeanor. Lee Ann asked her, "What can you tell me about this story, and where the hell is Peacock, Texas?"

Kim explained, "The funeral is on Friday, at 11:00 a.m. sharp. Don't be late. This is a military man's funeral."

It seems like she was suddenly encountering a number of absolutes. "Ok," she told her. "I promise I won't be late."

"I've made all your travel arrangements, and I'm glad you're going and not me," Kim said.

"Thanks for that," Lee Ann added anxiously waiting on the information she was about to provide.

Looking at various notes and her computer screen, Kim explained the itinerary. With a slight wrinkle in her forehead, she explained, "I don't think you'll like the last part of this trip. Here are your tickets on American Airlines, Flight 222 from La Guardia. You have a connection in Dallas to Abilene, Texas, on American Eagle, a twin-turboprop aircraft."

"Turboprop" is a generous description. Lee Ann later found out that the locals call these planes "puddle jumpers." No room for a roller-bag, carry-on. If it can't fit under the seat in front of you, they take it away at the gate, and all you can do is hope you'll see your bag again on arrival.

Kim continued, "In Abilene, you'll need to pick up a rental car; here's the contract for the car. Next, you'll need to drive seventy-seven miles to Aspermont, Texas; I have sent you a pin drop."

Her head was starting to swim a little as Kim continued, "You will overnight in Aspermont. Unfortunately, we didn't have much in the way of lodging choices. Aspermont has one motel."

Leaving no space for Lee Ann to ask a question, she announced, "Then the next day, you will drive twenty miles to the Double Mountain Cemetery in Peacock, Texas," and you'll be where you need to be. Again—on time, I hope."

She took it all in and organized the tickets Kim had just handed her.

A Soldier's Funeral

"I will be there. So, who is General Scott?"

Kim said, "I've found out very little about him. Maybe you will have better luck."

Later that afternoon, Lee Ann made time to do a little research on Clint Haddox, Robert Scott, Aspermont, and Peacock, Texas. Kim was right. She didn't learn much. She found the route to Aspermont and the motel where she would be staying, but she could find nothing about Haddox or Scott. It seemed as if they did not exist. Were these guys phantoms?

The flight from New York to Texas was uneventful, but the flight from Dallas to Abilene was horrible. The small plane had a rough time taking off with engines straining and a grinding sound filling the cockpit. Once airborne, they hit all manner of turbulence, causing the plane to bounce and move in dizzying lurches from side to side. Lee Ann white-knuckled the arm rest and started to pray a little.

She looked out her window; the engine cowling had a data plate from Rolls Royce. She looked out the other side of the aircraft at the engine cowling's data plate; it was from General Electric. She had a bad feeling, thinking, *What a piece of shit plane I am on! Will it land safely?*

The landing was a little better than the take-off, but not by much. By then, she was deadened to fear. Of course, they had to wait longer than usual to exit because a portable staircase had to be installed. They exited the plane using portable stairs like the ones in old movies or Air Force One clips. It was a long walk from the tarmac to the main building.

The heat was unbearable, over 100 degrees. She wondered how people live in this climate. She was happy to be on the ground and off that shitty plane. At least the Abilene airport is tiny and easy to navigate. She got her bags, retrieved her rental car, and headed out.

The drive to Aspermont was different from what Lee Ann was used to. What seemed to go on forever were open fields with brown grass, mesquite trees, weeds, cattle, oil field tanks, and pump jacks. It looked hot, dusty, and empty.

She saw rabbits. Some froze in place, others ran. Two of the rabbits that ran, she swears they wanted to commit suicide. All they had to do was stay off the road and run straight.

But they ran at top speed and turned onto the road in front of her

A Soldier's Funeral

car. Lee Ann wondered if that was a bad sign.

She saw feral pigs and deer in the fields, and one deer jumped a five-strand barbed wire fence with little to no effort. She saw a pack of wild dogs with bushy tails, learning later from the locals these were coyotes.

This trip also required that she adjust to a different brand of driving. The speed limit is 75 mph. Most people do 80 mph, some much faster, some slower.

The slow ones, including the trucks hauling crude oil and oil field equipment, move over and drive on the shoulder until the car behind them passes. Lee Ann had never seen this before. Almost everyone in the oncoming traffic waved at her as if they knew her. It was a lot for her to get used to.

Aspermont is a small town and the county seat of Stonewall County, with a population of 838. The distance from one end of town to the other is about two miles as the crow flies. The main street through town starts with two lanes and expands to four. The road narrows back down to two lanes at the other end of town. Broadway, the main street, has no stop signs or stoplights.

Driving through town, Lee Ann noticed abandoned homes and buildings in various stages of disrepair. Several are falling apart. One large house on the left side of the road must have been beautiful when it was built. It was a two-story home with carved woodwork on its eaves and overhangs. Now the roof has sections missing and sags. Windows were broken and missing. Doors were missing or hanging by one hinge. Lee Ann wondered what had happened to the family who lived here and how they or their ancestors could allow this to happen to their home.

About three hundred yards down the road and on the right side was another building. It appeared to have been a gas station or repair shop built in the forties. The front of this building had buckled outward by a foot or more about halfway down from one outside wall to the other outer wall. The roof had collapsed, causing the entire structure to become misshapen, creating a large opening in one of the side walls.

As Lee Ann drove slowly past, she could see a car inside through this hole. It appeared to be a 1969 Dodge Super Bee. When the roof of the building caved in, the vehicle was destroyed. Seeing the sad situation, Lee Ann suddenly thought about her dad who loves old muscle cars. He would have been heartbroken to have seen this.

Large empty lots in town were overgrown with weeds and mesquite trees. She saw kids driving golf carts and four-wheelers on the roads in town. Lee Ann found out later that the sheriff allowed this if they stayed off the main road. So much for law enforcement.

Her phone rang. It was Kim calling with the phone number of a local man named Ned. The cemetery was not in Peacock but was about seven miles away on a county road. Ned would guide Lee Ann to the graveyard since he was going out there anyway because his father owned land nearby, and he needed to tend to the cattle. Kim told Lee Ann to call him when she was ready to go.

She found the motel and paid for the room. Of course, the furniture was decades old, but everything was clean. Lee Ann was exhausted, so she showered and went straight to bed. She awoke several times that night to unfamiliar sounds; this was not the city she was used to.

She woke up at 6:00 a.m. in the morning. She had packed a black dress, thinking in this part of the world, people would expect tradition. Her only black dress happened to be very slim fitting, but she didn't have a chance to shop for something else, so this was it. She smoothed out the wrinkles and wriggled into it. Then she took a long look in the mirror, turning one way and then another, trying to decide if she'd attract any unwanted attention. She decided to add her Chanel scarf to soften the look and pull attention away from the accentuated parts of her figure. Thank goodness for the accessories.

She left the room about 7:30 a.m. It was hot again today, already 90 degrees. *Welcome to Texas*, she thought. She was hungry, so she stopped at the café for breakfast. Without hesitation, she opened the door and walked into the main room. As the door slammed behind her, everyone in the place stopped what they were doing and looked her way. They all had the same look on their faces that communicated one question: "What the hell are you doing here?"

The café looked to have been built in the 1940s and never remodeled. Fluorescent lights dimly lit the place, and what were once windows were now filled with air conditioner units. The tables and chairs were mismatched and from maybe the 1970s. Lee Ann hoped the food would be better than the decor. A quick glance at the clientele assured her that she was out of place here. She was in a genuinely nice black dress and heels, and everyone else wore jeans, overalls, and work clothes.

The server told her to sit anywhere. She picked an empty booth, pulled out her phone, and called the number Kim gave her for Ned. She heard the phone ring in her ear just as another phone rang in the café, and a man's voice answered, "Hello."

"Is this Ned?" she asked.

He laughed and said, "Yes, I am over here." He waved, then stood up and asked, "Will you join us?"

She slid out of the booth and went to his table. He shook her hand and said, "I am Ned. This is my wife, Ruby." Lee Ann shook Ruby's hand. Ruby gave her a polite nod. Ned said, "This is the only café in town, and we eat here every morning. I just knew you were Miss Bream, the New York reporter, the minute you walked in that door." She sat down and joined them. The server took her order and brought her a cup of extremely hot coffee.

Without hesitation, Ned asked, "Why all the interest in Will Chisum's nephew"?

Lee Ann explained, "I'm here to cover the funeral at the request of General Scott."

Ned said flatly, "I've never heard of him."

They finished eating, and Ned asked, "Are you ready?" Lee Ann tried to pay, but Ned had already paid the bill. "That's just the way we do things around here," he laughed and then asked again, "Are you ready?"

Lee Ann said. "Yes, I have all my gear in the car, and thank you."

As they walked in the parking lot, Ned told her, "I'm in that white Chevy truck," pointing to one of five in the parking lot. She pointed out her rented car. Ned said, "Follow me. I'll take you to the cemetery, and then I need to move my cattle."

Ned waited for her to pull behind his truck. They went through town and turned on a two-lane road. The landscape was more of the same brown grass, weeds, mesquite trees, and more Kamikaze rabbits. Lee Ann wondered how people lived under these conditions. They drove about fourteen miles on a paved road. Then it forked with a dirt road to the left. They took the dirt road.

Lee Ann felt on edge; she knew nothing about the man she was

A Soldier's Funeral

following, except that he'd been nice enough to buy breakfast. She wondered where he was taking her. Then thoughts turned darker, and she worried about the more sinister danger of depending on a stranger in the middle of nowhere. She wouldn't call this desolate goat trail a road. It was rough and full of potholes, rocks, and washboard bumps. They drove three miles and turned left at the top of a rise. The cemetery was on the downslope of the rise.

Ned stopped his truck, got out, and walked back to her and said, "This is it," and then he frowned, adding, "I don't know why anyone would pick this place to be buried. It's unkempt, unused, uncared for, and a forgotten place."

Lee Ann looked around the area. The grounds had not been mowed in a long time. The weeds were ankle to mid-calf high and covered all the headstones, and the fence around the graveyard had fallen in several places. Ned took a long look at the people who had gathered. "None of these people are from around here." Then he asked, "Why are they here?"

Lee Ann counted about sixty people at the gravesite. Their clothes were luxurious, well-tailored, and had a distinctive European appearance. It was obvious that they were designed outside of the U.S. She didn't know what to say, so she simply said, "Thank you for everything, and I hope to talk to you later," deliberately ignoring his observation and question.

She got out of her car and walked to the gravesite. As she approached, a man came toward her. General Robert Scott was a black man wearing an Army dress uniform with a Green Beret. Green Berets are the smartest, most lethal fighters in the world. About 5'8" and weighing around 270 pounds, he was an older man, and an imposing figure. His face was stern and lined. He smiled at her and said, "I am General Robert Scott. I asked for you to be here, and I am glad you came all this way."

Lee Ann shook his hand and asked the most important question on her mind, "Why am I here?"

The day was hot, still over 100 degrees and dry. The wind stirred up dust. Double Mountain Cemetery was not a pleasant place to be. When Lee Ann had arrived at the cemetery, someone or something was watching her, tracking her, or so she thought. She looked around but found nothing out of the ordinary. This premonition grew stronger with time. She had no explanation for this feeling, and it was unusual for her to experience the unexplained. She did not like what was happening to her.

General Scott said, "I want you to record the life of a man who was a throwaway child, an unwanted wayward drain on society. He became a soldier first, then special forces. In time he became the elite of all elites, a ghost. He lived two lives. For me, he was a hunter of men. He led a team of men just like him. As for others, he earned the respect and admiration of a city on the other side of the world."

Lee Ann stood there in silence and disbelief, finding it a challenge to comprehend what she'd just heard. She wondered why General Scott had requested her specifically? What would make him think she was the person capable of writing a story of this caliber about an enigma?

General Scott elaborated, "The people came here for the funeral of a man they knew as 'Akita,' my man Chief Warrant Officer 3 (CW3) Clint Haddox." General Scott's attitude shifted. He asked," Do you know how he died?"

She explained, "All I could find was the police report on the accident that killed him. I was unable to find anything more about Clint Haddox."

General Scott said, "Akita joined the Army at sixteen-years-old. When a member of my company dies past or present, I receive the police report. After receiving the information on Akita's death, I had the Director of the F.B.I. send agents to investigate how he died and interview Mr. Clay Jenkins. What I know was in the agent's official report. Akita was on his way back here from Lubbock in a thunderstorm. He stopped his truck when he saw a rancher trying to herd cattle off the road. He started helping, and when he finished a car hit and killed him."

This was all more than Lee Ann could take in for a moment.

Then General Scott clenched his fist and said with as much restraint as he could muster, "I want that mother fucking asshole that killed Akita." He stopped and said no more.

This was a lot to take in. "Do you want the driver to go to jail? For manslaughter?" she asked.

He looked at her hard and said, "No." He glanced around, then changed the subject, and said, "Peacock is a small town, and there are more people here at the funeral than the town's population. We had this group here early, and they are about to leave. Will you please hold your questions until they are gone?"

"Yes, of course," she said. When the people were leaving, she noticed that English was not the primary language being spoken. German (Deutsch) was the language everyone was speaking. Almost all of this group were women that she surmised to be between forty-five and fifty. After the ceremony, they hugged, kissed, and cried before leaving the cemetery.

A young man called for the group's attention and said, "My name is Alex. I work for Will Chisum. Will has asked me to guide you to the ranch."

As Lee Ann started to walk to her car, General Scott put his hand in front of her and said, "You need to stay."

Alex continued, "I am in the black Chevy truck over there. I will wait for all of you on the road, so you can follow me to the ranch." An older man let him know when all the people were in place and ready to leave. Alex drove slowly enough not to lose anyone.

General Scott and Lee Ann watched them slowly drive away.

She asked General Scott, "Where are these people from, and why are they here? How did they know Clint?"

He said, "They are all from Wetzlar, Germany. They were a part of his life when he was there."

Lee Ann wondered aloud, "What would make them travel so far? What was he to them? Where are they staying? The motel doesn't have enough rooms."

He explained, "They are staying at Will Chisum's Ranch, he was Akita's uncle and has asked them to stay with him at the ranch. We are supposed to join them there later. Will told me they have a Tex Mex style barbecue for all people here and the ranch hands."

She said, "We"?

He looked at her and said, "Yes, but first we need to make it through the next part of this."

Lee Ann questioned, "What's the *next* part?"

General Scott said, "I need to introduce you. The seven of us are the only ones who have been allowed to stay for the next part of the ceremony." Then he called them over and introduced Savannah, Petra,

Kirsten, and Sonia. General Scott said, "We have some time before the VIP's show. Please tell Lee Ann a little about yourselves. I need to call in the all-clear. Please excuse me." He walked away from them. All of them were standing in ankle-deep weeds and red sand, which was loose and gave way under the pressure of their high heels making it difficult for them to walk.

The older man who had helped Alex came over. "My name is Will Chisum," he said, extending his hand. Lee Ann introduced herself.

He was in his late seventies. His face and hands were worn from the sun and scarred from years of hard work. Will said, "The trip to the ranch will take them about an hour. I've invited everyone from out of town to stay at the ranch. Between the ranch house, bunkhouse, and a house built for Clint and his daughter Savannah, there's more than enough room."

After a brief exchange, Lee Ann found out Will Chisum was a Green Beret and had served three tours in Vietnam. After ten years in the Army, he left service to farm and ranch.

He hugged Sonia and said, "How have you been? It has been too long since you were here last."

Sonia introduced Will to the group. All the women except for Savannah were in their mid-to-late forties. Savannah had the kiss of youth and was probably just barely twenty. They were all stunning. They were all German. Lee Ann turned toward Sonia. The single word "beautiful" did not do justice to her. A goddess would be jealous of her face, deep blue eyes, flawless skin that had been kissed by the sun, long sandy blonde hair that went past her belt line, and an hourglass figure that could stop time. Sonia was wearing a tailored black silk dress with metallic gold lace edging the hem. After a round of introductions, she told Lee Ann that she's a physician, a G.P. with a clinic and hospital privileges.

Kirsten stood next to Sonia. Stunningly beautiful with a well-proportioned figure, she had playfully short blonde hair and piercing brown eyes. She looked directly into Lee Ann's eyes, making her feel like she was reading her mind. Sonia said, "When Kirsten wanted to, she could walk into a room, and everyone, men and women, noticed her." Kirsten, wearing a long black gown with a slit that showed off her muscular thigh, blushed a little.

A Soldier's Funeral

Petra chimed in, "One time, Akita overheard a lady say that look and that walk is pure sex!! Pure sex!! He often told her this fact."

Kirsten changed the subject and told her that she owned two beauty salons, one antique shop, and a car dealership.

Petra looked much younger than her age with the face and body of a supermodel, blue eyes, and shoulder-length brown hair. Sexy defined her. She explained, "I'm the owner of four clothing stores, and we export clothing to six countries." Her fashion sense was demonstrated in the short black dress trimmed with red that she wore. It was definitely tailored to show off her figure.

All three women were hard bodied with extraordinary muscle definition.

All Lee Ann could do was nod and ask, "How do you all keep so fit?"

Kirsten said, "All of us have years of martial arts training, weightlifting, and jogging. It is hard work but well worth the effort." Then she laughed and posed like a female body builder and asked, "What do you think?"

This time all Lee Ann managed to say was, "Wow."

Finally, she turned to Savannah who said, "I'm twenty-years-old. I'm in my third year of college. It hasn't been easy, but I've kept my 4.0. G.P.A. Akita was my dad, and he raised me by himself."

"I'm sorry for your loss," Lee Ann said.

Savannah was standing next to Sonia, and Lee Ann noticed they had a similar build. Savannah had more muscular definition and looked strong. Something about her exudes power.

She asked if they were related, but Savannah said they had just met for the first time. Lee Ann was surprised that two people who lived half a world apart could look so much alike and not be related. Sonia didn't say anything.

General Scott returned and said, "Now for the dog and pony show." He looked at the group. "I am sorry. I know none of you wanted this, but you cannot tell these people no."

Kirsten said, "They have a right to say goodbye. After all, Akita and the FRBs worked for them." Savannah and Sonia both looked uneasy.

Lee Ann couldn't let it pass and asked, "What does FRBs stand for?"

Together they said, "Fucking Rowdy Bastards." It was then that she

A Soldier's Funeral

noticed Petra, Kirsten, and Sonia were wearing identical necklaces, a gold pendant with three letters FRB hanging from a gold chain.

Lee Ann knew then this wasn't going to be the ordinary assignment that she had thought it might be.

At this time, the Secret Service and other heads of state security drove up in a motorcade of black vehicles. It was clear some especially important political people wished to say goodbye to this exceptional soldier.

Shortly behind the first group of cars, a second arrived. This group would consist of three Presidents of the United States and other heads of state. No one made any speeches. They said very few words except those expressing their condolences. Lee Ann had been around U.S. Presidents and heads of state before, so she wasn't star-struck.

President Bush shook everyone's hands and then said, "He was one of the most dedicated soldiers to serve under my command. Akita will be missed. The nation owed Akita a debt that could never be repaid."

Each one made sure to tell Savannah how proud she should be and how much Akita's service meant to them and the nation. The dignitaries left as quickly as they came. No one from town even knew this event had happened.

An uneasiness fell over the small group. Saying a final goodbye to someone you cared so deeply for was difficult.

This would be Lee Ann's first trip to this windy, God-forsaken place, but she suddenly realized that she was coming to love it from her first breath of dusty air. She couldn't have known that this story would take over her life. In fact, it would take over every person's life Clint "Akita" Haddox had touched, helped, or saved. Akita was a force of nature.

CHAPTER 2
A Grave Moved

Sonia flushed and was obviously upset. She turned to the two veterans and said, "So why the hell can't Akita be buried with his men behind the chapel on my family's estate in Wetzlar?"

The General hesitated, but before he could answer, the fraulein continued, "My ancestors built the chapel and the castle, and they have been buried there since the early 1300s. The FRBs asked me if they could be buried in my family's cemetery because Wetzlar was the only home any of them had known. I knew they were right. I was happy to do this for them. All the FRBs asked if I would have them buried with their brothers. Akita needs to be with his brothers."

Still upset to the point of being madder than hell, Sonia said, "My attorney told all the men. This request would need to be in their last will and testament. He filled out all the paperwork for the German and U.S. governments to have them buried in Wetzlar, Germany. All the men made me their sole beneficiary." Sonia looked intently at General Scott. "You know this, and you have copies of the paperwork."

For the moment, he let her continue.

Sonia went on to explain, "When three of them were killed in action. I received their bodies and buried them as to their request. They knew their lives would be short and have a violent end. I have eleven American special forces soldier's graves in my family cemetery, all FRBs. There is one that is missing—Akita. Why can't he be at home with his team of brothers? I want the only man I ever truly loved at home and at peace."

Kirsten interrupted, "You are *not* the only one who loved him. The three of us did, and all of us with our entire hearts." She looked straight at General Scott and said, "You need to understand that Akita made all our lives better than we ever imagined they could be."

With tears flowing down her face, Petra added, "I loved him. Akita was happy. He told me that Wetzlar was his home. I want Akita at home with his men where we can visit him on his birthday, Christmas, or whenever we need to. That is where he belongs."

By this time, all three women were in tears.

Sonia turned to Savannah and said in a voice cracking through the pain, "I am begging you, please let me take your dad home."

Savannah shook her head and cried. She addressed Will, "Please, we need to let him go. We can visit him. He will be home with his men and people who will never forget."

Will explained, "Clint told me once that he wanted to be buried with his family. I thought he meant here. His grandfather and older brother are over there. For that reason, I agreed to this location, even though I disapproved of anyone being buried here." Will looked at Savannah and asked, "Are you sure you want to let him go?"

Savannah took Sonia's hand and said, "I want my dad to be with you and his brothers."

Sonia grabbed Savannah and hugged her very tight. Tenderly, she said, "Your dad was my greatest love. Please come with me to Wetzlar. I want you to see where your dad will rest and the care and respect, we give him and his men."

General Scott, choking back tears, pulled out his cell phone and made a call. He said, "We need transport for CW3 Haddox's body today from Peacock to Wetzlar, Germany. Understand what I am telling you. Get a Chinook in the air now from Dyess Air Force base to here. I want it to land in the Peacock Cemetery. I need my jet at Dyess fueled and ready. We are going to Wetzlar today. Call me back in ten minutes with the confirmation."

General Scott looked at Will and said, "We need to let the funeral director know we will take Akita with us."

Will made the call. The conversation was heated. It ended with Will yelling, "He is my nephew, and I will move him. Do you fucking understand what I am telling you?" When he hung up, he continued, "I want my nephew buried with full military honors."

General Scott looked uneasy as he explained, "The Army will not allow it. It is impossible. His military records have been sealed. Akita's entire life was in the military in service for his country, and no one will ever know what Akita and the FRBs have done for their country and other countries." Then General Scott looked hard at Lee Ann and said, "I will tell you about Akita. When we get him to Wetzlar, I need you to print his story. I need his life to mean something."

It was clear to her that Akita had been important to General Scott. She simply nodded in agreement. She knew that she had a story from the little she had heard today, but she needed much more from Sonia, Kirsten, and Petra about when the FRBs were in Germany.

Lee Ann said, "I want the entire story. Clint—Akita's life before the Army. How did he get into the Army at sixteen? What did he do in the Army? What did the FRBs do that made three U.S. Presidents and other heads of state come to his funeral? More critically, why would three stunning, beautiful women love him simultaneously and know and like each other."

Sonia spoke up, "The only name I knew Clint by was 'Akita.'" It was hard for her to hear him called by another name.

General Scott explained to her, "I also called him 'Akita.' The only reason we were using 'Clint Haddox' was because of his family. I was concerned that Will would consider the nickname offensive."

Kirstin said, "Everyone thought 'Akita' was his real name, as did everyone that knew him in Wetzlar."

Savannah said, "I always called my dad 'Akita' since I was about two years old."

Will said, "I am not offended if you call him 'Akita'. I will try to use his nickname, also. After all, that's the name he preferred." Will asked, "How did he get that name?"

General Scott said, "He picked up the nickname after being in the unit for a little over three years. The FRBs came back from a mission. Four or five had suffered some injuries and were in the hospital. I went to check on them and heard the name 'Akita' for the first time. I asked what he had done to earn that name. No one would tell me. I only know that at first, he hated it and raised hell when anyone called him Akita. I still don't know how he got it. Only his team knew."

Sonia smiled, turned red for a moment, and said, "He did not like it at all. One night, the other guys were teasing me, telling me I was afraid to call him 'Akita' because then he would not like me. I told them that I didn't care if he liked me or not." Then Ed announced that if I was brave, I'd do it, so I had to stop them from messing with me. I knew they were playing around and trying to make me mad. So, I turned around, found Akita, and approached him. I smiled and said, 'Akita, dance with me.'

At first, he looked upset, but then he told me, 'Say that name again.' I did, and his expression stunned me. I will never forget what happened next. At the top of his voice, he said, 'I like it.' He gathered me up in his arms, lowered his voice, and told me that because of my accent, he didn't mind the name at all; in fact, he preferred it. Then he kissed me tenderly, a brief kiss it lasted less than one second. That single kiss sent shivers over me, and the hair on my arms stood up. I was terrified, this had never happened to me. I had been kissed before, but this was different. I remember I had to touch my lips.

Then Akita looked around at his team and said, 'All of you are a bunch of needle dick bug fuckers. Now I am Akita, a dog, it is still better than a bug fucker.' The entire room burst into laughter. That was the night I knew I loved him. I had never been so scared in my life. He was not the type of man I had envisioned loving.

Just then, she realized she had said too much. I am sorry. I remembered one night long ago. My story really doesn't explain the origin. I don't know more. I should not have spoken," Sonia said.

Savannah said, "Don't be sorry for good memories. I would like to know more about my dad when he was young. I know little about his life back then. He told me the three of you would always be with him, but that was all he said. I want to know more."

Kirsten said, "We can do that."

Sonia told Will that she'd make arrangements for everyone's departure from the ranch and their return to Wetzlar. To General Scott she said, "Please let me know when you arrive in Germany with Akita. That way, I can have my staff ready. I will have Klaus meet you at the gate. You will be in Germany a day before us. I will have my staff prepare a room for you."

Sonia then asked Savannah," Will you please come with Kirsten, Petra, and me? My plane will be ready tomorrow. You will be staying with me. After all, you are my daughter now."

Touched, Savannah said, "I never knew my mother. Why would you

A Grave Moved

say that I am your daughter?"

Sonia smiled, her eyes warm and inviting, "I always wanted Akita's child. Now I have his daughter. That is, if you do not mind having a German mom."

Sonia continued directing business. "I will also take you, Will. You've told all of us that you had more than enough room at your ranch. Now it's my turn. I have more than enough room on the plane and in my home. Please come and stay with me."

Before he could answer, Sonia said to Lee Ann briskly, "You will also come with me. I will give you the room and time for everyone to tell you about Akita."

Her reporter instinct was already on overload. "Thank you," she said. "I need to check with my boss and let him know where I will be." She walked away from the group, took out her cell phone, and called Mike. He hadn't wanted to send her to this backwater town in Texas. Mike was in his late 60s, and on such items, he was often right. In this instance, he was wrong.

Mike answered the call on the third ring. She blurted, "I have to go to Germany tomorrow. I have more interviews for this story."

Mike answered, "No, I need you on this White House story. I can send someone else."

She said, "This invitation is for me alone to tell the story of Akita and the FRBs."

Mike was silent for some time. This was unusual since he always had something to say. Finally, Mike spoke, and it was more of a question, "Akita and FRBs?"

Lee Ann said, "Yes."

Mike asked, "Are you sure?"

Again, she said, "Yes, I am sure."

I have heard whispers of the FRBs. I can send you a security team or send another reporter." Lee Ann *felt* more than *heard* fear in Mike's voice.

She answered, "So I'm too good to report on a soldier's funeral, but not good enough to write about Akita's funeral, life, and the FRBs." She was getting mad. She continued, "I'm doing this story whether you like it or not. I don't need security. So, tell me now. Am I fired?"

She heard an audible sigh and then Mike continued, "You aren't fired, but you don't know the world you're in now. The whispers I heard about the FRBs say they're the elite of the elite killers. It will be best if you're careful and check in with me daily. Will you please let me get you some security?"

Lee Ann said, "General Scott and Sonia want Akita's life story told. No one will speak to anyone else but me about this."

Mike asked Lee Ann if Sonia had a last name. She said, "Ludwig."

After a long moment, Mike said, "Shit! Do you know who she is? Is this Sonia Ludwig beyond belief beautiful? I mean Aphrodite beautiful?" Lee Ann told him she was that and more, plus she had been Akita's lover.

At this point, Mike was certain this was the Sonia Ludwig with the reputation, history and status. He continued, "She's descended from kings and queens. The Ludwig family is among the elites of European society. Her parents died five years ago, and she was their only child. She pursued and received a position in the Bundesnachrichtendienst Intelligence Service for the Federal Republic of Germany. Now she's second in command." He paused then said, "Son of a bitch, Sonia Ludwig is one of the wealthiest people in all of Europe. She lives in a 600-room castle."

"Why would she have anything to do with an American soldier?" asked Lee Ann.

"You need to find out," Mike replied.

"I *must* do this story," she said. With that, she hung up before he could reply.

General Scott approached and asked, "Do I need to make a call to your office and tell them you are coming with us?"

Lee Ann said, "No, but I need to know why you requested me for this."

General Scott looked at her directly and said, "I have seen your work. You have a terrible habit of telling the truth." He left it at that and provided no further information.

Lee Ann turned to Sonia and asked, "Did you have anything to do with this?"

Sonia smiled and said, "Yes, I did. I need Savannah to know her dad, that he was both good and bad. Savannah needs to understand why so

A Grave Moved

many people in the world loved him, why he meant so much to all of Wetzlar, and why I love him. Akita never told her. He couldn't. Now we can, and we must." This mission was coming Lee Ann's way.

Sonia continued, "She needs to know why I love her even when we had never met. I may not have given birth to her, but she is my daughter, not only mine but Petra and Kirsten's daughter. Can you understand this?"

Lee Ann didn't know how to respond to this, so she told her the truth: "No, I do not."

Sonia and General Scott smiled. Sonia said, "That's why you are here. You say what's on your mind."

General Scott chimed in, "When you talk to all of us and have all the facts, you will understand."

Sonia and Lee Ann joined Petra, making calls to get everyone to Wetzlar. She called her lawyer and said, "I have Akita. Please complete the arrangements for the funeral, and you know where I want him buried. When I die, I will be placed by his side."

Within fifteen minutes, they had all arrangements made to cover travel and rental cars returns for all the people from Wetzlar. Everyone would leave tomorrow.

Kirsten and Petra asked Savannah if they could help her pack, thinking this would be a good way to get to know her better. She accepted and said, "I would really like to get out of this cemetery, please."

General Scott looked at her and said, "You can leave. I am going to stay here and make sure that your dad gets to Wetzlar."

Savannah hugged him and said, "Thank you."

Will asked everyone to follow him to the ranch. It was decided that Lee Ann would spend the night at Will's, so everyone could leave for Germany together.

A moment later, when General Scott thought he was alone, he placed one hand on the coffin and said, "Your life was taken too soon. You left so many people who loved you. We are bringing you home. You will be with your brothers. I am happy that Savannah made this decision. She is strong in mind and body. I know you are proud of her. She lost you and gained three mothers. Please forgive me for the life I gave you. You deserved so much more."

Just then, the Chinook landed with four soldiers, all wearing Green Berets. They loaded the casket. General Scott left with them in the helicopter. At some point soon after, he called Savannah and told her tenderly, "Your dad and I are on our way. We will get him home."

CHAPTER 3
Broken Sabre Ranch Gathering

After Lee Ann collected her things from the hotel, she followed her guide Alex through the Texas wilderness. After an hour or so, she drove up a 20-to-25-degree incline, thinking that she was now in mountain territory. At the top, she saw several buildings, pulled into the driveway, and got out of her rental car.

She counted no less than forty-five pickups and twenty cars parked everywhere. She saw a group of people standing by a large two-story building and walked over to them.

The breeze shifted, and the smell of food cooking hit her. Large, sliding double doors at the front of the building stood open. The entranceway was about twenty feet across and opened to an area of sixty feet by forty feet.

On either side of the room two smaller doors opened outside. People filled the room, some standing and others sitting around tables talking. Kids of all ages ran around. Most of the boys and some of the girls wore cowboy hats and boots, and some wore spurs.

Will noticed Lee Ann and came over to her. He said, "I see you made it just in time."

"What's with the kids and their spurs?" she asked.

He said, "Well, it's basic. They needed them to ride."

With a hint of New Yorker incredulity, she posited, "They are too young and too small to ride."

Laughing right out loud, Will said, "They are *never* too young."

"What if they fall off?"

"They walk the horse to a fence, gate, or stump, use that as a step and get back on."

"What if they get hurt?"

Growing a little tired of her horse questions, Will sighed and said, "Believe me. It's a part of growing up. Every kid needs to learn how to ride and how to get back on when they fall off."

Then he changed the subject and explained, "We will start serving soon." He pointed to some tables at the back of the room. She saw ladies and men bringing in food trays. "The people here have been cooking for about twelve hours. The ones who are smoking the meat even longer. We wanted this to be enjoyed and give our guests a sample of West Texas flavors. Let me take you around, show you what we are doing, and introduce you."

He took her outside, where people were cooking meat in large smokers. The smell was good—rich and spicy. "We have smoked steaks for four hours and brisket for sixteen hours with mesquite wood." He smiled and asked, "Have you ever had mesquite-smoked meat before?"

"No," she answered. "I don't think we do all this in the city."

The ranch hands and their wives had the food set on tables buffet style with two-inch thick steaks, thinly sliced brisket, chicken, and sausage. Then she noticed the pinto beans with green chili and ham cooked in them, Jalapeno poppers, chili rellenos, potato salad, corn on the cob, tortillas, and cornbread, to name a few of the delectable dishes. She knew she'd have to try some of every dish.

When she finished and was wiping her mouth, Will asked, "Are you ready for dessert?"

"No, I can't eat another bite," she said.

Just then, the ranch ladies brought out the pies.

Will's wife Bernadette set a piece of her homemade chocolate pie in front of her and said, "Try this. It's like none other you have ever had."

She took a big bite; it was rich, deep, sweet chocolate with a taste she wasn't ready for: a hint of cayenne. Lee Ann could not stop eating it and asked for the recipe.

Bernadette smiled and said, "I will be more than happy to share it with you. Akita also liked this pie and put chili in his hot chocolate. If you're a fan of the pie, you should try it." For a New Yorker, this was foreign territory. Then Bernadette turned to attend to her other guests, leaving Lee Ann in a near-trance over the best-tasting pie she'd ever had the pleasure of putting in her mouth.

It was then that she noticed several cowhands gathered around a table telling stories. She walked over to listen, and when she saw an older man in his 70s or 80s, she moved closer to hear his story.

"It was his first paying job on a ranch," the old cowboy began. "Abe Rush and I were out gathering up strays and driving them to a holding pen. Abe saw a young mountain lion, which he pointed it out to me saying, 'I want to rope it.' I had known Abe since we were kids. He could rope anything. I told him not to, but at the same time, I wanted to see him do it. He pulled his lasso, kicked his horse into a full gallop, and started his run at the lion. He threw his loop, and it hit its mark. His horse stopped exactly as it was trained to do. All of you know that when you rope a calf, it tries to pull away from you when it hits the end of the rope. When that cat hit the end of his rope, it turned ass around, nose in the air. Its feet hit the ground. It turned and headed straight for Abe and his horse."

He started laughing at the memory and then continued the story." Abe was so scared, he shit his pants. He kicked his horse and tried to run away. The cat was still in the loop and coming fast. Abe let his rope go and galloped his horse hard. I thought he would run it until it died. He got away from the cat and later told me not to let him do anything that stupid again. I told him, 'I *told* you *not* to do this.'"

Everyone at the table, including Lee Ann, was laughing.

A young man walked up and said, "Hi, Grandpa, what's so funny?"

Another man who'd been listening said, "He's telling stories again."

The young man said, "I have one for you, and you won't believe it. Mr. Chisum had me take some hunters out today. I drove the four of them in the truck out to the lake on the back of the property. I stopped at the first gate. The passenger in the front seat declared that *he'd* open it. He got out and couldn't open a five-strand barbed wire gate! So, then I got out, opened it, got back in the truck, drove through it, stopped, and got out again to close it. I had to do this for the next gate. Then we went to the third gate. I had to do everything. These assholes from Chicago were not worth a fuck. On the final leg of the trip, I kid you not, the passenger on my side in the rear seat asked me, 'I was wondering . . . What kind of animal is it here that's smaller than a cow, but faster?'"

The people at the table started listing animals that fit this description. The young man said, "I told him I didn't know because too many possibilities came to mind, and that he'd just have to let me know if he saw another one. Not more than five minutes later, the guy shouted, 'There's one!' Well, I stopped the truck and looked where he was pointing. It was a fucking coyote."

The people at the table started laughing all around.

Broken Sabre Ranch Gathering

The young man continued. "I yelled, 'Why couldn't you say it looks like a fucking dog?' I told him that he didn't know his fucking ass from a hole in the ground."

Then the young man added, "I hope Mr. Chisum doesn't fire me over this."

The man he had called "Grandpa" said, "I'll talk to him. It would be best to be more careful about what you say to rich people who pay for hunts."

Lee Ann had seen coyotes on her drive here, but she didn't understand the Chicagoan's description: "smaller than a cow but faster." She thought they looked like dogs. She wished she could come back when she wasn't on official business and write all their stories down.

Just then, Will walked up to Lee Ann's table with a young girl. He said, "This is Blanca Martinez. She's the State 4H Small and Large Caliber Rifle Champion for her seventeen-year-old age group. She wants to tell you something."

Will left, and Blanca sat down. She had long black hair, a slender build, and a cute face, and Lee Ann asked her what she had to say to her.

She said, "I want to share some details about Akita. I heard from someone that you're here to write about him."

Lee Ann nodded and said, "Yes, that's right."

Blanca took a deep breath and began what would be a long, revealing story, "I was out on my ATV when I saw Akita shooting on the range. I was wondering. Do you call him Akita or Clint?"

"Akita. Why?"

Blanca explained, "Everybody called him Akita except Will." She continued, "I had been shooting with my dad and my brothers. I was a better shot than my brothers and always have been. I thought my dad was a good shot until I saw Akita shoot. Akita was hitting tiny targets at long range and making it look so easy. He was shooting with five different weapons. When he saw me watching, he asked me if I'd help him set up a shot. It took about an hour. We set the target (a .50 caliber empty cartridge) at the 200-meter mark with the hole facing the firing line. We placed sandbags behind the target, and Akita told me that they would stop us from losing the shell casing. Then we put his M82 Barrett rifle at the firing line. When everything was ready, he lay down, checked, and rechecked everything. Then he aimed. At this point, I asked him, 'Will you hit it?' I didn't get an answer. He was in his own world. When he fired, it was so loud it hurt my ears."

She continued, "He put his weapon away, and we walked to the target. We had to look for it. When I found it, I couldn't believe it! He put a half-inch bullet into the half-inch hole of the spent cartridge. I was holding the cartridge; the back end was blown out and deformed.

Akita told me not to cut myself on it. He let me keep it. Then I asked him if he could teach me to do that every time and whether or not he could do it every time. He said, 'Oh hell no. I'm lucky to hit it two times out of three.'"

Blanca looked at Lee Ann evenly and said, "I was twelve years old and wanted to be *that* good. I asked my mom and dad if they would let Akita teach me how to shoot. It wasn't an easy conversation. My dad simply said no without any further comment. When my mom asked him why, he said he didn't want me around Akita because he'd killed people. That didn't stop my mom. The next day she talked to Will and told him she wanted Akita to teach me to shoot."

Lee Ann could tell where this story was headed. Blanca continued, "Will told my mom he'd ask him. The very next morning, Akita arrived at my house and talked with my dad. When they finished talking, my dad asked me if I still wanted to have Akita teach me how to shoot."

Blanca took a deep breath, and then continued, "I was about to answer the obvious when Akita said, 'Before I commit to teaching you, I want to see how you shoot.' He wanted to go to the range right then. I was beyond excited to go.

Akita asked my mom to go with us. He drove and, on the way, he asked me why I wanted to learn. I told him about the 4 H Shooting Club. We talked about how to shoot correctly. We set up targets for me, and I started shooting right there and then. Akita watched every move I made. Then he had me get in and out of shooting position. He wanted to know what I saw when I looked through the sights. On the way home, he told me and my mom that I had some good habits but some I'd need to change. He said he was willing to teach me if I'd do exactly as he said. My mom considered what he'd just said and then told him lessons couldn't interfere with my school. She said it in her mom voice."

Broken Sabre Ranch Gathering

Lee Ann was becoming intrigued to see this side of Akita, a soldier with a soft side willing to teach kids a skill.

Blanca continued, "Akita told her I'd not only have to do my homework, but I'd have to keep my grades above the 80s. We were at the range every evening. Akita made me get up, take a shot, get down, and take another shot, over and over. He made me run two miles every morning before school and in the summer before anything else. He started me lifting weights. I was shooting my dad's old rifle and wasn't doing as well as Akita wanted. He got his rifle out, gave it to me, and told me to try it after he adjusted the sights for me. I fired three shots at the target. The bullets landed three inches apart. Not good enough for Akita. We adjusted the sights again. I had to repeat this four more times. We adjusted the sights after each time until I had a three-shot pattern the size of a dime. After completing this, I shot thirty rounds and didn't miss.

He went to the school and talked to the 4H teacher about the shooting rules. He only let me shoot his rifle for the next few weeks at the range. One day when I showed him my target.

He smiled and said, 'That's more like it. We still have work to do on your breathing, but you're doing well.'

He gave me a new German-made match grade .22 rifle a week later and told me that it met all the rules for my age. Then he showed me the targets used in the competitions. He told me, 'You will only shoot at these targets and only the way the rules are in the matches.'

Akita would play loud noise and music; he would throw pebbles at me! The first time I got mad and yelled at him. He told me in an exceptionally soft voice, 'You need to be able to tune all of this out and hit your target. It would be best if you had your full attention on your body position, how you hold the weapon, breathing, sight picture, target, and trigger pull.' Then he asked, 'What will you do if people mess with you at a match? Get mad? Throw things? All you will get out of that is losing. You need to turn off all your emotions when you're behind that weapon. You need to be as cold as polar ice.'

I trained like this for a year and a half. Everyday rain or shine. On weekends I spent six hours a day shooting. When the Army had Akita and he could not be there with me, my dad was. I was shooting 1000 rounds a week and hitting all my targets, even with all the distractions.

Broken Sabre Ranch Gathering

Akita and my mom came to my school to check me out one day to leave for a competition in Lubbock. We arrived at the location and found out where the weapons inspection was. I gave my rifle to the range officer. He took about ten minutes to tell me that it had passed the inspection. Akita handed me match-grade ammo and said, 'Shoot as you do with me every day.'

My mom was so nervous. At the time, I was mad that he had entered me without telling me. I didn't have time to prepare, but when I got behind my weapon my training took over. I turned my emotions off and put my full attention on shooting. This was when I first found out what he meant when he told me to be as cold as polar ice. I enjoyed that feeling. I won my age group and scored better than anyone in all the other age groups. On the way home, my mom was so proud of me."

Lee Ann noticed that Blanca, for all her strength, was becoming teary-eyed. She continued, "Akita told me, 'You did very well. I am proud of you. I didn't tell you about the competition today because I did not want you to be worried. The next time work on your breathing, and you won't miss.'"

Lee Ann understood the weight of Blanca's story. Akita had given a lot of himself for her to perfect her skills.

She continued, "I have *never* lost a shooting competition. Akita started training me in large-bore weapons that weekend. I was shooting both at the same time. I was shooting two thousand rounds a week. Akita took my dad and me to Tennessee to see his friend, a custom gunmaker named Tinker. Tinker measured me for a rifle stock. Then I had to shoot different calibers of weapons. He took more measurements of me in various places with all of them. Akita gave him the 4 H large-bore rules and told him, 'Push all the limits. Do not spare any expense on this one. She needs everything you can give her.'

Tinker told him the weapon would be ready in two months. When Akita offered to pick it up, Tinker told him that he would bring it to us because he needed to see me shoot. He wanted to make minor adjustments and fine-tune the weapon for me. As we were leaving, my dad told Akita that he could not afford such a special rifle. Akita cut him off and said, 'I didn't ask you to. I'm doing this for her because she is *that* good. Do you understand?' That was the only time I ever saw my dad back down.

I won enough shoots that colleges started looking at me. Now I have college scholarships. My dad will only need to pay for my food and gas for my car. When I got my first scholarship, I told Akita that he had done this for me, and he said, 'Hell no, I did not. You did all the hard work. You did it for yourself.'

Akita paid for my three rifles, all my ammo, everything I needed. He would not let my parents pay anything at all. I heard him tell my parents that all that was part of his teaching. Akita was a hard ass son of a bitch on the range. He expected perfection from me and would not let me accept less. I miss him. Now I will never be able to thank him for all this." Her eyes filled with tears. She took Lee Ann's hand in hers and squeezed it hard. "Thank you so much for listening to me," she said. I watched as she walked away.

Lee Ann was struck by a troubling, intuitive feeling that hit her hard and fast, and she simply could not make it subside. She felt certain Blanca was destined for a future beyond any human comprehension, a tragic future. She struggled to understand exactly why she had this strange reaction after listening to her story.

Just then Robin sat down and handed her a cup. "Thank you, I have a drink," she said.

Robin replied a little above a whisper, "Look inside the cup."

Lee Ann found a thumb drive inside it.

Robin explained, "You need to read all the emails and texts on that drive. After you have, you need to talk to Roy, Will, and myself. Please, don't tell anyone about what I just gave you. Do you understand?"

"I have questions for you *now*. Will you talk to me?"

Robin smiled a big, beautiful smile and said, "After you go through the information on that thumb drive, you will have hundreds of questions to ask, not just from me but many more people." She walked away without another word.

Just then Will approached and said, "It was good you heard Blanca out. Telling you her story helped. What did Robin want?"

Avoiding any comment about Robin, Lee Ann asked Will, "How could Akita be so kind to some people and live his life in the Army?"

Will explained, "Akita acted one way in his world and another way in

Broken Sabre Ranch Gathering

our world. I have no idea how he was able to do it." Then he completely changed the subject and asked, "What do you think of our country living?"

She looked around and said, "Your ranch and these people aren't what I expected."

Will said, "This ranch isn't mine. Bernadette owns it. Her family owned this land when it was part of Mexico. At the end of the war between the United States and Mexico, the Treaty of Guadalupe Hidalgo was signed. By its terms, Mexico ceded fifty-five percent of its territory, including parts of present-day Arizona, California, New Mexico, Texas, Colorado, Nevada, and Utah, to the United States. Her family has lived here and worked this land ever since." Smiling, Will added, "I married up."

"I don't believe that for a minute," she said.

"As far as the people here, most of the men we have working for us are former military.

We have six Green Berets and another ten Rangers, the elite soldiers with specialized training, and four Navy Seals," he explained.

"Do you recruit them?" She wondered aloud.

Will said, "No, they find out about this part of Texas and gravitate here."

Now Lee Ann's interest piqued.

Will explained, "When you're in combat at the elite levels these men achieved, you need to be around others like yourself. We're not the only ranch in this area with employees comprised mostly of SF soldiers. Four ranches have more than we do. Some come here not knowing much about ranch jobs, or how hard they can be, but they learn fast and become the best employees we've ever had."

The gathering continued well into the night. Savannah sat down next to her. "We need to get some sleep," she said. "Tomorrow will be a long day."

Lee Ann agreed and asked her, "Do you know where Will put my luggage?"

"Yes, it's in their house, and you can stay with me." Then she added, "The house has five bedrooms. You're in one, and I have Sonia, Petra, and Kirsten in the others."

They said our goodnights and departed for her house.

Showing Lee Ann to her room, Savannah said, "I'm exhausted. I'm going straight to bed. Make yourself at home."

After she left, Lee Ann showered and got ready for bed. Once she was horizontal, she couldn't sleep. She thought about everything that had unfolded today. The city sounds she was so used to were replaced with that of cows, horses, and other creatures. She had no idea what they were. She was unsure whether or not she was safe.

CHAPTER 4
Bernadette and Sonia

The following morning, Lee Ann woke up to the smell of bacon and coffee. She washed her face, put on her robe and went to the kitchen. Savannah and Kirsten were cooking and laughing. "What's so funny?" she asked as she sat down, making herself at home.

"Kirsten was afraid of all the sounds last night," Savannah said and winked.

Kirsten replied, "I didn't know the country was so full of noise at night. I thought it would be much quieter."

"I heard things in the night that made me get up and lock the door," Lee Ann admitted. They all laughed.

Just then, Sonia came in the front door. She smiled and said, "That smells good. May I have some coffee, please?" She was wearing jeans, knee-high boots, and a white silk shirt. Lee Ann asked her where she'd been.

"I went to the stables," she replied. "I wanted to see the horses. Bernadette was there, and we talked for a time. This is the first opportunity we've had to catch up since my last visit."

"At the funeral, Will said you'd been here before. I was wondering why?" Lee Ann asked, her reporter instinct kicking in.

Sonia turned and asked Savannah to call Bernadette. Then she looked at Lee Ann and said, "You need the whole story, not only what I know."

A short time later, Bernadette came in without knocking on the door. Sonia explained to her that Lee Ann was asking about the first time she had been at the ranch.

Bernadette made herself comfortable and said, "Will met Clint—or "Akita" as he was called—when Clint was about seven years old. I knew Will's sister had some kids, but that was all I knew. Will had heard things about her and her kids from his mom and dad. After his parents died, we never heard anything more. Years later, I don't remember which, I received a phone call from Lieutenant Colonel Scott, now General Scott. I had no idea why an Army Colonel would call here. Will had been out of the Army for years. LTC Scott told me that Akita had been in a training

Bernadette and Sonia

accident, that he was sending him here for forty-five days on medical leave, and after that, he'd return to active duty."

She continued, "So I asked him 'Why us?' and he told me that Will was Akita's emergency point of contact and sole beneficiary. He said that Akita needed time to recover from his injuries. He was already on his way, so he'd need to be picked up at the airport in Abilene. Then he gave me the arrival date and time and hung up. You can only imagine that I was mad and stunned at the same time.

I had to find Will. I had to go all the way to the backside of the ranch where he was working on a fence. I told him what had happened and showed him the time and date, only two days away. Will wanted to know what the injury was. I was still mad and said, 'No idea. He hung up the phone before I could ask anything.'

Will went on with his fence building and said we needed to prepare a room and be ready to pick him up. I pointed out that Akita wasn't our responsibility. Will shut that idea down and said, 'How would you feel if you showed up wounded and no one cared enough to pick you up? This is my sister's kid.'

Bernadette took a deep breath and continued, "Will and I drove to Abilene airport. They showed up early. Will always shows up early.

The flight landed on time. I wondered how we were going to know who he was. I didn't know what he looked like. Then Will pointed and said, 'I think that is him.' I saw a man with military dress uniform pants with bloused jump boots. The only reason I knew this was because Will wore his uniform this way when he got out of the Army. The man didn't have his dress coat, only a white tee shirt, and a green beret. The shirt had dark spots on it.

Will said quietly, 'He's been shot.' I asked how he knew that, and all he said was, 'I know.'

Akita had his duffel bags by the handle and started walking to the exit. He was leaning towards his side, the one with the dark spots. Will asked him if he was Clint Haddox, and as he was walking toward us, he said he was.

I noticed the muscles in his arms and under the tee-shirt. I thought he was fit. The closer he got, the madder I became. The dark spots were blood. His wounds had opened back up on the airplane and again when he was carrying his bag. We met, and he shook Will's hand, then mine.

'Training accident, my ass,' I said.

Akita didn't respond to that. He pointed out that we didn't know each other, so he'd get a room in town. Then Will let him know that he was coming with us and that he was family.

We had a chance to talk in the car heading home. Will asked him how he got shot. Akita told him that he didn't want to lie, but that he wasn't going to say anything except what the official military records say— training accident. We didn't ask any more questions. When we arrived home, Akita wouldn't even let us carry his bag in. All he said was, 'I can do it myself.'

Two days later, the sheriff in Aspermont called to tell us that a young lady was trying to find out where we lived. He told us that she had our address but couldn't find the ranch. She'd already driven out here but gave up and went to his office for directions. She told him that we had an American soldier staying with us who needed medical help. When I asked if she left her name, he said, 'Yes, it's Sonia Ludwig.' The sheriff guided her here.

Bernadette smiled broadly and added, 'One and a half hours later that "thing" over there walked into our lives.'"

Sonia hugged her, and said, "So I am still that 'thing'? I love you, too." Then she continued, "I came here to take care of Akita because I knew he would do a terrible job of it himself. When I left, I had a family here in Texas."

Bernadette said, "Will met her and the sheriff at the gate and led her the rest of the way here. Then he told her that he'd bring in her luggage and for her to go in the house. I didn't know what to expect. The door opened, and she walked into the living room. She was gorgeous. Her clothes cost more than some cars. I just sat there dumbfounded, and she walked over and introduced herself. When she spoke, I knew she wasn't from here, certainly not Texan or Mexican. I asked her where she was from. What a surprise when she answered, 'Wetzlar, Germany.' The next thing I asked without thinking was, 'What the hell are you doing here?' That put her off, and she was ready to start for the door. Just then Akita walked in and said something in German. Then this young lady ran, jumped in his arms, and kissed him. He groaned in pain.

Bernadette and Sonia

She said, 'I'm sorry. Let me fix it. You need your bandages changed.'

Then she turned to me and said, 'I have all I need in my medical bag. I will get it.' She turned and left out the front door.

I asked Akita what she was to him, and he was very sincere with his answer. He said, 'The best person in my life. I am sorry. I didn't know she was coming here. We will leave. I'll send her back, and we won't bother you again.'

Will had come in and overheard all of this and made a point to tell them that they were both more than welcome to stay.

Then Akita asked Will, 'Why are you doing this for me?'

Will was unequivocal and said, 'You have that green go-to-hell hat that unites us. You are my family. Let me do this for you.'

Sonia said to me and Will, 'I didn't want to cause trouble for you. I wanted to care for that 'thing' over there that I care for.' She pointed at Akita."

Bernadette continued, "That was when I started calling her 'that thing.'" Then she reflected, "I wondered what kind of woman would fly halfway around the world for a man. Not knowing anybody here and not telling anyone that she was coming."

Sonia said, "I was only thinking about Akita. I cared for him before the Army made him leave Germany and come here. He told me that he wanted to stay with me. I had some things I needed to take care of before I left. Akita had given me your address. I thought it would be easy to find. I didn't know the ranch was in the middle of nowhere."

Bernadette laughed and said, "Sonia was lost for a week. She was not used to living like this."

Sonia said, "I remember the first time I went riding with you. I've ridden horses, saddled them, groomed them, and fed them since I was young. I was not accustomed to western saddles. I had trouble saddling the horse. It was so embarrassing."

Bernadette said, "It didn't take you long to get the hang of it."

Sonia said, "I started liking the western style of riding. You were so nice to me. When I cooked for you and Will, you told me that it was good, but that I needed to add some spices to make it full-flavored. I learned so much from you and Will."

Bernadette asked, "Do you still remember your first chili pepper?"

Bernadette and Sonia

"Yes, how could I forget? Akita was eating them like candy and saying how much he missed them. I asked you how they tasted, and you said, 'Try one.'"

"I told you to take a small bite," Bernadette said.

"I know, but I took a bite like Will and Akita were taking. I chewed it about three times, and the heat hit me."

Bernadette laughed and said, "She turned red and was running for the water. I stopped her and gave her milk."

Sonia was also laughing at the memory. She said, "I yelled out, 'Why the hell would anyone eat this shit?'"

Bernadette laughed and said with a hint of nostalgia, "Will and Akita were rolling around on the floor. They were laughing that hard."

Bernadette said, "That 'thing,'" pointing at Sonia, "kept trying to eat chili the entire time she was here until she could eat one."

Sonia asked Bernadette, "Do you remember when Akita told Will about his mother and what happened when he was young?"

Bernadette asked, "Should we talk about this now?"

Sonia said, "I have never told anyone what you and I heard that night. We need to let people know how horrible Akita's life was and how he was forced to live."

Bernadette sighed and said, "Sonia and I were in the living room over there." She pointed. "I wanted to know about Sonia and her family, and I had asked a few questions. Akita got up and said that he'd be on the porch."

Sonia said, "His wounds were healing, and he was acting like a caged animal. Akita wanted to go on a run or work out. It was still too soon. I was afraid he would open his wounds again."

Bernadette explained, "Will went to the kitchen for a beer, and I told him to bring us all one and to take one to Akita on the porch, so Sonia and I could talk in peace.

Then Will went out on the porch, left the door open, and told Akita loudly enough for us to hear, 'You're in trouble now.'

Sonia and I started talking. It was a quiet evening. Then we heard Will's and Akita's voices coming from the porch. I told Sonia, 'And they say that we gossip.'

Sonia said, "I was going to say something back to her when I

Bernadette and Sonia

overheard Will say, 'You haven't asked any questions about your family.' Akita told him that he didn't have any to ask. Bernadette and I listened in silence as Will said, 'I know you boys. . . .'

Then we overheard Akita cut Will off. Akita's voice was cold as he said, 'Your sister ran off with her father-in-law. That day she destroyed two families. After that, she tore apart what was left of us. She was a cruel fucking sociopath. The only thing that pleased her was beating the hell out of us and having her lover, my grandfather, help her do it. She beat and starved us until she got tired of it. She laughed at us the entire time. I was nine years old and left for school one day. The house—if you could call it that—was a fucking shack. It had furniture and other shit in it when I left that morning. When I got home, it was empty. She left me three pairs of pants and three shirts on the porch. She had thrown me away like trash. All I felt at the time was happy that I would never see her again.'

Will took it all in and asked, 'What happened to your older brothers?'

Akita said, 'The police came and took them when I was six years old. I met them once after that and didn't want anything to do with them. I am better off without them. I like my life just like it is. At first, when I was left alone, I wanted someone to come and help me. I wanted to have what other kids had. I wanted to know what was wrong with me. When I knew no one was going to help, I got mad. I turned my anger on everything and everyone. I lived like that, not caring about anything, including my life. I fought to fight. Where was my family then?'"

Bernadette said, "I was going to tell Will that he needed to stop and come inside.

Then I heard Will say, 'I am not like that bitch when we were growing up. She had problems even as a child. From what little you shared, she got worse. I did not know any of this.

I was in the Army when she left. I couldn't do anything except try to stay alive in a war. It seemed impossible that anyone could endure that much fucking pain. I am sorry.'

Akita said, 'You didn't do that shit to me. Why are you sorry? So no, I do not have any fucking questions about this fucking family. Now, will you leave it alone?'

Will asked, 'What about that girl in there? Does she know about your childhood?'

BERNADETTE AND SONIA

Akita told him that Sonia didn't know anything, and that he didn't want her to. He didn't want her to ever look down on him, and he cared for her more than he should."

As she ended the story, Bernadette said, "Later, I told Will we had overheard them.

He told me that he liked Akita because he doesn't back down and says what he thinks, even if you don't like it. Then he told me not to let Akita know that Sonia and I had overheard their conversation."

Sonia said, "I didn't know that Akita had brothers. I still know nothing about them.

I never looked down on him. I know he lived in hell and was bloody in combat for the Army.

With me, Akita was kind and gentle. I held him that night like I never had before. I wanted him to feel the softness of a touch from someone who loved him. I had seen his scars and knew that not all were from combat. He had old, deep scars on his back, shoulders, and ass. I cannot imagine how much pain he suffered. I did not know until we heard their discussion that it was at the hands of his mother and grandfather. How could anyone do that to a child, and how could they enjoy the pain to that child? They were sick motherfuckers."

Bernadette changed the subject and said, "I was in awe of you. I had seen doctors take care of people my whole life. You took better care of Akita than any doctor I had ever seen.

You would not let him get away with anything. He also impressed me. He never raised his voice to you or called you a name. He did what you wanted most of the time. Once he felt better, he started messing with everyone. The month that you spent here with us was full of fun.

I learned strength from you. Do you remember the cowhand that tried to help you on a horse?"

Sonia said, "Yes, that son of a bitch grabbed my ass and acted like he had done nothing wrong."

Bernadette was laughing again, so hard she had difficulty talking. "You got off the horse, planted both feet on the ground and asked the guy if he got a good feel. He was trying to deny he had done anything wrong. Will had seen what happened and was heading your way. He stopped when you kicked the man in the face."

Bernadette and Sonia

Bernadette made sure she had everybody's attention and continued, "The man was about six feet tall, standing upright when she kicked him right in the face. You didn't stop there! When he was trying to get up, and he was on his hands and knees, you kicked him from behind in the balls so hard that his face hit the ground. Then you kicked his balls again. You were mad and didn't want to stop. Then Akita got to you, grabbed you in his arms, and told you to stop because the guy had had enough."

Will came in and recognized the story. Sonia looked up at him and said, " Hey, I never wanted to make you mad about beating up your cowboy."

He could laugh about it now and said, "Someone had trained you well." Everyone in the room was laughing.

Bernadette left to prepare for the trip, so everybody dispersed at the same time. Lee Ann went to her car, and laughter still hung in the air. Will said, "General Scott called, and he will be landing in Germany within the hour."

Kirsten said, "Then everyone should be ready to leave as soon as we can."

Will offered, "I'll lead you. We'll take the main road, then to Abilene."

Sonia came out of the house. She was on her phone. She hung up and said, "My plane is fueling now and doing preflight. As soon as we arrive at the airport, we'll be able to depart."

They lined up and drove off in their convoy. Lee Ann was sad to leave. She knew that she had wanted to see and do more here.

Sonia received a call from General Scott. His military jet landed in Frankfort, Germany. He said American soldiers had unloaded Akita's coffin and loaded it in a hearse.

Sonia told him that somebody named Klaus had made all the arrangements for the funeral home in Wetzlar to receive and hold Akita until the day of his funeral. He would be meeting him at the gate. After Sonia finished the call, she said, "I overheard General Scott say to the driver that he needed to go to the Ludwig estate in Wetzlar."

After boarding, Lee Ann had a chance to ask Sonia how much she knew about Savannah.

Sonia said, "Akita sent me pictures of Savannah all the time, and we spoke about her when he called me. I had wanted to know who had

Bernadette and Sonia

helped raise her, but I needed the right opportunity to ask." Now, Lee Ann gathered, it was too late.

Sonia's jet landed in Munich. Sonia, Kirsten, Petra, Savannah, Lee Ann, Will, and Bernadette disembarked. Four cars and Sonia's house staff awaited. Savannah attempted to retrieve her bags. A large, heavily muscled man held his hand up and said, "Please stop. This is my job." He spoke English very well with a German accent.

Savannah said a bit belligerently," I don't mind doing it myself."

Sonia walked over and said, "Please let him do this for you." Then she held out one hand as she turned and said, "Look, they are here to assist all of us."

Savannah then looked at the large man and said simply," Thank you."

He smiled at her, then looked at Sonia and said, "She looks just like you."

Sonia fighting back the tears, said, "She does look like me."

Savannah smiled and waited for him to retrieve the bags. She took Sonia's hands in hers and said, "Before you ask me if I would mind having a German mother, my answer is 'Yes.' I would love you as my mom if you don't mind having a Texan daughter."

Sonia could no longer hold back the tears, which made Savannah cry. They hugged; neither one wanting to release.

Savannah continued," I know why my dad loved you. You are beautiful, and your capacity for caring is unmatched."

Sonia hugged her harder and asked, "Did Akita raise you by himself?"

Savannah smiled and said, "Yes, when the Army did not have him. Will and Bernadette took over when he was gone."

Sonia smiled and said, "No one could have done a better job, you have what most people strive for and few achieve. Akita has surprised me again in how well he raised you."

Savannah smiled and said, "Thank you, sometimes I made it hard for him. Now I can't tell him how sorry I am or love him for keeping me safe, even when I didn't want it."

Sonia said, "He knew then and now."

Once everyone was in the cars, they departed for Wetzlar with all the luggage loaded.

BERNADETTE AND SONIA

At the same time a Lufthansa flight landed in Frankfort with people from Texas. They picked up their luggage and were met by cars to take them to Wetzlar. Arrangements had been made to bring everyone to the Ludwig Estate for another funeral and then to Kirsten's and Petra's homes.

CHAPTER 5
Taking a Story

Lee Ann returned to Texas from Wetzlar. She wanted to make sure that she had all aspects of this incredible story correct. Most of her final inquiries would involve the people from here. This story took over her life with the people's lives this soldier had touched, helped, or saved. She had her story completed and ready to send to her editor Mike.

Bernadette called her before she could send it and said, "Before you do anything, you have a meeting at Roy's ranch now. Malin will pick you up he will be there in a minute.

Just then, a knock on her door and a voice called out, "Lee Ann, I'm to take you to Roy's."

Lee Ann told Bernadette, "Good timing. He's here. I'm on my way."

As Malin drove her to Roy Walker's ranch for a meeting, Lee Ann was lost deep in thought. Malin was also unusually quiet. They'd said little by the time they arrived and were ushered into the house.

Roy, his wife Gaspara, Will, and Bernadette Chisum were at the meeting. Lee Ann had met all that were present and gained respect for them with the time she had spent here.

Will started the conversation, "Lee Ann, we cannot allow you to print your story."

She felt her anger rise. "Why?"

Roy said, "You don't have the entire story, and if you print what you have, some people here will go to jail."

Lee Ann was flabbergasted. She said," I do *not* understand. Everyone here gave me this story and should be proud of Akita and his men." She looked imploringly at Bernadette, "Please tell me what I have done to anger all of you. I can't believe you're asking me to kill a story that will tell all the good that has come from this part of Texas."

Gaspara explained, "No, you don't understand. You haven't done anything wrong. You don't have all the information that we have. You must not put this story in print. I will not allow good people to go to jail for doing the right thing. Even if it was illegal."

Taking a Story

Lee Ann was pissed off and said unequivocally," Fuck all of you. I have worked too hard on this. She turned to Gaspara. "*You* will not allow it? Fuck you. It's my story, and it will go to print."

Lee Ann stood up and continued, "Malin, you will take me back now." She walked out the door and slammed it hard behind her.

Bernadette followed her and stopped her at the back of the pickup. She lowered the tailgate and said, "Sit down. You may be angry, but you don't have the right to talk down to us."

Lee Ann said, "You don't have the right to kill a story that I have a year of my life in."

"What is one year of your life worth? Bernadette asked. "Is it worth one young person going to jail for life or worse? Is it worth Roy, Will, and myself going to jail as accessories?"

Lee Ann was stunned and asked, "Who and what crime?"

Bernadette said, "I can't tell you. We're trying to keep you and everyone else safe and out of jail. We're not telling you *not* to tell a story. Just tell a generic one. Please trust me. I would not ask you to do this if there were another way. We will not stop you by force. It is up to you. Lives are in your hands."

Just then, Malin walked up and asked, "Are you ready to leave?"

Lee Ann then looked Bernadette right in the eye and asked, "Am I still welcome to stay at the ranch, or do I need to go to the motel?"

Bernadette smiled and said," You will always be welcome at my home."

Malin shrugged his shoulders and went back inside muttering something to himself about not understanding women.

Later that evening, Lee Ann emailed Mike a revised story about the funeral of Clint 'Akita' Haddox. It was one deemed acceptable to everyone at the meeting.

Mike had thought this story was a waste of her time and talent. He had made sure to tell her that when he gave it to her. Mike thought she would be on this story one day, maybe two. It had taken much more time than they could have known.

Mike called Lee Ann the next day. He was furious when she answered

Taking a Story

the phone. He said, "You changed all the names in your report. Where are the names you had me do backgrounds on?" He did not let her answer. He continued, "Get your ass in my office now or find another job."

Lee Ann went to find Malin to tell him what she would face in New York and asked him if he would go with her. Kim would arrange for Malin and her to travel from Abilene, Texas, to New York.

Malin and Lee Ann arrived in the city late. They took a cab to Lee Ann's apartment. They were tired and wanted to stay in and watch TV, but they fell asleep before the show ended.

The next morning Lee Ann finished her coffee, dressed in a slim-fitting dark blue dress with six-inch gold stiletto heels and a gold belt around her waist. She made sure that her makeup was flawless. If she was going to be fired, she wanted to go out in style.

She asked Malin to call for a cab to take them to the office. "Let's go," he said as he put on his cowboy hat. He was dressed just like the first time they had met: boots, jeans, and a button-down western shirt. He worked for Will and Bernadette, and yes, he earned a Green Beret. Lee Ann had never been treated so well by anyone or felt so safe as when she was with him. Just as they were leaving the apartment, he grabbed Lee Ann by the arm and turned her toward him. Then he kissed her. It was soft, long, and filled with passion.

As she recovered from the surprise, she thought that this same deep feeling must be how Sonia felt when Akita kissed her for the first time. The thought was a kind of awakening.

They arrived at the main doors of her building. Malin got out of the taxi, walked around, opened her door, and offered his hand to help her out. She started to walk. He did not move. She had taken three or four steps and heard him say, "I will never get tired of the sights in the city."

When she turned to see what Malin was seeing, she realized he'd been staring at her. "You are stunning," he said.

Lee Ann walked back to him, kissed his lips, took his arm, and said, "I have an appointment. Remember?"

They walked to the front door, and the doorman opened it for them and said, "Good morning." His look was disapproving of Malin.

Taking a Story

Lee Ann took Malin's arm and walked into the main lobby. They made their way to her office. Kim was at her desk and said, "Good morning. Is this Malin, the man I have heard so much about?"

Lee Ann said, "Yes," and introduced her. Malin shook her hand and said, "Please don't believe anything you heard about me. I am probably worse than any of it."

For the moment, Kim just looked at Lee Ann and said, "Mike is expecting you." Lee Ann knocked on Mike's office door and went in.

Malin said to Kim, "Would you like a cup of coffee? I'll buy."

Starting to warm up to Malin, Kim said, "Yes, come with me."

As soon as Lee Ann sat down in front of Mike's desk, she could tell that he was still mad. He asked, "Why are all the names changed?"

Lee Ann said, "Multiple sources verified all I reported on this story."

"Then why change the names and places, and how did you erase my files with the correct names?" He wanted to know.

Lee Ann gathered herself and said, "The people the FRBs helped are not criminals and never have been. They do not deserve to go to jail or have their businesses taken from them. I will not be a part of that. Most of them, all females, could not afford college or just needed a hand up. The FRBs gave that to them. They all paid the loans back and are helping other women start businesses. The bank has been investigated, and no illegal activity was found.

The FRBs are all dead, and the U.S. Government can't find out where they got their funds from. If I leave the correct names and places in my report, people on both sides of the world will pay for something they did not do. The FRBs paid with their lives. Isn't that enough?"

That explanation didn't resolve Mike's anger. He said, "I want the list of names you took from my laptop, and I want to know how you erased it."

Lee Ann answered, "I met a young lady in Texas. I asked her for help with the list. She is a genius when it comes to computers and security systems."

"If you do not give me that list, you are fired," Mike replied.

Lee Ann stood up and said, "That is *fine* with me. I have a better offer

Taking a Story

in Texas. You have a beautiful day."

Mike's face went pale. He said, "You can't be serious."

Lee Ann left Mike's office and walked out to Kim's desk. Malin smiled and asked, "Are we going back home?"

She said, "Only if you call Texas home."

* * *

What happened over the next month is the stuff of fairy tales. Love at first sight or at least love at that first kiss happened before either Malin or Lee Ann knew what had happened. Lee Ann stayed in West Texas and married Malin. They purchased 390 acres of land just off one side of Bernadette's ranch. Ranch hands who work for Will and Roy built their large, three-bedroom house. It even had a deck for their rocking chairs and sunset evenings. This morning Lee Ann was on that deck with Yoyo, a 120-pound mountain lion that Malin brought home two years ago as a small ball of fur.

At the time, Lee Ann did not want her and told Malin, "She's a wild animal. I am afraid of what she will become. What if she is so wild that she attacks me?"

Malin promised, "We will only keep her until she can survive on her own. Plus, how bad can she be? She is a "Yoyo," explained Malin. "That's a word I use to describe people who are all fucked up."

Lee Ann laughed and asked, "How can something so small be a Yoyo?"

Malin smiled and said, "She's this small and ran away from home. She's a Yoyo."

"You just named her," Lee Ann laughed.

Malin said, "If she has a name, then she's staying. I'll call the vet and get some milk for her. Cow's milk will make her sick."

That was the beginning of a beautiful relationship. Lee Ann raised Yoyo on a bottle. They put her on the back deck after five months. She was free to go anywhere, but the deck became her home.

Lee Ann heard a vehicle pulling up and thought Malin had left something behind. She was wrong. Bernadette pulled her pickup into the drive and stopped. This was out of character for her. She had always called first to ensure that Lee Ann would be at home and let her know she wanted to talk.

Bernadette got out and said, "Hello. Do you have some time to talk?"

Lee Ann said, "Yes, please come up and have a seat. What's on your mind?"

Bernadette looked at Yoyo and said, "I thought you wanted her to be a wild mountain lion, not a pet."

"We put her out here thinking she would leave and be wild, but she has never left. She does keep the other wildlife away and still gets along with Nelly." Lee Ann pointed at their dog.

Bernadette asked, "Did you see yourself like this when you lived in New York?"

Lee Ann smiled and said, "Hell no, I thought the city was everything. I was wrong. I love living here."

Bernadette looked perplexed. "I'm at a loss," she said. I need to ask you something, but I don't know where to start, and I know it will make you mad. Before you say anything, let me start with this: I know you know that Blanca died in a head-on crash with a drunk driver. He killed her and four other kids on their way back to Texas A&M from a shooting competition in Lubbock.

Lee Ann almost started to cry. She was close to Blanca. She was a good kid, the first in her family to attend college. It was her shooting ability that got her a full-ride scholarship. Lee Ann said," Yes, I know."

Bernadette continued, "Roy was just diagnosed with brain cancer. The doctor told Gaspara he has no more than six months left."

Lee Ann did not know what to say. She liked Roy. She asked, "What can I do for Roy and Gaspara?"

Bernadette asked, "Do you remember the meeting we had years ago about your story?"

"Yes, how could I forget?"

Bernadette said, "With Blanca dead and Roy only having six months to live, no one can go to jail for any major time. Roy said you could interview him and some others now. He has asked everyone on this list if the story can be told now." Bernadette handed Lee Ann the list.

Taking a Story

Lee Ann read it, and said, "You are on this list. So do you want to tell me your part of the story now?"

Bernadette said, "You need to talk to Roy first. After Roy tells you what he knows about the night Akita was killed, you will understand why the story could not be told years ago. I will tell you what happened that night and what I did. You will finally have the whole story after you talk to everyone on that list.

Lee Ann was dumbstruck and said, "First, you tell me you can't do this story. Now you want me to forget about my pain and anger when I agreed to your demands and killed the story of a lifetime. I gave my boss a piece of shit story that no one would be proud of. He was pissed off and knew I was hiding something. Now you want me to do the story and add to it. Have you lost your fucking mind? Next, in three years, you will need me to forget the story again and say I never wrote it. No, I will not do this for you or anybody else."

Bernadette pointed at Yoyo and said, "You took the time and effort to nurse her to health. You wanted her to have a chance in life. You cared for her every need for months, and you did not stop there. You put her on your deck. You did not take her out to the cow tank and abandon her. You still care for her. You feed and water her. Hell, you brush her coat. I think you still care about this story, and you want to tell it. So, tell it. You know it is a once in a lifetime story."

Lee Ann looked at her long and hard, saying in slow, measured terms, "I will do this, but you have to tell me your part right here, right now. If you do not, I will never write it. Do you understand what I am saying?"

Bernadette smiled and said, "I need a glass of tea if I have to stay and tell you what I know."

Lee Ann spent the next nine months interviewing Savannah Haddox, Will Chisum, Bernadette Chisum, Leticia Martinez, Gaspara, Olivia Walker, Josephina Pena, Clay Jenkins, Texas Ranger Lieutenant Sergio Vega, Robin Smith, Roy Walker, and others. Walker died three months after his interview and had wanted to live long enough to see the story in print. Lee Ann was sad that she couldn't make that happen for him.

Lee Ann would work long and hard to gather the information she needed. At this point, she still did not have the whole story. The next phase of her investigation would involve traveling with Savannah and others. It would involve interviewing people and being involved in life-changing events that Savannah would initiate against the CIA and other government agencies. Lee Ann was determined to bring justice for Akita and the FRBs, even if it meant discoveries that might place blame on the CIA for their murders.

CHAPTER 6
THE LUDWIG ESTATE

The procession of black cars turned slowly off the public road onto a narrow, winding private road lined with tall oaks. They eventually arrived at the main gate and gatehouse. After a brief encounter with a gatehouse attendant, they drove another fifty meters, and pulled up to the magnificent entrance of a thirteenth-century castle.

Savannah, Will, Bernadette, and Lee Ann could do little but gawk out the window of the SUV they had traveled in, overwhelmed by the size and grandeur of the place. Sonia had just arrived in the car ahead of the group, but she was already standing on the front landing to welcome everyone to the Ludwig Estate. "Welcome to my home," she said as she launched into the place's history. "My ancestors built it in the late 1300s. My family has rebuilt it over the years and added to it. In World War II, the left-wing and gatehouse were bombed and almost destroyed. My grandfather had everything repaired, rebuilt, and added the two outbuildings to give the staff living quarters. Each staff member's quarters have four bedrooms and at least two bathrooms. Their homes had been damaged or destroyed in the war. He modernized the estate with electrical wiring, plumbing, restrooms, and gas heating. My father updated all the buildings. They now have alarm systems and Wi-Fi. He also added a wing that attaches the main house to the keep."

The house staff was unloading luggage, and Sonia took the opportunity to introduce them. Sonia pointed out Kerstin and Petra and told two of the staff, "I think you already know these two." Then she smiled a very devilish smile, and all three laughed.

Sonia continued, "Some of my staff do not speak English. If you need anything or need to go somewhere, please ask Christina or Monika, both excellent English speakers. They will help you with everything. Kerstin, Petra, and I will also be more than happy to help. Kerstin and Petra will stay here until your return trip.

Sonia turned to Monika and said, "Lee Ann will need to use my office. Make sure she has internet access and anything else she needs to do her job."

"Please come this way. I will show you the office first, and then I'll take you to your room. Do you need to call anyone before we start?" Monika asked.

Lee Ann said, "No, thank you. I can call later."

The next day, everyone gathered at the chapel for the service. General Scott and Will expressed reservations to Sonia, wondering whether or not the service would be simple since a ceremony had already been held in Texas. General Scott, with an air of exhaustion, explained, "We can't see putting everyone through it again."

Sonia responded unequivocally with steel in her voice, "The people here will not understand; they want to say goodbye; we will let them take the time to do so. I want *all* the people he helped to have the opportunity to speak."

Will whispered to General Scott, "She just put us in our place."

General Scott whispered back, "Yes, she did." The two turned and walked away. The issue seemed to be closed.

Having had her say with Will and General Scott for the moment, Sonia said to Lee Ann, "Please come with me. I need you to hear and see this for your story."

Inexplicably, they walked back over to General Scott and Will. Sonia said, "You know no one from the U.S. has visited the FRB's graves. At my insistence, I have taken them on as my responsibility. The men wanted to be buried without anyone present, then to be left alone. Also, this is my home, and I did not wish to have it invaded."

General Scott said stiffly, "I know. They told me the same, and you have honored their request. You and your lawyers blocked attempts by the U.S. government to gain access to your family cemetery. My men made their demands to this effect in their last will and testaments. You are their named beneficiary."

Sonia said, "Yes, I have their wills, but I also have Akita's, and I'm not his beneficiary; Savannah is. Akita also asked to be buried here with his men."

General Scott looked upset and said, "Why did you ask to move him? Why didn't you just use his will and take him?"

Sonia explained, "I wanted it to be Savannah's decision. I wanted

THE LUDWIG ESTATE

him here, but I wasn't going to be the one to move him if she wanted her father in Texas."

General Scott quizzed Sonia: "Why are you allowing the public in today?"

Sonia said, "I need this. I want Savannah to know Akita was loved. The three of you must come with me to their graves now while we have time. I need you to see the headstones. When we buried the first three men here, Akita and the other men told me what the team wanted to have carved on the headstones. Each man gave me the list and the placement of what would be on the stones for the three I was ordering and for their own. I need to explain what is on the headstones." She took them out the back door of the chapel to the Ludwig family cemetery.

The grounds were expansive. The boundary, covered in red and white flowering vines, consisted of precisely trimmed hedges, keeping the interior closed off from the outside world. Lee Ann noticed large stones, some standing upright, others lying on their sides.

"Are those headstones?" Lee Ann asked.

Sonia said, "Yes, this is an ancient burial ground. The headstones were here before my family settled this land in the 1300s. Would you like to see how beautifully carved they are? We have some time, and I love to see the effort that was taken so long ago by people to say goodbye to their loved ones."

General Scott pointed as he stated, "I would also like to ask you about the headstones over there." He was interested in a group of headstones that had swastikas and German WWII helmets on them.

Sonia answered, gazing intently at General Scott, "We have time to look at both areas. All families have had people on both sides of every war ever fought. We may disagree with what they did or stood for. I don't believe in what some of my people did in WWII. However, we still need to honor the right of those left behind to bury their dead." General Scott nodded and was silent.

As they walked to the ancient grave markers, Lee Ann noticed how well kept the grounds were. The grass cut evenly, and all edges are trimmed. Nothing out of place. Some older markers were tilted off center or lying down due to time and weather. She asked Sonia, "Will the stones be straightened or placed again?"

Sonia said, "No, we do not know where all the graves are. If we dig or move a stone, we may disturb another place of rest. No one in my family wanted this, and neither do I."

She stopped and addressed the group, "When I set up the area for the FRBs, we used ground penetrating radar and discovered graves we didn't even know about. I had them marked, so they will never be disturbed. I had to expand the search area to outside the cemetery. Now they all have their final resting place. One grave could never be identified, but I had it marked and fenced. I was going to keep searching, but then decided against it. FRBs spent their lives protecting people they did not know. Now they keep that unknown person safe." They continued to walk through the large headstones in relative silence. They had been carved with circles, geometric designs, and other shapes.

Lee Ann asked, "Do you know what these markings say? They are beautiful to say the least."

Sonia said, "What you asked has been lost to time. All I can do is care for them as if they were mine." Then Sonia turned to General Scott and Will and asked, "Do you still want to see the WWII graves?"

Will spoke up first. "No, they fought for what they believed in or were forced to fight for. You are right about war and family. I have some in my past that I'm not proud of, nor will I ever be, but they are still my family.

General Scott added, "Sonia, I'm sorry if I offended you. It's not my place to judge what happened in the past with your people."

Sonia said dismissively, "You have nothing to be sorry for. Now we need to hurry. Time is getting short, and I must explain what is on the FRB headstones." They walked to a corner of the graveyard where an archway led them to a large space where eleven headstones stood. Sonia's grounds crew had prepared the place where Akita would be laid to rest. All the headstones were white marble, all the same shape and size.

Next to where Akita would be buried was the grave of his associate Ed. At the top of his headstone carved large were letter "FRB." Next, his name, dates of birth and death, and his rank appeared lower and in the right quarter of the stone. Then down the left side quarter even with the name were his special skills tabs, the arches displaying words signifying a special skill that a soldier has earned and received orders for. From top to bottom, Ed's identified him as "Phantom Warrior, Ghost, Hunter-Killer, Special Forces, Ranger, Airborne, Soldier, and Wayward."

Sonia explained, "All eleven headstones are uniform in the placement of this information."

General Scott, visibly irritated, asked, "Why are the tabs wrong? Only three are real. The rest are shit."

As Lee Ann gawked at General Scott's nerve, Sonia said evenly, "The FRBs were the best special forces soldiers anywhere in the world. The bond between them was unseen, but it was stronger than steel. It could not be broken, and you know it. They ranked each other this way. After missions, they would assess how well each other performed. To earn the tabs above "Special Forces," they had to perform all mission tasks to their standards for two missions. The team would vote and then award the tab. Not all the FRBs have all the tabs. The two lower tabs were what they were before you recruited them."

General Scott fell silent and then said, "I did not know any of this."

Sonia continued, "This was their way of honoring each other and you."

A little unnerved by the direction her remarks were taking, General Scott asked, "How does this honor me?"

Sonia pointed to the lower tabs. "They were 'Wayward and the Soldiers' before you." Then she pointed to the top tabs: "This is what *you* made them. I wanted you to see this before we place Akita's headstone." Quietly, she then asked, "Do you understand why they wanted this on their headstones?"

General Scott sighed and said, "The FRBs were the wayward son of bitches even in death."

Sonia said, "Yes, they were. Now do you approve?"

General Scott said with a hint of nostalgia, "Yes, I do. I wonder how they would rank me?"

Sonia said, "I still have the paperwork listing all they had to do to earn each tab. Do you want it?"

General Scott perked up a little and said, "Yes, please, but I don't want to take it from you."

Sonia smiled and said, "I know they would want you to have it, and it pleases me to give it to you."

Will interrupted, "As you know, I was Special Forces. I earned my tabs. May I see what it took for the other tabs?"

Sonia said, "Yes, of course, and can one of you explain this to Savannah, please?"

General Scott said, "Yes, of course. I will."

CHAPTER 7
Saying Goodbye

A brief time later, Akita was placed where he would remain for all time. Over one hundred people attended the service.

Lee Ann was close enough to Savannah and Sonia to hear Savannah's heartfelt question: "Did all the people there know my dad?"

Sonia said, "Yes, and some have asked to speak about your dad."

Kerstin, at the microphone, announced in a voice barely above a whisper, "We are here to honor Akita's memory. If you wish to speak, please come up, and take the time you need to tell us what he meant to you. Your story will help others say goodbye. For me saying goodbye to him is exceedingly difficult. He did so much for so many, and I loved him."

Kirsten was crying. Petra walked up, hugged her, and helped her to a seat. She was in tears, also.

Sonia asked, "Savannah will you speak?"

Savannah, "I can't. It is all I can do to be here. Are you going to speak?"

"I am not that strong," Sonia explained. "I'll fall apart before I get to the mic."

Savannah slid one arm around Sonia's waist. Sonia placed her arm over Savannah's shoulder and said, "I am glad you are here with me. I have another question for you."

"Please ask what you want to know?" Sonia said.

"The necklace you're wearing, the pendant, has FRB on it," Savannah said as she took a long look at the necklace around Sonia's neck.

Sonia explained, "Yes, your dad gave it to me. I am never without it."

"Did he gift all the others as well? Most of the women here have them," Savannah observed.

Sonia laughed very lightly. "No, he did not. The FRBs gave them to the ones they cared for or loved. Your dad only gave three: Kerstin's, Petra's, and mine. He had them made from 24k gold."

That answer satisfied Savannah. At least for the moment.

CHAPTER 8
The Interviews

Lee Ann found the information Sonia was sharing with Savannah about the necklace fascinating. Then her reporter instinct kicked in. She saw a man approaching the FRBs' graves. He was wearing a Navy dress uniform, and he looked fit. Then she noticed he had a slight limp.

She approached him, noticed the Trident on his chest, and asked, "Did you know these men?"

He looked at her, thinking that she was a little forward, and then briefly replied, "I met them in the Hindu Kush once."

Lee Ann wasn't sure why she found him intriguing enough to ask more questions, but she continued, "Are you stationed in Germany?"

"No, ma'am. I came here from the States. General Scott called me and let me know where the FRBs were buried and that Akita would be buried here today," he explained.

Now her journalistic sensibilities were on high alert, and she asked, "If you only meet them once, why would you come, and why would General Scott call you?"

He looked at her in a measured, direct way and slowly lifted his pant leg. He was sure his first instincts about her were right. She was a bulldog. His lower left leg was prosthetic. "I lost this the day I met them," he said as he pulled his pant leg back down.

Before she could offer any explanation regarding why she was asking him questions, General Scott approached them. He shook the man's hand and said, "I am glad you made it. It looks like you've already met Lee Ann. She's a reporter here at my request. She is writing about Akita and the FRBs. I would like you to tell her what happened in the Hindu Kush. Can you share that?"

So that explained everything. The man smiled, answering, "I was going to tell her, but I knew I would have to clear it with you first."

General Scott said, "When you tell her, make sure you tell the good and the bad. I want their story to be the facts, all the facts."

Then he turned to Lee Ann and said, "So, now you've met James Elwes, Lee Ann. James, this is Lee Ann Bream."

Just then, Petra walked up and said, "May I borrow the General?"

The Interviews

General Scott smiled at the two of them and walked away with her.

"Now that we've officially met, and my story has been officially sanctioned, would you like to talk over a cup of coffee?" James said.

She answered, relieved that they had completed the niceties, "Yes. When do you want to meet?"

He smiled and said, "Tomorrow morning, please."

"Where are you staying? she asked. "I will pick you up."

"The Michel Hotel."

"Ok, I will be there at 07:00."

As soon as Lee Ann reached the hotel lobby, instead of finding James Elwes waiting for her in the coffee shop, General Scott greeted her.

"Hello, Lee Ann. Unfortunately, Elwes is unavailable. He's been called back to duty. Needed in the Middle East," General Scott explained.

She was surprised and disappointed that his story would have to be delayed. Who knows what insights into Akita that battle might have afforded her?

CHAPTER 9
Anna Meier

After making plans with James Elwes, she continued to take in her surroundings. It was then that she noticed a tall, platinum-blonde lady at Ed's grave. She was unusually tall, probably 6'4". Her hand trembled as she reached out to touch his headstone.

Lee Ann decided that it was a good time to talk to her. "Are you all right?"

She took a minute to collect herself and answered, "Yes, I am fine."

Lee Ann introduced herself. Then the tall woman said politely, "I am Anna. Nice to meet you."

She decided not to waste any time and dove right in explaining, "I'm here to record the story of Akita and the FRBs. So how did you know Ed?"

Anna said, "I met him years ago in Berlin."

She asked, "Can you tell me how you two of you met?"

Anna sighed as if she knew she was dealing with the inevitable and said, "I am an archeologist. I was in Berlin on a research assignment at the Pergamon Museum. There was a concert in the underground club Tresor. It's a small club and very hard to get into. My brother had tickets and wanted me to go with him. He'd broken up with his girlfriend and didn't want to go alone. I told him yes because I wanted to unwind from work."

Lee Ann nodded to encourage her to continue.

Anna took a deep breath and continued, "We went in his BMW M1. When he parked, the car was *very* close to the curb. As you probably know that car sits extremely low to the ground, and it was awkward when I tried to get out of the car. I was wearing a miniskirt and high heels. The low car and elevated curb made it impossible for me to get out of the car, and my brother was not helping."

Lee Ann smiled, already having a sense of where this tale would be going.

She continued, "I was getting mad when a man appeared out of nowhere. Then he offered his hand to help me out of the car. I took it. He pulled me up about halfway, and I lost my balance. He grabbed my other hand, pulling me up and out of the car. He reached his arm around my waist and steadied me. It all happened so fast, but I was then able to look at him closely for the first time. The man holding me was about 6'8" with longish brown hair and brown eyes. I could feel his well-defined muscles. In a word, he was beautiful. I know it's a cliché to say it, but in that moment, he took my breath away."

Her eyes were a little wispy, but she continued. "He asked if I needed anything else, and when I told him I was fine and thanked him for his help, he took a long, hard look at my brother and said that my *boyfriend* should have helped me. I told him that the driver was not my boyfriend but my brother, and he never helps."

All Lee Ann could do was nod in understanding. Anna wiped away a tear and continued, "After Ed introduced himself, I noticed he was with a group of friends, so asked him where everyone was from. He explained that the women were all German, but the men were Americans. And that when they were in-country, they liked to visit unfamiliar places, learn about the history, and try new things. I was a little surprised when he asked me to join them. I told him that I couldn't abandon my brother. Ed being Ed, he told me to bring him. His philosophy was '"the more, the merrier."'"

Lee Ann could tell that Anna was lost in the memory. She continued with more details of her first encounter with Ed.

"I told my brother that I was hungry and that I wanted to eat before the concert. I literally gave him no time to refuse. I grabbed Ed's arm and said, 'Lead the way.' We went to a small restaurant, and to my surprise, we had a great evening with food, drinks, and extraordinary service. I discovered that this group of Americans were called FRBs, and the women went everywhere with them when they were in country. This is when I first met

Akita, Kirsten, Petra, and Sonia. We talked about our work, our families, and what we did. I remember clearly that it was Akita who asked what the evening's plan was. A tour of the city had been arranged, and Ed asked me if I wanted to go with them."

Despite her desire to get to more important matters, Lee Ann simply nodded, awaiting more details.

Anna continued, "My brother told me to have fun and that he didn't mind going to the concert alone. Being protective, he asked if Ed would make sure that I got home safely. Of course, Ed said yes. Ed and I had such a wonderful time that I asked him if I could see him the next day." Then Anna went silent.

"Are you all right?" Lee Ann asked her for the second time in the last few minutes.

She smiled and said, "I have years of good memories with Ed. I loved him dearly, and it started with a stranger helping me out of a car."

"Will you share the rest of your story with me?" She asked.

Anna said, "Now that all of the FRBs are dead, and no one can get in trouble, yes."

Lee Ann was stunned by her answer and asked, "What do you mean?"

She said quietly, "Not here and not now. Meet me at my office later, say at 19:00. This is the address." She gave her a business card.

Lee Ann left Anna at Ed's grave. She desperately wanted to continue the interview, but she had learned long ago not to push too hard. She didn't want to lose the trust she had already built because people will never reveal what they know.

CHAPTER 10
African Royalty

Lee Ann felt as though she was making some progress. She saw the possibility of another opening to meet a person who might have an interesting story to share. She was hoping she could earn their trust and encourage them to talk at this time of great loss. She slowly approached a man and woman standing together. Without any hesitation, the man standing next to a strikingly beautiful, exotic looking woman turned to her and said, "This is Valiane. She is an African Royal from the Grand Lodge. She was the Sword-bearer of the Grand Lodge of England."

Before Lee Ann could reply, Valiane said, "And this is Bediako, First Warrior of the Blood Oath."

Lee Ann decided the direct approach would be best with this couple. She asked, "How did you know Akita, and why did you come to the funeral?"

Valiane said, "I met Akita when I was nine years old. My country was being torn apart by civil war. My father called the U.S. president and asked for help, but he also asserted that the help sent could not be tied back to the U.S. When the men arrived from the U.S. that evening, my father was mad that the president had betrayed him. My father had been expecting enough men to guard the palace. The president had sent only twelve men, and our home, The Palace of the Empire, was about to be overrun by enemy troops. My father had to get to the capital."

Valiane gave her a chance to take all this in and then explained, "One American told my father that he would split his men and my family into two groups, and each would take a different path. When my father said that he wanted to keep us all together, the American explained plainly that if we did it my father's way, when the enemy attacked, our whole family will die. His way, some will survive. Of course, my father then agreed. The Americans split into two six men teams. My mother and I went with one, my father and brother went with the other team. My father took his armored sedan. We did not take any of my father's soldiers because we could not know where their loyalties lay. The American who talked to my father and devised the plan introduced himself as 'Akita.' We had only a few minutes to prepare and the plan was to take the path through the mountains. I was mad at him. He split up my family and was not showing my mother the respect she deserved.

My father was also furious, and I remember that he told my mother and me, 'Do what they say, we all must live.'"

It was clear that she had met Akita in the most difficult of circumstances. She continued, "Akita did not let us take anything with us. We started out by truck and drove for about three hours. Akita had one of his men ahead of us in a jeep. Then the man circled back, stopped us, and talked to Akita. The American's told us to get out of the truck. Then they drove the truck into a ditch. My mother was so mad, and when she asked how we would get to the capital now, Akita told her that we would walk and run.

She continued, "Akita split his men up. One far out front of us, one right in front of us. Then my mother and me. Two behind us and one far behind. We walked for six or seven kilometers. I fell and said that I could go no further. Akita was relentless. He told me that we would all die if I didn't get up. I tried. I just couldn't. He pulled off his pack, took everything out, distributed it to his men, and they put it in their packs. He cut holes in the sides of his own now-empty pack. He picked me up and put my legs into the holes and put me on his back. Then we were walking and then running. When the men were walking, my mother walked. When they were running, two of them, one on each side, would lift her by her armpits. She had no choice but to keep up. Then the man scouting in front of us came running back and told us that we had company ahead. Akita wanted to know how many. The man told him there were at least three on the trail and more, at least four, on the north side of the brush."

Valiane, now deeply immersed in the memory, continued, "Akita told my mother to lie down on the ground and to stay down. One man stayed with us, and the others left. Fifteen minutes later, all of us were moving again. We passed bodies on the trail, and there was blood everywhere. We did not stop for another three or four hours. When we stopped, Akita took me out of the pack and gave me water. I remember telling him that I was hungry. He had one of his men give me a chocolate bar. The man forward from us came back and told us that there were around a hundred men two kilometers up on the trail. Akita took out the map, clearly, he had a plan."

Relating significant details, Valiane explained Akita's strategy. "He opened his map and said to his men, 'We need to go here, then turn here, run the canyon to here.'"

"One man added, 'The hard way.' I remember," Valiane said, "that another man observed, 'This shit just keeps getting better,' and Akita told him that he wouldn't have it any other way."

She continued, "We left and traveled for another two hours. When we stopped. Akita said one-word, 'Recon.' Two men left, one going ahead of us, one going back down the way we had come. Mom and I drank more water. Akita gave me another chocolate bar. I was starting to like him. The men came back and said everything was clear, so Akita told everyone that we could rest for now and move out before first light. He told us that we'd need to be at the cliff before they caught up to us, with the bottleneck leading to it because when the fight broke out, we would have the advantage. It was then that my mother asked Akita if we would ever make it to the capital. Akita told her that he and his men would do everything they could to get us there. Then my mother asked him why he was doing all this. Akita told her, 'We received orders; we are following them. If not us, then who?'"

"The following morning before the darkness had lifted, Akita woke us. Within five minutes, his men were ready to go. He put me back in the pack, and we moved. He told me to stay quiet. Then the man behind us came running up and said that we had trouble and only about six hours to spare. Akita said that everyone would need to double-time to the cliff. We took off. When we were at the bottom of the cliff, Akita called one of his men over to us. The man was the biggest man I had ever seen. Akita told me that the man's name was Ed and that he would carry me up the cliff. Akita took me off his back, and Ed put me on his."

Valiane wiped a tear away, gathered herself, and then continued, "Akita told his men that he would buy them some time to ascend the cliff. I know that Ed gave him a weapon and ammo and told him he'd need more firepower."

Valiane was leaving nothing out of this drama. Continuing the saga, she said, "One of the men asked Akita if he was sure he wanted to do this, and Akita told him, 'No, but if not me, then who?' Then Akita smiled and said, 'Into the lion's den.' I will never forget his words."

"We started the climb. Later I learned that the cliff we climbed was 152 meters high and another 400 meters to the ridge. Halfway up to the ridge, I heard gunfire. Ed yelled for us to keep moving. That was when I realized what was happening. Akita stayed down there to take the fight to the enemy. He was alone. I started to try and get away from Ed. I was yelling, 'They are killing him.'"

"Ed backed up, pushing me against a rock. Then he whispered, 'Listen.' I stopped and listened. Then Ed asked me if I could hear the rounds, one right after another and sharp. I told him I could, and then he asked me if I could hear the one that was by itself and deep, and I answered in the affirmative again. Then Ed smiled and told me, 'That is Akita. They are not killing him. He is killing them. If Akita were dead, you would not hear any gunfire.'"

Relating the story was taking a toll on her, but she never stopped. She continued, "We made it up to the top of the ridgeline. We followed the ridgeline to a small clearing, which took another six hours. Ed decided that's where we'd camp. My mother had tripped and fallen on the way up the ridge and was hurt. Ed got on the radio, and I heard him say, 'The Queen needs medical care above what we have.' Then he gave them some numbers from the map which signaled our location. Later, two men parachuted in. One man started helping my mother. I was amazed they dropped out of the sky.

A radio call came in that said we should stay in place because we were safe. They said they'd send in reinforcements. That night we received a supply drop of food, ammo, and six more men. The men would not say anything about Akita, so I knew he was dead. The next day we stayed in place. The Americans were camouflaging the area where my mother and I were. At midday the following day, I heard a voice from outside the camp. It sent chills down my spine. Only one word was spoken, and that word was 'Ed.'

The men reacted in one heartbeat. All had weapons up and ready. They moved like jungle cats, looking, listening. Then the voice again said, 'Ed.' I knew that voice. It was my American Akita, I started to run toward it. Then one man grabbed me, pushed me to the ground, and lay on top of me. He said simply, 'Keep quiet.' Then Akita said to Ed, 'I do not want to get shot. May I stand?'"

Ed told him yes, and Akita rose, ghost-like. He was closer than the men thought he would be, and I could tell that it scared them. Ed's weapon was trained on Akita, and he asked Akita if he was alone. Akita told him that he had eighteen men with him. Ed wanted to know if they were friends or not. Akita told him that he wouldn't be alive if they weren't friends."

"Then Ed told Akita, 'Have them stand, hands out to their sides.'"

Akita turned and said, 'Show yourselves hands out. If you touch a weapon, you die.' The men stood up and held their hands straight out from their sides. They were thirty meters behind Akita in the cover of the tree line."

Ed told them, 'Walk forward to here.' He pointed to the ground. The men moved slowly. They did not want to get shot."

Akita told Ed, 'They needed to give the Queen their oath of loyalty and that they will keep it.'"

Ed and two other men took the weapons from them and patted them down. Then Akita told Ed that we needed to allow them to give their oath to their Queen and then give the weapons back."

"Ed took some time, then said, 'They have not shot you, so we will try it.'"

The first man Bediako kneeled in front of my mother. He looked up and said, 'My Queen, I swear to you on all the blood I have spilled, and all the blood spilled for you. I will defend my country, its citizens, my fellow soldiers, and the royal family against all enemies, foreign and domestic, until I draw my last breath.' He stood and moved behind her. Each man gave the same oath, then took his place behind his Queen." Ed returned their weapons.

Akita told my mother, 'They will only take orders from you now. Will you have them see the medic, then get something to eat?' My mother did so.

When Akita had finished, I went to him. I wanted to tell him that I was sorry. He was dirty; he had blood all over his clothes, and he smelled like rotting meat. He looked at me and said, 'Your mother needs your help. Would you please go and help her?'"

It was only after my mother's men had seen the medic and received care and food, that Akita told Ed, 'I need a medic.' Then he turned and walked to the tent."

A medic arrived, and when the medic finished and exited Akita's tent, he said, 'I need help. Akita has two bullet holes in him.'"

"Bobby offered to assist. Three hours later, Bobby told Ed that they had done all they could. Ed told my mother, 'We need to find out how he got shot and who did it.'"

"Bediako stepped forward and said, 'We did not know he was injured. He was probably shot when he attacked us. We tried to fight back. We did not want to die. We were shooting.'"

Valiane looked at Bediako and said, "You tell Lee Ann about what happened at the bottom of that cliff." Then she turned to Lee Ann and said, "I know the story, but I was not there. Bediako lived it. He needs to tell you what my American did."

Bediako said, "We had eighty men when we started. General Kojo and ten of his men were in black uniforms instead of the Army's tan ones. He told us, 'I am your ruler now.' He made us hunt the royal family. He told us if we did not, he would kill us. To make the point, he shot a man in the head. We had followed a group for days. Kojo told us that the king was in this group, and they would get tired. Then the group turned into rough terrain. It was hard going, and it got worse. Kojo looked at his map and said, 'They are boxing themselves in. We will have the king.' We started down a canyon and passed through a place where the walls were about twenty feet apart. We could see the cliff now. Kojo said, 'We have them now, they cannot go up that.' He pointed, and as soon as he did, his head snapped back, and blood sprayed. He hit the ground. His men were yelling and pointing. Our men were firing at everything and nothing. The men that were pointing were dying. We were pinned down. Some men tried to run back up the canyon. They fell dead after three or four steps. Then automatic fire came in on us. I had men all around me screaming, crying, and calling for their mothers. The firing stopped. I looked up and saw a man running towards us. He was killing the men we had on point. He picked up their weapons and killed the men closest to him. He was alone and attacking us. I thought that he was out of ammo. I got up and tried to get the men to fight back. He was close and closing the distance. I saw him pull a small shovel, an entrenching tool, from his back. He swung it at one man and hit him in the neck. He swung it at another and buried it so deep in the man's head he could not pull it out. I pointed at him and yelled out. Before I finished, he had me, and my back was towards him. His left arm was around my head. His right hand was at my neck with a knife.

He pulled the knife to my neck and said, 'Tell them to drop their weapons, or I will kill everyone here who is big enough to die.'"

"I yelled, 'Drop them, drop them,' and they did. He then asked me why our uniforms were different, and I told him that they were going to kill us if we did not come with them.

He pulled the knife again. This time blood ran down my shirt."

"Then he said, his voice was hard and cold, 'Swear on all the blood I have spilled, and all the blood you have spilled that you will defend your country, its citizens, your fellow soldiers, and the royal family against all enemies foreign and domestic until you draw your last breath.'

I gave my oath. It was an oath I always wanted to give to my country, but not like this.

He gave me the knife and told me, 'Make all my men give the oath. If they do not give the oath to their country. Then pull the blade through their neck. We do not need them.'"

"I did this, and I had to leave five men there. I counted men, and I had thirty men left.

The American man turned to me and said, 'Get your weapons and come with me.' We walked to the cliff. He told us, 'Start climbing. Do not stop, or you will fall. If you fall, you will die. If you fall, do not grab the man next to you because both of you will die. If you fall, do not fall on the man under you, or you will all die. If you live or die, it is up to you.' We did not stop. He would not stop and rest. All of us wanted to stop and rest or give up. He pushed us. He said that we were almost there. I wanted to know where "there" was. We got to the top of a slope. We were still in the tree line. In a small clearing, we saw the camp.

He stopped us and said, 'Do not make a sound, do not move until I tell you to. If you do, all of us will die.'"

Then Bediako said, "Valiane has already told you what happened when we got to the camp."

Valiane added, "Lee Ann, my American Akita climbed that cliff and made it to the camp. Then he made sure all the men were taken care of first, and he had bullet holes in him.

Only Akita and eighteen Warriors of the Blood Oath made it out of all the men who started the climb. You asked me why I was here. My father and brother ran the first chance they had to another country. Our group had not made it to the cliff before they ran. Akita did not run away. My mother and I lived because of him and his men. Akita made the Warriors of the Blood Oath. Akita made my mother the Queen of the Blood Oath Warriors. He stopped the coup without knowing it by killing General Kojo, who started the coup. That is why I am here as they started to walk away."

Bediako said, "Lee Ann, you should know this also. I asked Akita why he had first killed the men in black uniforms? I was sure he would say because of the uniform, but he told me it was because they were pointing and that a man in charge or one who thinks he is in charge will point. I asked him if that was why he grabbed me. He said, 'You pointed, and I had nowhere else to go. I was dead, and I knew it.' Then he smiled at me and said, 'When you are in uniform and in a group, do not point. You never know who is watching or what they are willing to do.'"

Then Bediako looked at Lee Ann directly and asked, "What kind of man does what he did?"

After taking this all in, all Lee Ann could say was, "I do not know the answer to that."

CHAPTER 11
General Scott Interview

Lee Ann felt as though she had been preparing for this interview her whole professional career. The opportunity to interview General Scott came at a price. She knew she should be prepared for anything after coming to understand the intensity of his connection with the FRBs. The most important thing was to relax and give him a chance to talk. She had prepared her questions with a knife's edge precision, hoping to glean as much as she could to bring some clarity to Akita's story. She took a deep breath and began.

How did you recruit the men in your unit?

"I had people on the training bases looking for the hard skills I needed. They would find a soldier in boot camp or a class with a high skill level. I had a phone number they called. I never acted on the first call. I had the soldier surveilled to determine if they maintained a high skill level. Then I sent someone to talk or test them to determine if what we offered interested them."

What skill did Akita have that was reported to you?

"The first time on a firing range, he was given 80 rounds and 80 targets. He did not miss and took less time than allowed. The next time, he had the same result. Then I got another call. I was told he had an altercation with a drill sergeant. The sergeant had him in the position of attention and was yelling about something. He accidentally spit on Akita. It took four men to pull him off. Akita was sixteen years old and weighed 125 pounds. The sergeant was twenty-nine and weighed 220 pounds.

The company commander wanted to have Akita dishonorably discharged from the Army, but he couldn't because the Army was Akita's legal guardian. The State of Texas had custody of him and signed it over to the Army. He was in a long-term detention facility. They gave all new residents the ASVAB test, and he scored in the top five percent of the country. The Army made a deal with Texas: a high school diploma if he enlists for three years. The commander was pissed off. Six drill sergeants took Akita behind the mess hall and beat his ass. He put two in the hospital before he went down. I became extremely interested in somebody who could fight like that. I talked to JAG about the Army's legal guardianship and was told they could change his contract and issue him a new one, so I sent people to talk to him."

Why was he in the detention facility?

"He had been beaten at home from the time he was about two years old. When he was nine years old, he left for school one morning. When he came home that evening, the house was empty. He raised himself the only way he could in order to survive. He stayed in trouble for fighting, stealing, and much more. Once, a group of high school boys wanted to kick his ass. He took out the leader with a brick. As the group of boys hit and kicked him, Akita beat the leader in the head with a brick. Akita spent three weeks in the hospital. The State called it self-defense. You can read Akita's medical records from the entrance exam."

Do you remember so much detail about all your people?

"Yes, when it was the FRBs. All twelve of them had it that bad or worse. I gave them pride in themselves, a reason to be the best in a job only they could do." (Lee Ann made an additional note of this, thinking something about his answer was off.)

What did Akita have to do before receiving his invitation to your unit?

"I recruited him at seventeen years old. He had to graduate from airborne school, ranger school, jungle school, desert training, sniper school, and special forces school to be considered for entry into the unit."

How did you get involved with this unit?

"I founded this unit at the request of the President of the United States. This unit answered only to the President and to me. Akita agreed to change his contract. He passed all the schools and was in the top three in each class. I had his orders for the detachment processed. Akita accepted them and understood that his military identity would be sealed from that day forward. He was now part of a unit that did not exist officially. This shadow unit was a detachment of the 5th Special Forces. Akita had not only joined the unit, but also, within ninety days, he had been placed on a team. I was an LTC at the time. I put this team together because their hard skills and psychological profiles matched, making an unmatched fighting force, at least on paper.

I also considered that the men did not have a family to worry about. All of them were beaten at home by their parents and kids at school.

General Scott Interview

They had been starved and forced to live in conditions that would make others sick. They had learned how to fight, even when it was five or ten on one. The only help available was self-provided: fighting abilities, skills, and the ability to make others pay. When they took a badass whooping, they started with the biggest one, doing everything to him that he was doing to them. Make him pay, pick up anything, hit him with it hard, and often. If you hurt him enough, the others will leave you alone. Either way, you will be in the hospital. They became thieves and beggars for money on the street. Growing up in this way, most kids became broken, subservient, or in prison, but these men became hardened fighters. They did not fit into society. They were unwanted, throwaways, wayward, and indifferent." Scott stopped talking.

What is wrong? Do you need a break?

"No. I don't. I had psychological profiles done on all my soldiers. A researcher at the Department of Defense trying to enhance muscle structure pulled my profiles. My higher command ordered me to send twenty-four of my people to a research facility in New Mexico. The orders were for six months. I sent them as ordered. I had no updates for eighteen months. When I was called to headquarters for a briefing, I was told my people had been part of an experiment to enhance the muscular structure. I found out details later from a report. A friend liberated top secret files in DOD as a favor to me. On the first day, the men were tested for strength. All the weights lifted were recorded and run times, also as a baseline.

The report also said that the doctor first devised a way to turn off one-half of two genes and splice two others together. This manipulation creates an abnormality that can be passed on to the next generation. The doctor had worked under a genius in the genetic field for years. Then he stole all his work and defected to the U.S. This was his first job. He experimented on my men and gave them a virus to deliver this into their system. One man died from the virus. The others were sick for weeks, and the medical staff would give them nothing for their symptoms that might interfere with the test.

With the treatment the men were receiving, they decided not to lift any more than they did on the first day or run any faster. In fact, most lifted less and ran slower. The doctor got very pissed off that his experiment was failing. He was going to lose his funding and face disgrace. That is when he implemented a drug regimen, forced physical training ten hours a day, and double rations. They were strapped to a bed the last two weeks with an I.V. concoction of untested drugs fed into them. The tester said that the drugs caused significant pain. My men's psychological profiles were the only reason they were picked—my unwanted or throwaway soldiers, the ones that no one would miss. This was my fault. I sent twenty-four of my men; thirteen came back. At the time I have no idea what happened to the others— if they died or washed out. All thirteen men were over 200 pounds, two of them 300 or more. They wanted to tear me apart. All I could say was that I followed orders and didn't know what they were going through. Akita asked for the name and address of the person who ordered the program. I could not tell him for fear of what he'd do.

When they returned, I needed to see if they had the skills required. I promised to give them all the tools they needed, then turn them loose on an enemy, and lead them into the fight. I promised I'd fight alongside them, show them how to lead, and then let them lead. I had to do all this to gain their trust, respect, and loyalty back."

When did you realize this team of the unwanted had become the unmatched fighting force you needed? Did what happened to them have anything to do with it?

"They were stronger, much stronger. As for psychological, it's hard to tell. Their mental and emotional state of mind had always been challenging to understand. They were different from other men under my command."

How did you test them to find out if they were mission-ready?

"I gave them light missions to test their skills. They were doing better than expected. As a group, they asked for missions with more difficulty. I told them I would investigate and let them know. When the team left, Akita stayed behind. He instructed me that if I didn't give them a worthy mission, I'd lose them as a team. He passionately said that I needed to let them do what I'd put them together to do. I remember what Akita said: 'Send us into the lion's den and let us kill lions.' He spoke to me so inappropriately that I ordered him out of my office. I was mad. I had several missions, but only one that was difficult. So, I relented. I called them in and handed over the mission. I thought they would try to get

General Scott Interview

out of this one or ask for help. Instead, they thanked me and said it was about time. They were all smiling. I was stumped.

Most of this mission is still classified, but I can tell you this. On their first difficult mission, all went well for the first two-thirds of it with buildup and deployment. They were eight months in and still in hostile territory. When exiting, a firefight broke out. This new young team brought hell down on everything that was not one of them. The enemy did not have a chance to run or give up. We had to use the secondary extraction point to get them out. They were so driven to accomplish the mission I gave them. Nothing else mattered. They made sure to master all the associated tasks within the parameters of their mission. The team received only minor wounds. After this mission, the team was given one week to recover and debrief what they could have done differently, more efficiently, and more effectively or better. They made sure everyone knew how well they had done during this time, and that no one could have done it any better. This was done very loudly."

How did the name FRBs come about?

"They played tricks on each other and everyone else, tricks they had learned in detention homes, jails, group homes, and other places they had to live in growing up. All this mayhem did not sit well with the company's regular people, who started calling them 'Fucking Rowdy Basterds.' This nickname was supposed to be derogatory. None of the FRBs had any family to speak of. Out of the twelve men, only Akita had an uncle he had never met, and Ed had a sister he did not know. That was it, no other family. This meant that the team's decisions would be mission completion only without the goal of returning to a caring family. When they took the derogatory name and made it a nickname to be proud of, I knew I would have to contain some fallout this team would cause. Their mischievous and twisted nature would be trouble for all around them when they were idle."

What about the connection to Wetzlar?

"I had to devise a way they could focus on other items besides messing with the soldiers around them. I came up with the idea to relocate all team's R&R time to Germany.

This would allow all detachment personnel to see how they impacted others. Show them the missions they were on. The accomplishments that

General Scott Interview

they were making would have positive impacts. Like their predecessors had done in World War II. My decision would change lives here in the United States and Germany. I would make Kirchgoens, Germany, the location where this unit would take R&R after six months or more out on missions. Kirchgoens (Ayers Kaserne) was a U.S. Army installation built in 1952. It had one barracks set back from other living and motor pool areas. I signed for it. Now it belonged to the 5th SF. I was unaware that Wetzlar, a town seventeen kilometers away would become the focal point for FRB activities.

The FRB's finding out about Wetzlar was by mistake. Akita and Ed were at a motor pool collecting parts for the vehicles they needed. Sergeant E5 James was commenting he was going to Wetzlar one evening to see his girlfriend and others. He planned to take them to a bar for a night of dancing and to a restaurant for excellent food. Akita and the others had very little to do on the Kaserne, and Kirchgoens was no different. So, Akita got the directions to the bar and Sergeant James offered to introduce the FRBs to the friends he had made there. This single insignificant conversation would lead to a twenty-five-year relationship between the FRBs, the almost inhuman American soldiers, and over 110 Wetzlar residents."

It was clear that General Scott was finished. He began shuffling papers on his desk. Lee Ann knew it was time for her to go. She thanked him, gathered her materials, and stood up to go. "Thank you so much for your time, General. I'm so grateful for the time you've taken to give me so many details."

"Do me proud, Lee Ann, and just tell the story straight. That's all I ask," he said.

Lee Ann nodded and turned to leave, knowing that she had much, much more to learn about this enigmatic group of men, and especially more to know about Akita.

CHAPTER 12
Retrieving Three People

Lee Ann rubbed her eyes as she looked over her notes that she had taken during her interviews with General Scott. He was proving to be a most reliable source. She could only imagine the intensity of the situation.

On the second mission, Akita and Ed were on overwatch. The other team members were retrieving three people from some Colombian army deserters working for a drug dealer. They had not been told who the people were. Just that they were being held against their will. The CIA needed them back.

The team had worked their way into the camp. So far, the intel had been correct, and the camp's layout matched the aerial photos. They had killed six people using knives, then lowered the bodies to the ground, and moved them so they were out of sight. They were trying not to make a sound. A noise broke out in one building, and everyone froze.

Suddenly, a door opened, and men started coming out. All had weapons. Someone inside the room with the door open yelled something indistinguishable in Spanish. One of the men outside went back to the door. He was handed a small case. He rejoined the group that had gotten in two pickups.

Both trucks went to the gate. A guard opened it and let them pass. The team waited until the trucks were out of sight. Akita had seen the men load a footlocker into one of the trucks.

Then watching them leave, he whispered a question to Ed, "Patrol?"

Ed replied in a whisper, "Looks like they are going to a meeting with the box and case."

Akita said, "I had a count of six."

Ed said, "That's what I got."

The team found a small building guarded by two men. The intel they had received told them this was where the people should be. They split into three teams. Two teams would come in from behind and take out any guards, one team on the left and one on the right. The third team would go straight in from the front. The guards would see them and respond to them. The teams right and left would act and kill them silently. The team on the front straight-in approach would get in and get the people out.

Retrieving Three People

General Scott had told them, "Take the people even if they do not want to leave and get out." The teams outside would provide cover for their exit.

The plan worked. They had their people still tied and gagged. They worked their way to the perimeter. It was hard work getting the three people outside the wire, carrying, lifting, and pushing them all the way. They were bound. They could not help and had no idea what was happening to them. They were scared, and one man even pissed on himself.

In time, the team had the people and were outside the perimeter of the camp.

Inside the camp, a guard found a dead man. The man's throat had been cut so deeply that his head was only held on by bone. The alarm went up, and the jungle came alive with the soldiers from the camp.

Akita was in the prone position with his 308. He aimed and fired. Ed moved to where he was 90 degrees on Akita's right side. When the four rounds in the weapon had been fired, Ed fed one round at a time into the breach. This allowed Akita to fire continuously without time to reload.

V-man was carrying one of the people on his shoulder. He ran down one side of a ditch. He was halfway up the other bank when three men met him with weapons up, ready to fire.

V-man pulled his weapon up to fire. When he saw the first man's head thrust back hard, this man was dead before he hit the ground. The second man on his nonfiring side (left-hand side for V-man) had a pink mist spraying out his head, and he fell to the ground. The third man's head went sideways as half of it disappeared.

V-man made it to cover, turned, and fired. Other team members found people around them falling in front and behind, all people they had not shot. Akita was doing his job. Ed was amazed at how fast Akita was on the trigger, and his aim was not missing.

The team maneuvered into place. That put the hostile force between Akita and their firepower and a gorge to the rear. Akita was taking targets at will. Half of the team would move, and the other would provide cover fire. Ed noticed rounds coming into their location. Akita kept shooting.

Akita heard Ed yell, "Move, mother fucker, move."

So, he moved to get a better shot position. Akita heard Ed tell him

Retrieving Three People

to move two more times. He did and got a better shot position each time. Akita was shooting movement. He would see movement, shoot that movement, one eye looking some 700 meters away for movement, the other sighting targets through his scope. He was so focused on his task that he did not know rounds were coming into their location. Akita had four hundred 308 rounds. Ed had four hundred 308 rounds. Akita thought he had fired fifty rounds and spent maybe thirty minutes on the weapon. He had six rounds left, and Ed had fifteen. He had been on the weapon for an hour and a half as far as time.

Then Ed had told him to move because of incoming rounds.

After this gun fight, Akita and Ed moved about five kilometers away to an abounded house. The pickups from the camp were there. Two men were at the door.

Akita said," I will work my way to the far side and take that one out. He pointed. You have the other. We must be quiet. We cannot let the ones inside know we are here."

Ed said, "We have six to deal with."

"Another day in paradise," Akita said.

Ed said, "Akita, you are one sick mother fucker."

The two men at the door died at the same time when their throats were cut. Akita and Ed readied themselves. Akita pulled out his M1911 .45 pistol. Ed had his M4 and nodded his head. Akita kicked the door hard. The house was so old the door went into the house six feet before crashing to the floor. The men inside were sitting at a table. They were startled by the door and by two men coming in shooting. They died without getting a hand on a weapon. Ed had put three rounds in every man. Akita had put one round in each man's head, reloaded, and moved through the rooms clearing the house.

Ed stayed at the door so no one could enter. Akita yelled, "Clear" when he left each room. This was the assembly area for the team. Once all were present, they would move to the extraction point. The team made it to the house and secured the area.

Bobby asked, "What the hell happened?"

Ed said, "We had uninvited guests."

Bobby asked, "Did you shoot then enough?"

"We wanted to make sure they were dead. Now we know they're

79

dead. How are those three?" Akita asked.

V-man said, "Good to go, but can I beat his ass for pissing on me?"

"You might want to find out who he is first. Somebody wants them back bad to have us get them," Bobby observed.

Ten minutes later, the team was moving to the extraction point. The exit was a success.

CHAPTER 13
Indifference Towards the Enemy

LTC Scott sent another team out to confirm the after-action report. This team found Akita had kept the enemy from moving. All they could do is "spray and pray." This meant raising their weapons above what they were hiding behind. Only the weapons and their arms could be seen. Then they shoot on fully automatic, moving the weapons from right to left from behind whatever cover they had found. When the enemy did move, they were shot either by Akita or the ten-man extraction team fighting their way out.

Akita had been a force multiplier and had allowed his people to escape. They found that the enemy soldiers were trapped between sniper fire, heavy fire from the ten-man extraction team, and a gorge to their rear. They told LTC Scott that Akita and the others had shown brutality and indifference almost to the point of being inhuman (not like American soldiers should be).

The other teams wanted this new team disbanded due to the amount of indifference towards the enemy, overkill, and seemingly the lack of respect for other teams.

Some asked if they had an exit plan. This team cared only about the mission completion. To all others in the unit, they did not have contingency plans for evac. This was wrong; the plans were there and talked through, but the job at hand came first.

They slowed down to not make mistakes and became more efficient, which made them faster. Akita kept raising the standards for his team. When they would meet that standard, they set it even higher to what should have been unachievable. When they reached that goal, still unsatisfied, they again set a new standard. They became the standard for all others to follow.

CHAPTER 14
Interview General Scott: Columbia

General Scott began with one startling fact: "I received a mission from the President." Then he relayed the details of yet another unbelievably dangerous adventure.

CIA agent, Jim Skinner in South America, had gone rogue. He teamed up with General Mendoza, who was involved in drugs, prostitution, sex slavery, and other vile shit. Several organizations tried to shut down the operation and capture or kill the general and the CIA agent, but none were successful. All of them had failed because of the unpredictability of where the general would be at any one time. The general had several homes that he had confiscated. He would also often see a house he wanted, kill the occupants, and take it over as his own. He never spent two nights in the same place.

General Mendoza had more than thirty cars. He would have one car drive him to a location, and another drive him from that location along with six or seven other vehicles to add to the chaos.

Our CIA man was always at his side. A man in the general's trust twisted the schedule of his routes, where he slept, and who he slept with. This puzzle was unpredictable and remained unbroken by any intelligence agency or armed force. The only pattern he had was that he would go to an armed compound in the jungle forty miles from the nearest village. This compound was in a clearing with a perimeter of ten meters from the first fence. The second fence was another ten meters beyond that. It had 100 full-time armed personnel.

The compound contained six large barracks and two small outhouses with an office at the front gate. Just outside the compound, all the vehicles parked in a parking lot. Only one road led into the compound.

General Mendoza went there to oversee his drug operation and money delivery system.

My orders from the President were to find and kill the general and capture or kill the CIA agent. Shut the operation down and make it look like a rival drug lord or militia overthrew and killed them.

I issued orders to Akita by phone to return to Fort Benning, Georgia. He was to leave the FRBs in Wetzlar. I informed him all transportation

INTERVIEW GENERAL SCOTT: COLOMBIA

arrangements had been made and were in place, and a car would pick him up in two hours. Akita was picked up in Wetzlar by Army military police and transported to Rhein-Main Air Base. He was handed off to Air Force personnel. They drove him to a C5A aircraft waiting for him on the runway.

Akita arrived in Fort Benning seventeen hours later. The CIA briefed him an hour after he landed. The briefing lasted two hours, then another hour of questions and answers.

Akita waited for the CIA personnel to leave. He wanted to get eyes on the target, and he didn't trust the intel.

Akita said that if we had a soldier who defected, we would get him ourselves. We wouldn't go to an outside entity to do it for us. He was sure that something was wrong with this situation and that there were things they weren't being told.

I agreed that we needed more details. Akita told me that he wanted two of his men, Ed and Joe, to go with him to South America. I arranged for the transportation and got the men to the states. We briefed them on the mission and told them that we needed more reliable intel.

It was Ed who said, "We get our own Intel gathering mission this time. We won't be in the dark. Cool." The three spent forty-five days in the jungle, running silent (silent operations are the most dangerous to execute).

Six hours into the third day, Joe was on point and did a hard stop. He made no more movements. Ed and Akita followed his lead.

Akita whispered, "What do you have?"

Joe quietly said, "I have movement at eleven o'clock on top of the rise. Just passed the ditch."

Akita moved slowly to a location where he could see the area Joe had told him about, he took out his binoculars (binos) and found the movement. It was two men. One was talking on a radio and waving his arms around. It looked like he was trying to get someone's attention. They were having communication (commo) problems. The other man used a spotting scope to survey the route Akita and his men would take.

Akita said in a low voice, "We are a day ahead of schedule. It looks like we have two surveillance locations being set up. This one 400 meters to our left and another one somewhere over to our right." He turned

Interview General Scott: Colombia

to Joe and said, "Find the other one. We need to know what we are up against."

Ed quietly said, "You were right something is wrong with this. I am glad you wanted to get an early start."

Joe smiled and said, "One day early, we find out we are being watched. I will find out who he is waving at." Joe slipped away silently.

Ed was watching the men on the rise and said, "They do not have any training or are just not using it because we're not supposed to be here until tomorrow. I do not think they were military. I think they are CIA. Or they do not know about us, and they are hunting."

Akita said, "I have never seen white people in the middle of this shit set up a lookout post to hunt."

Joe returned and reported, "Three men are setting up another camp about 700 meters away and on the high ground. We need to travel between both points to recon the compound."

Akita took out his map. He had cut out the section they needed to plot their course. This way, he did not have a white paper the size of a small table flapping in the breeze. He put a mark on the map of the left camp's location. Without saying anything or being asked, Joe put a mark where the other one was.

Akita said," We must cross the river and climb this rise. Mother fuck, they have a clear field of view. We can't cross here without being seen on the river up the incline and on the backside going down to the compound. We need another way." He smiled and asked," How do you feel about the long, hard way?"

Ed asked, "When do we *not* go the long, hard way?"

Akita gave the map to Ed and pointed, "Go this way. It is a day or so longer and steeper, but they will not see you."

Joe looked carefully and said," You are right. It is hidden from them." Joe knew Akita was planning something and continued, "You are not going with us. You give us your map and tell us to go this way. What are you thinking, and where will you be?"

"I want information," he explained. To get it, I need to be very close and listen. With the commo problems and the fact that they do not know we are here, I should be able to find out some of what we need." Then Akita slipped away silently.

Interview General Scott: Colombia

Joe told Ed, "It is scary how he does that with no sound."

Ed observed, "You should work on missions with him shooting and moving to get a better shot position. The man is stealthy. Working with him, I have learned how to move quickly and quietly, but not like that."

CHAPTER 15
Targets: Akita and the FRBs

Akita worked his way to the lookout point. Four hours later, he was as close as he needed. The last fifty meters took an hour. He could hear what was said in a normal voice. The men were bitching about being there and waiting on the three people they were sent to gather intel on.

Akita slowly took out his mini recorder. All the teams were issued and used recorders in the field. They were used primarily in meetings with people who were supposed to be allies. When they talked amongst themselves in a foreign language, the team would record everything and give the tape to the interpreters, who would tell the teams what was said and what it meant.

Akita wanted hard evidence in case this opp went sideways.

About one and a half hours after Akita got into his position, the radio cracked to life. A voice on the other end said, "L one, this is L two radio check over."

One of the men Akita was watching grabbed the hand mike and said, "It's about time you got that fucking thing fixed."

The voice on the other end said, "Bill, what time tomorrow are they supposed to arrive? Do you think they will be late? Or are they not coming?"

Akita now knew that his men were the target, and one of the men he was watching was named Bill. Akita carefully pushed the record button, hoping the sound would not be heard.

Bill replied to the caller and said, "Leroy, the men coming here are good at what they do. Keep a sharp eye out. We know their starting point for this recon. This is the only way to that compound. They must come this way. We have their radio frequencies, so now that yours is working, listen and write everything you hear in your log, and remember, all we need to find out is their extraction points. Once we have that, we can make all other arrangements."

In a disagreeable voice, Leroy said, "That fucking doctor wants them dead because they are his failed experiment. So, we get this group of fucked up experiments to kill Skinner, a fucking CIA traitor, and the doctor gets us to clean up his fuckup. We must also retrieve their bodies and transport them to his research facility. What else do we need to do to eliminate other people's messes?"

Bill said, "Keep that to yourself. We are in charge of this. The army has been told that we will handle their men's exit. Their men make the call that the mission is complete and tell us where to pick them up one of two places. We will have enough men there to take them out. We are here for one reason only: to retrieve the extraction points."

"I need to know one thing. After this is done, how will we cover it up?" Leroy said.

Bill was unequivocal. "That is not your job or mine."

Akita was angry. He waited until the camp was quiet. He left back the way he had come.

Akita began working out a plan as he made his way to the meeting place where Ed and Joe were. Akita decided to tell Ed and Joe what he had heard. "Do your job," he said, "and act like no one is watching. After we get this job done, we will deal with the fucking CIA."

Ed asked, "Do you think we have an army informant working with them?" Akita had done reconnaissance on the camp from inside the camp. He had been under all the buildings and found the floors were half-inch thick wood planks, and no one ever checked under the building. On day forty-three, Akita made a radio call to the mission support CIA team with the extraction points his team had decided on. He gave precise map coordinates for two points that his team would use to be extracted. The names of the points were Alpha and Bravo.

The first and only radio call Scott received from this recon mission was from Akita requesting evac. With a hint of pride, Scott said, "The evac went as planned. Four days later, my men were back."

CHAPTER 16
Insane

General Scott was looking weary, but he continued telling the story. He knew how important this was.

Akita did not follow protocol. He did not go through the medic station, shower, or turn in weapons. He pushed his way by a captain and my company clerk. Forced his way into my office."

He said, "We need to talk now."

General Scott didn't like this interruption, but he could see the anger in Akita, so he told his clerk to hold his calls and reset his appointments for the rest of the day. He waited for the door to shut. Then he told Akita, "You stink. Can this wait until you shower?"

In an uncompromising voice, Akita said, "No, what I have to tell you is more important than anything you will hear today."

"Take a seat, and tell me what you think is more important than the health of my men," General Scott said. Akita pulled out his pocket recorder and pushed the play button.

"Listen to this," he said.

The general listened to the recording. It had background noise and was faint at times, but what Akita had recorded was clear to him.

Before he could say anything, Akita said, "The CIA is watching the compound, and after we take care of their traitor Jim Skinner, they will take us out. No one will ever know."

General Scott stood abruptly and said, "I will cancel this opp."

Akita said, "No, I have a way to get the compound eliminated, remove Jim Skinner, get our men out, and at the same time, take the doctor out of play."

Scott sat back down to hear what Akita was thinking.

Akita started, "First, you know where the doctor is. Nothing gets past this office."

Scott said, "The doctor entered the U.S. about three months ago, and my contact told me the Army wanted nothing more to do with him, but the CIA was interested in his experiments."

Akita paused and asked, "What will happen if the doctor gets our bodies autopsied? He will find out that his experiment was not a failure. As insane as he is, he will sell the tech to anyone around the world. We cannot allow him to find out about us. You need to send a team to recon his location. We cannot move on him before we take out the compound in South America."

Scott said," I can coordinate the two opps from here to go off simultaneously."

"We will have three opps. The doctor, the compound, and our exit," Akita explained.

Akita looked hard at Scott and said, "I need you to contact your old friends in South America. They cannot have CIA or Army ties. It would be best if you went outside the normal communication types. Arrange for them to transport us out. We will need less than normal vehicles. You will need to write everything down, and we do not need to use radios or phones.

I will give your orders to Bobby. He will get everyone out, and I will stay behind with Ed, Joe, and Kevin. You need to get us out the same way a day or so later."

Scott asked, "Why do you need to keep everyone in the dark, and what do you need to stay for?"

Akita asked, "How did the CIA know we would be there and our point of entry? I have a way to stop the CIA in the field. If this works, the four of us will have a four- or five-hour window to work with before the CIA can call in reinforcements. I will need Kevin to leave in two or three days with weapons and ammo that cannot be traced back here. I have a list of what we will need. He will hide them in the field and then return to leave for the mission. Only the four of us and you will know what we are doing."

Scott said thoughtfully, "I need time to get this set up. Go check in with the medical and shower. You fucking stink, and you have my office smelling like you."

A short time later, Akita returned to his office. He had cleared the medics and showered.

Scott handed Akita two evac plans and asked, "How will you implement this in the field?"

Akita said," I will call in one of the evac sights the CIA knows about. I will have Ed on high ground watching both sights. The CIA should move their people to the point I say we are going to. When Ed keys his mike twice, I will give your orders to Bobby. If anyone raises hell about the change, we will secure them. I will tell Bobby to keep them secure and not let them see the light of day until we are back in the states. Will this work for you?"

Scott said, "Yes, we need to know if anyone is in the other camp. How will I know when to kick off the opp to remove the doctor?"

Akita said, "Bobby will call you on the radio freq 3030. He will use the call sign 'Greenland'; your call Sign will be 'Iceland.' After you acknowledge 'Greenland, this is Iceland,' Bobby will only say one word, 'Go.'"

Akita continued, "The four of us will take out the CIA personnel that are there to kill us. Then we will follow your evac plan. Now here is the plan I have for the compound. I need twelve more men to make it happen."

Akita presented his mission plan and gave General Scott a list of men he wanted to take with him. All men on the list were Noncommissioned Officers (NCO'S) who were not married. Akita was emphatic that if any of the men had children, he didn't want them.

General Scott said, "I will pick the people to do this mission."

Akita said, "That list has the best men on it."

Scott asked, "Are they good enough to be FRBs?"

Coldly, Akita answered, "There will never be any more FRB'S. If one of us dies, the person you replace them with will not fit in."

General Scott asked, "What makes you think that?"

Akita said, "You forged the twelve of us into a single blade. If part of that blade is taken away, it becomes unusable and breaks. You need to forge more weapons made of hard men who will defend a society that has rejected them, men who like being in the lion's den."

General Scott observed, "I can't, or do you not remember Kin Weeks?"

Akita shook his head then asked, "Do you know why Kin died?"

"Yes, he went into a biker bar where he attacked and killed seven fucking people to include the leaders of the biker gang," explained General Scott.

Akita said, "Yes, he fucking did that. Do you know why?"

General Scott said, "The fucking drugs they pumped into all of you made him go crazy."

Akita said, "You really do not know even after all this time. Did you know he had a sister?"

Insane

General Scott answered in the negative.

Akita said, "He had an older sister. She worked every job she could get to keep the two of them together. She had a good paying job down the street from that bar. She walked to work because they didn't have a car. Her boss took her home when she worked late. One night he had to go home because of sick kids or some shit like that. She walked by the bar on her way home. I will tell you what a biker told us. One of the bikers was drunk and started fucking with her for fun. Wanting a kiss, telling her that he would buy her a drink, that kind of shit. She said nothing and tried to walk on. He called her a bitch and grabbed her ass. She fought back, and he pushed her to the ground. Then he yelled, 'I am going to fuck you.' The other bikers started telling him to do it and that she would love it. She got to her feet and slapped him. He took out a knife, cut her and kept cutting her. That's when several others kicked her until she stopped moving.

They picked her up and dumped her body in a dumpster."

General Scott, stunned, shook his head, and said, "I did not know."

Akita said, "Kin joined the Army to get strong enough to avenge her death. That was his only goal in life. That is when someone decided it was a good idea to pump him full of that shit and turn him lose."

General Scott wondered how he had heard the details. Akita smiled that devilish smile of his and said, "Because very nicely, we asked one of the bikers who was there. Kin was one of us, and we wanted to make it right, but he already had. Kin was not your fault. You need to make more weapons. When you do, remember: no family no kids along with the criteria you found us with."

General Scott asked, "What happened to the other men that I sent?"

Akita said, "I know some died and others the drugs did shit to their brains. They did not give everyone the same shit." At this point he changed the subject and said, "My plan will work but only with the right people who want to be in the lion's den. I need the people on that list."

"You are insane," said General Scott with an edge to his voice. "What you want to do is not feasible. Go back and figure out how it could be done correctly."

CHAPTER 17
A President's Orders

General Scott had informed the President that Akita and his men had returned. He wanted to know if they'd found a way to alleviate the problem. They were out of time. Basically, the President observed that this "fucked up" CIA agent would sell intel on our ops in South America, and he needed to be stopped at all costs.

General Scott presented Akita's plan, explaining, "It's too risky. All the men would be killed."

The President said," If this is the only plan you have, we have no choice. Get this plan of Akitas done ASAP."

Akita was already on a plane going back as General Scott had ordered. They were only three hours out, so General Scott had their flight turned back. He had all the gear Akita wanted on the ground ready for him when he landed. He called the rest of the FRBs back from Germany. He then ordered all the men on Akita's list to prepare for combat and arrange for their transport to meet The FRBs in Colombia.

When Akita landed, General Scott told him his team and the men on his list were in the air. They would meet him in Colombia.

Akita smiled and said simply, "Into the lion's den."

General Scott shook his head and answered, "There's something broken in you. You're fucking crazy."

When the plane landed in Colombia, the twenty-three-man team met him and unloaded their gear. The gear was unpacked and inventoried. Steve said," Christmas is early, and I like the gifts this year."

Ed picked up a claymore and asked, "May I keep this one? We have so many no one will miss one."

Steve asked, "Are we blowing up a camp or a city? You have enough here to take out a small country."

The twelve new men were silent and stunned. The FRBs were joking, messing with each other having fun. They had never seen the FRBs doing this. Everyone was excited and ready to start this mission. The gear was split up and loaded in packs and carrier bags. The men and their bags were loaded on a Chinook. The flight took two hours. The Chinook hovered and the ramp lowered, and the men with all their gear exited. Only Ed joked, "Now the fun begins."

They started on the twenty-two-kilometer hike with 200 pounds of gear along with weapons and ammo. They moved through the thick jungle in eighty-degree heat and ninety-five percent humidity without being seen or heard.

Akita's plan was simple: surround the camp with minimal personnel. Once they accomplished that, he would sneak into the camp and place M18 Claymore mines under the buildings on the ground, face-up, and shaped charges under all buildings except the office. (The Claymore fires steel balls out to about 110 yards within a sixty-degree arc in front of the device. It's used primarily in ambushes and as an anti-infiltration device against enemy infantry.) This part of the operation could take two weeks.

Akita would have to get in and out of the camp multiple times. Akita was fucking nuts to think he could do all of this without getting caught or killed. He could have assigned this to another man, and General Scott told him to do so, but Akita insisted that he couldn't order anyone to do something he wouldn't do himself. Akita's thought process is different from the others, allowing him to analyze all situations from areas others wouldn't think about. He was too valuable to lose.

Six other men would place M47 Dragon shoulder-fired rockets in an area to fire them into the parking area. Then they would wait for the general to arrive. All the explosives would be set off by remote at the same time the vehicles were destroyed by rocket fire. The fourteen other men (seven two-man teams on M60 machine guns with four thousand rounds) would surround the camp and shoot and kill any enemy men.

Akita and three men would enter the camp to secure the office and deploy flash bangs to disorient everyone inside, so they could enter unimpeded and kill everyone in the office, burn the office on the way out, and meet the team at the extraction point. Akita and his team decided to bring Jim Skinner out alive, so the fucking traitor would be brought to justice in front of the entire world for his crimes.

The mission went as planned; Akita came close to getting caught several times.

Once Akita was about to be exposed, the team was ready to assault the camp. They were setting on go, then Akita killed the man before he could sound the alarm.

In one smooth motion, he pulled his knife, stabbed the man in the heart and left the knife in the wound, so the man would not bleed. He then grabbed the man with one arm around his shoulders. Using all his strength, he pulled the man's body into his side, making it look like he was a drunk friend he was helping. He walked the man to the outhouses. Once he had the body inside, he pulled his knife out, lifted the seat, and disposed of his body down the shit hole in broad daylight.

After the operation was complete, V-man started teasing, saying, "Akita had that man hugged up so hard I could hear bones breaking, and I was a hundred meters away."

Joe asked Akita, "Why did you hug that man? I thought you liked girls."

Ed cut in and said, "I saw you looking at him sweet like, and then you grabbed him up and hugged him and walked to a small room where you two could be alone."

The other twelve men who were here at the request of Akita found this banter funny. The FRBs were getting away with teasing their leader about an action he had to take to complete this mission, but none of the twelve felt comfortable enough to join in. One of them in the rear of the marching order asked the man next to him, "Would you have thought to do that?"

The answer he got was, "No, I would not have. Why is it so funny to them? We could have all been killed because of that."

Akita told them, "The exit plan has changed." Then he looked at Ed. Without being told Ed left.

Akita handed Bobby the handwritten orders and said, "Follow this to the letter. You will not be comfortable, but you will be alive."

One of the extra men on the mission got furious and said, "No, we follow the mission as it was given. You can't change it. We go to the extraction point you radioed in for. The men there will be waiting for us."

Bobby hit the man hard on the jaw knocking him out.

Joe tied his hands and asked, "Anyone else want to defy orders?"

Akita told Bobby, "Keep both of your prisoners safe and quiet. Do

A President's Orders

not let them see or speak to anyone. General Scott will take charge of them when you arrive in the states.

Now go and make your call. Take the extra bags with you. Give the bags to counterintelligence officer Julia Dietrich only." The bags were handed over, and the two groups split up and left.

CHAPTER 18
The Hunted becomes the Hunter

Ed had struggled to get into a location in time to see both locations. He keyed his mike twice for Akita, and then said, "Move."

Akita replied, "Move your ass. We have work to do." Akita looked at Kevin and said, "I called in point Alpha as you wanted. Let's get the weapons."

Kevin said, "We had to use Alpha. The area around is easier to navigate without being seen. We can go up the backside and surprise the mother fuckers that want to kill us."

Ed walked up quietly and said, "It is me! Don't shoot."

Joe jokingly said, "Nice of you to join us. We were going to have all the fun without you."

After the four got the weapons and ammo, they started up the backside of point Alpha. Once in position, Akita gave the hand sign. All four men busted on scene with weapons firing on targets that had already been chosen. Several CIA men went down. The pilots were selected first. Others tried to run or find cover, but there was little cover. The site was picked because it was large enough for helicopters to land with no trees in the way. Joe and Ed took out the runners.

Akita and Kevin killed all the others.

When things had quieted down, Ed asked, "Why didn't they try and fight back?"

Akita said pointing, "They were expecting us to walk up from there and open fire to kill us in that small, closed area. The only reason this worked is because we are better trained. Now put all the bodies in one helicopter and torch it."

Then he turned to Joe and said, "You have more flying time than we do. Get the other chopper started and ready to fly. "All personnel in the detachment transported regularly on rotary or fixed wing aircraft received flight training. The pilots were the ones that did this training, and they called it seat time. With this seat time, if the pilot was unable to fly or had been killed, someone could fly and land the aircraft. This ensured not all onboard would die.

Joe said, "I have more flight time, but Ed has takeoff and landing experience."

Ed said, "I will do it."

The bodies and chopper were rigged to blow. Ed operated the controls and got the chopper off the ground. It turned a quarter turn on takeoff. Ed pushed on the foot control, and the bird straightened out. Joe set off the charges on the other chopper and said, "No one will know what happened here."

Akita told Ed, "We made it this far. Don't kill us after all the work is done."

Ed said with a smile, "Fuck you."

An hour later, Ed landed in a small clearing. Charges were set to blow the chopper.

The men started their hike to a village where a boat was waiting for them. When they were a safe distance away, Joe blew the charges. Two hours later, they were on the outskirts of the village.

Akita said, "Look for a small brown and red boat. We need to talk to a man named Ronald."

Ed said, "Over there is a thing you might call a boat, and it's brown and red." They made their way over to the boat. A man came out of a hut to meet them.

He smiled and said, "My name is Ronald. General Scott told me to take care of you, and you needed a boat. He also said you have weapons you do not need to take back or get caught with."

Akita smiled and handed over the weapons they used on the CIA men. He and his men kept their weapons. Akita told Ronald, "We need to leave now."

Ronald told the men, "Come with me, please." He led them to another boat. It was a little better than the one on the bank. "It is slow, but it doesn't leak. When you get to the shore, leave it there in the open. I will pick it up later."

The men shook hands with Ronald and left down the river.

Ed asked, "What is next, a car from the 20s?"

Akita said, "Scotts orders say we will be picked up by plane, then we catch a barge. The barge will take us just off the coast of Georgia. We will swim ashore, and our people will pick us up."

The barge got them five miles off the coast. The captain told them,

The Hunted Becomes the Hunter

"I can't get any closer. The Coast Guard will think I am dropping off drugs." The four men said nothing. They just stepped off the side and started the swim. When they came ashore, Harold was there and smiling.

He said, "I did not think you would ever get here. Now get in the bus before anyone sees you."

Hours later, they arrived at Fort Benning. General Scott met the bus and said, "I am happy to see the four of you. Get showered and get some sleep. I will see you at 05:00."

The soldier who did not want to follow the changing orders was removed from the unit and placed in another with no charges or disciplinary action taken. The doctor was brought into Fort Benning. General Scott's men had him cuffed and shackled and placed him in a windowless basement room. General Scott told them that he would handle this issue personally. The doctor was never seen again or heard from worldwide.

CHAPTER 19
Anna: A Second Interview

Anna wanted to be interviewed after General Scott. Lee Ann called a cab and asked to be taken to the address on Anna's card. She arrived at a large building, the Reichskammergerichts Museum.

She walked in and asked the lady at the entryway for Anna Meier. The receptionist asked, "Are you Lee Ann Bream"?

Lee Ann answered in the affirmative.

"We have been expecting you. Please come with me," she said as she led Lee Ann to Anna's office, tapped on the door, and entered. The office was a small room with books, maps, and paperwork neatly stacked everywhere. Anna was sitting at her desk.

She stood and said, "Please take a seat. Would you like something to drink?" Lee Ann declined, "No, thank you."

Anna said, "Please excuse the mess. The museum lets me office here even though they aren't involved with my work."

Lee Ann took a seat. "My boss's desk and office make this look very well organized," she declared as she looked at Anna's well-decorated enclave.

Anna smiled. "That is kind of you to say. We use a large storage building eleven kilometers from here to clean and categorize the finds my team makes. Many discoveries are housed there until we have a permanent place for them."

Lee Ann asked if the museum supplied the storage building for her. Anna told her that they'd had trouble with people taking artifacts from their last location, and she told Ed and Akita about the problem. They told Julia, and then they found and bought the building. It was Julia's bank that provided the security.

Lee Ann asked, "How can Army personnel afford to do everything the FRBs did?"

Anna said, "They can't."

"So how could the FRBs do it?"

Anna paused for a beat and then said, "I want to tell you, and I want you to understand everything."

Lee Ann said, "I've heard that the FRBs owned several businesses

Anna: A Second Interview

here."

"You don't have half of their story," Anna replied.

"Okay, what do I not have, and what are you willing to tell me?" Lee Ann replied.

Anna took a deep breath and then wanted to know what Lee Ann would do with the information if she did choose to share it with her. Lee Ann explained that General Scott asked her to tell the truth about Akita and the FRBs.

Anna laughed and replied, "General Scott is a good man, and he cares for all his men, but the FRBs were special to him. You should know this by now, but he doesn't know anything about what they did or how they came to own the most lucrative bank in Germany. So, please be specific. What will you do with the information I give you?" Anna asked a second time.

"I will try to verify what I am told, and if I can verify the story, I will tell it as truthfully as possible," Lee Ann replied.

Anna took another deep breath and said, "Some of what I'm going to tell you *cannot* be verified because the operations executed by the FRBs were silent ones. The people who ordered the missions will say nothing. Some of what the FRBs did during the missions and after, only they knew, and they never told anyone because they didn't want to go to jail."

"I understand what you are telling me," Lee Ann said. "What do you expect me to do with what you tell me?"

"I want you to record everything. Take in what I tell you and what others tell you, especially General Scott. Merge all the information, and you will have most of the truth. Then I want you to print it for the world to see. Will you do this for me?" Anna asked.

"I will try my best, but I can promise nothing," Lee Ann said straightforwardly. She then settled more deeply into her chair, making herself comfortable as she took out her notebook and pen. "Well," she said, "If you're ready, I'm ready. Shall we begin?" Without waiting for Anna's answer, Lee Ann posed her first question.

Do you know where the FRBs got their money from?

"One night after Ed and I had been together for about three years, I asked the same question. Ed told me a story about an operation in Colombia. He did not say much about the mission but said he and Akita had to clear an assembly area for the team. There were some armed people there. Ed and Akita had to take them out. After that, Akita cleared the rest of the rooms, and Ed stood watch at the front door. Akita found the footlocker-sized box, and he checked it for explosives. He found gold bars. He took the gold and put it in his rucksack, where the ammo he used had left space. Akita told Ed what he had found and replaced Ed at the door.

Ed put the rest of the gold in his rucksack. Akita and Ed had 800 pounds of gold, and no one knew about it. This empty house was a meeting place for arms and drug deals with payments made in gold. Ed told me about this part of the mission, so I could understand what happened. This was the assembly area for the team. Once all were present, they would move to the extraction point. The team made it to the house and secured the area. The exit was a success, and just like the other missions, no bag check. General Scott had the team flown to Frankfurt and then trucked to Kirch Goens, Germany, also known as Ayers, Kaserne. Again, no bag check. At Ayers, Kaserne, Akita and Ed told the team what they had.

It was Bobby who remembered that Uwe Dietrich's sister was a banker. Dietrich was the guy they had helped when he was getting his ass kicked. He was also part of the German mafia. Since Joe had spoken to her before when they took her brother to the hospital, he volunteered to call her."

So it was Julia who had the bank connection and told them what they needed to do?

"Yes, she told them to split the gold between them and go to bullion banks, turn it into cash, then receive the paperwork they'd need to deposit the money in a bank. She offered to take the deposit at her bank, on the stipulation that one of the FRBs open an account there. She was the manager. They spent all the next day researching bullion banks in all the countries of Europe."

This was quite the operation. Did they run into any problems?

"Luckily, no. Each team member took gold and boarded trains. It took three days for everyone to return, and they were all smiling when they came back. When they made a count, the team had $172,803,553.00."

Anna: A Second Interview

So, then they opened the accounts?

"Yes, Akita opened the accounts in Wetzlar with the plan that they would all be on all the accounts. He told them to go in one by one and deposit the cash as Julia had told them. Also, Akita made a point to tell them to spend nothing. Then he had another idea and proposed getting all the girls together for a trip—just for fun. He asked Joe to make the arrangements."

Did Julia give them any other advice?

"Just the basics: she stressed that if they didn't want to get caught, they should spend only what their combined pay would allow. That and to stay in-country. They all agreed."

Was this the only time something like this occurred?

"Actually, no. Ed told me three years after this that they brought back five duffle bags full of cash. They also gave those to Julia. She took care of everything for them and made legal deposits. Ed and Akita were the only ones who could sign for money over five thousand euros. If you have enough for today, I have another meeting in a few minutes."

Thank you for your time.

With that, Lee Ann shook Anna's hand, stashed her notebook in her purse, and left to contemplate her next move. Later she discovered that she couldn't verify the story's details; however, the bank in question has been certified, and all its business is legal.

CHAPTER 20
Domplatz

The next day Sonia and Savannah invited Lee Ann to spend some time with them exploring Wetzlar. Sonia and Savannah were becoming inseparable. Sonia asked Savannah if she'd like to see where she and Akita had met. Savannah just smiled and beamed. It was clear she was excited to learn this personal information about her father and Sonia. Lee Ann was delighted to be along. She was eager to learn not only where they had met, but also, how they'd met.

Sonia decided that before their adventure began, they should have a good lunch, so she took them to Grillstuber Restaurant. The meal was delicious, the staff excellent. One of the servers even complimented Sonia and Savannah on their beauty. As they both blushed, Savannah placed her hand on Sonia's in another moment of bonding. Sonia's driver was waiting by the curb as they exited the restaurant. Sonia instructed him to take them to the Domplatz. The Domplatz is a medieval church built in the Twelfth Century.

"I met your father there in the parking lot. I was going to a friend's house. There was an accident over there," she pointed. "Five cars all piled up. Two were on fire when I arrived.

Someone had pulled most of the people out of the cars and lined them up. The bad ones here, the ones who had cuts and broken bones there, those who were just hurt here, and the dead there altogether. Eighteen people. It was horrible. No one was around, so I started treating the people who needed it most."

She paused to let Lee Ann and Savannah take in the scene. They could tell she was reliving the tragedy of it all. A heady mix of emotions stirred. Sonia continued, "I heard a painful growl that ended in a yell in pain. I ran to the sound. Then I saw a man ripping open the door of an overturned car that was ablaze. The flames were all around him. I tried to get to him but couldn't because it was too hot. I watched in horror as he dove into the cab of the car. I thought for certain he was going to die. It seemed like an eternity before he appeared from the flames with a young girl in his arms. He took the girl to her mother. The mother was among the people with broken bones. She had a broken leg. It was when I ran

DOMPLATZ

over to see how severely injured the child was that he yelled confidently, 'I promised I would get her.' I stood in frozen disbelief that he was speaking English. He was an American."

Sonia continued, "After he gave the child to her mother, I was amazed. In all the chaos, two men ran onto the scene. One said, 'I ran as fast as I could to get Bobby.' They didn't look like soldiers. They had long hair, and one had a beard. They asked their friend where they should start. It was clear they were used to him issuing orders. He said, 'Help her. Do everything you can.' One of the men had a medical bag, and he went to work silently."

Sonia was reeling from relating the dramatic rescue scene where it had happened. It had taken a lot out of her to share the details. She looked a little teary-eyed when she said that when she'd tried to look at the rescuer's arms, he barked at her to help them and gestured toward the wounded.

Sonia continued. "The American with the doctor's bag was fast and exceptionally good. He did things I had never seen before, techniques entirely novel to me. He worked tirelessly, seamlessly transitioning from one injury to the next. He worked furiously until authorities and healthcare professionals finally arrived.

When I looked for the first American, he was gone. I was worried, so I asked where he'd gone. In response, he remarked, 'You possess a remarkable proficiency. What university are you in?' When I told him I was a doctor, he told me I looked too young to be one."

"I knew that the man needed help, and something about his heroism made me extremely interested in him. After the arrival of the authorities, we decided our job there was done, and 'Bobby,' as he introduced himself. I said, your friend is injured and in need of our help. Please tell me where he is. His reply was curt, 'Follow me.' I took a chance and went with him. We walked into the dark bar, and Bobby said, 'Akita. This lady wants to see if you are OK.' Then he turned to me and said, 'Sonia. This is Akita.' I couldn't believe my hero had cleaned up, changed his clothes, and was sitting there drinking a beer. He had bandages on his right arm and his hands. The bandages looked like a child had put them on. He admitted he had put them on himself."

Lee Ann was starting to see a whole new side to Akita. He was obviously stubborn when it came to taking care of himself. Sonia continued, "I borrowed Bobby's medical bag and told Akita that the care he had given himself looked like shit care. I heard laughter from a group of big men standing around us. One of them told him that Akita was good at a lot of fucking things, but applying his own bandages wasn't one of them. I sat down next to him and unwrapped them. He had skin missing where he had grabbed the door, his arms had second-degree burns, and his hair was singed. I told him that he was lucky, and that I'd been sure he was going to die when I saw him go into that burning car.

One of the men said, 'That is Akita, and you can't kill him. He is too fucking stubborn.'

"I used supplies from Bobby's bag and treated Akita's arms and hands. Then Bobby introduced me to the men standing around the table. I remember vividly exactly who was there: Ed Johnson, Kevin Viraman V-man, Jon Laws, Steve Jackson, Kody Lunsford, Sam Hawke, Paul Martinez, Harold Powell, Joe Metcalf, and Jodie Lucero. All of them looked to be over 200 pounds."

"I introduced myself. Bobby said that he had assisted me during the accident. I told Bobby, 'You did most of the work and are highly skilled. You were exceptional. I couldn't have managed without you.' Paul jokingly said, 'Don't tell him that. His ego is big enough already.'

Curious about the accident, Ed asked, 'What caused the crash?' Akita quickly pointed at me, stating, 'It was her.' With a mischievous smile, he stood up and said, 'She attempted to hail a taxi.' Striking a pose swaying his hips, raising a hand, he called out, 'Taxi!' Laughter sent through the bar, not exclusively from this group.

Despite my attempt to explain, 'I wasn't present during the accident,' my words fell on deaf ears. Ed insisted that I had to run to catch the cab. He stood on his toes, taking tiny steps as if in high heels, and swaying his hips from side to side, while yelling, 'Taxi! Taxi!!'

Laughter filled the air even more, causing me to feel embarrassed. A few other men attempted to mimic a seductive lady's stride and hailed a cab. The sight of them, their large build with their attempts at femininity, was utterly absurd. I couldn't help but burst into laughter alongside them.

I refused to take the blame, laughing all the while. It was then that I realized this group of strangers treated me like I belonged. Akita said, 'I am sorry, but I had to. Then he asked me for dinner, holding out his hand for me to take. I could not say no. We went to Grillstuber."

The reason was now clear why Sonia had taken Lee Ann and Savannah there for lunch. Sonia, lost in another world, reminisced, "Your dad did everything for me. He opened the door, pulled out my chair, said 'Yes ma'am, no ma'am, please and thank you.' After we finished, he walked me to a taxi. As we walked, I asked him why he had risked his life for that child. I'll never forget the exact word he said: 'If not me, then who? I did not risk anything.'

I knew I wanted to see him again, so I told him I'd come change his bandages again. Then he smiled and invited me to a birthday party. The rest, as they say, is history."

Savannah asked Sonia, "Will you tell me about your relationship with my dad? I know you two loved each other. I want to ask a question, but I do not wish to offend you."

Sonia said, "Ask. You need to know." Trying to lighten the mood, she added, "But I will not answer anything about sex." Then she laughed quietly.

Savannah smiled and said," No, not that. I want to know why a lady like you would have anything to do with a man like my dad."

CHAPTER 21
Julia

Sonia smiled, put her arm around Savannah, and said, "When we return to the house, we will sit down, and I will tell you, but now we have an appointment with Julia and Klaus, my lawyer. Klaus will be representing you at the meeting until you retain your own lawyer."

Savannah nodded in recognition and said, "I have met Julia. She came to the ranch a little over three years ago. I think Dad told me that she was his banker. She brought paperwork from the bank here in Wetzlar for my dad to sign, and he had put me on his account." She couldn't imagine why she'd need her own lawyer.

Sonia said, "The meeting today is about your father's estate."

"My dad has an estate? I don't know anything about it." Savannah said.

Sonia answered, "Yes, he did, and now it will be yours. Lee Ann, you will come, too. I want Akita's complete story told."

Lee Ann smiled and said, "I would be honored to attend with you."

They got in the car and left. Julia was waiting for them at the bank. Julia greeted them and directed them into her office. It was nicely appointed with a large sitting area. Julia appeared to be in her 60s, tall, slender, with short black hair. She was well-dressed and looked very well put together. Banker Chanel. Klaus had already arrived. He stood up, introduced himself, and motioned to Julia to start the proceedings.

Julie smoothed her skirt, took a deep breath, and began, "Before you ask anything, let me tell you this. The first time I met Akita, he walked in without an appointment and asked to speak to the manager. That was me. He said that he needed to open business and real estate accounts. I have all the board members' names and other information you need. The real estate account will have the same board members. We filled out all the paperwork.

About a year later, the bank was closing when Akita came by to say he'd found a building he wanted to buy. He gave me the address. When I checked his accounts, he had more than enough money to make the deal. This was the first time he had helped a woman own her own business."

Julia's assistant knocked, came in, and gave Julia a folder. Julia opened

JULIA

it and separated the papers into four bundles. She handed a bundle to Savannah, Sonia, and Sonia's lawyer Klaus.

Julia said, "I want to start simply by saying this is not Akita's last will. Akita came here over three years ago and had me start the paperwork to take his name off his accounts and put Savannah's name on them. I traveled to Texas to finalize his request. He also had the property titles transferred to her. He has two safety deposit boxes here. The titles are in one of the boxes. The keys for the boxes are in your packet, Savannah."

In disbelief, Savannah was looking through the papers. Quietly, so almost no one in the room could hear her, she muttered, "I own this bank."

Julia said, "Yes, you own this, plus three other buildings, and several businesses are paying off loans to you."

Savannah said, still in shock, "My dad didn't tell me any of this."

Julia said, "Savannah, you're worth more than two billion dollars, plus this bank. Your father and I worked for over twenty-five years finding and financing female-owned businesses. We also put money in the stock market. When the bank where I worked was closing because of bad business deals, Akita bought the building, and my husband remodeled it into a bank. I completed the paperwork, inspections, and a license. He transferred all his accounts to it. I had only his accounts to manage at first."

Savannah asked, "What do I have to do now?"

"I need you to read and sign all the documents," Julia explained. "Everything is in your name, and legally we need your signature. I will do the same for you that I did for your father. You are my boss now. As of this moment, your life will never be the same. After you read the documents, we will talk again."

Klaus asked, "Sonia, may I speak to you privately?"

Sonia said, "Yes, but I want Lee Ann to join us." They walked out of the office and stopped in the hall.

"Are you sure you want her here?" Klaus asked.

Sonia simply answered, "Yes."

Klaus asked, "When are you going to tell her?"

Sonia said, "How can I tell her?"

Lee Ann asked Sonia, "Tell her what?" She did not get an answer.

Julia

Klaus said, "Her father did not tell her any of this and look what it is doing to her. It would be best to tell her before she finds out that she is your sole beneficiary. What happens if Julia tells her by mistake?"

Sonia said, "I know I need to tell her." The three of them walked back into the office.

Sonia made some excuses to wrap everything up quickly with a promise to return the next week after they'd had a chance to review all the documents and secure Savannah her own personal lawyer.

Julia said, "Yes, of course, call me with the details."

As the group left each was lost in thought, knowing that several of their lives would never be the same again.

Later that day when she was alone, Lee Ann called Mike and updated him. She wanted more information about Julia and her brother Uwe Dietrich. Later that evening, Mike called to inform her that the bank Julia Dietrich had previously worked for closed because it had been investigated for money laundering, and the president was sent to jail for four years. At the same time, Julia's brother Uwe was investigated for having ties to a powerful criminal organization.

Mike had found an article in the local Wetzlar paper that said Uwe Dietrich was severely beaten by several gang members and had told polizei that three English-speaking men stepped in and saved his life by "beating the shit" out of the six men attacking him. He said the three men appeared to take pleasure in crushing his attackers. The paper reported that Uwe had told polizei the men had taken him to the hospital. His sister Julia had offered a reward for the names of his saviors.

CHAPTER 22
Nikita Wolf

Sonia, Savannah, and Lee Ann left the bank, parted ways with Klaus, and shortly arrived at Sonia's Clinic. They took a minute to catch their breath in the car.

"I've been noticing how fit the ladies I've met here are," said Savannah.

"You mean the FRBs girls? asked Sonia. Savannah replied in the affirmative.

Sonia had more stories to share before going into the clinic. "One girl in our group was beaten by a drunk German. He didn't like to see her with an American even though he didn't even know her. That was when Akita started making us take martial arts training from him and his men. They were trying to teach us what they knew, but it wasn't working so well. Then Nikita Wolf, Sam Hawke's girlfriend, volunteered to train us, so we could take care of ourselves. She had trained in martial arts since she was five. Her father held world titles. She kept the classes going after the FRBs left. All of us still take the classes. Then your dad came back, we were much better prepared to train with them. I had fun beating on your dad in class."

Savannah said, "My dad never hit me or called me names. He only yelled at me once, maybe twice. I miss him so much.

Sonia said quietly, "He was a good father and a good man. He would never have been violent with a woman. I miss him, too. I remember we came back from a trip once. We were in the bar relaxing. It was full of people, some dancing, some just having fun, and some drunk. This GI was mad at a girl for spilling a drink on him, and he stood up from the table and yelled, 'You bitch!' and hit her.

Akita picked him up and slammed him to the floor. It all happened amazingly fast. The rest of the FRBs were up, also, and quickly spread out in the room. They moved like wolves, and I watched as they took the entire room. Akita handed the woman to Bobby to see if she needed care. Then he let the man get up. Two of his friends moved toward Akita. Ed and Jodie restrained them. It looked as if it took no effort. Akita lectured the man. He told him that any man who hits someone weaker was nothing but 'a fucking asshole.' He advised him that if he really wanted to prove what a man was, he should hit the biggest, ugliest man in the face, right then and there. Win or lose, he'd be the 'fucking biggest and the ugliest.'

Then Akita asked him if he'd recovered enough to fight back. The GI had no time to react before Akita hit him hard in the face. I heard bone break. The guy didn't get back up. One by one, Akita confronted the guys who had pitched in to help the GI. By the time he got to the last one, the man pissed his pants. Then Akita stood in the middle of the floor and made an announcement: 'Please, guys, do not hit women.' Your dad did that for a woman he didn't even know."

Now that they had time to think about Akita's staunch code of ethics where women were concerned, they exited the car and walked into the clinic. Sonia said, "Please come in. I need to check and see if my supplies have arrived."

The clinic's waiting room was large, open, and clean with attractive, comfortable furniture. An area off to one side was filled with children playing and toys.

The receptionist greeted the group and said, "Dr. Ludwig, how are you today?"

Sonia smiled and said, "I'm always good. You know that. Meet Savannah Haddox and Lee Ann Bream. Lee Ann and Savannah, meet Christina Schaefer. Is Dr. Gillibrand in?"

Christina said, "Yes, in his office."

Sonia walked down a hallway, opened a door on the left, and went in. A few minutes later, she came out with some paperwork, which she handed to Christina and said, "Please order this." Christina picked up the phone and made a call.

With her task completed, Sonia was ready to go. As they were leaving, Lee Ann commented on how lovely the clinic was. Sonia thanked her and told her that she didn't practice anymore but that she enjoyed overseeing the operation. Sonia asked Savannah, "Did your dad tell you about this clinic?"

Before Savannah had a chance to answer, Sonia continued, "He owns this building. I mean, you own it. He gave me this floor for the clinic. Julia's husband remodeled it for me. When I started, all my patients were General Scott's men. Not only the teams, but also, the support personnel——all 630 of them. He sent them here when they were in-country. Getting and keeping patients took three or more years of hard work."

Savannah had only one question as she tried to understand everything: "Where you, Dad's doctor?"

"Yes, I was " she answered.

CHAPTER 23
Mom

Sonia said, "Savannah, I have something important to tell you." Then she fell silent.

"What is it?"

"Ask me when we get home."

They got into the car, and Sonia told the driver to take them home. The trip took about forty-five minutes. Nobody made small talk.

Will and Bernadette were waiting for them at the door, and then Sonia ushered everybody into her office and closed the door. Will and Bernadette sat together on a sofa. Sonia was in a chair next to her desk, and Savannah sat next to Will in a chair. Lee Ann took a chair on the other side of the sofa.

Will cleared his throat and began. "Savannah, about fifteen years ago, Bernadette and I were in debt with the ranch. We were going to lose it. Your dad found out and asked why I hadn't told him. We were just too proud. Then your dad called his bank, and all the bills were paid in the next few days. I told him I didn't know how I'd pay him back. All he did was smile. He never said another word about it, and he wouldn't let us pay him back. After that, the ranch was doing well, so Bernadette and I talked about it and had the title for the ranch put in your dad's name. He never knew. Now, we want you to have it. We don't have kids, and we helped your dad raise you, so we consider you as ours."

Bernadette added, "The ranch is rightfully yours."

Savannah was incredulous and objected, perhaps more loudly than she should have, "No! It's *your* land. Please don't say anything else about it."

Bernadette insisted, "No, it isn't. End of discussion. Your father owns it, and now you do."

She stood up and hugged Savannah. Will took his wife's hand, and they left the office. Savannah sat in disbelief. She looked at Sonia and said, "What else did my dad neglect to tell me?"

Sonia took a deep breath and said, "I must tell you this before I lose my nerve." Sonia's complexion turned ghostly white. She looked and felt sick. Tears rolled down her face. She took a deep breath and continued,

Mom

"Your dad had been gone for three years when I met a man and married him. It was a mistake. All he wanted was my money. It took me years to end the marriage. Akita told me that he'd met a woman from Houston during this time. He took her to Will's ranch, and she lived on the ranch with him for about four years. She wasn't happy there. She didn't like traveling an hour and a half to Abilene to shop or eat at a restaurant. She missed the city. She wanted a child, but doctors told them she was infertile. The only way for her to give birth was to have a donor egg."

Sonia took another deep breath before continuing, "Your dad found a donor willing to give her eggs. After six months, she was pregnant. Your dad was so happy to have a baby girl when you were born. Your mother didn't know how to be a caring mother. Ranch life was too hard for her. She became more bitter every day. She reached the point that she hated your dad and her life on the ranch. The day she left. She told your dad she was leaving you with him. The egg had belonged to another woman, so you weren't hers anyway. I know this is hard to hear."

Savannah was taking in the information as best she could. Sonia took her hand and said earnestly, "She was only the woman that gave birth to you, but she is not your mother. You can think of her as a surrogate."

Savannah started to cry. Between big sobs, she said, "Dad never told me any of this. Now he'd dead, my mother left years ago, and I'm alone."

Sonia, also crying, said, "No, you are not alone, and you never will be as long as I'm alive. I was the egg donor. You are my daughter, my blood, my genes." The room went silent.

Savannah asked, "Why didn't he tell me?"

Sonia replied, "He was hurt deeply by her. He didn't want you to be hurt by his failure as a husband. He was determined not to fail you as your dad. He did everything in his power to give you a life full of people you loved and who loved you. He wanted you to have a stable home. He never wanted you to feel it was your fault she left. So, he raised you on the ranch. He tried to give you the childhood he never knew. Your dad loved you more than anyone will ever know."

Sonia said, "I wanted to live with you and your dad in Texas. I was willing to give all this up for you and for him, but he wouldn't let me make the sacrifice. He wouldn't interfere with my marriage and that he'd file for a divorce. He told me he would make a good life for you. A life

MOM

full of wonders. Your dad sent me pictures of you all the time. When you were old enough, your dad hoped you would understand why he came to me for my eggs and why I said yes. We had plans to tell you after your college graduation."

Savannah asked Sonia why Akita had come to her to be a donor. She wanted to be sure she understood fully. Sonia gave the answer Savannah knew in her heart—that Akita loved her and wanted the child to be hers. It was the only way because they were both married at the time.

Akita's divorce was final three years after the woman left, and Sonia's a year before his. Then life happened. Akita and Sonia stayed in touch and had made plans for her to come to Texas for Savannah's graduation. He was retiring, and Sonia had hired a doctor to take her place at the clinic.

Sonia bit her bottom lip to hold back the river of tears as she continued, "We were making plans. Did you know that your dad proposed to me? He wanted me to marry him. I told him yes. I asked him why it took him so long to ask me."

Savannah hugged her.

Sonia said, "I should have been there for you. I should have gone to Texas when your dad told me no. If I had been there, maybe Akita would be alive."

Savannah said, "You cannot do this to yourself." She looked hard at Sonia and said, "*Mom*, please don't blame yourself. His death is not your fault."

They both realized what had just happened.

Savannah said to no one in particular, "I have a mom."

"I am here, darling Savannah, and I am not leaving."

CHAPTER 24
KIRSTEN

Lee Ann was as uncomfortable as she was speechless, thinking she shouldn't have been included in these private discussions. Just then Monika knocked on the door and Sonia invited her in. She brought news that Kirsten was waiting and that she wanted to see Savannah. Savannah, still shaken from everything she'd been told, asked for time to pull herself together.

She said, "No one should see me like this, and I need to fix my makeup." Monika escorted her through the back way to her room and then stepped outside as she said, "I will be here if you need anything." When Savannah was ready, she called for Monika, and they made their way to the library.

Monika knocked on the door and said, "Lady Sonia, Miss Haddox."

Sonia said, "I just told Kirsten about us. She didn't know."

Kirsten gave Savannah a hug and said, "I should have. You are a mirror image of Sonia." I could not be happier for you." Kirsten was overcome with joy. Akita and the FRBs meant so much to her, more than she was going to be able to convey adequately to Savannah, but she had to try. She had plans to take Savannah and Lee Ann to her own home. "I will share my story about Akita, but I want you to see how far I've come from my beginnings thanks to Akita. You need to know what kind of man he was for me."

Sonia reached out and held Savannah's hand and said, "Don't let her keep you too long."

Kirsten said, "You worry too much. She's in good hands."

They left through the massive front doors. In the center of the drive sat a dark red 1969 e-type Jaguar. The three of them stood there for a second before Kirsten observed that they'd need to use one of Sonia's cars. A few minutes later, they were on their way.

Kirsten's house was set back from the road and surrounded by trees, and the yard had nothing out of place. They pulled into a garage large enough to hold eight cars with room to spare, parked, and went into the house. Kirsten's home was modern, clean with no clutter. Kirsten gave Savannah and Lee Ann tea to drink, and she made snacks. Everyone sat at the kitchen table, and then Kirsten began. "Savannah, are you harboring any anger about what you've just learned?"

Savannah said, "No, of course not. If they hadn't done all of this, I wouldn't be here."

Kirsten said quietly, "If I had not met your dad, I would not be here either."

Savannah looked at Kirsten and asked, "What do you mean? How did you meet him?"

Kirsten said, "I was twenty years old and very poor. I lived with my family in a part of town where Russians were moving in. They brought the mob with them. It was not a safe part of town. Late one night, I was walking home when a rough gang of Russian men surrounded me. They started yelling at me, telling me what they would do to me. They were touching me, pushing me to each other, ripping at my clothes. One knocked me to the ground, kicking me. I felt the gravel pierce my skin as another one jumped on top and banged my head against the stone street. I was beyond scared. I tried to get away, but I couldn't. I had six big men on me. Then I heard someone speak in English. It was not a yell, but a hard, cold voice. From the dark, I heard him say that he'd kill all of them if they didn't leave me alone, that it was their choice to live or die. He moved suddenly, but smooth like a leopard as he attacked. I saw glints of steel, and then the Russians screaming in pain and falling to the ground. The attack lasted less than one minute. The last man holding me ran.

As painful and as vivid as Kirsten's memories of the event were, she continued, "When it was over, five men lay unmoving on the ground. One man stood in the middle of them. He asked me if I was all right, and I told him I was. My English was not particularly good at the time. He took my hand and asked me if I was hurt. He was handsome and built like a truck. It was then that he introduced himself as Akita. Then I passed out."

Lee Ann and Savannah were enthralled by Kirsten's story. It was another case of Akita stepping in to help a stranger. Kirsten continued, "When I came to, I was in a bar. Akita's friend Bobby was bandaging my wounds. Fortunately, he arrived there quickly after the guys called and told him to come with his medical bag. I was a mess. I had blood on my face, scrapes all over, and my clothes were in shreds. As I sat up, I saw that a group of men had gathered round. I started shaking. Bobby told me to calm down and that I was safe. I wanted to know where Akita was, but nobody answered me. It was then that I first heard the name 'Petra.' Bobby sat with me, and Petra appeared. She told me to come with her and that Akita had sent her to get some clothes. I knew I was a mess. Somebody gave me a blanket to wrap around me, and we went to a clothing store. Of course, it was closed, but Petra opened it. I went to a dressing room, handed over the rags I had on, and she started pulling outfits for me to try."

Kirsten took a beat for Savannah and Lee Ann to grasp the situation she'd been in fully. Kirsten explained, "I told her I didn't have any money, but she said that didn't matter because Akita or she'd be paying for them. Just then, Akita arrived and asked me if I was all right.

I didn't have time to answer before Petra interrupted to point out that his clothes were a mess, too. Petra had him strip down, and she put his bloody, ripped clothes in the bin. He stood there naked like a little boy being chastised. He was heavily muscled and scarred, and right then and there, I quickly ascertained how much pain he must have gone through."

Lee Ann and Savannah were speechless as Kirsten continued to tell the tale. Kirsten continued, "He told me his wounds weren't as bad as they looked. I knew I wanted to know this man, my hero now. He asked Petra if she'd give me a job. She offered it and a place to live upstairs as soon as he suggested it. Then he asked me a question that would forever change my life. He asked me if I had any ideas about what I wanted to do in life. I shared with him something I had only dreamed about, that I wanted to work in a salon."

Kirsten stopped for a moment and wiped away a tear before she went on with the story. Akita asked Petra to take a picture of me, so I would never forget where I came from. He emphasized that Petra and he would help, but that I'd have to do the challenging work myself. Everything would be up to me. When I was not in school or working at the store, I went everywhere with Petra. I learned demanding work from her and much more about life. She was two years younger than me. She still amazes me. Your dad saved my life that night. Then Petra and your dad gave a life to me. All I am today I owe to them."

Savannah asked, "When did you fall in love with my dad?"

KIRSTEN

Kirsten smiled. "I finished school, worked in the store with Petra, and worked in a salon. Your dad's banker Julia found a salon for sale. He put up the money for a two-percent loan. I went right to work. It was about a year after that the FRBs came in. Your dad was wounded, and Sonia was taking care of him. I went to see him and give him an update on my progress. Sonia was trying to keep him in bed. He was in pain, but he wasn't complaining. All he wanted was to know about my life. Sonia told me that I was part of the FRB family now and that I would be an official FRBB, a Fucking Rowdy Bastard Babe. The title came with some responsibilities. I had to take martial arts training and travel with them on occasion. The more time I spent with them, the more I realized how I felt about your dad. He was different from other men I knew. He defended me and helped me. He had not asked for anything in return. Around the other women, he was kind and sweet. He was always laughing, joking, teasing them, and playing jokes on his men. They also played jokes on him. He enjoyed all of it. He lived life at full throttle."

Lee Ann and Savannah gave Kirsten a big hug. When they separated and she caught her breath, Kirsten observed, "I did not want to love him because I knew that he loved Sonia and Petra, but one night I couldn't help myself. I kissed him. He kissed me back, deeply. He held me, looking at me with that gaze that went through me to my soul. I fell deep into his embrace and stayed there for two days. That was it. All I wanted was your dad. I had no idea what I was going to tell Sonia or Petra. They had been so good to me. They were my friends. I was scared, but I had to tell them what I had done."

CHAPTER 25
Betrayed Friendship

Kirsten had been unable to help herself, even though she knew Akita had a deep connection to Petra and Sonia, one that she didn't quite understand. It was deep—soul-level deep, so she knew she had to confess. When she had the talk with them, the first thing they wanted to know was what she thought his attraction to her was. Kirsten had thought long and hard about that very topic and had decided they had terrible backgrounds in common. They had been in miserable life circumstances, and when given the chance, they'd pulled themselves up by the bootstraps.

The three women knew that Akita wouldn't be willing to give any one of them up, so they reached a compromise. It would be Akita with all three or none of them in his life. What Kirsten had thought Petra and Sonia would see as a betrayal turned out to be a spiritual communion of sorts among the three of them.

As Kirsten explained everything to Savannah, she was fearful that she was going into too much detail, but she forged ahead and explained, "That night, we agreed not to have sex with anyone else, so no chance of diseases."

Savannah just looked at her wide-eyed. Kirsten continued, "What your dad and I had was only shared between the two of us. I loved him deeply and still have love in my heart for him. I miss him."

Savannah said in a measured tone, "You are married."

"Yes, and I love my husband and my family. Your father is in my past, but I will always love him."

Savannah hugged her, then sighed and said, "I thought I knew dad."

Kirsten cut her off, "You do know him better than any of us. He made a life for you, his daughter. You knew a father's love." Kirsten hugged Savannah. "All of us were his past. You were his life. It's getting late. I need to take you home."

Savannah smiled and said, "To be here and have to go home sounds strange and good." It's hard for me to understand the fact that I have a mom."

Kirsten said, "Sonia is a good person and friend. I know she loves you. Your dad made his decision. It was her and you. I wish you, Akita, and Sonia had more time as a family."

Lee Ann had said nothing as she learned these details about Akita's love life, but she took note, and this story, like more that were to come, told her volumes about this man who was shaping up to be more superhuman than she had originally imagine.

They arrived back at Sonia's and lost in thought, Savannah and Lee Ann emerged from the car. Kirsten said, "Hold up, I'll walk in with you. I want your mom to know I brought you home safely." Savannah turned and looked at her intently, laughed, and asked, "What is on that evil mind of yours?"

"Nothing at all," Kirsten replied. "You sound exactly like your dad."

CHAPTER 26
LADY SAVANNAH

Savannah planned to knock on the door, but Kirsten just walked in like she owned the place. Monika met them in the entry. She smiled and said, "I hope you had a good evening." Then she turned to Savannah and said, "I have moved you into a castle apartment near that of Lady Sonia's at her request. Lady Sonia has her dressmaker here for you. Please, all of you, follow me. Monika led them through the castle's hallways. When they arrived, Monika knocked on the door and announced, "Lady Sonia, I bring you Kirsten, Savannah, and Lee Ann." She moved to one side and let them in.

Sonia smiled and said, "I know it's late, and you've had a long day, Savannah, but this is Natalie, and she needs your measurements."

Savannah said, "Sonia, I appreciate this, but I have enough clothes."

Sonia smiled and said, "We've been invited to a formal dinner with Annette Mann. Both of us need new dresses."

Natalie took Savannah's measurements and remarked that her measurements were similar to Sonia's. Then a discussion ensued about a suitable dress color, and a decision was made: gold. Then Savannah added, "I'd like black and pale gold." Again, the women agreed. It was late, so they all hugged and said good night with plans to meet again the next day for lunch. As everyone was preparing to leave, Sonia found a quick opportunity to share important news with Monika. In little above a whisper, Sonia said, "I need to tell you something important. Savannah is my daughter. She just learned the truth. Will you please tell the rest of the staff?"

Monika kept her composure and said, "Yes, Lady Sonia, I will."

Just then Savannah announced that she needed some rest. She hugged Sonia and said good night.

Monika said, "I will take you and Lee Ann to your apartment." As they walked down the marble hallways, Monika said, "So, you are Lady Sonia's daughter."

Savannah said simply "Yes, I am."

Monika smiled and said, "I thought you looked like her, Lady Savannah."

Savannah laughed and responded, "Please, call me Savannah."

"I cannot now that I know who you are," explained Monika. They arrived at an inset door. Monika pushed it open, walked Savannah and Lee Ann through the six rooms and showed them everything.

Savannah had been happy with her other room, and she told Monika, "This is too much."

Monika said, "That room was not for Lady Sonia's family. This one is for Lady Savannah. Do you need anything else?"

Savannah said, "No, and thank you," Then with a giggle, she added, "Lady Monika."

Monika did not see the humor and said, "Please do not do that again." Then she turned to Lee Ann and offered to take her to her room. Lee Ann was grateful for the offer because she was relatively sure she'd never be able to find the location again. She yawned as she hugged Savannah good night and thought about the fascinating things she had learned.

CHAPTER 27
Petra

Another deep attraction and connection Akita had was with Petra, and now it was her turn to tell her story. As they settled in and made themselves comfortable, Petra began, "The first time I met Akita, I worked as a clerk. He walked into the store and looked around at this shirt and then another. His clothes were too small and ugly."

As Petra's eyes became teary, she related the story with sensitivity and detail.

Akita asked me, "Do you have clothes that will fit me and look better than this?"

"I thought anything would look better, but what I said was, 'What size are you?'

He answered with the explanation that the PX didn't have anything bigger than what he was wearing. I thought he was good-looking, so I offered to help him find something. He picked up a brown shirt. I was thinking, oh hell no, but I told him he should try it on. It was a size too small in the chest. I had him try on multiple options until we finally found one that fit. He was delighted and asked for five of that particular shirt. Then he decided to try on pants."

Petra could tell everyone was envisioning Akita in a little dress shop and that the very thought of it amused them. She continued, "Everything was going well until my boss came in. She heard the English we were speaking and became angry.

As he was checking out and leaving, my boss said loudly enough for Akita to hear, 'Americas are not welcome here!'

A week or so later, he walked in with a woman, introduced himself, and asked if I remembered helping him. I told him that he looked much better than the last time I saw him.

He smiled, introduced me to Julia, and told me that she was his banker.

Julia shook my hand and then told me, 'This is your lucky day!'

I'm sure that by the look on my face, Julia knew how confused I was. She didn't give me a chance to say anything before she delivered the news that Akita had bought the building. I simply could not think. My mind went blank. I was speechless.

Then Akita told me that he wanted to speak to my boss, so I went to her office with the news that a man wanted to speak to her. She became terribly angry when she saw him and demanded, 'What do you want?'

He looked at me, then at her, and announced, 'You will no longer manage this store. You're fired.'

Julia cut in and told her that Akita now owned the building and that her services would no longer be needed. My boss, becoming red in the face by the minute, shouted, 'You can't fucking do this to me. I am calling the Polizei.'

Then she picked up the phone and called the Polizei, telling them to come and arrest some trespassers. They arrived in about three minutes and asked what happened. Julia told them and showed them the bill of sale and explained that Akita had fired her. After a brief conversation, which I had to translate for Akita, the officers shook his hand and told him good luck with the business. Then they told my boss to leave and not to return."

Petra could tell her little audience knew there was more to the story. Petra continued, "The shocking surprise came next. Akita took my hand, looked into my eyes, and said, 'This building will be yours. You will manage and own it.'

Julia smiled and said that I would need to come by the bank and sign some paperwork. Everything would be in Akita's name until I paid him back for what he'd spent. She said she'd be happy to help me with the business. I was speechless.

Akita said, 'My men need to come in and buy some clothes. Would that be okay with you?'

I told him my name was Petra. That is all I could think of.

He smiled and said, 'I know.'

When I could finally think I asked him how many men and what sizes they were. He smiled again and said, 'Eleven men, and I am the smallest.'

So, you now know that Akita gave me my start in business. He had only met me once and did all this for me. I now own four clothing stores and export clothing to six countries. I have loved him almost all my life. I miss him. All I want is for him to be at peace. I want you to know how far we would go for Akita and how far he would go for us."

CHAPTER 28
The Dance

Petra smiled and said, "I like this memory. It is my favorite. Akita did not know how to do the Texas two-step."

Lee Ann asked, "The dance?"

Petra said, "Yes, I still think this is funny. He was born in Texas, and even though his childhood was difficult, he grew up in Texas and did not know how to dance the two-step."

"Why would he need to do that dance here?" Lee Ann wondered aloud.

Petra said, "Kirsten and I were planning a birthday party for Sonia. Kirsten wanted a dance, and she wanted to have it Texas style or what we thought Texas style was. We had seen cowboys, cowgirls, the big hats, and the boots, all of it on the TV show *Dallas*. Kirsten wanted the two-step. All the girls that dated the FRBs knew how to do the two-step. The FRBs had been in-country for two days, but Akita had to go to Washington DC for meetings and wouldn't be back for a week.

We were making plans, and the guys were helping. They thought it would be a good idea. Sonia did not know what we were doing. We had two weeks before her birthday when Akita arrived in Frankfurt. This time he wasn't hurt. I picked him up. I was so excited on the way back here that I told him about the party and the dance. That's when he told me that he couldn't dance and that he didn't know what the two-step was. I didn't give him a choice. I told him he'd have to take dance lessons, so he could have the first dance with Sonia.

I called the dance studio. Camila, the owner, was teaching a class, so I left her a message. About fifteen minutes later, I received a call from Camila, and our conversation was comical. I asked if she could teach Akita the two-step in time for the birthday party.

She asked me, 'Can he dance at all?' I said that I didn't think he'd *ever* danced. She laughed and said, 'I know the time is short before the party. Bring him to my studio tomorrow. We will start, but you must help.'

When Akita and Kirsten returned, I told him that I had scheduled him for a dance class the next morning. He took the news well, and we spent the rest of the day and night together. When we arrived at the

The Dance

studio, Camila was teaching a class of young girls. She's Puerto Rican with one of those hard bodies from years of dancing. When she walked, her leg muscles rippled and bulged. Her arms were well defined. Her face was captivating, and she had long black hair.

I remember exactly what Akita said: 'Just shoot me, please.' I assured him we'd have fun and that he'd like it eventually. He said he thought getting shot was probably better.

When Camila finished her class, she walked over to us and introduced herself. She shook my hand and then Akita's. She looked him over, smiling. She said, 'I don't know if I can teach you to dance, but you will do if I need a bodyguard.' Then she explained that she'd have someone else teach her regular classes and that she'd do this for Lady Sonia. It was then we discovered that Sonia donated to Camila's studio.

Akita looked uncomfortable at first, but she reassured him and told him that she'd teach him more than one dance, so he would have more fun when he went out. Akita said, 'We have fun everywhere we go. I'll learn to dance from you. Then you will learn to have fun with us.'

Petra was remembering an array of details about that special time in her life. Camila asked, 'What kind of fun?' Petra continued, I tried to warn her. I told her, "When the guys are in, we pick things for them to do with us, and they pick stuff for us to do with them. We have fun most of the time, but I have been scared."

Akita interrupted, 'Do we have a deal?'

Camila looked at Petra and asked, 'Should I?'

Petra nodded and said, 'Yes, you will have fun on a trip with us.'

Camila said, 'Okay, then yes, we have a deal.'

"We spent the day with her. Akita was trying, but he was getting in his own way. He didn't want to hurt her, step on her foot, or worse."

Then Camila came in closer and said, 'You will not hurt me. Hold me like you are in my bed, and we are making love.' Akita put one arm around her waist and held her shoulder with his hand. He lifted her to his level, leaned in, kissed the side of her neck, and asked, 'Like this?'

He put her back down, and she didn't know what to do. Camila smiled as though she hadn't been caught off-guard and said, 'See, you did not hurt me. Tomorrow, we start at 08:00. You will get it. Both of us will make sure.'

The Dance

Akita said, 'We need the others in here. I know they cannot dance. They never learned either. Camila, can you teach them, so we do not make fools of ourselves?'

Camila asked, 'How many people are we talking about?'

"I counted on my fingers and answered, 'Twelve men and twenty women, but the women can dance. Then Camila wanted to know if all the men were like Akita. I told her they were all wild, aggressive, and mentally deranged. Then she wanted to be sure we'd issue an invitation to the party for her week of hard work."

Petra paused, but nobody seemed to have any questions, so she continued the tale. "We spent hours trying to teach them to dance. All of us were laughing, teasing each other, and having fun in the class. I danced with Akita on the last day of class, and he could finally do a presentable Texas two-step. After everyone else left, Akita and I stayed to help Camila clean up. Then Camila started teasing Akita. She observed, 'You were born in Texas, but you had to learn the Texas two-step in Germany from a Puerto Rican woman. What the hell is up with that?'

Akita danced with Sonia at her birthday party and was so proud of himself. Sonia did say that he wasn't a very good dancer, but being his dance partner was by far the best gift of the night."

CHAPTER 29
Wedding Plans

The day Clint Akita Haddox was killed began like any other. He finished looking at stock (pregnancy-tested cows) to buy for the Broken Saber Ranch. He had traveled to Amarillo with the ranch owner, Bernadette Chisum, his aunt. She had married his uncle Will after he returned home from the army.

His seventeen-year-old shooting student Blanca Martinez was along. She was twelve years old when he started training her. Now she competes at the highest level and wins most of the competitions she enters. Her younger sister, ten-year-old Leticia, tagged along on the trip, and so did Josefina Pena, the thirty-eight-year-old ranch office manager.

While in Amarillo, the ladies dropped Akita off at the stockyard and took the truck and twenty-four-foot utility trailer to stock up on supplies for the ranch and ammo for Blanca.

Will and Bernadette kept a small store on the ranch, so the families living there would not have to travel seventy miles to buy necessary items. The trailer would be filled with enough groceries to resupply the ranch store.

In the meantime, while the ladies were out, Akita didn't find any stock worth buying. He started calling other stockyards and decided to drive to Lubbock to look at more stock. While he was waiting for his truck, he called Germany.

A week prior, he had asked Sonia Ludwig to marry him. She had answered, "Yes! What took you so long?"

They first met when he was in the Army. They had a history. Akita had worked twenty years in the military and now works in the Department of Defense. He had submitted his retirement papers and would be out of service in fifteen days. No one knew about the plans he and Sonia were making. Akita had always had a mischievous and sometimes playfully devious nature when dealing with his friends.

He convinced Sonia to help him play a little trick on Bernadette. He would ask Bernadette to call Sonia on their way back home, and Sonia would ask Bernadette if she could have a wedding at the ranch. Earlier,

Wedding Plans

Sonia had told Akita, "Okay, that sounds like fun. I'll take my sweet time and drag it out. I love being devilish almost as much as you." Before the ladies returned, he called Sonia three more times to work out everything.

Bernadette drove up, and Akita told her that he wanted to go to Lubbock before returning to the ranch. They drove to the Lubbock stockyard, and Akita spent three hours looking at the stock. He found twenty head and bought them. The cattle would be delivered to the ranch in three days. With the unplanned trip to Lubbock, no one had eaten, and Leticia felt ravenously hungry.

By this time, clouds were building up, turning the sky dark, and rain had started falling. The weather was getting much worse.

Akita said, "Okay, we will stop and get something before Leticia tries to eat the north end of a southbound skunk."

Leticia said," I would never eat a skunk, but you would," and pointed at Akita.

Laughing, Josefina said, "You may not eat a skunk, but I think you were nibbling on the seat."

"No, I wasn't," Leticia insisted.

Blanca said, "I need to buy more ammo. I have the state shooting competition coming up, and I need to practice so I can be perfect."

They got everything done and left for the ranch at one o clock in the morning. Sheets of rain had pounded them for the last two hours. Streets flooded, and the flashes of lightning often blinded Akita. The thunder boomed so loud that none of the passengers could sleep. He guessed the raindrops were the size of dimes. It was hard to see out the windshield.

Before passing through the town of Ralls, Akita asked Bernadette to call Sonia. Bernadette took Akita's phone and made the call.

When Sonia answered, Bernadette told her, "You are on speakerphone, and we have little ears in the truck with us. Akita wanted me to call you and put the phone on speaker because he is driving, plus we are in a bad thunderstorm. I can only see twenty feet in front of the truck."

Akita said to Sonia, "I need you to ask Bernadette for the favor you need."

Sonia started laughing, "So you want me to take it easy on you

Wedding Plans

because of the rain?"

"Yes, please," Akita said.

Bernadette said, "All right already. What no good thing are the two of you up to?"

Sonia asked, "May I host a wedding at the ranch next month?"

Bernadette, "Why would you want to have a wedding there when you have your place? I've seen photos of your home. It's magnificent."

Sonia said, "Because of who is getting married."

Bernadette said, "You didn't have to ask. You are family."

Sonia said, "Not yet I'm not, but I will be next month."

Bernadette's mouth opened, trying to say something but all that came out was, "W-h-h-h-a-a-a-t do you …oh shit! You and Akita!" The next thing was, "Why didn't you tell me?"

Akita said, "We are telling you now."

Bernadette hit Akita's arm. The girls in the back were screaming so loud that they drowned out the thunder. Then in her happiness and surprise, Bernadette hit Akita again. Sonia laughed hard and asked, "May I have my wedding at the ranch?"

Bernadette, "Yes, we can decorate the houses, the yard, and all the barns. We can put on the best barbecue west Texas has ever seen." Sonia was laughing again and even harder.

Bernadette said, "Well, hell, this is not my wedding. It's yours. You tell me what 'you want, and we'll get it done."

Sonia said, "I need you to help me with everything, and I want you in my wedding."

Blanca asked excitedly, "Can I be in your wedding?"

Leticia said, "Me too, please."

Bernadette asked, "How long have the two of you been planning this? You should be ashamed—giving me a heart attack!" Bernadette hit Akita again. She said, "Sonia, you have been hanging around this thing too long. The devil in him is rubbing off on you."

Sonia said, "I have always been this way and have fun because of my devil. He is sitting next to you."

Bernadette, laughing, said, "I expected more from you."

Akita stopped paying so much attention to the phone call and more

137

Wedding Plans

on driving. This storm was unrelenting. Bernadette and Sonia continued making wedding plans. They were now between the small communities of Crosbyton and Dickens. Akita braked hard and swerved to miss a cow. He pulled over on the shoulder and stopped the truck.

Akita told Bernadette, "Look," and pointed at a man, trying to move the cattle off the road and into a field. "He needs help."

CHAPTER 30
The Death of the Last FRB

Akita hopped out of the truck into the rain and red mud and started helping the rancher herd loose cattle back to the field. The task worsened as lightning and thunder spooked the cows. Flashes lit the night sky almost non-stop, followed by loud bangs and rumbles of thunder.

Soaked, both men struggled to hurry in the mud. Akita slipped and fell as often as the other rancher.

Bernadette was laughing and giving a play-by-play over the phone to Sonia. Finally, all the cattle were back in the area, and the men repaired the fence.

The rancher told Akita, "Thank you for the help. My name is Clay Jenkins." They shook hands.

Akita introduced himself and said, "A friend of mine owns the land over there," and pointed across the road.

Clay said, "You know Roy Walker? I lease this field from him."

Akita said, "Yes, he's a hard ass, but one of the best men I know. I've helped him out a time or two, and he's always willing to help servicemen. Do you need any more help?"

Clay replied, "No, you have helped me more than you know. I need to get out of the rain, and so do you. Thank you again."

Akita said, "I was happy to do it." Clay got into his truck and left. Akita walked back to his truck and checked the rear trailer doors, then the hitch and safety chains. He stepped out from between the truck and trailer and started walking along the side of the truck. He was about to get in the driver's seat.

Just at that moment, a speeding car with its lights turned off swerved on the road and hit the truck at the back door of the crew cab. The vehicle's passenger side collided with the truck's driver's side with such force that the truck slid sideways a foot and a half. The three young women in the back seat were knocked to the truck's floorboard. Bernadette was slammed against the front passenger door.

Akita was between the two vehicles. On impact, he was crushed from his chest to his knees and torn in half. His lower body was dragged a short distance down the road and was left in an unrecognizable pile.

The Death of the Last FRB

Bernadette yelled into the phone, "Akita was hit." Then she ran around to the driver's side of the truck. When she saw Akita, she cried, "No, God, please, no." Then she threw up.

The vehicle that hit Akita stopped and backed up. The car's passenger side was mangled, and the door glass was broken. Bernadette looked through the missing glass and saw the man aiming a pistol directly at her. Then he fired, missing her by a foot. She moved quickly and pulled her old Browning Hi Power from her waist, returning fire. She could see the fear in the man's face. He stopped the car, put it in drive and accelerated hard to get away.

The girls were attempting to get out of the truck. Josefina was using all her strength to keep them inside it. Blanca forced her way out of the truck, hoping she could help Akita. She had heard the first pistol shot and saw the muzzle flash inside the car that hit them. Without hesitation, she reached into the truck's cab from the open front door on the passenger side and grabbed the rifle (a custom-made 308) that Akita kept between the front seat and the console. She heard another pistol shot, so she thumped the safety off and took up a kneeling shot position at the passenger front fender. She aimed, breathed out, and turned off her anger as Akita had trained her. Her heart was now as cold as polar ice.

CHAPTER 31
A Shots Fired

Blanca fired as lightning still lit up the night sky. She saw her shot was high, hitting the top of the man's scalp. The weapon was sighted in for Akita, not her. She adjusted her aim and fired again just as another bolt of lightning flashed across the sky. The round hit its mark slightly above and behind the man's ear. The weapon was loaded with 175 grain Hollow Points. (Hollow point bullets expand once they hit a target. This expansion creates a wound channel and brings down large game such as moose or bear). When this round exited, it destroyed the left side of the man's face from his eyebrow and nose to his jawbone.

The man was dead as Blanca fired again at the same spot. She placed two rounds less than one-fourth of an inch apart. This round jellified his brain, and it sprayed out onto the road.

She again adjusted her aim and fired two more times; she hit the right side of his chest, tearing apart his heart, lungs, and left side rib and depositing it all onto the door and floorboard of the car. Blanca had fired five rounds from a bolt action rifle at night at a moving target in a thunderstorm and hit her target in less time than it took Bernadette to fire three rounds from her pistol.

Sonia was still on the phone yelling frantically, "What happened? What the hell just happened? Tell me! Let me talk to Akita."

Bernadette walked around the truck; her hands were shaking. She picked up the phone through the open door and told Sonia, "Akita is dead." She had to say this three times before Sonia could understand what she was saying.

Sobbing uncontrollably, Sonia repeated the same word over and over and over, "No, no, no."

Bernadette had no way to console her. She was still in shock, herself. She said simply, "I need to call the police," and hung up.

CHAPTER 32
A Cover Up

Bernadette did not call the police. Instead, she called Will. Shocked and horrified, her speech was still unintelligible. Crying, she told him what had happened. Will tried to calm her down, so he could make sense of what she was telling him. When he could hear her breathing become a little more regular, he asked, "Where are you?"

She said, "We're between Crosbyton and Dickens at the ranch road before White River."

Will said, "I'm calling Roy Walker. That's his ranch road. He will help." Then he told Bernadette to keep everyone in the truck. He knew the girls didn't need to see Akita like that if Bernadette's description was accurate. He continued, "Do not call the cops yet. Take everyone's phone away until we get this sorted out. I'm on my way."

About ten minutes later. A tow truck and pickup pulled up at the gate on the opposite side about two hundred yards down the road. Bernadette recognized Roy and Olivia Walker. Their families were friends and had been since Roy needed some help about five years earlier. Roy, a tall, slender man, was driving the tow truck, and Olivia, his daughter, was driving the pickup.

Roy got out and said, "Will called me. We need to get everyone out of this shit and get them dry and warm. What I need now is everyone except you to go with Olivia now. She will take them to our house. They'll stay there until Will picks them up." Roy noticed the body parts on the road and motioned for Olivia to move her truck forward until her front bumper was against the front bumper of Akita's truck. He parked the truck there, so the girls wouldn't see the body parts. Bernadette helped Josefina, Blanca, and Leticia as they dashed to Olivia's pick up.

The storm was still raging. Roy said, "Will told me that you think Blanca killed the man in the car."

Bernadette said, "He shot at me, and I shot back. Then I heard rifle shots. When the car stopped, I saw Blanca fire the last round."

The mud where both trucks were parked was slimy and slick underfoot. Roy asked, "Has Blanca told anyone about what she has done?"

A Cover Up

Bernadette said, "No she hasn't."

Roy walked over to Olivia's truck and told Blanca that he needed to speak to her alone.

Even though it was still pouring, she got out of the truck and walked down the road with him far enough that no one could hear what was said.

Roy said," I have some things to take care of before returning home. When I'm finished, I want to talk to you about what happened tonight. Until I do, please do not say anything to anyone. Not even your mom and dad when you talk to them on the phone and tell them that you're not hurt. Do you understand what I am telling you?"

Blanca said, "Yes, I do. I will not say a word."

Roy looked at the scene and said, "Will and I will fix all this shit." Blanca returned to Olivia's truck. Olivia backed up, turned around, drove to the ranch road, opened the gate, went through it, and closed it behind her.

Roy waited until she was out of sight. Then he said to Bernadette, "You and Akita made this supply run today. No one else was with you. I will take care of the car and body. I owe Akita and you much more than this. One more thing. I need your pistol and the rifle Blanca used."

Bernadette gave Roy the weapons and said, "I'll tell the police that we were alone, and this was a hit and run."

Roy said," I need to take this car now. You need to call the cops when I leave and tell them a car hit your truck and killed Akita. The car did not stop. Do you understand"? She nodded yes.

He went through the car quickly and removed the cell phone and laptop. He pulled the batteries from both and bagged them. With his wench, he loaded the car onto his truck and drove away into the dark, damp night quickly.

The local sheriff received the call and asked Bernadette, "Are you hurt? Are you sure that the man with her was dead"?

Bernadette said, "I'm not injured. Akita's body was in two pieces."

The sheriff, not waiting for further explanations or descriptions said, "I am on my way."

He hung up and called the justice of the peace and told him about the accident and the death. The sheriff needed him there to verify the death.

A Cover Up

While Bernadette was waiting for the sheriff, she called Savannah. Before she could say much more than, "We were involved in an accident," Bernadette started sobbing.

As Savannah felt the fear creep into her, she asked, "What happened to my dad? Is he OK?"

Bernadette said, "He was hit by a car. Savannah, baby girl, he is dead."

Savannah screamed, "Stop lying to me. My dad can't be dead. He may be hurt, but he is not dead."

Bernadette said, "Baby girl, I am sorry."

"Where is my dad? I want to see him," Savannah said between sobs

Bernadette said, "You can't see him the way he is. You don't want to remember him that way."

Savannah replied, "Tell me where he is. I will leave now. I must see him.

Bernadette said, "You can't, and if you could, I wouldn't let you see him the way he is."

Savannah hung up after saying, "I will find him myself." Then she collapsed onto the floor. She could not move; all she could do was cry.

Bernadette waited about twenty minutes before the Dickens County Sheriff and the ambulance arrived. She was cold and wet. The paramedic escorted her to the back of the ambulance, gave her a blanket, and assessed her condition.

The sheriff asked her questions about the car. She said, "It all happened so fast, and with this storm, I couldn't tell him what color the car was."

The sheriff was going to call a tow truck when Will arrived with the ranch tow truck.

Bernadette ran to Will, crying. She hugged him.

Will told the sheriff that he'd take Akita's truck and trailer back to the ranch. The ambulance took Akita's body. The sheriff gave Will the address where Akita's body would be taken. The sheriff said, "We need to get out of this storm. I'll call you if I need anything else." Then he got in his car and left.

Will waited for him to get out of sight, drove to the ranch road, turned onto it, stopped, got out and opened the gate, went through, and

A Cover Up

then locked the gate behind him. He then drove to Roy's house. When Will and Bernadette arrived, Will dropped Bernadette off and told her he had to take Akita's truck and the trailer back home. Will waited for Bernadette to get inside Roy's house, then turned his truck around and drove home.

Will drove to the barn, unhooked the trailer, and unloaded Akita's truck. He put the tow truck away and started walking to the house. Savannah had seen the tow truck with her dad's truck on it. She ran from her house, stopped Will, and demanded, "Where is my dad?"

Will reached out and hugged her. All he could get out was, "I am sorry."

Savannah said, "No, he can't be dead, not my dad. My dad is one of the toughest men on earth. He can't be dead."

Will said, "We will know more in the morning. I must go and get the others now. They're at Roy Walkers. I'll get someone to stay with you."

Will went to Blanca's house and told her mother, "Both girls are okay. Then he told her that Akita was dead and asked her to stay with Savannah until morning?

She agreed and left to stay with Savannah.

CHAPTER 33
Eliminating Evidence

The sheriff and the ambulance arrived at Bernadette's accident scene. Roy had driven fifteen miles to the backside of his land. He stopped his truck where a D9 High Track Cat dozer he had been using to build a cow tank was parked. Roy had built it himself to catch rain runoff, so the livestock would have water in dry months. At 1000 feet long by 600 feet wide and 60 feet deep, it was lined with two feet of clay on the bottom and sides to prevent water loss due to saturation. The dam was U-shaped. The 150 feet thick base tapered to eight feet at the top.

He unloaded the car. Then he removed the man's body and placed it next to his truck.

Roy got in the dozer's cab and pushed the car into the cow tank. Then he started using the D9 in the center of the tank at the dam, the deepest part of the tank. Roy pushed the clay liner fifteen feet towards the inlet side of the tank until he had a seventy-foot long by a ten-foot-wide hole in the two-foot-thick clay bottom. By doing this, he created a dam inside the tank for him to work behind, unimpeded by the rainwater filling the cow tank.

This quickly constructed dam was five feet high and shaped to seal off both ends of the work area. He placed the clay in this manner to reuse it to seal the tank's bottom when he finished. He then dug a hole in the bottom of the newly constructed cow tank behind this small dam. This trench was twenty-feet deep and forty-feet long. When Roy had finished digging the trench, water was lapping at the top of his small dam, and he was running out of time.

Roy quickly pushed the car into the trench, opened the dozer door, and threw Bernadette's pistol and Akita's rifle in with the car. He ran the dozer over the car multiple times, crushing it down to about one foot in height. Once he was satisfied with the car's shape, he started backfilling the trench and burying the car with the dirt he had removed. When he finished this task, water came over his small dam.

He hurriedly pushed the clay back in place. Now the water level was at the bottom of the dozer doors. Roy had to move quickly to move the dozer out and onto the high ground. He was pleased with himself. The

Eliminating Evidence

tank would be halfway filled by morning. This car would never be found.

Roy loaded the man's body onto the back of his truck and drove to a bend in the river where he knew feral hogs bedded down. He carried the body about a half a mile through thick brush and dumped it where he found hog tracks, uprooted grass, weeds, and other plants.

He wanted the fingerprints. A friend of his could ID this shit head, but this process was impossible in this weather, so he cut off the right hand and put it in a bag. He knew the hogs would eat every body part, including the bones. Tomorrow no one would be able to find anything even if they were standing right where the body lay.

Roy drove to his house. He was wet and muddy, so he parked in the barn. He kept a clean change of clothes there because he had been in trouble too often with his wife for tracking mud and cow shit into her house. He changed clothes. Then he removed the hand from the bag, dried it and cleaned off the mud. Finding his stamp pad and paper, he began the task of fingerprinting. He took photos of the unusual ring on the little finger with his phone. He put the fingerprint paper in an envelope and sealed it.

Roy called Olivia to tell her that he'd be out for another two hours. Olivia told him that she had given some dry clothes to the three ladies, but they were still on edge. Roy and she agreed that it would take some time for them to recover.

Next, Roy put on gloves, cleaned the hand with bleach, and put it in a clean bag. He then got into one of the old ranch trucks that he generally used for feeding cattle and fencing. These trucks never leave the ranch and aren't registered, nor do they have license plates. The police can't trace them from photos. The last time this truck was registered was in the early 70 s. Roy started to drive towards Aspermont.

Roy stopped at a ranch gate and pulled some baling wire off a fence post that had been left there for fence repair. He pulled the hand out of the bag and twisted one end of the wire around the middle finger, making a hook out of the other end. He placed the hand back in the bag and continued driving to Aspermont.

Outside of town, Roy stopped long enough to place a bandana on his face and put on an old ball cap, pulling it down over his ears. At this time of night and in this storm, he doubted anyone would see him, but

Eliminating Evidence

he didn't want to be identified. He continued driving and when he arrived in town, he drove to the courthouse, stopped, and got out of the truck. Using his gloves, he removed the hand from the bag and walked to the courthouse's main entrance. Using the hooked end of the wire, he wired the hand to the handle of the door with the backside of the hand facing out towards the sidewalk. Then he curled the fingers into the palm, making it flip off whoever would find it.

He wanted law enforcement to identify this man if his friend couldn't. The body had no ID, and the car was clean except for the phone and the laptop. The ring was the only thing possibly identifiable on the body.

Roy returned to the truck and started driving home. On the way there, he called his wife Gaspara. She was visiting her mother in Puebla, Mexico. He began to tell her about the accident.

Gaspara told him that Olivia had already called her. She asked, "Do you need me to come home early?"

Roy answered, "No, stay there with your mom. It's been too long since your last visit, and I will handle everything here."

Gaspara said, "I love you."

Roy replied, "I love you, too" and hung up.

Roy was tired, but he called Will next. When he answered, Roy explained, "We need to set a trap with the phone to see what we catch. We also need to have someone watch the courthouse in Aspermont who'll be able to tell us what happens, and when any other law enforcement comes into town."

Will said, "I'll have Alex there early and have him call in every time something new happens. What are you thinking?"

Roy said, "The shit head in the car did not have ID, wallet, or credit cards, nothing at all. The car was too clean, not even a scrap of paper. I think he was sent to kill Akita. He found his chance and succeeded, but he had to return to take care of the witnesses. That girl stopped him. Will, do you know how good of a shot she is?"

Will said, "Clint—Akita was training her, and she won shooting matches for 4H. He told me she was outstanding, which is high praise from him."

Roy said, "I checked the body and found that she placed two rounds

ELIMINATING EVIDENCE

a quarter of an inch apart in his skull, put two in his chest less than an inch apart, and one round took off his scalp. Now for the good part, she did it with a bolt action rifle at night on a moving target in a thunderstorm. That's better than outstanding. That fucking no name ass hole didn't know who he was fucking with when he went back. Now we need to try and catch whoever sent him."

Will agreed and said, "If we set a trap, we'll need the high ground around the accident scene."

Roy asked, "Are you at my house yet?"

Will said, "I'm at your road now. With this storm, it took longer to get Akita's truck back to the house than it should have."

Roy said, "When you get there, stay the rest of the night. We have more than enough room. No reason to travel in this storm when you don't need to."

Will said, "Thank you. I think we'll take you up on that."

"I want to talk to Blanca," Roy said, "and tell her how many lives she saved. That man would have killed everyone. I'm about an hour out, and I'll need to get some sleep before starting. I'll call Olivia and have her wake me four hours from now. Will, we need to use our trained men for this, but we can't force them to help. It wouldn't be right."

Will said, "I'll ask all of mine. I'll also get a map of the area and find out where to place people."

Roy breathed a heavy sigh of relief, said good night, and hung up. Then he called Olivia and told her that Will would be there soon to stay overnight. Then he told her when he would be home and when to wake him. As their conversation was winding down, he asked, "How are the girls? Were they able to go to sleep?"

Olivia answered, "They're in bed except for Blanca."

Roy said thoughtfully, "I'll speak with her when I get there. Please tell her to try and sleep."

Olivia answered, "I will. Get home safe." She hung up the phone.

Roy arrived at his house and parked the truck back at the barn. He walked to the house. No one was up. The house was dark, and he quietly went to bed.

CHAPTER 34
A Hand Found

In the morning, Dolores parked her car and pulled out a set of keys from the glove box. Her job for the last ten years was to clean the inside of the courthouse. She always unlocked and entered through the main door.

Today, she made her way to the door while talking to her son on the phone. Distracted, she reached out to the door handle to unlock it and grabbed the hand. She looked at it, not yet understanding what she was holding. Then it hit her. She let the hand go and started stomping her feet in tiny steps, yelling at the top of her lungs, "I touched it, I touched it, oh my God, I touched it. "

Her son, still on the phone, shouted, "Mom, what's wrong!?" Then the phone switched off. Dolores had dropped it.

Alex, watching from across the parking lot, was laughing to himself.

Dolores was so loud and so out of control that people ran to help. One man grabbed her by the shoulders to try to calm her down. He asked if she was going to be all right when it was obvious at once that she would never be all right again.

Dolores, still visibly upset, pointed toward the door and shouted, "I touched it!" Then she gazed at her own hand and began wiping it frantically on her shirt, crying, "GET. IT. OFF. OF. ME!" She then vomited on herself and on the man holding her.

The man released his hold on her and started to gag.

A woman who also worked at the courthouse had just arrived. She saw all the commotion as she was walking to the door. When she saw the hand, as well as the state of Dolores and the man, she covered her mouth and nose with one hand. With the other, she pulled out her phone and called the sheriff. Fortunately, she was the voice of calm.

The sheriff was at his home when he received her call. At first, he didn't know what to think. He immediately drove to the courthouse. When he arrived, several people were standing in the doorway. "Move aside," he said officially.

He examined the hand to ensure it was a human hand. Then he told everyone to use the other entrance. On both sides of the door, he draped

A Hand Found

yellow and black police tape with the warning "do not enter" printed on it. He then called the State Police.

The State Trooper took less than two minutes to arrive. He looked at the hand briefly and explained, "I must call the FBI and have them help. With it being placed here like this, it looks like someone is making a statement. They're telling us 'I killed this person, and you can do nothing about it.'"

The State Trooper took pictures of the hand, the wire, and the ring. He then unwired the hand from the door handle and placed it in an evidence bag. He asked the sheriff, "Do you have a place to store this until the FBI gets here from Abilene?"

The sheriff replied, "The only thing I can think of is the coolers at the hospital. I'll call the doctor and ask if we can use the cooler."

The State Trooper agreed, and they left with the hand.

Alex made his call.

CHAPTER 35
Morgan

Early in the morning, Olivia knocked on Roy's door and said, "Dad, it's time."

Roy woke and dressed, went to the kitchen for coffee, and found everyone up. Breakfast was waiting for him. They sat at the kitchen table and bar to eat. When Roy finished eating. He looked around and asked, "Where is Blanca?"

Olivia replied, "She's finally sleeping."

Roy asked Olivia to wake her up, so Olivia left to wake her.

Roy leaned over to Will and said quietly, "The phone and laptop are in that bag."

He pointed to a small table under the coat rack. "When I found the phone, I used the dead man's thumbprint to open it. It didn't take long to open and read an email that had a CIA heading. Then I took the time to disable the passcode before I pulled the battery and sim card. I want the info on that phone. I also want all the information on the laptop's hard drive."

Will said," I know someone who can get the info off that phone. She gets paid to hack into the company's IT security systems. She worked for me when she was in college. I'll call her."

Roy nodded. "We need her now. I'll pay her."

Will replied, "You don't have to. I will." He stepped out of the house and made the call.

Savannah was in disbelief that her father was dead. She had only slept off and on all night. Her phone rang. She was not going to answer, but she picked it up to see who was calling. It was Robin Smith. Savannah answered, "Hello, I can't talk now, please."

Robin cut her off and said, "Do not hang up. I have Will on the call with us."

Will said, "I need your help."

Savannah asked, "What do you need?"

Robin said, "I don't know how to get to Roy Walker's house. Will you meet me in Dickens and take me there?"

Will said, "We think your dad was murdered. We need Robin to retrieve all the information off a phone and laptop, and she'll have to do her work here."

Savannah answered, "I will be there," and hung up.

When Savannah went outside to leave, she saw the ranch hands loading horses, weapons, ammo, and other items. She noticed all the men doing this were former military. She asked one, "Are you going to Roy's ranch?"

He said, "Yes, Will and Roy need us. We're going to catch the mother fuckers who killed your dad."

Savannah went back into the house. She remembered when she was getting ready to leave for college, her dad gave her a small decorative box. He wrote down a name and phone number on the back of the ranch's business card. She had not thought about this since then.

Her dad had told her that he owned C&M Security, a private security company. The card had the contact information of the man who runs the day-to-day operations. Akita's exact words at the time could be taken as a warning or a premonition, "Call him if you ever find yourself in trouble, and I'm not around. I've told him who you are, and if something happens to me, the company and everything else is yours. You will be his boss." Savannah opened the box and dialed the number.

A man's voice answered, "C&M Security." Savannah asked to speak to Morgan.

The man asked, "Can I have your name, so I can tell him who is calling?"

"My name is Savannah Haddox, and I need to speak to Morgan now," Savannah replied impatiently.

The man said, "Hold, please."

A short time passed, and another man's voice said, "Morgan, speaking ma'am, how may I help you?"

Savannah asked, "Do you know who I am?"

Morgan said, "Yes, ma'am, I do. You're the daughter of Akita, my boss, and owner of this company."

Morgan

Savannah said, "My dad told me to call you if I was ever in trouble and needed help. My dad is dead, and people here have a phone with emails and text messages that make them think the CIA killed him."

Morgan said simply, "All of the men here are ready to help. We will do anything necessary to get to the bottom of your dad's death."

Savannah replied, "I don't want to get to the bottom of anything. I want the mother fuckers to pay with their lives. Can you help me with that?"

Morgan paused briefly and then said, "Your dad was my friend, and I owe him more than I can ever repay. Every man here owes him. I need all the information you have and can make available before I make the arrangements you're asking for. Do you understand what it means if the CIA killed him on U.S. soil?"

Savannah said, "No, I don't understand all that it means, but I know that the CIA can't operate inside the U.S. I'll give you the information you need as I can get it. In the meantime, you need to start putting a plan together."

Morgan replied, "Right now, I can do little, but I will get all I can on the area and routes that we think they'll use. Once we get intel, we will gear up. You're my boss. Whatever you need, we will do."

Savannah hung up with Morgan and made another call. It was to General Scott.

The General answered the phone on the second ring. Savannah told him about the plan to trap the people who would undoubtedly come to find their missing man; however, she didn't tell the General about Morgan and her plans.

General Scott said, "Sounds like a good plan, but they need law enforcement with them. I have an idea. I'll call a friend of mine in the Texas Rangers. I can get them out there to investigate the accident, but I won't tell them what the ranchers are doing. Please tell the landowner Roy to expect them and act accordingly.

Savannah responded, "I will, and thank you. I don't need anyone else in trouble if we can help it." She hung up, found her truck keys, drove to the barn, and hooked her horse trailer to the truck. Then saddled her horse and Blanca's, loaded both, and drove back to the house. Methodically, she took her pistol, a 12-gauge shotgun, and a 308 rifle with ammo with her. She also loaded three five-gallon water jugs and a large bucket for watering the horses. Then she started the drive to Dickens.

CHAPTER 36
SETTING THE TRAP

Will returned to the kitchen to speak to Roy. "Robin is on the way," he said. "I told her about the laptop. She told me to have it ready, and she'll try to retrieve any info on it. She didn't know how to get here, so she turned my call into a conference call with Savannah. They're friends from when Robin worked for me. They'll meet in Dickens and come here."

Roy said, "She'll need to do the phone first. We need it turned on and in the impact area. I want whoever sent that piece of shit to know where to start looking for their man."

"Yes, I'll do that," Roy confirmed. "We need to get everyone in place. We need overwatch and containment if they take the bait. I asked our men, and they will be ready."

"I asked my men to help. They're all coming and will bring horses to cover more ground," Will said.

Blanca and Olivia went into the kitchen. Blanca's lack of sleep was apparent.

Roy looked at her and said," I need your help at the barn. Will you come with me, please?"

Blanca said, "Yes, but I need to eat something first?"

Roy smiled and said, "Please hurry. We have a lot to do."

To Will, Roy said, "Please don't do anything until we get back."

When Savannah and Robin arrived in Dickens. Savannah parked and checked her trailer and the horses. Robin pulled up in a new BMW. Savannah greeted her and said, "We have to drive on ranch roads, and that car is too low to make it. Load your stuff in the truck and leave your car here. No one will mess with it."

Robin loaded her gear in the truck, and the women started to Roy's house.

Roy looked at Blanca and said, "Are you ready?" Blanca answered in the affirmative, and they walked to the barn without saying anything. Once they got there, Roy asked, "Can you drive?"

Blanca looked at him with a questioning look and then said, "Yes, of course."

Roy pitched her the keys to his pickup and said, "You drive."

SETTING THE TRAP

"Where are we going?" Blanca asked as she jumped behind the wheel.

Roy smiled and said, "I have a place where we picnic. Let's go there. I'll tell you which way to go." Roy gave the directions, and they arrived at a little clearing with a table and fire pit. Roy got out and sat down at the table. Blanca joined him.

Blanca asked, "What are we doing here?"

Roy wrinkled his brow and said, "Will you tell me what you think happened last night?"

Blanca's eyes teared up. She said, "I killed that man."

"Stop," Roy said. You did not kill him. He killed himself when he backed up his car and shot at Bernadette. If you hadn't acted exactly the way you did, everybody there would be dead. You would be dead, and I think being alive is better than being dead. Don't you?"

Blanca said, "Yes, but how do you know he would kill all of us?"

Roy said, "He was there to kill Akita, and he did that. He backed up to kill all the witnesses. You stopped him. Now I need your help and skills. Will and I are going to set a trap and see if we can get someone to come to find out what happened to their man."

Blanca's eyes were blazing with anger, and she asked, "He was *there* to kill Akita?"

Roy said, "Yes. Now, do you understand what I said? The killer killed himself."

Blanca breathed in and out deeply, mentally going to the place Akita had trained her to go.

Roy noticed as her face changed, and she showed no emotion.

She looked him in the eye and said, "I will help get the mother fuckers who killed Akita."

Roy became uneasy. He had seen this before from seasoned warriors or snipers but never from someone so young. He said nothing for a time, then simply said, "Let's go to work."

Blanca and Roy moved from the table to the truck. She started the engine, and said, "I am ready." Roy got in, and they drove to the house.

When they arrived, Roy's and Will's men were waiting. All had horses in trailers, weapons in trucks, pistols strapped on hips, and enough food and water to last for weeks.

Blanca was impressed. She said to Roy, "If the phone is the bate and

Setting the Trap

these men are the steel jaws of the trap. I would not want to be the one you are after."

"This may be overkill," Roy said, "but I would rather have too many men, guns, and supplies than not enough."

Will had the men gather around. Roy walked to the front of his truck and asked Will for the map. They had marked where they wanted the men to be placed. Roy put the map on the truck's hood and said, "Before we start, I want everyone to understand this plan might not work. Whoever sent the man that killed Akita probably won't take the bait."

Roy looked around at this group of hard men; some worked for Will and the rest worked for him, badass elite soldiers trained well and forged in the fire of battle.

Roy continued to address the men, "With what we are planning, if they come, we'll have a fight on our hands. Win or lose, all of us can and will go to jail or die. Speaking for myself, if you don't want to be a part of this, I will never hold it against you, and if you work for me, your job is still yours."

Will stepped up to the truck and said, "I feel the same, and if you work for me, and you don't want to be here, go back to the ranch and go to work." No one moved.

Malin, one of Will's men, said, "I owe Akita. He told me about Will's ranch, and when I showed up, Will hired me on the spot and me without any ranch or farming experience. I want to make whoever did this pay."

One of Roy's men spoke up next, "He was one of us. I am in." Everyone agreed.

Savannah and Robin arrived and parked. They got out and approached Will. Robin hugged Will and asked him where the laptop was. Before he replied, he hugged Savannah and asked her if she was all right.

Savannah said nothing. She just squeezed him tightly and sighed.

Will told Roy, "I'll get the laptop for Robin."

Savannah took Roy's arm and guided him away from the group. Once out of earshot, she said, "I called my dad's General. He'll have one of the Texas Rangers out here. The Rangers won't know what you're doing. General Scott told me to tell you to "act accordingly." I think he wants you to put the Ranger back on his heels until you've done what you need to."

Roy smiled and said, "You're three steps ahead of me. I have an idea

Setting the Trap

about how to deal with the Ranger. This will be fun. He hugged her. "Your dad would be proud," he said as he noticed that Will and Robin had rejoined the group.

Activity was starting. Savannah and Blanca unloaded the horses.

Will escorted Robin into Roy's house and gave her the phone and laptop. He told her that they needed the phone's info first. When he returned to the meeting, he noticed that Savannah was there.

Roy turned to the map and said, "If they are smart, they'll take the high ground here and here before they search this area for the phone. So, we need to be here, and here again, pointing to three additional areas on the map. Further out from here, we can watch every move they make. I've asked the landowners if we can place men on their land because we're trying to catch cattle rustlers. We have their permission. In these parts, it's common to shoot somebody for stealing cattle. So, if you are asked why you're there, your answer is 'looking for rustlers.' Then Roy added, "I want the best shots we have in place there."

Malin said, "We have two men with Barrett .50 calibers." The two men stepped forward.

One of Roy's men said, "I'll take one of the positions." Roy gave them walkie-talkies.

Then Roy told the group, "We don't know how long this will take. Be prepared to be out for ten days or so." He turned back to the map and said, "When our guest arrives, we move in here, and he pointed to multiple locations. They will have no escape. For the people involved in this part, I want you to have campfires, play music, all that shit. That way, they'll think we're working in the area. I'll have a truck bring hay and water for your horses." Roy thought more a minute and then added, "I need trucks here. When we spring, the trap moves them across the road. I don't want anything getting out." Roy handed out walkie-talkies to each team of people.

Robin walked up and said, "You need to see what I have from the phone."

Roy told Will directly, "I'll finish here and get everyone in position. You go with her and take Savannah with you."

CHAPTER 37
Robin in Control

Will and Savannah left with Robin. When they entered the kitchen, Will was surprised at how much electronic gear Robin had amassed.

Robin said, "Someone pulled the battery out of the phone and laptop, an action that made my job easier and didn't allow anyone to track it. The first thing I did was disable the Internet connection and location tracker on the phone. So, we are safe. The person who used this wasn't up on security or password protocols. It took me less than five minutes to gain access to the emails and text messages on the phone." Robin, feeling proud of herself continued, "Look at this. He's CIA and operating in the US. He sent emails to this IP address. I still have not found where it is, but here are the emails sent and received."

Will told her to copy everything to a thumb drive.

Robin was ahead of him. "Already done, and with what this is, I made six copies."

Will observed, "Then we have all the evidence here. Akita was killed by the CIA."

"Not so fast," Robin said. "All we have is evidence that this man followed Akita for months. He also told someone what he was doing. We can't prove that he killed Akita or that anyone ordered it. (Robin and Savannah didn't know that the man was dead, and Will would not tell them). "I still have hours of work to do, and we may not be able to prove anything."

Will said, "Roy needs to see this," and left.

After Will left, Savannah moved closer to see what Robin had on the computer screen. She took some time to read the one email that Robin had shown Will. She finished reading and asked, "Are you sure that The CIA was involved?"

Robin explained, "Yes, the man driving the car that killed your dad was CIA, but I have more work to do before I am able to say *if* the CIA ordered his death."

Savannah asked for one of the thumb drives, and Robin gave it to her. Savannah then excused herself to make a phone call. She stepped out of the house and walked a short distance away for privacy. She called

Morgan again and told him about the email on the CIA phone.

Morgan asked, "Can you send me a copy of that email?"

Savannah borrowed Robin's laptop and sent the email to Morgan. Then she deleted it from the sent mail and cleared the deleted mail files. No one needed to know what she was doing yet. She would tell them later if Morgan had to act on the information she was giving him.

She returned to the house, gave Robin the laptop back, and thanked her.

Robin said, "Will hasn't come back with Roy yet. Please stay with me."

Savannah and Robin had been talking for ten minutes when Will and Roy stepped into the house. He asked Robin to show Roy what she had so far. She did and answered several questions from both men.

Roy asked, "Can you stop working on this now and come with me? We need you in the field. I'm taking the phone back where we found it."

Robin asked, "Do you want me to get all the information off the phone and leave the tracker on?"

"Yes," Roy said. "We need someone to come looking for their man."

Robin said that she'd remove the hard drive before they left. She then handed a thumb drive to both men and said, "You need to put this in a safe place, and we need to give one to the police. I'll need fifteen minutes here, and then we can go."

Roy loaded a generator on the bed of his truck. Robin needed it for power in the field. Then he drove Robin and Will to the accident location. They got out of the truck.

Roy opened the tailgate and asked Robin, "Can you use this as a table to work on?"

Robin said, "Yes, that's more than enough room. Give me a few minutes to set up, and then I need the phone.

Will said, "I'll find a good place to hide the phone." Roy nodded his approval.

When Robin had everything set, she asked Roy for the phone. Roy pulled the phone out of his pocket and handed it to her. "Here we go," she said.

Before installing the sim card and battery, she set up a program to clone the phone. With everything ready, she installed the battery and card.

Robin in Control

The phone came to life, and her equipment started the cloning process. Within two minutes, she had a phone with all the information on it.

She gave the original phone to Will and said, "I have all I need. She looked at Roy and said, "I need all of my other equipment, so I can give you the contents of this phone on a thumb drive."

Roy started to say something, but Robin looked at her equipment and said, "Someone just pinged that phone."

Will asked, "How could it be this fast?"

Robin said, "They were looking for it, and when its signal went out, that is all it took. They will know where it is soon."

Will said, "I need to take this phone to the accident area now and find a good place to put it. I'll make it look like it was thrown from the car on impact."

As Will was leaving, Roy said, "Don't make it too easy to find. We need them in the right place for at least five minutes for the road blockade to work. If they want to fight their way out, that will not happen."

As he looked back, Will answered, "I hope they try. I want them to pay for what they have done." He stopped himself before he said anything else.

"For Savannah's sake, so do I," Roy said. "It was not right what they did to Bernadette and Akita."

Roy then turned to Robin and said, "I'm going to put guards around you."

Robin asked why he'd do that.

Roy explained, "Others may want what you found on the phone and laptop and will stop at nothing to get it back. I will not take chances with your life."

"Do you think this will go that far?" Robin asked.

Roy said, "No, I do not, but I want to be careful." Then he asked, "Can you work out of a twenty-four-foot stock trailer with a living area?"

Robin said, "Yes, but I will need a little time with the more sensitive equipment to finish the work on the laptop."

Roy asked, "How long do you need? I will start having the trailer set up for you."

Then Robin said something that made Roy stop what he was doing

Robin in Control

and pay very close attention: "I have six drones we can use with the large area we need to cover. I'll need some friends of mine to operate the drones. That way we will be able to see everything. Let me call them now and get them headed this way."

Roy said, "Have them go to the house. I'll have someone pick them up and take them to the trailer." He kissed her cheek. "That is a game-changer. We have the high ground! Have them call when they get to the house."

Roy drove Robin back to the house.

Robin said," I'll need three hours on the laptop before I can tell you if I can get past the security on it. Then it'll take at least an hour to copy everything on the phone to a thumb drive. I'm going to make six or more copies of everything. I will need to know how many copies you and Will need."

Roy said, "You pulled the hard drive. Can you leave that work for later? I want you away from the house and in a place closer to us for safety reasons."

Robin said, "Yes, in that case, I need an hour at your house on the phone clone, then I can start in the field."

Roy called Olivia, and when she answered, he told her, "Clean out the six-horse trailer and make sure to stock food and water in the living quarters."

Olivia answered, "I will, but first I need to feed Crusher and Shaker."

Roy said, "Feed your dogs before they eat my horse."

Olivia laughed and said," Dad, they are not that bad."

"Robin will work in the field with us. I need you and your dogs in the field. I need to know that you are safe," Roy said seriously.

Olivia said," I will bring my horse with me." With that, she said goodbye and hung up.

Then Roy asked Robin, "Can you set up something at the house that will show a large electronic signal? If we have uninvited guests, I want to make sure they come to the house."

Robin thought for a while and said, "I think I know what you want. I will get it set up. I will also put a remote switch on it. We will be able to trigger it anytime you want." Robin then offered, "I have surveillance equipment I use on companies before I try to break into their systems to find out what people do before and after work. I take their habits and use them in my plans. We could place items where you think they will be and see what they are doing."

Roy smiled and said, "I could kiss you again! You do some of the same things I used to do for the Army in my job."

Robin said, "Take me home now, and I will get what I need."

"Now?" Roy asked.

Robin said, "Yes, I will also get the equipment I need to work out of the trailer. If Will had told me everything you needed, I would have brought it."

Roy turned the truck around and called Olivia again. She answered quickly. Roy explained, "I'm taking Robin home to get more equipment she needs. I will be back in an hour and a half."

Olivia asked, "More stuff. Doesn't she have enough?"

Roy said, "She needs more in case our plan works."

Olivia said, "Okay. Can you bring back burgers from Dickens? I'm hungry."

Robin added, "That sounds good. I'm hungry, too. I'll call ahead and order. How many burgers do we need?"

Roy thought and said, "We will need forty and all of the fixings." Robin called and placed the order.

When they arrived at Robin's house, she collected everything she thought she would need and more. Then they drove to the burger joint and picked up their order, turned around, and headed back to the ranch.

Olivia had the trailer stocked, clean, and ready for Robin at the ranch. Roy drove up and parked his truck by the trailer. He walked to the barn, got his one-ton Chevy Duramax, backed up to the trailer, and hooked it up. He took Robin's equipment out of his truck and loaded it into the trailer.

Robin went to the house, packed her equipment, and took it to the trailer. This took three trips.

Roy told Olivia to take his truck and give the burgers to the ranch hands. Then Roy and Robin took his one-ton and trailer to a location next to the accident area where he thought it would offer the best protection for Robin, a place that would allow her to collect all the information and send it to him and his men as quickly as possible.

Robin in Control

Robin asked, "Can we put the field surveillance equipment out now? Before we set up here? It will make this part easy later. I overheard you telling the men you would block the road with trucks and trailers."

Roy said," Yes, that way, no one gets in from the outside, and we can use the area on the blocked road to hold the people we catch."

"I can put listening equipment on the blocking vehicles, so you hear and record everything in that area," Robin explained.

Roy unhooked the trailer and leveled it. "The trucks and trailers we will block the road with are there," he told Robin as he pointed to them. "Please set up what you think we need on them. After you are done here, let me know, and we will head out to the field and wire it, also."

An hour later, Robin walked over to Roy and said," I am finished here. Can we go to the other areas now?" Roy drove Robin to all the spots he thought would be used by anyone doing surveillance and shooters on overwatch. She placed listening devices, motion detectors, and other items at every location and synced everything to her laptop. Robin started unpacking and hooking up equipment, and she was not shy.

"Roy, can you put this over there, hook this up, and place this on top of that?" she directed. They put all the large items in the trailer and wired them to her monitor's laptop and some sensitive equipment in the living space. Then she asked, "Roy, do you want to jam their radios and cell phones?"

Roy was shocked, and his answer was a simple, "Yes."

She smiled and said, "What, you didn't think I could do that? Help me set antennas and a satellite dish on the top of the trailer." Once they finished, she said, "I need to make sure all of this is working."

Roy noticed that the more she worked, the better her mood became. She was in her world and enjoyed being in control. He asked her, "How much do I owe you? I do not care what the amount is. This is worth it."

Robin said, "Nothing. Savannah is a friend. I met her when I worked for Will. I lived with him and Bernadette. When her dad was away, Will and Bernadette took care of her. That is how we met. She is younger than I am, but she is braver and more intelligent. We had fun doing all kinds of stuff and occasionally got into trouble," she said, smiling at the memories.

CHAPTER 38
Unwanted Guests

Robin took a minute during the preparations to tell Roy something she remembered. She said, "When Savanaha's dad was home, I stayed at her house more times than I can count. The first time her dad didn't know I was there. He was cooking breakfast. We walked out, and he saw me and said, 'What do you want to eat? We have bacon, eggs, and pancakes. If you want something else, you can cook it yourself.' I told him that those options sounded good to me. He smiled and said, 'I thought so.' Then he made more of everything."

Robin continued, "I asked him if I could have coffee. He said, 'Oh hell no, I will not share my coffee.' At the same time, he was pouring me a cup. Akita was always nice to me. I need to do this for them."

Roy asked, "Will doing this interfere with your job?"

Robin said, "No, I have contracts with several companies, and I set my hours."

Two hours later, they finished setting and checking her equipment. Roy gave her a walkie-talkie and said, "Call if you need anything or if we have intruders."

Robin said, "Wait here." Then she started moving the hard-sided cases of her gear. "Here you are," she said and then opened a large case. Next, she pulled out another case about the size of a briefcase, opened it, and smiled. She turned to Roy and said, "Your walkie-talkies can be hacked. These can't." She held out an earpiece. "With these, all communications will be encrypted.

I have fifty, and I will sync them with my equipment. With the listening devices we placed today, I will hear and record everything in real-time. If we have intruders, I can let everyone know where they are."

Olivia drove up with her horse loaded in a trailer.

Robin said, "Have your men keep their walkie-talkies. Tell them to talk about being pissed off with you for having them out looking for rustlers."

Roy said, "You are cunning. I will hand these out today and have everyone follow your instructions." As he got in his truck, he thanked her, and said, "You may have to stay here for a while. Will you be okay out

Unwanted Guests

here at night?"

Robin said, "I go camping with my family in tents. This is so much better."

Before he drove away, Roy told Olivia that he had to make some rounds but that he'd come back before he went home.

Within the hour, Robin got a call from a very confused ranch hand on her company phone.

He said, "There are five ladies here. They want someone to take them to you."

Robin said, "May I speak to one of them, please?"

The man handed the phone back to the owner. She said, "Robin, we are here. Sorry, it took so long. We got turned around."

Robin said, "Hi Linda, that is fine. Do you want to stay out in the field with me or in the house?"

Linda asked, "How much room do you have, and what house?"

Robin told Linda, "Go to the main house. I will call Roy and let him know you guys are here and will stay the night. The ranch hand will show you the way and let you in. Linda, I am calling Roy now, I will conference you in."

Roy answered, and Robin told him, "I have you on a conference call. The girls are here and need to stay at your house."

Roy said, "They can stay in the den and guest room just off it. I'll show them when I get there and make sure they have everything they need. It should be about fifteen minutes."

Linda said, "Thank you."

"Get some sleep," Robin said. "I need you out here at 6:00 AM."

Linda replied, "You are a terrible boss!"

Roy said, "I will get them up, feed them breakfast, and drive them out first thing."

Linda said," Well, aren't you sweet?"

"Wait until you find out what first thing means on a ranch," Robin added. "Good night and thank you for coming. Roy, do you need anything from me before I hang up?"

Roy said, "No, I am good so far." The call ended, and the ranch hand was still confused.

Roy woke the women up at 4:00 AM. He had already made breakfast

Unwanted Guests

and coffee and thought this morning would be like herding cats. He was wrong. The women got up, dressed, ate, and were ready to go quickly.

He asked Linda, "Can you teach Olivia how to get ready like you just did?"

Linda smiled and said, "Have her come to work with us for one month. She will know what it is to have Robin as a boss."

At this time, they left the ranch house for the field. Roy pulled up to the trailer where Robin was up and working at 5:45 AM.

That morning around 7:00 AM, Robin was startled when her motion sensor alarm started going off. She got on her radio and set it to signal all radios synced to her base.

She spoke into the mike and said, "Wake up, we have unwanted guests."

Her speaker went wild: "We know! Where and how many? Thanks for the wakeup call. We have this!"

Roy said, "It looks like we will have fun today. Get in place and report on everything and try not to kill anyone."

A voice on the radio said, "You take the fun out of everything."

Robin was shocked. All the men were looking forward to this fight. They were happy and joking about going into battle. Robin changed her settings and called Roy. When he answered, she asked, "Why are the men acting happy?"

Roy laughed and said, "This is what they trained for. Now we are giving them a way to show how good they still are without the military laws holding them back. Our friend is dead, and the men coming here are involved. We will not let this go. We will win today or die defending what we believe in. Do you understand now?"

Robin said, "Please don't ever get mad at me."

Roy said, "I am not mad at anyone. I miss my friend. Today we'll find out why he had to die. Then we will make the people responsible pay. I will never think of you as anything other than a daughter of Akita, Will, and myself. Do you understand?"

Robin, choking back tears, said, "You are sweet. Now let's get to work. We have some fucking bad guys on your land, and we need to catch them."

After getting into position, the ranch hands stayed motionless and silent. Roy took this opportunity to call his lawyer. He told her, "Call the courthouse and have them look up the lack of legal easement on the road that split the property and make sure that information will be conveyed to all law enforcement that call for it."

She said, "I will ensure they do as you ask."

Roy said, "Thank you," and hung up.

One spotting position called in and said, "We have six getting out of a car and walking down the road. They're hunting around for something."

Roy called back and asked, "How far from where we need them to be?"

The voice returned, saying, "The men are right where we need them." He stopped short. Then he came back on and said, "The car is in position, also."

Other positions started reporting in, saying the same thing from various locations, "We have two over here setting up spotting opps."

Will called Roy and asked, "Have you ever heard of setting up your lookouts after you start your opp? Who is running this fuck up? It is clear they don't give a fuck about their men."

CHAPTER 39
A Texas Ranger

Roy called Robin and told her, "Broadcast to everybody. Close the fucking road now!"

Robin changed her settings and put the call out, "Close the fucking road now and hurry. No one gets away!"

Roy had to smile. Robin was getting into this. The ranch hands assigned to blocking vehicles quickly moved their trucks with stock trailers and blocked off the road and ditches on both sides of Roy's land, trapping everything for one and a half miles on the road.

The men on horseback moved to capture the men in the spotting positions. Gunshots rang out.

Roy and Will were on the radio asking, "Who fired?"

One of Roy's men called in and said, "Roy, they just killed two of your calves. The calves stumbled on their location. I think the men got scared and shot at the sound before they knew what they were shooting at, or they just shot for the hell of it."

Roy said, "Get them under control before they do any more damage. You can use as much force as necessary to secure them."

Roy got a call from one of Will's men. He was on guard outside the barricade.

Roy answered the radio and asked, "What do you have?"

"A Texas Ranger is here, and he looks unhappy," the man replied.

Roy said, "I will be right there."

Texas Ranger Lieutenant Sergio Vega had been called into headquarters in Lubbock Company C. When he arrived, Captain Castillo called him into his office. Once inside, Castillo told Vega, "The Chief has assigned you to investigate a sensitive case. A car crash killed a soldier on U.S. Hwy 82 outside of Crosbyton. Before you get pissed off about a car crash, look at this file." Castillo handed him the file from Sheriff Miller of Dickens County.

Vega started looking through it. He found a statement from Bernadette Chisum and photos of a truck and its surrounding area. He studied them and moved on to the next set: the man's upper body near the truck, and the lower body some distance away. He said, "Jesus fucking

Christ."

Then he started looking for more photos. He asked, «Where are the pictures of the other car?»

Castillo said, "This was a hit and run. That is all we have."

Vega said, "What the fuck am I supposed to do with this shit? A rookie ranger would have done a better job."

Castillo chuckled and said, "You are not wrong. The dead man in the photos is Clint Haddox. His general, General Scott, called the Chief late last night and woke him up. He wants an outside entity to investigate how his man died. He told the Chief this was an assassination and that he wanted someone to pay.

Vega asked, "How can he call the top man in the Rangers and get everyone to jump?"

Castillo said, "The Chief and General Scott served together."

Vega said, "The good old boy shit, and I am in the middle."

Castillo, trying to stay on task, said, "After the Chief got off the phone with Scott, he called Sheriff Miller at home. He told Miller to deliver his report to me before 07:00 AM this morning."

Vega asked, "How did that go over?"

Castillo said, "Miller was not happy, but he did what he was told."

Vega looked at the photos again.

Castillo told him to take them with him, and added, "Call the Sheriff and find out what is missing from that file. Then go to the scene and find something that the Chief can take to General Scott to prove one way or the other what happened."

Sergio said, "I do not know enough about accident scene investigation. Can you get a state trooper who is good with them to help me?"

Castillo said, "Yes, I'll call and request their assistance. I will give your number to them, and you can let the trooper know where and when to meet. Do you need anything else?"

Vega said that he didn't and left the office.

Criminals often do not let state or national borders hinder their attempt to escape. It is not unusual for a Ranger to travel out of the state or even out of the country in pursuit. Lieutenant Sergio Vega was looking at a road that had been blocked with trucks and stock trailers and a hard-looking armed man. Another man arrived on the scene from the other side of the trucks. This man, also armed, started walking toward Vega's pickup. Vega got out of his truck and started to say who and what he was doing here.

Roy cut him off with pure anger and yelled at the top of his voice, "Every time I have rustlers, I call law enforcement. They say they're two or three hours away and that they'll have someone out to me as soon as possible. By the time they get here, I have lost stock. So now, I decided to do your job for you and save my cattle. They send one man. What did you fuck up to get sent here? Who did you piss off? How fucked up of an individual are you? Well, will you answer me or stand there like a dumb ass?"

Vega said, "I'm not here for cattle rustling. I'm here to investigate an auto accident."

Roy again cut him off, "Well, now that makes sense. The mother fuckers will send you out here for some auto accident but not for my livelihood being stolen. My name is Roy Walker. Now get the fuck off of my property."

Vega said, "This is a public road, and you have no right to block it. Move your trucks, or I will have them towed and put you in jail."

Roy smiled and said calmly, "This is not a public road. I own the land over there and pointed to one side of the road, and I own the land on that side also, I have it leased out now, but I own it. They did not get a legal easement through my land when this road was built. So please, put me in jail. I will sue you and your Rangers, the State, and anyone else I see fit, and I will win. You need to call the courthouse to find out who you are fucking with and who owns this fucking road."

Vega took out his cell and made a call. He asked whoever answered, "Can you check on an easement for me? The property belongs to Roy Walker. I need the answer now. It is urgent."

Trying to gain control, Vega said to Roy, "I have a State Trooper on the way to help with the investigation. Can you use our help?"

Vega's phone rang, and he answered the call. The call lasted less than one minute. Vega said, "Thank you," and hung up. Vega told Roy, "You are correct, no easement. The office told me your lawyer called this morning and told them to expect my question and have the answer ready for anyone that asked."

Roy smiled and said, "Good, now get the fuck off my land."

Vega said, "Mister Walker, I still have an investigation. You are blocking the accident scene. I need access to the area."

Roy turned and said, "You have it, but if you interfere with me or my men doing your fucking job for you, there will be hell to pay, and you will pay it. Do you hear me? Your truck will remain out here. Get the shit you need and come with me."

CHAPTER 40
HELPING A FRIEND

Robin's team put their drones in the air. They were up for a short time when Robin called on the radio: "We have men on the high side of the leased pasture at the tractor just off the road."

She received a reply: "We have them in sight and are moving to their location."

Robin answered, "I see you." Then her voice cracked, "We have a rider down. He is in a ditch one mile from Roy's barn. There are men about a half mile from him. I will zoom in closer." She stopped mid-sentence. "It's Blanca."

Robin heard Savannah say, "On my way. Walk me into her."

Malin and Savannah were together. Savannah knew her horse was a good ranch horse but lacked speed. She needed speed. Malin had a very fast, almost uncontrollable stud. No one had been able to get the horse to work the way it was required on the ranch. Most studs are a handful, but this one was worse than that.

Malin had taken off the saddle and gave the horse a break until he needed him. Savannah and Malin were going to do clean up sweeps on both sides of the road after the opp was over to make sure no one got away.

Savannah grabbed the reins and yelled to Malin, "I am taking your horse. He's fast, and I need fast." She leaped on its back and put spurs into the horse's sides. The horse lunged forward with tremendous power. He tried to buck, but Savannah had been on a horse since she could walk, so she was in control.

Savannah's dog wasted no time moving her 155 pounds and easily stayed with the horse. This dog was an Army-trained dog that broke its leg in Afghanistan while working with Akita.

The Army was going to put it down, but Akita could not let that happen. After all, his nickname was the breed of this dog. He put the dog on a military aircraft and took it home to Savannah.

It took three operations from the vet in Haskell, Texas, to repair the leg. It took Savannah one day to call this dog hers, and she named it Jo.

Savannah called to Robin, "I need the fence cut at your location on both sides of the road. Tell Will and Roy."

Robin heard Olivia call, "I need that fence cut now. I am about five hundred yards away and will not slow down."

Roy was leading Vega to the accident location when he heard Savannah, and then Olivia, call for the fence to be cut. They were riding hard and fast. Blanca had been pitched off her horse, and they were not going to let anything more happen to her.

The next thing Vega heard was Roy yelling, "Get that fucking fence cut and have two men standing on each side of the cut." Roy called to Olivia, "Make sure you go between the men at the fence."

Just seconds later, Olivia blasted onto the road, put spurs to her horse, and yelled, "Tell her we are coming." Her dogs were next to cross the road. They were pushing hard to keep up.

Vega was startled and almost hit by a young girl commanding others from the back of a horse.

Robin called out to everyone, "Savannah is here and moving fast." The men ran back to the fence opening to show her where it was. Vega heard the deep thud of hooved feet pounding the ground before he saw the terrifying sight of a black horse with its ears laid back, white teeth bared, nostrils wide open, and heading straight for him. Roy and Vega were standing in the middle of the road on the left side of the hurriedly opened fence. Roy grabbed the back of Vega's shirt collar and pulled hard.

Savannah and the stallion jumped the first fence. The feet of the black beast cleared the five-strand barbed wire fence by over a foot. Savannah had seen the opening too late. She gave the horse his head and urged him to make the jump. He not only cleared the fence, but the jump was also long. His front hooves landed just short of where Roy was standing. Although Roy was trying to get Vega out of the way, the big horse, or the rider, grazed Vega's shoulder hard enough to rock him back.

When the horse's front feet hit the ground, Savannah yelled, "Move your fucking slow ass." Her dog had jumped the first fence, also and was on Savannah's left-hand side.

Jo saw the man in the way and lowered her shoulder the way the army had trained her to do when she was up-armored on patrol. She hit Vega between his knee and hip hard and at speed. (This is one way the

Helping a Friend

army teaches dogs to take out people on the battlefield.) Vega's legs were thrown up, and his body spun 90 degrees in the air before he came to rest face first on the pavement.

Savannah steered her mount through the second gate, just missing the man at the left fence post. Jo picked up the lost speed and jumped the second fence effortlessly on the other side of that man at almost the same time. Roy helped Vega up to his feet.

Roy was mad as hell. He started yelling, "Who the fuck put her on that sack of nuts without a fucking saddle? Who is that fucking stupid? She is going to kill herself."

Vega asked, "Who is she calling a slow mother fucker?"

Roy smiled and said, "The horse, but when you see a horse running straight at you. It would be wise to move out of the fucking way. Don't you think?"

Vega said, "You were pulling me back. How did that horse hit me?"

Roy started laughing so hard he could not speak. He finally gathered himself enough to talk. Roy said, "If that horse hit you at that speed, you would be dead. Her dog hit you."

"That's bullshit, "Vega said. "There was no dog."

Still laughing, Roy said, "You are the best investigator I have ever met. You didn't see that large dog that knocked you on your ass."

Vega asked, "Who was that?"

He did not get an answer.

Robin called Roy, "Come here. You need to see this." Roy went into the trailer Vega followed him. Robin pointed to her screen and said, "She is catching Olivia."

Roy watched as Savannah and her dog overtook Olivia, moving about one and a half times the speed of Olivia's horse."

Savannah called, "Where is she?"

Roy spotted the men about a half mile from where the women were going. He got on the radio and told them, "You have men with guns. You need to wait for some backup."

Savannah yelled out to Robin, "Where are they?"

Robin answered her, "Straight ahead of you."

Savannah said, "Walk Olivia into Blanca's position. I will take care of the men."

Helping a Friend

Roy was furious and told Savannah, "Stop what you are doing. You're going to get yourself killed. Wait for backup." Watching the screen, he knew she was not listening. She was going to run straight into trained men with guns.

Roy asked Robin, "Who is close enough to help her?"

Vega could not believe what he was seeing and hearing. Roy told Vega, "Get the fuck out of here. You have no business being here."

Robin did not answer. She was making the call to a spotting point in the area.

The man said, "Yes, we see what is happening, and I am going to help."

Robin called Olivia and said, "You must turn right and follow the ditch. Blanca is about one fourth of a mile away. She's on her feet, but her horse is about three hundred yards away. You need to get it to her."

Olivia answered, "I will get her back to your trailer. There's a first aid kit in it."

Robin said, "Oh shit." She pointed to the screen. Roy was already looking.

They saw Savannah ride her horse at full speed into the men. They were surprised they didn't know anyone knew they were there.

Roy said, "Son of a bitch." As he watched, Savannah plowed through both men. The impact was so intense that men, weapons, and gear went flying. As soon as she hit the men, Savannah pulled back on the reins hard. The big horse planted his legs to stop this causing his rear end to lower close to the ground. Savannah turned and slid off the horse before it stopped.

She hit the ground running. She grabbed one man while he was still on the ground. She stood over him from behind with a hand full of his hair and a knife at his neck. She yelled angrily, "Who killed my dad?"

The two of them watched as a voice on the radio said, "Did you see that shit? I have never seen a person unass a horse like that." Then he said, "Savannah has one man, and that dog has the other one by the shoulder and is shaking him so hard his body is leaving the ground. Then he asked, "Roy, are you sure she needs help?"

CHAPTER 41
JO

Roy yelled at Lucas, "Her dad is dead, and she thinks the men there had something to do with it. So, get your fucking ass over there and help her before she kills them."

Olivia found Blanca and asked, "Are you hurt?" Blanca had a bloody spot on her head that she was holding with one hand.

She said, "Only my feelings. A snake spooked my horse. Will you get her for me?

Olivia called Robin and said, "Blanca has a head wound. She seems to be okay. Where is her horse? I need to get it so she can ride." Robin told Olivia where to go and get the loose horse. Olivia gathered up the horse and returned to Blanca. She handed the reins to Blanca and said, "You owe me."

Lucas, the man Roy sent to help Savannah, rode up, stepped off his horse, ran over to Savannah. "Don't kill him," he said.

Savannah looked first at Lucas and then at his horse. She ordered, "Give me one of the repair wires you have. (Repair wire is a two- to three-foot-long section of barbed wire used to splice together broken and damaged fence wire)

Lucas pulled one of the sections from the bundle behind his saddle. He gave it to Savannah. Savannah turned the man's hair loose and tied his hands behind his back with the barbed wire splice. She turned to Lucas and said, "We'll cut his clothes off down to his underwear. Take any phones, radios, electronics, and wallet and keep them with you. Take the weapons, bundle them up in his clothes and tie them to your saddle."

Savannah then turned and yelled, "Jo." The dog looked her way. Savannah stomped her left foot and pointed her hand at the ground on her left side. Jo started dragging the man she had by the shoulder. The man started yelling out in pain. Jo pulled him to Savannah's left side. She got there and did not let the man go. She waited for her next order. Savannah told Lucas, "I need another wire."

Lucas stopped what he was doing and got her the wire. When he saw the man's shoulder, he said, "I'm glad that's not me." Then he went back

Jo

to gathering up all the weapons and clothes.

Savannah commanded Jo, "Drop." Jo let the man go, moved her nose to his head, and growled. Savannah put this second man's hands behind his back and tied them with the wire. She cut away his clothes, collecting his phones, radios, electronics, and wallet. She was almost finished when Blanca and Olivia rode up. Olivia's dogs were sniffing and growling at the men that were tied. Savannah smiled and said, "I am glad you could join us."

Olivia laughed and said, "Do you think I'm going to let you have all the fun?"

Robin called on an open call. Everyone could hear her say, "Savannah, you have a man just over the ridge to your left about six hundred meters away. He can't see you now, but he is coming your way. He pulled up in a 4X4 truck but is on foot now."

Savannah looked at Olivia and said, "Give me your rope. You need to take these men to your dad and take Blanca with you."

Olivia gave Savannah her rope and said, "I will call dad and let him know we are on the way."

Savannah put the rope around the first man's neck, then made another loop and did the same to the other man. She handed the loose end to Olivia. She turned to the men and said, "Her horse is a ranch horse. It is used to dragging four and five-hundred-pound steers around. If you don't walk, you will be dragged. Look at her dogs. They will have fun eating you if you try and get away or anything else. Do you understand what I mean?" Savannah looked at Olivia and said, "Don't stop for anything. Get them there in any shape you can."

Olivia smiled and said, "I told you. You could not have all the fun." Olivia and Blanca headed out.

Savannah told Lucas, "We have another one to catch. You need to go around that point. It is the long way, so hurry. I will ride up and over the ridge. We will have him between us with nowhere to go."

Lucas said, "No, you need to take the long way. He will see you coming."

Savannah said, "I want him to see a girl out for a ride. He won't think he's in danger. This will work if we do it my way, and I have a weapon.

Jo

She patted her pistol and then pointed to Jo.

They rode to intercept the intruder. Lucas rode hard and fast. Savannah rode slowly as if joy riding. She spotted the man and rode towards him. When she was close enough for him to hear, she asked, "May I help you? Are you lost?"

The man smiled and said, "No, I'm not lost. I'm looking to buy some land to hunt on. I heard this place is for sale." The man heard Lucas's horse running up from behind him. He turned to look.

Savannah said, "Jo." Then gave Jo the hand sign for attack. Jo went straight for the man in full combat mode, jumped up, grabbed his neck, and took him down without difficulty. The man tried to fight, but Jo clamped down on his neck and shook her head. The man yelled out in pain.

Savannah dismounted, walked over to him, and said, "If you struggle, she will break your neck. Lucas walked up with a fence splice and tied the man's hands behind him. Then he started cutting away his clothes. When he was finished, he gave Savannah a leather badge wallet with a government ID card for the CIA.

Savannah called Jo off and said, "Good girl." Then she asked Lucas, "Will you call your friend from the lookout point and have him drive the 4X4 truck back to where Roy and Will are? I will take their horse back with me." Lucas did so. In about five minutes, his friend rode up.

Savannah gave him the keys and said, "Call Will before you get there. He will let you in." She said to Lucas, "Take this shithead to Will and Roy. I'll bring this horse with me."

Lucas smiled and said, "Yes, Ma'am. Can I drag him if he tries anything?"

The man started yelling, "You mother fuckers have no idea who you are fucking with."

Savannah pulled out the case and said, "Yes, we do. You are some low-level shithead from the CIA. The question is, do you know just how much shit you are in?"

Lucas started riding toward the assembly area.

Savannah walked over to the stallion, rubbed his ear, and said, "I have asked a lot from you today. I have one more thing we need to do, and I

JO

will give you water, food, and a good grooming. She took the reins from the ranch hands horse in her right hand. The reins for her horse in her left hand, then mounted and rode to the assembly area.

CHAPTER 42
STATE TROOPER

At the road blockade, a guard called on the radio and said, "We have a State Trooper out here, and he is all kinds of pissed off."

Roy, still upset, called back and said, "I am on my way. "

Outside, Roy yelled at Vega, "Come with me. Your Trooper is here fucking up everything."

Vega, tired of being told what to do, said, "You go tell him to come in here."

Roy stopped walking and yelled, "You wanted him here, so get your ass over here and come with me. If you fucking don't, I will tell my man to shoot him. The choice is yours."

Vega, not knowing if Roy would do this said. "On my way, tell them to hold fire."

Roy and Vega walked through the blockade to find the guard with his weapon muzzle down stock on his shoulder, telling the Trooper, "Stop where you are. Keep your hand away from your weapon."

Roy walked up, placed his hand on the man's shoulder, and said, "We have this from here."

The Trooper was angry as hell and said, "You are under arrest stay where you are."

Roy shot back at the Trooper, "Who the fuck do you think you are? You cannot arrest anyone here. If you could, what would the charge be?" Roy began walking fast toward the Trooper.

Vega sped up, cut Roy off, and said, "I will explain what is going on here. I have this under control." Vega walked over to the Trooper, looked at his name tag, and said, "Smith, you need to calm down. We are here to investigate an auto crash. The landowner is trying to save his livestock from being stolen. The rustlers are on his land and armed."

Smith said, "They can't block the road or have armed guards stopping the public and law enforcement from using it."

Vega said, "There is no legal easement for this road. The landowner can build a fucking fence across it, and there is nothing you or anyone can do about it. As far as the weapons, did you see the purple corner post? (In Texas Penal Code §30.05, if a property is fenced, posted with at least one sign, or marked with purple paint, it is illegal for anyone to enter. The fine or jail time for trespassing in Texas can be up to $2,000 or up to 180 days) Look around all of this, and the people are within the marked land boundary. Do you want to go to court and tell the judge he was on his property with a weapon? He never threatened me with it. The owner had blocked a road and put guards on it so cattle would not be lost."

Smith said, "No, I do not. The case would be thrown out, and I would look like an ass."

Vega said, "Tell me what you see when you look at the ranch hands."

Smith said, "They are like all other cowboys I have dealt with."

In a disgusted voice, Vega said," I hope your scene interpretation is better than your assessment of people. Let's find out what happened in this car crash."

Smith asked, "Do you have the accident report and photos? I was told that will be all we have to work with."

Vega walked to his truck, retrieved the report, and gave it to Smith.

Smith opened it up on the hood of Vega's truck, looked at it, and said, "Where is the rest?"

Vega said, "That is all we have, so let's get started."

Vega and Smith walked through the roadblock. Vega looked around and found Roy. He waved Roy over and asked, "Where did the accident happen?"

Roy pointed out Will and said, "Will was the one that hauled Akita's truck off the road. He will be able to show you where the truck was." Vega and Smith walked over to Will.

Vega introduced himself and Smith and told Will, "Roy told me that you could show me where the truck you hauled away was. We need a starting point to try and find out what happened."

Will said, "Come with me."

Will walked to a point in the road and pointed out the tire marks in the mud where Akita's truck was hit and knocked sideways off the road. Will said, "That son of a bitch slammed into Akita's truck, killing him. My wife was in the truck. You need to find him fast and bring him to justice."

Smith said, "You keep saying 'him.' Do you know it was a man?"

Will said, "Do you think a woman could do this and leave? If you do, then you are nothing but a fucking asshole." Will walked off acting mad.

Olivia and Blanca arrived at the assembly area. They had used a game trail to make the journey easier for the men they had captured. The trail split at the fence and went both ways. This put the group around one hundred and fifty meters from Robin's trailer and the opening that had been cut in the fence.

Olivia called her dad with her phone and not the radio. She wanted him to know before anyone else that they were coming. She knew her dad would prepare for Blanca's medical care and their prisoners.

Roy took the call and was relieved to hear that Blanca was alert and seemed fine except for a bump on the head. He told Olivia, "Come straight here. We still have the fence down, so you can use the opening to get here. I'll take the men off your hands. You need to take Blanca to the trailer. I will have someone there to look at her head."

Olivia turned her horse toward the assembly area and said, "Good news for you fucks, we have a shortcut. You will not have to walk to the gate and down the highway."

Blanca asked, "Can we take them around anyway? Their friend killed Akita. Someone must pay. The longer walk will help them tell us what they know. We could shoot the mother fuckers and find more of their friends. Eventually, we will find one that will talk."

Olivia smiled and said, "Good idea, but dad wants to talk to them. If he doesn't get what he wants, I'll feed them to Crusher and Shaker." She pointed at the dogs. The group made the rest of the way without talking.

Upon the small group's arrival, the State Trooper saw the men and started yelling, "Stop where you are." He started to climb the fence. His foot was on the third wire from the top when he found himself facing the barrel of a twelve-gauge shotgun and two rottweilers at the fence growling.

Still on horseback, the woman behind the weapon said, "Get your fat ass off my fence. I am the one who has to fix fences here, and I do not like it. So, get your fat ass off now."

Vega saw another woman on horseback spin a scoped rifle out of its scabbard and aim it at Smith. The barrel of the weapon was steady. Vega knew this woman would shoot. Then he noticed the men and what they were doing. Their weapons were at the ready, not as ranch hands or civilians would do, but fully tactical. Something had seemed off to him since he arrived. Now it hit him like a ton of bricks. The men here are not ranch hands but highly trained military personnel.

Vega ran up to Smith and said, "Get off the fence now before you get shot." He grabbed Smith and pulled hard. Smith hit the ground hard.

Vega looked at the young lady and said, "I am sorry he will not damage anything else. Please lower your weapon. He does not deserve to die over being stupid and fence repair."

Roy ran up to Vega and said, "Olivia lower the weapon now." Olivia lowered her shotgun and said, "We have people trying to steal from us and will kill not to be caught. Now the people supposed to protect us are attacking us and fucking up my fence."

Vega looked around. None of the men relaxed their position. Still on full alert, he looked at the girl on horseback. Her weapon was in a firing position, the barrel still unmoving.

Vega said, "Mister Walker, please have that young lady lower her weapon." He pointed at Blanca.

Olivia looked where Vega was pointing and said, "Blanca, let's get your head taken care of before you get an infection."

Blanca lowered her weapon, rode up to Olivia, and said, "I would like that. I am not thinking straight."

The group rode to the opening in the fence and gave the prisoners over to Will's men.

Olivia took Blanca to the trailer, set her down, and was going to get the first aid kit when one of Will's men walked up with a medical bag.

He said, "I have it from here."

Olivia said, "Thank you," and walked towards her dad, the Texas Ranger, and the State Trooper. Before she made it to them, another ranch hand showed up with a prisoner in tow. Right behind him was Savannah with a horse in tow.

Savannah said, "We have a vehicle on the way that this one was driving. He has cut a fence somewhere to get in."

Roy called out to one of his men, "Ride the fence, find and fix where he cut it."

Smith asked, "How many people are you going to mistreat and abuse? I don't care if they are rustlers. You do not have the right to do this."

Roy walked up to Smith, stood right in his face, and said, "I can hang them if you would like. It is still legal to do so."

Vega said, "I checked with state and local law enforcement to find out how many times Mister Walker has requested help for cattle rustling. He has called eight times in the last two years. The help was either late or never showed. He does have a right to protect his family and his property. Would I prefer this to be done differently? Yes, I would, but we have failed him every time he has asked for help. So, the way I see this is we are as much to blame for the treatment we see here as Mister Walker. Pull your head out of your ass, and let's finish our job."

Vega then turned to Roy and said, "No more of this. You can walk the men here, but you can't drag them."

Roy got on the radio and said, "Don't drag anyone. You can walk them here. Use all force necessary to achieve this without killing anyone."

Roy looked at Vega and asked, "Will that work for you?"

Smith said, "I will have you up on charges for this."

Roy laughed and said, "Good luck with that."

CHAPTER 43
Lessons Learned

Savannah tied up her horse and the ranch hand's horse. She walked to her truck and took the container for holding water and a five-gallon jug of water. She shouldered the jug and had the container in her hand on the opposite side. She put the container on the ground in front of the horses and filled it with water. The stallion and Jo were drinking at the same time, and the other horse did not drink until Jo stopped. Savannah went back to her truck and got another jug and a brush. She walked back, poured a little water on the back of the stallion and brushed him. She repeated this until the jug was empty. She took the jugs back to her truck, pulled out the badge and wallet, and took pictures of the ID and other paperwork inside the wallet with her phone.

Then she sent them to Morgan's email along with a statement: "We have several prisoners here. This is the only one with an ID."

Less than a minute later, Morgan called. When Savannah answered, he said, "Do not say a word, just listen. CIA will not let you have their men. They will do anything to get them back. What they are doing there is illegal. I have a contact in the agency. He told me no one has an operation in your area. This is completely off the books." He could hear Savannah breathing, so he continued, "When I found this out, I put men together, and I am in the air headed to you. I also have men on the ground headed your way. How long until you have to move the men, and how will you move them?"

Savannah said, "We are not finished rounding them all up yet. We were going to take them to the local sheriff as cattle rustlers. We have a Texas Ranger here assessing dad's accident. We can give them to him, but he does not have a way to transport them to Lubbock. I could call General Scott and ask for help."

Morgan said, "I know General Scott. I will call him. I have a plan in mind. Give me some time, and I will call you back."

Savannah walked to the trailer that Robin was working out of and knocked on the door.

Robin said, "Come in."

Lessons Learned

Savannah entered, sat down, and asked, "Robin, can you run a background on someone and a company for me?"

Robin said, "Yes, I can. Who and what company?"

Savannah said, "Lieutenant Colonel (LTC) Morgan James, and a security company named C&M."

Robin asked, "How soon do you need this?"

"As soon as possible, Savannah explained. "I have reached out to Morgan who runs C&M. My dad owned the company."

Robin said, "I will start right away."

Savannah said, "Thank you," and left the trailer.

Vega and Smith collected samples of glass, blood, and other items not washed away with the rain. Vega found what he thought to be bone and blood, but it was in the wrong place to be part of the auto accident. Blood, tissue, and glass were at the point of impact on the left side of the truck and the right side of the hit and run vehicle. The blood and tissue here should belong to Akita. More glass was found when the car had backed up and stopped hard again on the left side of the truck and the right side of the hit and run vehicle. The bone and a small amount of blood were twelve feet away from the impact area on the left side and in the oncoming traffic lane.

Vega collected it and marked the sample unknown.

Smith was using a measuring wheel to determine the speed of travel and speed at braking. Smith told Vega, "We need to find out if the car was speeding and hit the truck by accident or if the car accelerated into the truck. We need to inspect the road to find any evidence."

Vega asked, "Will that evidence still exist with the heavy rain they had here? We barely have enough glass and other evidence to say there was an accident."

Smith answered, "With what I have seen, this looks like the car hit the truck on purpose. Then it backed up hard and fast. Something happened, and it changed directions and sped off. We should find acceleration marks in the mud and on the blacktop if I am right."

Vega said, "Let's get to it and find the marks or not."

Will saw the pair of law enforcement officers leaving the assembly area. He hurriedly walked over to them and asked, "Are you finished?"

Lessons Learned

Vega said, "No, we need to find out if the car was speeding or lying in wait to hit the truck."

Will asked, "So you do not think this was an accident?"

Smith said, "We need to rule out all other possibilities. At this point, we do not know."

Will said, "Please keep me in the loop," and walked away.

Vega and Smith left to look for evidence.

Robin's women had kept three drones up at all times, with the others charging for their next time out. Men started to be walked in with hands tied behind their backs. Mounted ranch hands yelled out orders. If the orders were not followed, they rode into or roped whoever was not paying attention. After this treatment, the captives did as they were told. Some ranch hands led horses without riders. The men who owned them were driving confiscated vehicles. The vehicles were parked and searched outside the blockade. Some riders rode back out to help with the other prisoners being moved.

Malin found Will and told him, "The only reason we did not have anyone killed on either side was because they're a bunch of stupid fucks and were not paying attention to anything around them. They acted like they would not meet any resistance at all

Vega and Smith returned and found Will. Smith said, "The car was parked on the side of the road and left tire marks in the mud and road due to hard acceleration. It looks like this was murder, but we need more than we have now. We need to find the other car and go over the truck you hauled to your ranch."

Will said, "Akita's truck has not been touched. You can inspect it any time."

Olivia was walking by Vega and Smith, going to Robin's trailer to check on Blanca.

Smith recognized her, grabbed her arm, and said, "You are under arrest for assaulting a law officer."

Vega told Smith, "You need to leave this alone. She is trying to protect her home."

Olivia yelled out in pain, "I am going to fucking kill you."

Savannah heard Olivia and ran over to her. She saw what Smith was

Lessons Learned

doing. She grabbed Smith's hand, twisted it towards his thumb hard, and forced him to release Olivia.

She stood in front of Smith and told Olivia, "Run! I have this."

Savannah said, "You are nothing but a fucking bully. You hide behind that badge and gun. Take them off and show me what you are made of."

Savannah took off her pistol belt and gave it to Vega, and said, "Hold this for me."

Savannah looked at Smith and said, "You hurt my friend. Now I am going to hurt you."

Smith said, "I am a State Trooper."

Savannah cut him off and said, "No, you think you're a man, but you are nothing but a scared little boy. I bet that you don't have a dick. If you do, it is inverted. Do you still piss the bed at night? What is wrong? Oh shit, I am right."

Smith swung his fist at her. She easily moved out of the way. Smith had swung so hard that he almost lost his footing. Vega started to move in and put a stop to this madness.

Olivia moved and stood in his way. Olivia said, "Do not interfere. He has been an asshole to everybody, and you know it. Now he has thrown the first punch. No one here will let you stop this. Vega looked at the men around him. All three were shaking their heads no.

Smith took another swing. Savannah made him miss badly.

Olivia said, "Smith is a dumbass. If you took his brain and shoved it up a gnat's ass, it would look like a BB in a boxcar. I have five hundred on Savannah. Will you take the bet?"

Savannah told Smith, "What a pussy swing. I know you can do better.

Smith said, "Fuck you, I am going."

Savannah cut him off again and said, "You can't fuck. You don't have a dick."

This sent Smith over the edge. He swung so hard this time his body weight carried him around and to the ground.

Savannah said, "Get the fuck up and fight like a man. Or are you finished?"

Smith got up and was so mad his face was red.

Savannah took her first punch it landed hard on Smith's nose.

Lessons Learned

Vega noticed Savannah had pulled the punch. Savannah ducked the next punch Smith threw, caught his arm held it, kicked his nose three times, and let him go.

Vega told Olivia, "She is not trying. She is pulling her kicks and punches. What is she doing?"

Will walked up and said, "Savannah, stop playing patty cake and get this over with. We have more important things to do."

Savannah said, "Yes sir." Vega watched Savannah attack for the first time, and she threw one punch. It landed on Smith's ear. Smith turned and fell face first on the pavement.

Savannah said, "I made the mess. I will clean it up." She got her pistol belt back from Vega and then picked up Smith. Vega estimated his weight at over two hundred pounds.

Savannah had picked him up without effort, put him over her shoulder, and walked toward the trucks blocking the road.

Vega followed her in disbelief. She continued through the blockade, walked to Smith's car, and slammed him down on the hood.

Vega heard Olivia behind him say, "Are you glad that you did not take the bet?"

Vega looked at her and said, "What is wrong with all of you?"

Will joined them and said, "Savannah's dad trained her. When he was out of the country, I took over. When I could not teach her anymore, others on the ranch took over. Her dad freed a man and brought him here until his paperwork for citizenship was granted. That man also trained her. He was Spetsnaz (Russian special forces). His training also ended when he had taught her everything he knew. Every time her dad was here, her training with him continued. She has worked at the ranch since she was very young. Training and hard work have made her what she is. She does not like to see people she likes bullied or hurt by others."

Vega said, "I do not ever want to piss her off. She did this while pulling all her punches, and she was not mad." Vega's phone rang.

Savannah looked at Will and said, "I need to talk to you privately. We have a problem."

Will said, "Let's talk in the trailer."

Savannah said, "Good idea. Robin needs to be in on this." Will and

Lessons Learned

Savannah were starting to leave when Vega stopped them.

Vega told them, "I just got off the phone with my boss Captain Castillo. He wants this mess cleaned up. He said he would have more State Troopers sent here if I tell him we need them."

Will looked over at Trooper Smith and asked, "How has that worked so far? Before you do anything, let me talk to Roy and Savannah and see what we can do."

Will and Savannah walked away. Will asked, "What is wrong?"

CHAPTER 44
Arranging Transport

Savannah explained to Will, "My dad owned a security company. Morgan, the man in charge of that company, is on his way here by air, and he has men on the ground coming here."

"How long have you known this?" Will asked.

Savannah said, "I found out some time ago. I have Robin doing a background check on him and the company. I just got off the phone with him."

Savannah also relayed that Morgan had told her that the CIA will not allow their men to be detained; they will do anything to get them back. Morgan also said that what the CIA is doing here is illegal. He has a man inside the CIA, and they do not have an operation here.

Savannah continued, "They do not know we have their men. We're safe for now. I want to hand the men over to the Texas Rangers. Tell the Rangers the men are cattle rustlers and trespassers. Then add property damage, assault, carrying concealed weapons without permits, no ID, cutting fences, killing cattle, the two calves they shot, and anything else we can think of. We have enough charges to put them in jail and keep them there."

Will said, "Without IDs, the Rangers can keep them until someone comes forward to identify them. I will find Roy and let him know all this. I will meet you at the trailer."

While Savannah was waiting for Roy and Will, she called Morgan and told him the plan.

Morgan said, "You told me that the Texas Rangers did not have a way to transport the men to Lubbock. I took it upon myself to have my men rent a bus. They're leaving Abilene now. I will arrive in ten minutes. Where can I meet you?"

Savannah said, "I will meet you when you land."

Will and Roy arrived at the trailer. Savannah told them about the bus and that Morgan should be landing soon.

Roy observed to Will, "We don't want law enforcement here now. When we are finished here, get one of my ranch hands to drive that fucking cop Smith in his car to Lubbock. Have Vega follow them. If

Arranging Transport

Vega asks why, tell him I don't want Smith to say that someone stole his shit. Have one of our trucks follow so we do not have a hand stuck in Lubbock."

Will said, "I will handle it. I know who I will send."

"I waited until we were together to tell you this," Robin said. "I have recorded everything the men out there have said. You need to hear this." Robin then turned to her keyboard, selected one item from the playlist, and started the recording.

A man's voice said, "We were sent here to find out what happened to Arthur. He was sent here to eliminate some asshole that was a threat to national security, and now this bunch of half-wit-backward-sister-fucking-country-fucks think we are fucking cattle rustlers. The fucking CIA does not pay me well enough for this shit."

Roy smiled and said, "I am happy you are here and smarter than all of us on surveillance. Please make several copies of that recording. I wish we had it on video."

Robin said, "I am not smarter than you. I have been taught a new way of doing this. Now, do you think I would bring all my equipment out here and not set up cameras? We have this on video. It's not the best picture, but I can clean it up. Once I get a clearer picture, I'll put the video on the same thumb drive with the phone information."

Will said, "We have them by the short hairs now."

"Not so fast, Will," Savannah said. "With this, all we have is hearsay. We don't have anything that will prove the CIA had dad killed. We need Arthur, and we need him to confess."

The sound of a helicopter landing stopped the meeting. Savannah, Will, and Roy left to meet Morgan. Morgan stepped out of the helicopter before the engine wound down. Savannah walked up, shook Morgan's hand, and introduced herself. She then turned and introduced Roy and Will.

Morgan asked, "Do you have a place we can talk? I have much I need to share."

Roy said, "What is your interest in what we are doing?"

Morgan said, "Akita owned the company I work for. Now it belongs to Savannah."

"I had Robin run background checks on the company and you,"

Arranging Transport

Savannah explained. "The company is large and boasts over 9000 personnel, light and heavy ground vehicles, cargo aircraft, helicopters, and many other toys. You are Army Special Forces Lieutenant Colonel Morgan James, retired twenty-one years in service. You left the Army to operate C&M Security company."

Impressed, Morgan said, "When your dad and I started the company, it was much smaller. The tasks we took paid well, and our reputation for satisfactory results kept new clients wanting our services. The company has grown considerably, and some of the best warriors in the world flocked to us. We pay well and expect excellence from our employees."

Roy said, "We can use the trailer. Robin, our IT person, will show you our evidence.

Robin showed Morgan what they had collected. Will laid out the plan to turn over the prisoners.

Morgan said, "I have a bus and six up-armored SUVs coming. They will be here soon. If you let me, I will take some of your men to Lubbock by air, so we have eyes on the drop off location. They'll need to be unarmed and blend in with the locals. We can land here at this small airport just outside Lubbock. We'll need someone to get them to the Ranger building."

Will said, "I have a friend that will do this for me. I'll call him and get it set up."

Morgan explained, "The helicopter can take eight at a time. We can make two trips before the bus leaves. Then come back here to provide air support for the bus and the trucks you want to take."

"Why do you have armored cars coming here? What did Savannah tell you we are doing?" Roy asked.

Savannah said, "I am right here. I told him we had CIA people here and that we needed to move to Lubbock. He told me the CIA would not appreciate their agents being our prisoners. They will stop us if they find out what we are doing."

Morgan said, "I told her I would get this job done, so I brought the tools and personnel necessary to complete the task."

Just then, Roy's phone rang. He answered it, listened for a while, and then said, "Thank you, let them in. We will meet them next to the trailer."

Roy hung up and said, "The bus and SUVs have arrived at the

barricade; they are coming in. Where do you want them?"

Will suggested, "Have the bus turn around using your road. The SUVs can park alongside our trucks."

Savannah said, "I will guide the bus and get it turned around." She left the trailer.

With the bus turned around and in place, Roy asked Morgan, "Do you want to send the first group to Lubbock?"

"Let's get them in the helicopter," Morgan said. "The sooner we start, the better. We need to wait to load the people on the bus until we have everyone placed in Lubbock."

Roy agreed saying, "I need to start moving the horse's trucks and trailers back to the ranches and repair the fences. Get this cluster fuck off the road. We can hold the men between the fence and the road until we leave."

Will and Roy sent trucks to Lubbock after the helicopter made its second trip and before the bus was loaded. The barricade was removed, and the fence was repaired.

CHAPTER 45
The Hand Over

Olivia gathered the confiscated weapons, phones, and electronics. She loaded the items into one of Morgan's SUVs. The items will be turned over to the Texas Rangers as evidence against the prisoners. She kept the CIA ID wallet separate. Savannah had asked for it. Olivia found Savannah in Robin's trailer and handed the ID wallet to her. Olivia asked, "What are you going to do with it?"

Savannah said, "We need the Texas Rangers to arrest and charge them. If we give this to them, we lose, and all of this will be for nothing.

The helicopter returned. Some of Morgan's men were armed and had weapons at the ready loaded on the bus. The prisoners were loaded next, then ranch hands, also armed and ready, boarded.

Roy observed to Morgan, "This reminds me of how we traveled when I was in a foreign country."

Morgan said, "It is a damn shame that we have to do this here and with U.S. Agents as prisoners. Someone high up in the food chain needs to go to jail for a long time for killing my friend."

Roy said, "They won't make it that far if I find out who ordered Akita's death. I will take care of them my way."

Morgan agreed and said, "You will have to beat me there."

Morgan's SUVs lined up on both sides of the road, heavily armed men inside.

Morgan, Roy, Will, Olivia, and Savannah boarded the helicopter. The bus and SUVs pulled away. The helicopter lifted off the ground and assumed a position above the convoy.

The Texas Ranger office is small and located inside the State Police building, a two-story constructed like a strip mall. The bus pulled into the parking lot and stopped at the entrance. The SUVs parked in front and behind the bus. The helicopter circled the complex. Once Morgan was satisfied that the threat level was low, he told Roy to make the call.

Roy called Captain Castillo and explained, "We are here to transfer prisoners to you. We have several that need medical treatment. Some of my men have trained as medics and treated them at the ranch. We have two that got themselves bitten by a fucking dog. The others have broken arms, jaws, and minor cuts, but nothing to fucking worry about."

Castillo asked, "What do you mean nothing to worry about? The injuries you just listed are major. You and your men had to use excessive force in their capture."

Roy said, "They should not have been on my land trying to steal cattle. They killed two of my calves, and they tried to get away. I could not allow that. The ones that did not point weapons at us or try to fight are fine. By the way, where the fuck were you and law enforcement when I called for help over the past years? I fucking bet you were here in town sitting on your ass."

Castillo asked, "Do you know who you are talking to?"

Before Castillo could say another word, Roy said, "Yes, the mother fucker that never showed up to do his job. So, I fucking took it on myself to do it for him." Roy paused, then added, "Vega will need to receive them. I am willing to press all the charges that Vega has the evidence to charge them with. Can my men deliver them inside without getting shot?"

Castillo said, "Vega has informed me that you arranged the transport of cattle rustlers. He said you captured them in the act and could get them moved faster than we could have a bus at your location. You can unload them now, but please have your men leave their weapons in the vehicles."

Roy hung up and called his man on the bus. Roy told him, "It is safe to take them inside now, but go unarmed."

Roy called Castillo back and told him, "My men are bringing them in now. We need to land. It will be fifteen minutes before I return to fill out the complaint."

"We are ready," Castillo said. "Why do you have heavily armed men and SUVs around my building?"

Roy said, "I do not want them to get away. I've spent too much time, money, and manpower getting to this point. I don't want to chase anyone down." Roy hung up and then told the pilot, "Let's get this bird on the ground." The helicopter pulled up and turned to leave.

The ranch hands debussed the prisoners and walked them through the front doors.

The Hand Over

Morgan's men stayed outside and were posted around the bus, trucks, and SUVs.

Once inside, the State Troopers took over the prisoners under the supervision of Ranger Vega. The Troopers did not appreciate the men's hands being rope tied behind their backs.

Then one Trooper found a man with his hands tied with barbed wire. He angrily stated, "This is inhumane and illegal. He called to Vega, "Come over and look at this."

Vega walked over, looked at the barbed wire bindings, and said, "You will find three more like this. The ranchers had to use what they had to restrain these men. After all, they did the job that the police should have done but were too busy to be bothered with. They did your job."

The Trooper was not pleased and said, "It is still inhumane and illegal. I will see whoever is responsible for this arrested and charged."

Vega shook his head, saying, "Good luck with that."

Will, Roy, Morgan, Savannah, and Olivia walked in the front door and were escorted into the processing area.

Vega walked over to them and asked, "Where are the weapons, phones, and other evidence you have? Without it, we may not be able to charge them."

Roy smiled and said, "Olivia will show you where it is. There is a large bundle, and it's heavy. Will you help her carry it in please?" Vega agreed to help and told Olivia to lead the way.

Several Troopers took statements from the ranch hands, Roy, Will, Olivia, and Savannah. The process took hours. When a Trooper was taking Morgan's statement, he asked, "Why were you involved in this situation? You don't have a vested interest in the ranches."

Morgan answered, "The owner of C&M Security wanted my assistance, and she ordered me to use any company assets needed to ensure a satisfactory conclusion."

The Trooper was confused and asked, "Who is the owner of your company?"

Morgan explained, "My boss is Savannah Haddox." Morgan pointed to Savannah and said, "She's right there."

The Trooper looked where Morgan was pointing and said, "You are

THE HAND OVER

full of shit. I searched your company, with its age, assets, and capabilities. She's too young to own the company."

Morgan laughed aloud and in a loud voice said, "Savannah, this asshole told me I'm full of shit. He doesn't think you're my boss. Tell this fucker how wrong he is."

Savannah, with everyone watching, walked over to the Trooper's desk, leaned against it, and said, "Do not ever insult one of my employees again. If you do, I will sue you for defamation or order the employee to kick your ass. Did I make myself perfectly clear?"

Savannah walked away without letting the Trooper respond.

Morgan looked at the Trooper and asked, "Are we done here?" Then he stood and walked away saying loudly, "I have the best boss ever."

Vega approached Savannah and asked, "Do you own the company?"

Savannah said, "Yes, I do."

Vega started to leave. Savannah laid her hand on Vega's forearm. He stopped, turned, and asked, "What do you need?"

With all the interviews completed. The prisoners had still not been identified. Vega told Roy, "We have all we need from you and your people. Everyone can leave now. If I need anything else, I will call."

Roy shook his hand and said, "We got off on the wrong foot. For that, I am sorry. Thank you for all your work. Will you please let us know what you find on the auto accident? The man that was killed was a friend."

Vega said, "I will do my best to determine who was involved."

Savannah told Roy, "I will get a ride home with someone. I have one more thing to do."

Roy said, "I will ensure someone stays here for you."

Once outside, Roy told Morgan, "This went smoothly, but when phone calls are made, the CIA will try to get their people released. We need to leave someone here to let us know when that happens. Savannah will not go with us. She told me she had one more thing to do. Will you have one of the SUVs stay here and give her a ride home?"

Morgan said, "You're right. I will have someone on overwatch. The CIA will rase hell to get their men out of jail. We will know when that happens, and yes, I'll make sure that my boss gets home safe."

The Hand Over

Savannah told Vega, "I need to talk to you privately. I have something you will need."

Vega took her into an office and asked, "What do you need to tell me?"

Savannah said, "I have information linking this investigation to my dad's auto accident. It proves that he was murdered. This information will lead you into dangerous territory. If I give it to you, your life may be at risk. You will be going against powerful forces with a long reach. Are you willing to see this to the end?"

Vega said, "My job is to find the truth. I do not see how you can link cattle rustlers to your dad's accident. Are you sure or are you looking for someone or something to blame?"

Savannah unbuttoned one button and pulled an envelope from underneath her shirt just above the waistband of her jeans. The envelope's contents made it bulge. She handed it to Vega and said, "Inside, you will find a phone, two thumb drives, and a CIA ID wallet. It would be best to look at it before you ask me a question like that again. All hell will break out when the CIA finds that you have their men in jail. The phone we found on the side of the road —that is what the CIA was looking for. It belonged to the man that killed my dad. One thumb drive has the contents of that phone on it, and the other has audio and video of the prisoners talking at camp when they thought no one was listening. It also has video only of what they were doing on the ranch, including killing calves."

Before Vega could say anything, Savannah walked out of the office. She looked back to see Vega in a state of disbelief. Vega plugged in the first thumb drive. It had the contents of the phone on it. He read the text and some of the emails. After processing what he had read, he called the IT section. He said, "I have a thumb drive and a phone. I need you to go through the phone and tell me if anyone altered the information, and I mean all of it, emails, texts, call logs, everything. Can you come to my office and pick it up, please?"

Vega then plugged in the other thumb drive. He watched all the videos with audio. He then listened to the audio. He opened the ID wallet, returned to the videos and found what he was looking for. He played the video of the man complaining. The man said, "We were sent here to find out what happened to Arthur. He was sent here to eliminate some asshole that was a threat to national security, and now this bunch of half-wit-backward-sister-fucking country fucks think we are fucking cattle rustlers. The fucking CIA does not pay me well enough for this shit." The ID belonged to this man.

CHAPTER 46
A First Date

Vega stood up and went to Castillo's office, knocked on the door, and entered. "I have something to show you," he said. You need to see it now."

Both men left Castillo's office and went to Vega's office. Vega handed Castillo the ID wallet and then played the video. Castillo asked simply, "Where did you get this?"

"Savannah Haddox stayed behind when the others left. She handed it to me along with a phone and this thumb drive. It has the contents of the phone on it. I gave the phone to IT and asked them to see if it had been tampered with," Vega explained. "We have circumstantial evidence here that Clint Haddox was murdered."

Castillo was pissed off and said, "They fucking played us. They are all a bunch of fucking cowhands, and they played us like fools. They brought CIA personnel in here and had us jail them as cattle rustlers, and all along they had this shit. Now we will have to let them go."

Vega said, "We have them jailed on good charges that we can prove, and Savannah gave it to us."

Castillo, still pissed, asked, "What about this shit? If we start investigating the fucking CIA, our careers are over. "FUCK ME." We must follow this and find out what happened on that road. I will tell higher up what you have and get some help. We are so fucked. You know that."

Vega said, "Another thing. You called them cowhands. I have a feeling that they are much more. The way they handled weapons and everything else tells me they are trained. Maybe military. I will have their names run to see what we have."

Castillo yelled, "Oh fuck me all over again. Do what you must. Find out who the fuck we are dealing with and dig deep into why that fucking Clint was killed."

Vega said, "Yes, sir."

Castillo left Vega's office, still pissed off and unsure of what was next.

The next day Vega received the intel on all the men they had interviewed the day before.

He went through the intel page by page. When finished, he left his office and went to Castillo's with all the paperwork. He knocked on the door and went in.

Castillo looked up and asked, "How are you going to fuck up my day?"

Vega said, "I was right about your cow hands. All the ones we interviewed are either retired Special Forces, Marine Recon, and Navy Seals with combat time in Vietnam.Or Special Forces, Marine Recon, and Navy Seals with several tours of combat in the Middle East. They are all badasses. Cowhands did not play us. They handed us this investigation on a silver platter. I want to find out why."

"Go find out and make it quick," Castillo said. "The shit is already rolling downhill, and I do not want us stuck in it."

Vega smiled and said, "I did not know you cared so much for me." Then he left Lubbock and drove to the Walker ranch. He arrived two hours later and pulled into the driveway, parked his truck, and walked to the Walker home's door. He knocked and said, "Mr. Walker, this is Ranger Vega. May I speak with you?"

The door opened, and Olivia said, "Mr. Vega, my dad is not here. What do you need?"

Vega said, "I have questions about the accident that killed Mr. Haddox. I also have questions about all the activities on the ranch the other day and cattle rustling."

Olivia said, "As I just told you, my dad is not here. May I help you?"

"Has your dad told you anything about the auto accident?" Vega asked.

Olivia looked at him in disgust and said, "How can he tell me anything about that? We found out that Akita was killed from Bernadette. She told us when their ranch hands showed up here to help us. Why are you asking stupid questions, and by stupid, I mean shit you already know? What the fuck is wrong with you?"

Vega was set back on his heels and said, "I am sorry if I have offended you. That was not my intention." Olivia started to close the door. Vega continued, "I have been on the road without anything to eat. Let me take you to lunch and make up for this misunderstanding.

A First Date

Please?"

Olivia looked at him and asked, "Are you asking me out on a date?" She did not let him answer. She just continued to fire question after question: "Do you think that is wise? Or are you just making fun of me? I do not know you. Why should I go anywhere with you? I will tell my dad that you came here to date me. Is that what you want? Well, tell me? Or are you at a loss for words now?"

Vega held up his hands in surrender and said, "I am sorry I did not want to offend you again. Please accept my apology. I will leave now."

Olivia knew she had bested him and was pleased to have done so. She said, "I am not offended. You caught me off guard. I have not had anything to eat either." Smiling, she asked, "Does your offer for a date still stand?"

Vega knew at that point this young lady outmatched him, and he was in trouble. He smiled and said, "Yes, it would be my pleasure. Where would you like to go?"

Then Vega's phone rang. He looked at the caller ID. It was his IT department. He said, "Excuse me, I need to take this." He walked several feet away and answered this is Vega. The call was from Mary in the IT section.

Mary said, "You have a DNA match on the blood evidence you collected on the road at the Walker ranch."

Vega said, "Please continue. What does it look like?"

Mary said, "You have two matches. One is Clint Haddox. Your deceased victim, the other one, matches a hand found at the Stonewall County courthouse. That is all I have."

Vega asked, "What do you mean hand?"

Mary said, "I called the sheriff of Stonewall, and he told me the hand is all they have. It was left hanging on the door of the courthouse."

Vega said, "Oh fuck me, what will be next? Fucking UFOs?" Then he said, "Mary, thank you, and I am sorry for the outburst. This case keeps getting better and better." Then he pushed the button and hung up.

Vega turned to see Olivia locking the door and heading his way.

Olivia said, "Abilene, please, the Texas Steak House will do." Again, Vega smiled, knowing he was not in charge of this day.

Olivia asked, "Will you tell me your first name? I have been around

207

servicemen all my life, and I refuse to call someone I am on a date with by their last name."

Vega said, "My name is Sergio."

Olivia said with a devilish grin, "You can call me Ms. Walker."

"Are you kidding? You want me to address you that way?" Vega asked.

Olivia, still smiling, said, "No. Can't you take a joke?"

Smiling, Sergio said, "Olivia, you are just mean. Please get in the truck and accompany me to the Texas Steak House."

Their first date went well. It would not be their last. They started seeing each other.

CHAPTER 47
Unsolved

Vega was in his office going over the case evidence. He was at an impasse. He decided to go to Stonewall and find out all the facts about the hand and whether it had anything to do with his case. Vega spoke to the Stonewall County sheriff and the state troopers involved with the hand. He discovered the hand had been fingerprinted and sent to the FBI in the Abilene office. He gathered all the evidence from Stonewall to include the fingerprints. He sent the fingerprint card to the lab in Lubbock. He put a rush attached to it. He then went to the FBI office in Abilene. He spoke to the agent in charge. He was told there were no matching fingerprints in the federal system, and the DNA was not on file. When he was out of the FBI office, he called Mary. When she answered, he asked her, "Can you please run the DNA from the accident and the matching hand through outside sources?"

Mary said, "You are hoping to find a family match in civilian databases, aren't you?"

Vega said, "Yes. I think the FBI, or some other agency is hiding the ID of this man. If we find a family match, I will have the ID. and maybe get some answers. Who he was, who he worked for, what he was doing in Texas. I want to know if he was killed on the road or if he was in the car and dead already. If someone was transporting his body, it would explain why they left the accident scene. I have questions, and I hope you can help me with the answers."

Mary said, "I will do my best. I will let you know if and when I find anything."

"Thank you," Vega said and hung up.

Vega was in Castillo's office giving his update when his phone rang. He looked at the caller ID and said, "Let me get this. It's Mary in IT." He stepped out of the office and answered the call.

Mary said, "We have a match on the DNA. I got it from a civilian ancestry agency. It is the man's mother. I also got you her address and phone number."

Vega asked, "Can you email it to me? I am in a meeting now."

Mary said, "Yes, it is on the way. I hope it helps." Then she hung up.

Vega returned to the office and told Castillo, "I have new information I need to follow up on now."

Castillo said, "Go. We need something on this before all this shit is too deep to shovel."

Vega called Miss Woods and asked, "May I have your son Arthur's address?"

Miss Woods said, "Arthur died in the Middle East. He was in Army Intelligence. His funeral was over three years ago. Why are you asking?"

Vega said, "Ma'am, I am so sorry. I have the wrong last name and phone number. Please forgive me." He hung up before she could ask anything more.

Vega burst into Castillo's office and said, "I have a positive ID on the DNA. His name is Arthur Woods."

Castillo asked, "Don't you know how to knock? Have you lost your ever-loving fucking mind? I am on a call. Can this wait?"

Vega said, "Sorry, it will wait." Then he left the office.

Shortly, Castillo called Vega into his office and asked, "What have you got?"

Vega said, "His name is Arthur Woods. Do you remember the recording the ranchers made? The name Arthur was on it."

Castillo said," Yes, I remember. Do you have anything else?"

Vega said, "I called his mother she told me he died in the Middle East three years ago."

Castillo asked, "How the fuck can his hand show up in Texas three years after he was killed in the Middle East?"

Vega said, "He had to be CIA. He either died on the road at the Walker ranch or was dead in the car and being transported for disposal."

Castillo asked, "Are you still seeing the Walker girl? Have you any new information on the accident?"

Vega said, "Yes, I am still seeing Olivia. I don't have any new information. Bernadette Chisum was the only one involved in the accident and has not changed her story."

Castillo said, "So we are no closer to closing this. We're still in the dark about everything. Is this what you are telling me?"

Vega said, "No, now we have more questions than we had yesterday. The only thing we have is his name. Do you have a contact we can use to find out what the fuck is going on?"

Castillo said, "No, not really, but I can make some calls." Vega left the office. He never came close to closing this case. It was one of three that he still wants answers and closure on.

Sergio and Olivia soon married and live on the Walker ranch.

Olivia never revealed anything to Sergio about the night Akita was killed or the actions of others in the following days.

(Sergio, I am sorry that you will find out this way. Please remember the bond between Olivia, her dad, and all the men she grew up with on the ranch. Family loyalty is everything.)

CHAPTER 48
Leadership Meeting

It has been five months since the CIA people were rounded up and jailed.

Lee Ann was awakened by her phone. She picked it up and looked at the time. It was 3:30 in the morning. She was mad. Who is calling now? The caller's I.D. was unknown. She was going to hang up when Malin rolled over and said, "Answer it."

So, she pushed the button and said, "This better be important." The voice on the other end said, "I have finely accessed all the data on the hard drive." Lee Ann recognized the voice, and it was Robin. She asked, "What hard drive, and why are you calling at this time? Please call back later."

Robin said, "This will not wait. I need your help now. Please wake up and listen. All the FRBs were murdered by the C.I.A. and all but three on AMERICAN soil."

Sitting straight up in bed, Lee Ann asked, "What did you just say?"

Robin said, "I got passed the security on the drive. It has taken this long because I didn't want to damage or lose anything. I also didn't want anyone alerted that we had the drive. I have all the information on it now. I have a list of the C.I.A. agents that killed the FRBs. The list includes names, dates, locations, and how they were killed."

Lee Ann could not comprehend what she had just heard. She asked, "Are you sure?"

Robin said, "You need to come over here now, and I mean now. Do you understand? RIGHT NOW."

"Why me? Lee Ann asked, "If what you have is real, you need to call the sheriff or Sergio Vega."

Robin, almost yelling, said, "We must tell Savannah." She knows her dad was targeted and assassinated." She calmed and said, "We have known that the man that killed him was CIA No one knew why. Some thought he had a vendetta against Akita."

Lee Ann replied, "Yes, I know, but we were unable to prove they knew each other."

Robin said, "The C.I.A. assassinated all the FRBs, and I know why. I

213

LEADERSHIP MEETING

need your help. We must tell Savannah and the others what we know. Then we need to decide on what we do next."

"I am on my way," Lee Ann answered. Please don't tell anyone else until I get there. All of our lives are on the line now."

She hung up the phone and started to get out of bed. Malin held her arm and asked, "What do you mean all our lives are on the line?"

She said, "Robin has unlocked the hard drive from the laptop Roy took from the car that killed Akita."

Malin said, "I will go with you."

Lee Ann looked at him and said, "No, not now. If I need you, I will call. Robin is freaked out and may not want anyone else there."

She got in her pickup and drove to Robin's house. When she arrived, Robin met her in the drive. She had a pistol in her hand and looked scared. "Come in," Robin said. "I will show you what I found."

They went inside her home and made their way to her office. Then Robin informed Lee Ann that she had made several copies of the drive. She handed Lee Ann a thumb drive and said, "This is just the list I told you about. I have all the other information from the hard drive on this thumb drive. Put them in a safe place."

Lee Ann said, "I will. Now please show me what you have."

Robin's computer was already powered up. She pulled up the list on a form she had saved. Robin said, "Here it is." She turned the monitor so Lee Ann could see:

FROM: Michael Skinner, the Deputy Executive Director of the C.I.A.
TO: Agents Liam Smith, Noah Johnson, Oliver Williams, Elijah Jones, James Garcia, William Miller, Benjamin Davis, Lucas Wilson, Henry Anderson, and Theodore Thomas.

RE: *Traitors to the United States of America*
U.S. ARMY personnel Clint Haddox, Ed Johnson, Bobby Wade, John Laws, Steve Jackson, Kody Lunsford, Sam Hawk, Paul Martinez, Joe Metcalf, Jody Lucero, Harold Powell, Kevin Viraman
The agency orders the personnel listed above to be eliminated at all costs. This order is Top Secret and authorizes you to operate inside the United States on this single issue.
Report directly and only to D.E.D. Skinner. The personnel herein have killed

LEADERSHIP MEETING

innocent U.S. and foreign military and civilian people. The appearance of accidental death would be favorable and should be considered first but not necessary.

Lee Ann looked at Robin in disbelief and said, "How could they do this?"

Robin said, "The FRBs brought Skinner's brother Jim back from South America. He was tried, convicted, and sentenced to death for treason."

Lee Ann said, "I remember the whole family was persecuted in the press. They lost almost everything trying to defend their son."

"Michael Skinner issued this order without authorization from the leadership above him. He was getting his family's revenge using his position with the C.I.A. If we are not careful, we will be next," Robin explained.

Lee Ann asked, "What else is on the drive?"

Robin said, "Let me show you. The agents reported when, where, and how they killed each soldier. The first three were killed in a firefight on an operation in the middle east. The agent shot them from behind and at a distance. Everybody assumed the enemy had killed them. The fucking C.I.A. did. We have all the evidence we need for their arrest and conviction."

Lee Ann said, "Savannah will be devastated to learn the country her dad fought for his whole life killed him and all his men."

Robin offered, "I will give her all the information on the hard drive and tell her."

"No," Lee Ann said. "We will do it together. What do you think she will do?"

Robin said, "She loved her dad and has not been the same since his death. She will want revenge, justice, or both. I don't know what she will do. If I know her, it won't be good."

Lee Ann called Savannah from Robin's house. She answered on the second ring.

"Savannah, Robin has unlocked the hard drive from the C.I.A. laptop. We need to show you what is on it," Lee Ann explained.

Savannah said, "Please tell me."

Robin said, "Tell her we cannot do this over the phone."

Leadership Meeting

Savannah heard this and asked, "Where are you? I will drive there now."

Lee Ann answered, "I'm at Robin's house." The phone went dead. Lee Ann looked at Robin and said, "She hung up on me."

"She's on her way. We need to be ready to answer all questions she'll have," Robin said.

Lee Ann said, "Show me the rest of the material on the drive. Send a copy to Malin. I am calling him now to explain that he needs to put it in a safe location."

Savannah arrived sooner than they had expected. She said, "I drove over one hundred all the way here. What is on the drive? Why couldn't you tell me over the phone?" Robin showed her all the data.

Savannah sat silent for a while. They could see the rage building in her. Then her appearance changed. She looked at Lee Ann and Robin and asked in an indifferent voice, "Who else have you shared this with?"

Robin said, "We sent a copy to Malin, and I have ten copies on delayed emails set to be sent if I do not reset daily."

Savannah said, "I need to make some calls. Both of you need to pack for an extended stay in Germany."

Robin said, "I can't just drop everything and go to Germany."

Savannah said, "Robin, I am buying your company right now. Name your price. I will pay it." Robin wrote down the price on a scrap of paper and handed it to Savannah.

Savannah said, "You will have it in your account today if you agree to work for me and double your staff before we go to Germany."

Robin said, "It's yours as of right now. I work for you. I have twenty employees now. I can get some good I.T. personnel tomorrow."

Savannah looked at Robin and said, "I do not need IT. I need expert hackers, ones that can break into any system F.B.I., C.I.A., and banking here in the U.S. and overseas. Can you get me the people I need?"

Robin said, "I know what people you need. I use them myself. I will get you the best, but it will cost you."

Savannah said, "The cost is not important. I will pay for results. I will need six or more to go with us. The rest will be online from here. You will control them from wherever we are. They need to understand this will be twenty-four hours a day, every day. They will take breaks when we

LEADERSHIP MEETING

do not require their help. I will pay extra for what I need when I need it. You will keep track of the ones that do that, and I will double their pay. Make sure they know what is expected from them."

Savannah turned to Lee Ann and said, "You don't have your whole story now, and you won't have it unless you go with me. Now, please call Morgan for me and tell him about the kill list. Then tell him we're going to Germany, and he will have at least fifteen men go with us."

Savannah, Robin, and Lee Ann started making phone calls. About an hour later, Lee Ann had everything she needed to finish. She was still determining who Savannah had called and what she would do. Lee Ann knew Savannah was angry when they told her what they had found, but that wasn't all of it. Savanah was immediately thinking about what to do, and when she was finished, she went into action. Now Lee Ann was thinking what the fuck she had gotten herself into.

Morgan had one of the C&M Security planes loaded and ready to go the following day. They arrived at the airport. Morgan's men loaded their bags. Lee Ann noticed the cargo bay was full of hard-sided boxes strapped down, and she asked one of the men what they contained.

He smiled and said, "Whatever we need to complete this operation." Then he turned and said nothing more.

They all boarded the plane.

Morgan explained, "We will be airborne in ten minutes and land in Germany in eight hours."

During the flight, Morgan and Savannah sat together. They looked at floor plans, roadways, and other items on a tablet. Several people were making phone calls, Savannah and Morgan among them. Savannah said, "If you cannot be there on time, you need to find another fucking job because I will have no further need for you."

Morgan was arranging for rent to be paid on a building, explaining, "Have all of your guests off the floors we have rented by the time we arrive and have the conference room set up the way we laid out to you."

The group arrived in Germany thirty minutes late. Cars were waiting to take everyone from Frankfurt to Wetzlar. Trucks were there for the boxes in the cargo area. Luggage was placed in the cars as soon as the trucks were loaded, and then they departed. No one went through German customs. No one checked passports or anything else. They

LEADERSHIP MEETING

arrived at the hotel one and a half hours later. At the check in desk, the clerk explained, "You have the top three floors, and the conference room is set the way you wanted. Most of your guests have checked in. Only one group has not arrived. We expect them soon as they left the airport in Munich a short time ago."

The hotel staff took the luggage to everyone's rooms.

Savannah wanted to inspect the layout of the conference room and asked Morgan and Lee Ann to go with her. The conference room was large, and Savannah had it set up. In the front of the room, four tables with six chairs each faced the room's rear. Also, ten chairs on one side of the tables faced the back of the room. The tables and chairs had reserved signs on them.

Three groups of eighteen chairs faced the front of the room. Each group had the company name on them: Sharpest Edge Security, Spearpoint Security Company, and White Rock Security Specialist. The chairs on both sides and the back of the room were labeled reserved. A space in the rear of the room, about ten feet by ten feet, was empty.

Savannah's mom Sonia entered the room. Hotel staff followed her, saying, "Lady Sonia, we didn't know you were coming."

Sonia dismissed them and quickly hugged Savannah. "I have missed you," she said. "I have news. When we spoke about what you intend to do when you learned who ordered the deaths of the FRBs and your dad, you said you wanted them to pay with their lives. You said you wanted blood for blood. I was against you becoming just like the men you are hunting. I told you I did not want a murderer for a daughter. You now have a way to achieve justice and ensure everyone involved with the FRB's deaths pay. I used the fact that you are my daughter to secure dual citizenship for you. I also pulled in a few favors. You are now an employee with the Bundesnachrichtendienst (BND). With this position, you have a passport and diplomatic immunity." Sonia handed the passport over to Savannah.

Savannah smiled and said, "I missed you more than you know. Mom, I did not know you were doing this for me. I cannot thank you enough for this gift. A job with the BND is more than I could have hoped for, and diplomatic immunity. I heard you when you said you did not want me to be a murderer, and I do not want you to have a reason to think of me that way. I do not know what to say." Then she asked," Are Kirsten and

Leadership Meeting

Petra with you?" She had no sooner asked when Petra and Kirsten burst into the room. They hugged Savannah.

Petra asked, "Why are you staying here? Your home is much better than this."

Savannah introduced Morgan to the group. Then she told them why she had asked to buy their security companies. Lee Ann observed, "This was the first time I had heard Sonia, Kirsten, and Petra had security companies."

Savannah explained, "Each company was set up by my dad and was given to the women as a gift. He wanted to know that they were safe. This was his way of doing it.

Each company has between 6000 to 8000 employees. They work worldwide in war zones and for individuals who need their skills."

Morgan added, "Akita started C&M Security. Also, we have 9000 full-time employees, plus some others we can call if needed. Savannah now has well over 27,000 hardcore SF and elite soldiers from around the world in her employment."

Savannah said, "I also have Uwe's organization of 12,000 worldwide and Robin's company.

Lee Ann asked her, "Why do you need this fighting force? Are you planning to go to war?"

Savannah asked, "Why do you think we are here? I will find, capture, and bring to justice the mother fuckers who killed my dad and his men, the FRBs. This is the beginning of a war with the CIA, and it will not end until I have everyone on that list, and then I will deliver them and all the evidence to a law enforcement agency. Once that is done, I will go gunning for Michael Skinner." Lee Ann was stunned that Savannah made this happen quickly. What was she going to do now?

The following day everyone was in the conference room. The company's leaders had taken their places. Robin and her crew were at the tables with laptops and other gear. All were working on a list they were given. Lee Ann walked around the table to see what they were doing. They were looking up military and financial records from countries around the world. Some were on the phones with Robin's people in Texas. Data and paperwork were on all the tables.

Lee Ann asked one woman, "How long have you been at this?"

LEADERSHIP MEETING

She looked up from her work and said, "We started this in Texas and have been working on it ever since."

Morgan yelled, "Listen up, this meeting starts now." Everyone fell silent. "My name is Morgan James. The people up here," he said, pointing to the chairs where Sonia, Petra, Kirsten, and others were seated, "are the former owners of the companies you work for." Then he pointed at Savannah and said, "This is the new owner of all your companies. Her name is Ms. Haddox."

The man in charge of White Rock Security shouted, "We have more important shit to do. I'm taking my men and leaving."

Savannah stood. She wore a lite silvery gray Stetson hat. The brim was styled flat on the sides, down an inch in the back, and slightly more in the front. It had a gold metal hat band half-inch wide that was faceted to reflect the light. She wore a snug fitting white silk blouse and a thin gold chain necklace with a gold pendant. Her dark, red, skintight pencil skirt ended three inches above her knee. A six-inch-wide gold metal belt in front had two buckles, one above the other. On each side, the metal was attached to black leather straps that met in the back and fastened with a single buckle. The belt enhanced her hourglass figure, tiny waist, ample breasts, attractive hips, and shapely butt. She wore six-inch stilettos with highly polished gold heels. People who had seen Savannah in jeans often noticed how her jeans would strain against her thigh muscles when she walked. Her thighs could be described as somewhere between those of a ballet dancer and a bodybuilder, heavily muscled with deep tie-ins.

Savannah started walking towards the empty space in the room. She crossed one foot around and in front of the other in a gliding motion like a ballroom dancer, which caused a more noticeable hip and body motion while she kept her head level.

Kirsten whispered to her table, "She's walking the way I showed her when she wants to be noticed."

Those close remembered the comment about that walk. Kirsten would do it just because she could. The comment was, "That look, and that walk is *pure sex! pure sex!*" The quote fell dreadfully short of what everyone was seeing. Savannah was exquisite at this moment. Everyone in the room, male and female, had their eyes glued on her.

One of the women who worked for Robin said, "I am straight, but

LEADERSHIP MEETING

she makes me want to be gay."

Savannah had the men in the room in a trance. She arrived at the empty space and stood in the center. She turned around and looked at the man from White Rock Security and said, "I had the hotel staff set up this space. I knew that someone would challenge me."

Savannah then looked at Robin and asked, "What is his name?"

Robin answered, "Edward."

Savannah looked at Edward and said, "Please join me here. Or are you a coward as well as a thief? Do you think you can steal from the company? Take my company, men, equipment, and weapons, and do whatever you want to? I thank you are a pussy. I don't think you have a dick. I think you have a little flap of skin down there that stops dust from getting in." Savannah looked around the room and added, "He thought he had three hairs down there until one of them pissed on him." The room erupted in laughter.

Edward was pissed. He stormed over to her, yelling, "I will show you, bitch."

Morgan started to move. Savannah put up her hand to hold him back. Edward reached her and tried to slap her. Savannah moved out of the way and said, "You even fight like a girl."

Edward threw a punch and put everything into it. Savannah moved as the punch went wide. She then set and placed a kick into his chest. The toe of her foot impacted his sternum. The heel of her shoe plunged deep into his solar plexus. There was a popping noise as Edward's sternum broke. He let out a whooshing sound as he lost all the air in his lungs. He went backward five feet from the impact and crumpled to the floor.

Savannah looked at all the men in the room and asked, "Does anyone else have a problem working for me? Do any of you want to steal from me?"

Savannah turned to Morgan and said, "Have your men take everything from him. Leave him with his pants only and take him to Sonia's clinic."

Savannah asked Robin, "What does he have in his bank records?"

Robin said, "He has one million dollars above what he has made from the company. He has no stocks. He did not have money when he started to work for White Rock Security."

Leadership Meeting

Savannah asked Morgan, "Is there a way he made this money without stealing from the company, clients, and me?"

Morgan said, "No, ma'am, it is not possible."

Savannah told Robin, "Clean out all his bank accounts, give half back to the company coffers, and give the other to Wetzlar's orphanage. Ensure that safe deposit boxes are placed on company property accounts, and the passwords changed. Revoke his access to company computers, buildings, and accounts."

Another man from White Rock Security stood up and said, "You can't do that. You do not know where he got his money. You are stealing from him."

Savannah turned to Robin, but before asking her question, Robin said, "He was stealing from our clients, and we have the proof. We are sending the information to law enforcement in the states. The man standing is Jeff Stringer. He has more money than he has made or saved in the five years working for White Rock Security. He doesn't have stocks or anything else."

Savannah asked, "How much money are we talking about?"

Robin said, "Three hundred thousand dollars."

Savannah asked Jeff, "What do you have to say in this matter?"

Jeff started to leave.

Morgan said, "I would not leave if I were you. I have men in the hall that will stop you and bring you back to answer the question."

Jeff stopped and said, "I will fuck you up, lady."

Savannah smiled and said, "Well, I better get ready then."

She stepped out of her heels and removed her skirt. She was wearing shorts that were the same color as her skirt. She carefully folded the skirt and placed it behind her shoes, and said, "Okay, I am ready, your move."

Jeff walked over, got into a stance, and said, "Let's see how you do when you have to attack."

Savannah moved. She was fast, extremely fast. She kicked his knee first, then his mouth. His knee and jaw were broken.

Savannah said, "If you want to see me attack, you must be awake." She hit him with a right hook that broke his orbital bone and knocked him out. Savannah stepped back into her heels and picked up the skirt. Her hat was still in place and did not require straightening.

Leadership Meeting

Sonia was standing proud, her ample chest pushed out, her head raised, and a devilish smile on her lips. She said to Kirsten and Petra, "She looks like me but acts like her dad."

Petra said, "She is a daughter to all of us."

Some of Robin's women looked horrified. Some of the men were in disbelief.

Morgan, with delight and pride, said, "That is my boss, and she is no one to be fucked with."

Savannah walked up to the table where Robin was working, placed her skirt on the table, and turned to face the room. She looked at Morgan and said, "Please put your men in place."

Morgan keyed the mike on his headset and said, "Secure the doors." Then he said, "Ma'am, the room is yours."

CHAPTER 49
WARRIOR QUEEN

Savannah said, "Morgan was going to introduce the other women and me before he was interrupted. My name is Savannah Haddox. I own ninety percent of the companies you work for, and if you haven't noticed, I am female, and I am young. I know what every swinging dick in this room is thinking. *We are fucked she will fuckup everything because she does not know what we do or how we do it. She will get us killed.* You are right that I have not had to apply battlefield tactics and techniques or apply overwhelming firepower. I do not know how to retrieve a person from the enemy. That is why Morgan has agreed to be my C.E.O. If you don't know Morgan, he and my dad started C&M Security. I have had background checks run on your company's performance and financials. C&M has outperformed all your companies combined. From today, Morgan leads all operations. He will give assignments and receive all reports."

Savannah continued, "The woman behind me in the black cowboy hat is Robin. The other people at this table and overseas are running background checks on everyone in this room. The checks are extensive and include your finances in the States and abroad, your work history, and much more. You will be allowed to leave this room once you have been cleared. For this reason, Morgan's men will collect all phones and other electronics. You will get them back before you leave."

Robin spoke up and said, "We have a problem." Morgan's men started collecting the electronics. Savannah turned her attention to Robin. Their discussion took about five minutes.

Savannah turned to the room and asked, "Tom Sellars, will you please stand?"

A man working for Spearpoint Security Company stood and said, "I am Tom Sellars."

Without being requested, Robin stood and asked, "Mr. Sellars, What intelligence agency do you work for?"

Before Tom could answer, Robin informed him, "We will find out, and it will not take long. So, you can save everyone time and tell us. "Morgan's men moved towards Tom and restrained him. The room was tense, no one knew what to expect.

Tom said, "I don't know what you are talking about."

Savannah said, "You did not exist until six years ago. Someone made a lot of effort inventing your history, but not good enough."

Another woman wearing a cowboy hat said, "I have it. His name is Lowell Webb. He works for the F.B.I. He spent nine years in the Tenth Mountain Division."

Savannah told Robin, "Find out how he has infiltrated my company and what he is looking for."

Robin was on a call with her team in the U.S. and working furiously on her keyboard. She looked up and said, "Yes, ma'am, I'm already on it. This may take some time."

Savannah again turned her attention to the room and said, "While Robin is working on this problem. I want to let you know why you have been invited here."

Someone yelled out, "Invited my ass. We were told if we did not come to look for another job."

Savannah smiled and said, "That is my way of inviting you. I do not think you want to find out how I demand your presence. I have a mission for you. You can and will do this one while working on the assignments that Morgan gives you. I will discuss it when we get Mr. Webb's problem resolved."

Robin again spoke up, "Mr. Webb is investigating Salvador Garcia. Salvador's father, Humberto Garcia, owns a company that ships multiple products worldwide. He has been accused of smuggling dope, but this has never been proven."

Salvador stood and yelled, "You son of a bitch, getting close to me trying to be my friend. I am going to fuck you up." Savannah quickly moved and stood in front of Salvador.

She asked, "Why are you working for this company? You can work for your father and not risk your life protecting people you do not know."

Salvador still pissed off, said, "I do not want the life he offers. I like the work we do. I get to do things no one else wants to do."

Savannah turned to Morgan and said, "I just found you a new employee. He will be a good fit with your men."

Morgan said, "Salvador take your place at the door with my men."

Robin said, "I have transferred his employment records to your company."

Salvador smiled at Savannah and asked, "May I kick his ass now for spying on me?"

Savannah said, "No. We will send him back to the states unharmed. He was ordered to do this job. His job is the same as ours. We interfere with other lives with what we also do."

Morgan's men escorted Lowell Webb out of the hotel and into a cab with instructions to go home.

Robin announced, "We have the background checks complete on the men in this room. We are working on the rest of the company's employees."

Morgan spoke on his headset and ordered someone on the other end to bring the cases in now. As he stood beside Savannah, he said to everyone, "We have a list of people to be captured. This will be a worldwide search, and once they are in custody, you will send them to a holding facility. We have the list on tablets that will be issued to you shortly. All the information we have on each man is provided on the tablets. All the men are CIA agents. You have where they have worked in the country, town, or village, as well as who they were working for or against; what intel they were gathering; who they were trying to kill, and who they killed; the station chief they reported to; if they used drugs or gambled. If they did it, we have a record of it, including their background investigation the CIA had on file. The reason we have this information is because of the hard work of the people at the front table, and others we have in our employ. If you need anything more, contact me. You have my company email. I will get the info you need. A secure phone number is provided on the tablet. It is manned 24/7. It is the only number you will use."

Morgan took a breath and continued, "When you find a man on the list, call the number. If you need help with his capture, call the number, and you will receive all the help you need. If the man is in jail or worse, we will extract him. If you have him in your control, call, and you will receive instructions for the evacuation of your man to a holding facility. Ms. Haddox has authorized the company to pay $25,000.00 for the individual who finds one of the men on the list. She has also authorized $50,000.00 for any individual who captures one of the men on the list.

Also, after all the men are in custody, everyone involved in the captures will receive an additional $10,000.00. This is on top of your current pay."

To his enrapt audience, Morgan continued, "We have the tablets on the company's intranet, not the internet. They will not send or receive emails from outside the company. You will only use the tablets to send and receive information about the list. Do I make myself perfectly clear?" After a brief pause, he said, "All of the evidence we have of their involvement in the deaths of the FRBs has been handed over to the Texas Rangers because four soldiers were killed on Texas soil." Morgan's men started handing out the tablets from the hard cases that had been strapped down in the plane's cargo area.

Savannah said, "My dad told me the foundation for all warriors is their ability to defend themselves in hand-to-hand combat. I believe this is true, and it should be tested. That way, you know what you must work on to become more proficient. While we have time, if anyone wishes to test their skills against mine, please join me in my world." She pointed towards the empty area in the room and started walking to it. Once she was inside that area, no one took her up on the offer.

Morgan's men finished handing out the tablets. Morgan said, "Again, all the information you need about the people on the list has been uploaded on the tablets. Please follow them. We need them alive and in one peace. Now for better news, a meal has been prepared for all of us. You are invited. It will be served at 18:00 in the dining hall. We have one more item before we adjourn with four companies combined under one banner. Savannah, what is the new company name? We will need it for everything from advertising to taxes."

Savannah was about to say something when Sonia spoke up, "The FRBs had a way of ranking themselves. They used tabs placed above the Army Special Forces tab. These tabs had to be earned, and the men set standards for each. After one man met that standard, the team voted, and the tab was given. The highest one was Phantom Warrior. I think Phantom Warriors Security is a good name for this new company."

Several men yelled out, "Oh hell yes!

Morgan got Sonia's attention and said, "Akita spoke of you often. I was impressed at how much he cared for you. Savannah told me that you would be here. I needed to know more about the mother of my new boss and Akita's life love. So, I researched you and your family. Your family is of noble descent, and you would be a queen after your father died. Then Savannah would be next in line for the crown."

Sonia smiled and said, "You would be right if it were one hundred years ago. She would be royalty and have the title of Queen." Sonia looked at Savannah, tears rolling down her cheeks, and said, "My daughter Queen of the Phantom Warriors."

Morgan turned and addressed the room, "We have a Queen leading and watching over us. I am honored to present Savannah, Queen of the Phantom Warriors."

The room filled with the cheers of hard battle tested men. One man said, "I have never met a queen. Now I work for one."

Savannah was in a league of her own, no one was her equal. This West Texas, ranch-raised woman was now lifted atop the shoulders of twelve of the most elite warriors the world has ever known, the FRBs. She now has an army with aircraft, armored vehicles, and weapons to command. She also has access to the Bundesnachrichtendienst (BND) because Sonia is second in command from the top of the BND. She also has access to U.S. intelligence through General Scott. One organization that everyone needs to be aware of is the lawless criminal one that Uwe Dietrich is the head of. Savannah is now one of the wealthiest and most powerful people of her time. The Stetson on her head is now a crown, and she is madder than hell at the CIA.

CHAPTER 50
Mom's Way

After the meeting, Savannah told Lee Ann, "I have to make a call. I want you to take part in it."

She asked, "Why do you want me to be involved with your calls?"

Savannah turned and looked straight at her, a hard look as if she should have known the answer before asking, and said, "Like it or not, you are part of my world. Your job is to find facts and write the truth. How can you tell the truth without all the facts?"

She did not give her a chance to answer. She didn't breathe before saying, "This call will give you information that you will not get any other way. Do you want the hard, uncomfortable story or just the one you wish to write?"

Anger washed over Lee Ann, and she almost yelled. She said, "You know I will not write anything that I cannot verify. Your world, as you call it, has consumed every aspect of my life. Sometimes I wish I had never met you."

Savannah said, "I am sorry that you feel that way. I like you, and I respect your work ethic. I think of you as family. Now if you don't want to be part of my world, I understand, and you can leave anytime. You are not my prisoner. I will have Robin arrange travel for you. Where do you want to go, Texas or New York?" Savannah turned to walk away.

Lee Ann said, "Savannah, I do not wish to leave. Texas is my home now, and you should know that. You are part of my family. I think of you as my sister, but please tell me why it's so important for me to be on this call with you?"

Savannah stopped, turned, and said, "You need to hear what I am going to do. After the call, I want your counsel, Sis. I want to know what you think the pros and cons are. I also want to know if you would take this action if you were in my place."

Lee Ann smiled and said, "I will tell you what I think, Sis." They went to Savannah's room to make the call. Savannah called Uwe Dietrich and put the call on speaker. Uwe answered on the fourth ring.

Savannah told Uwe, "I have you on speakerphone. Lee Ann is here with me. I hope you don't mind."

Mom's Way

Uwe said, "That depends on the subject. What do you want?"

Savannah told Uwe, "I need the call center we spoke about up and running. I gave my men the capture order and contact number today."

Uwe said, "I owe Akita my life on more than one occasion. I will never be able to repay that debt. My debt to him is now my debt to you. All you ever have to do is ask. I do not care what it is. I will do it."

Savannah said, "Your debt will be paid in full."

Uwe cut her off and said, "No, it will not. What You are asking of me does not come close to what Akita did for me. My life is worth much more as far as I am concerned my debt will never be paid. Understand this I owe you, and I always will."

Savannah said, "It was not my intention to offend you. I am sorry. I will not take advantage of you. As you and I discussed, once my men have apprehended the fuck heads who killed my dad and the FRBs, they will call the number you gave me and hold the men until you have made the arrangements to pick them up and smuggle them out of the country they are in and into Germany. Once we have all of them, you will smuggle them into Texas. Before you wanted to shoulder this expense, I cannot allow you to pay for any of this. I will pay for all the man hours, transportation, housing, and food. All I want in return is for you to hold them, take everything away from them except their underwear, and not torture them. Savannah's demeanor went beyond cold. The vile disgust she held for the CIA men was evidenced in her voice. She continued, "My dad and his men would be on a mission for months without hygiene of any kind. So, no showers or anything else. If it was good enough for the men they killed, it should be good enough for them. Do we have a deal?"

Uwe said, "I will do this your way, but if the motherfuckers try to escape or anything else, I will have my men stop them and beat them until their fucking actions will not be repeated. Do we have a deal?"

Savannah said, "Yes, we do. Keep all of them alive. I know you want them dead, as do I, but we need the world to know what they did. I need to have them in a courtroom and receive the death penalty. Can you do this for me?"

Uwe said, "You have my word. I will deliver them to you alive. Now I must get everything in place."

Savannah said, "Thank you. I will not forget this." Then she hung up the phone.

Savannah looked at Lee Ann and asked, "Have I done the right thing now, or should I have just killed them fucking bastards?"

Lee Ann answered, "I know this is not what you want, but Sonia has asked you not to take their lives. I don't know if I could have your restraint and strength with this. You are doing the right thing."

Savannah hugged Lee Ann and said, "Thank you. I could not ask for a better sister. If you were not here with me, I would have gone against my mom's wishes and simply had all of them killed."

Witnessing all this scared Lee Ann to her core. She wondered what the hell she was now a part of.

CHAPTER 51
Dining with the Boss

That evening at the table, Sonia, Kirsten, Petra, Robin, Morgan, and Lee Ann were waiting for Savannah to arrive. They were at the rear corner of the room, surrounded by the men working for the newly formed company, the Phantom Warriors.

Sonia said, "Savannah sent a message to her employees today. I didn't know she could take out men twice her size with no effort. She made it look easy."

Morgan said, "I've never seen anyone do that much damage to the human body with so few punches or kicks. I don't think anyone in that room, including me, could beat her in that setting. She is a monster."

Robin said, "A monster wrapped in a sweet, beautiful body. I have known her for years, and never in my wildest dreams or imagination did I think she could destroy men that easily. She is a badass, and now everybody knows. I am glad that she likes me. I don't want to be on her bad side."

Kirsten said, "I have seen that power and speed only once in my life, the night Akita saved me. She controls it just like he did and only lets it out when necessary. She made all the men there respect her. Do you think anyone in this room will challenge her orders?"

Lee Ann added, "I have seen her working alongside young men, old men, and children. I haven't seen her argue with anyone or get mad. You should see her with Jo, her dog, running and playing like a child without a care in the world she is kind. Now I know she is also deadly."

Morgan said, "When you know how to fight that well, it makes no sense to get mad because you can maim someone without trying. You are right. She sent the message *I am the boss, and don't ever forget it.*"

Savannah entered the dining hall. She had changed into jeans, a red shirt, boots, and her hat. Again, she had the attention of everybody in the room. She scanned the room, found the group, and made her way to their table. Men said, "Good evening, ma'am," as she passed.

She smiled and returned, "Good evening. How are you?"

Morgan got up and pulled her chair out for her. Savannah said, "Thank you, I am sorry I am late. I called Bernadette and let her know that the meeting went off without a hitch."

Petra asked with an evil-looking smile, "Were you at the same meeting we were at?"

Savannah smiled and said, "Whatever are you talking about? A boring meeting with nothing out of the ordinary happening."

Sonia said, "Your dad would be proud. You handled yourself well as you took control of the room and used just enough force to make your point."

Savannah said, "My dad was a good teacher, an excellent soldier, and the best dad anyone could have. He taught me many things that have helped me. I used one lesson in the meeting today. When someone opposes you on the battlefield or anywhere else, bring hell itself down on them and make them regret crossing your path, annihilate them or make them dead. I did not have to use the last part today."

Morgan said, "That works on the battlefield but sometimes not so well in business."

Kirsten asked, "Can we stop, shop, talk and enjoy our meal?

Savannah, the necklace you are wearing is beautiful. Where did you get it?"

Savannah said as she touched it lovingly, "Mom gave it to me today."

Kirsten asked, "May I get a closer look?"

Savannah took the necklace off and handed it to Kirsten. The pendant was gold, about two inches long and one-and-a-half inches wide. It was the SF unit crest, the words *De Oppresso Liber* had been replaced with *You are my one love*. Kirstin turned it over, and on the back side was the name Akita.

Kirsten said, "Sonia, this is stunning. When did Akita give it to you?" Sonia said, "Several years ago. He made it for me from gold he found somewhere in South America on a riverbank. It's 1.0 kilograms (over two ounces). He had twice that much in weight. The jeweler kept the rest as payment. I had the diamonds placed on the knife blade and arrowheads and rubies set on the arrow fletches by the same jeweler later. I think adding the jewels made it stand out. Now my daughter has a gift from her dad and me." The piece was beautiful, but the meaning behind it was unsurpassed. The necklace was passed around the table and then back to Savannah.

Dining with the Boss

They ate a well-prepared meal and discussed the history of Texas, Germany, and royalty. They also talked about family, good friends, and other things. Savannah stood and said, "We must return to Texas in two days. I want to spend time with my mom. If she will have me after today."

Sonia said, "There is nothing I would like more than spending time with you. You have done nothing today to change that."

Everyone in the room was finishing and leaving. The employees took flights the next day to various parts of the world. Kirsten and Petra went home to their families and their work.

The day after that Savannah was at the Ludwig estate in her office when she called Ranger Vegas Lubbock's office. The receptionist answered the phone and said, "Lubbock Texas Rangers. My name is Sue. How may I help you?"

Savannah said, "My name is Savannah Haddox. May I speak to Ranger Vega, please?"

Sue informed her, "Vega was not in the office and asked, "How may I help you?"

Savannah said, "If you don't want an international incident attributed to your office, you will put Ranger Vega or Captain Castillo on now. Or do you still think you can help?"

Sue said, "You cannot threaten me or this office," and hung up.

Five minutes later, Captain Castillo called Savannah's phone. When her phone rang, she looked at the caller ID and did not answer. She looked at Lee Ann and said, "My call to the Chief worked. Let them stew and see how long before he calls back."

Lee Ann asked, "Why do you have to be mean about it? The receptionist had no way of knowing who you are or the office you hold."

Savannah's phone rang again. She looked at the caller ID and said, "That was quick."

Then she answered and put it on speaker phone. She said, "Bundesnachrichtendienst office, my name is Savannah. How may I be of assistance?"

A voice on the phone said, "Miss Haddox, this is Captain Castillo in the Lubbock Texas Ranger office. Before we start, I want to apologize for my receptionist. I want to tell you what has happened. Chief Harden called her, and before she could get her greeting out. This is what he did.

237

He said, 'This is Chief Harden. Then he yelled, asking her, 'Who the fuck do you think you are hanging up on, a fucking German Diplomat? Get Vega or Castillo to call Mis Haddox back right now. When you finish that, explain to Captain Castillo why you don't need to be fired. Do you fucking understand?' He hung up the phone before she could answer. Now that I have that out of the way. What may I do for you?"

Savannah said, "I have given your office all the evidence needed to have a judge issue arrest warrants for the ten CIA agents who murdered U.S. Army soldiers on American soil and three U.S. soldiers in the Middle East. I want the warrants on my desk here in Wetzlar tomorrow by 13:00. Do you understand?"

Castillo said, "Mis Haddox, I do not have the authority to send any warrants to Germany."

Savannah said, "Look at the email you just received from your Chief. That is all the authority you need. Or do I need to make another call?"

Castillo took a few seconds to respond. He said, "You will have them on your desk."

Savannah said, "Thank you for your cooperation. The BND is currently searching for your rogue agents. We will bring them in and hand them over to your office when we find them." She did not give him a chance to respond before she hung up.

CHAPTER 52
Capture Worldwide

It has been six months since Savannah gave the order to capture the CIA agents responsible for the deaths of her father and his men, the FRBs. Today the first call came into Uwe's call center. Liam Smith and Noah Johnson had been found by former Spearpoint Security personnel in Istanbul. Savannah called and notified Morgan that she needed a team in Istanbul, but he explained to her that he didn't have any way to insert a team into Istanbul.

Without hanging up on Morgan's call, Savannah picked up her other phone and called Uwe. He answered, "What do you need me to do?"

Savannah said, "I need a team placed in Istanbul, and time is short. We have found two."

Uwe said, "No problem. Have your team meet me at the Port of Algeciras in sixteen hours."

Savanah answered, "Let me see if Morgan can get them there." She picked up the other phone.

Morgan said, "I heard. I can have them there in time. Give me Uwe's number, and I will make all the arrangements with him. I'll call and keep you in the loop." She gave him the number and hung up that call.

Then she told Uwe, "Morgan will call you and set everything up. Please keep me informed. I want to know when you have them and when you lock them up."

Uwe said, "With pleasure. I have waited for this day as I know you have. If Morgan's team arrives on time, I should be able to have them in Turkey no more than three days from the time we meet in Port of Algeciras. I will also have them taken to Istanbul unseen." Uwe hung up.

Savannah then called Lee Ann. "I had to call and tell you the good news. I need you here to record what happens from this point forward." Then she filled her in.

Lee Ann said, "Call me when Morgan is in Turkey. I will free up all my time after that."

Days later, Savannah called. She stated, "Morgan's heavy team is in Turkey. They're on their way to Istanbul. Can you make it here within the hour?"

Lee Ann said, "Yes, I'm on my way." Savannah hung up before she could say goodbye. Then Lee Ann drove to the Chisum ranch.

She and Savannah waited patiently with no news for around thirty hours. Then the phone rang. Savannah put it on speakerphone and answered, "Yes, what do you have for me?"

Morgan said, "We have them. We had to take them by force. This was a bloody gunfight from start to finish."

Savannah asked, "Are you okay? Is anyone hurt?"

"I have one man with minor injuries, and one of Uwe's men also just minor stuff. Nothing to worry over. Tell Uwe I am impressed with his plans and how his men carried them out," Morgan said.

Savannah said, "I will. Please call when you arrive in Germany."

"You got it, boss," Morgan replied and hung up.

Savannah looked at Lee Ann and said, "All we need now is the other eight."

Lee Ann was about to say something when the phone rang. Savannah answered, "I know you have them moving to Germany now." She listened, then put the speaker on and said, "I have you on speaker. What did you say?"

It was Uwe. He said, "I have another call. Your men in Tajikistan have Lucas Wilson captured and need me to transport him. They stumbled upon him at a market, followed him, and an opportunity to take him occurred. They have him, and no one knows. I wish all of my shit was this easy. I will have him late tomorrow. I will let you know when I get him to Germany."

Savannah said, "Thank you. Morgan wanted me to tell you that your plans and men impressed him. So let your men involved in Turkey know I will double their pay."

Uwe laughed and said, "I will tell them, but if you keep this up, you will spoil them." Then he hung up.

Savannah looked at Lee Ann and said, "I don't believe this."

Lee Ann reassured her, saying, "We will get the rest of them soon." Then she asked, "What do you think Michael Skinner will do when he finds out about missing men?"

Savannah said, "I hope he starts to wonder and worry. I think he will after we take out three or four more of his men. I'll help him become paranoid. I have a plan, but I will need you and Robin to help. Will you?"

Lee Ann asked, "What do you have in mind?"

Savannah said, "I have an idea, but I need some information to make it work. Let me work it out, then I will tell you."

With the wind down, Lee Ann left and went home. Once more, she was asking wondering what Savannah was going to do next. Later, she was watching World News. Their top story was a gun battle in Istanbul and chase that covered several miles on crowded streets. Thirty-five police and military personnel had been killed. A man hunt was ongoing, but no one was in custody. Everyone would be alive if the CIA had not killed Akita.

Three days later, Savannah called Lee Ann. She said, "I need you here. We have another call. Please come as fast as you can."

"I'm on my way," Lee Ann said and hung up. She drove to Savannah's house, parked, and walked to the back door. Before she could knock, Savannah opened the door and said, "Get in here." She grabbed her arm, pulled her in, closed the door, turned, and said, "Three more have been located. We have a few details now."

"Savannah, I'm not sure I want to be part of this anymore," Lee Ann admitted.

Savannah stopped in mid-stride and, with a misunderstanding look on her face, asked, "Why? What brought this on?"

Lee Ann explained, "Your men have killed people. I know you want justice. The price for your justice is already too high."

Savannah said, "The fucking CIA killed my dad and his men. We do not know if they were the only ones. My dad and others were experimented on, and we do not know if they were the only ones either. The CIA will kill to keep this covered up, and you know it. So, what price should be paid to stop them? Do you want me to stop? What is my dad's life and his men's lives worth?"

Lee Ann said, "I do not know how to answer your questions. All I know is lives were lost in Istanbul."

Savannah replied, "My men killed them in self-defense, and you know that, also. Now you need to choose "in" or "out." You're smart enough to know that on the very first day we started this, it would be bloody. The people who were killed were trying to kill my men. What would you do if you were in my place? So, are you in or out?"

Thoughtfully, Lee Ann explained, "I know everything you just laid out is true. I just don't like the fact people have been killed, and more may die. Can you please keep the deaths of others to a minimum?"

Savannah said, "I feel bad, also, but if my men get shot at, they will shoot back, and they are deadly accurate. Are you with me or not?"

"Savannah, you know I have been with you from the start, and I will remain with you," Lee Ann said.

Savannah said, "Good, now let's get to work. I need coffee. Do you want a cup?"

They took their coffee to her office. Savannah called Uwe and put the phone on speaker.

Uwe answered, "I was going to call you. I have more information. We know that one man is in the capital city of the Congo, Kinshasa. There may be another. I am waiting on another report."

Savannah said, "Call me back when you know. I will call Morgan and give him the heads up."

Uwe said, "Good I will call you with an update when I know more."

Lee Ann asked Uwe, "I know you have the others in Germany. Where are you holding them?"

Uwe said, "They are safe, and escape is not possible."

Savannah interrupted and asked, "When you have more guests at your location, may I visit? I want to tell them why they are your guests and what will happen to them."

Uwe said, "It would please me to do this for you. I can tell them you do not have to do this yourself."

Savannah said, "Thank you for your offer, but I want to see them and look at their faces when I tell them who I am and why they are on my list."

"I understand it is personal, and you must deliver the message yourself," Uwe replied.

Savannah said, "Yes, I do. Start making the arrangements now for myself and Lee Ann to visit, please."

Uwe said, "I look forward to seeing you," and hung up.

Savannah asked, "Will you stay with me until Uwe calls back?"

Lee Ann affirmed, "Yes, I will. I need to call Malin and tell him where

I am and that I may be late getting home." She called Malin and told him what was happening. Wanting her to stay safe, he told her that if it got too late to stay overnight. Some twenty hours later, Uwe's call came in.

Uwe told Savannah, "I do not have all the information, but the CIA has something big going on in Kinshasa. I am told we have three men on your list there."

Savannah said, "Okay, the men I have there have done well. They called and gave me the information, also. I have them in Kinshasa doing surveillance for a customer on another issue. It seems that we have an overlap. Good for us, bad for the CIA."

Uwe stated, "I also have a few people there for my business interest. My reports are we have other forces in the area also. We do not know what is happening there, but whatever it is, tensions are heating up."

"I will have Morgan call you for the details. We will get a plan together and let you know. Okay?" Savannah asked.

Uwe said, "Sounds good. Let me know what you need" And hung up.

Lee Ann told Savannah that she needed to return home but that she'd be back soon. Savannah understood and told her to return as soon as she could.

Lee Ann returned home, showered, dressed, and cooked a meal for Malin. She also fed her pets. She was about to go back inside. Yoyo decided Lee Ann had to pet her. She would not leave her alone until she got her way. Lee Ann didn't mind, but she had a 120-pound bundle of teeth and claws playing and trying to be gentle with her at the same time. Lee Ann had to smile. A New York City girl on a ranch in Texas playing with a mountain lion. She realized at that moment what a good life she had and how happy she was.

Malin came out and sat with her. He smiled and asked, "Are you okay?"

Lee Ann said, "Yes," and hugged him. Then she told him, "I must go back to Savannah's. They're making plans to get more men on the list."

Malin said, "I hope they get all of them and make them pay with their lives."

Lee Ann asked, "You mean to pay in a courtroom, right?"

With an uneasy look, Malin said, "Yea, that is what I meant." Lee Ann knew the conflict in him. The CIA killed U.S. Service men, and he wanted blood. She chose not to push it.

Lee Ann yawned, stood up, and said, "You need to pay attention to your cat."

Malin said, "I love you, too." Then Lee Ann left and drove back to Savannah's.

Later that evening, Uwe called and said, "It is confirmed Theodore Thomas, Henry Sanderson, and Benjamin Davis are at the CIA station in Kinshasa. The whole city is in unrest. Police and military are everywhere."

Savannah said, "Thank you, I will pass it along. I do not know if we will try the apprehension with all the unrest. I will let you know either way." She hung up.

Savannah had Morgan on the phone for an hour, then put the speaker on.

Morgan said, "I think all the background shit will give us cover. We can take them at the station, and no one will be able to stop us. Give me the go order. I have everything in place."

Savannah said, "I will give it to you, but first what are your estimated casualties for us? I do not want to put men at risk if you don't think we can get this done."

Morgan said, "We can do this."

"Go get this done," Savannah demanded.

Morgan said, "Thank you for believing in me and your men. I will call when it is over, and we hand them over to Uwe. He has been informed about the pickup point." Then he ended the call.

As soon as Savannah hung up, her phone rang. She answered, and after a few seconds, she put the speaker on.

Savannah said, "Robin, I have you on speaker. Please tell Lee Ann what you just told me."

Robin said, "We know where William Miller, James Garcia, and Elijah Jones are. They are in the States"

"Where?" Lee Ann asked.

Robin said, "The CIAs training site Camp Peary. Savannah, we have their class schedule. They are training new recruits."

Savannah told Robin, "I will put you on a conference call with Morgan. Once you are on the call, I will leave. I need to call Uwe and make arrangements."

Savannah put Robin on the call with Morgan and hung up. Then Savannah was on the phone with Uwe. Lee Ann overheard her say, "I need you to smuggle three out of the States."

A few seconds later, she said, "Get it done. Thanks," she said before she hung up.

Savannah looked at Lee Ann and said, "We need to be in Wetzlar the day after tomorrow. Are you ready to travel?"

Lee Ann replied, "Yes, I have to call Malin."

In the next few minutes Savannah called Sonia and asked for the jet to be sent to Abilene. She thanked her and ended the call. The next call she made was to Robin, asking for the private number to Skinner's office." After a little while, she said, "I need it tomorrow at the latest."

Then another call came in, and she hung up the other call. She told Lee Ann, "The jet is on the way. We'll leave as soon as the crew and aircraft are ready. Go home and pack for a week."

CHAPTER 53
A Head Taken

Savannah and Lee Ann arrived at the Abilene airport. Some of Sonia's flight crew met them at the main door, and their bags were taken to the aircraft. They only had to show their passports. Then they boarded and were in the air within minutes. Over the intercom, the captain announced, "The flight time should be eight hours or less."

About an hour in the air Savannah's phone rang. She took the call, got Lee Ann's attention, and placed the call on speaker, informing Morgan that he was on.

Morgan said, "We have the men you wanted in Kinshasa. It was easy to get them with all the other shit going on. However, transport to a safe area for turnover to Uwe was another matter."

Savannah asked, "What went wrong?"

Morgan explained, "One of the assholes tried to escape. When this happened, the team handled it well. He was put down hard in the middle of the street by having his legs taken out from under him. Then he was dragged back to the truck and beaten until he was forced back inside. Some of the locals tried to help him. They were persuaded not to interfere. Four of them are dead. We have already handed them off and are returning to the States."

Savannah said, "After you get the men back safely, I need you in Wetzlar. I have been informed by the heavy team you assigned that the men we want from Camp Peary meet after classes at a bar, and they stay for some time. They asked me for six more men to assist with the extraction. I told them you would make that decision and give the order. So please make the call and let me know."

Morgan said, "I will take care of it and meet you in Wetzlar."

Savannah smiled at Lee Ann and said, "Now we start fucking with Skinner. I want him disorientated, scared, and unsure who he can trust. I have Robin and her entire section working on it as we speak. A man that General Scott trained is a CIA agent now and is assigned to CIA headquarters. He will keep us informed of Skinner's movements."

"Is this man loyal to Scott or the CIA?" Lee Ann asked.

Savannah said, "Scott told him that Skinner killed his men. Men he served with. He is loyal to the U.S. and its laws and Scott."

Lee Ann asked, "How does Scott instill and maintain this level of loyalty in his men even after they leave his unit?"

"He has that same level of loyalty for them," Savannah explained. "He will back them in front of others no matter what. Even if they are wrong, and he knows it. He will tear their shit up from one end to the other when they are alone. He gets his pound of flesh, and the men will not make the mistake again."

The rest of the flight was uneventful. They landed In Germany at 03:00. Sonia met them at the airport, and her driver drove them to Wetzlar.

Upon their arrival, Savannah told Sonia what had happened and why they were in Germany.

Walking into Sonia's home still took Lee Ann's breath away. Again, even at this time of night, Monika took them to their rooms, looking completely put together and not showing a lack of sleep.

Later in the morning, Sonia's staff prepared and served breakfast in style. Lee Ann and Savannah had been used to country life, and this lifestyle was so far outside their normal, in a word, it could be described as "uncomfortable" to them. Sonia joined them. She said, "I called Uwe. He will be here within the hour."

Savannah asked, "Will you go with us to see the men that took so much from us?"

Sonia said, "No. If I do, I am afraid I will shoot them myself." They finished their meal and prepared for the trip.

Monika knocked on Lee Ann's door and said, "Miss Lee Ann, Uwe has arrived and is waiting on you and Lady Savannah."

"Thank you. I will be right down," Lee Ann replied. As she left, she went down the main staircase and saw Savannah and Uwe in the entrance room.

Savannah said, "Uwe just told me we have about a two-hour drive. Lee Ann, do you need anything for your work before we leave?"

"No, I have all I need," she answered.

Uwe said, "Please come with me." He turned and started walking to the door. Savannah and Lee Ann followed him out to the car. Uwe's driver was waiting for them and opened the car doors. When they were inside, Uwe told the man, "You know where we are going. Get us there quickly."

When they were about thirty minutes into the trip. Uwe told them, "We are going to a bunker and housing area built fifty meters underground during the war. I bought it for my business. I have repaired most of it. The area where we are holding the men is secure. It is where I keep sensitive cargo. The walls are one meter (three foot) thick reinforced concrete, and the steel doors are fifty millimeters (two inches) thick."

Savannah asked, "Do you have another place to hold one man without the others knowing?"

Uwe said, "Yes, but it is in part of the bunker that I have not repaired yet. The conditions there are not suited for humans."

Savannah asked, "Once you have them in this location, can they escape?"

Uwe said, "No."

"Perfect, we can use it," Savannah replied. "I will ask one in the group a question, and when he does not answer, I will tell you to kill him. You take him away, and the other men never see him again. You then come back and say it is done. They will think he is dead, and they will not want to be killed, so they will tell us what we need to know."

Uwe said, "Yes, we can do that. I have sixteen men there now, and the other three will arrive before we do. I also have a man there that I have a contract on. I am trying to increase my fee. I need to put him in with the others. If you do not mind."

Savannah said, "I do not mind, and I will not interfere with your business."

Uwe made a call. They overheard him say, "Has Emil's man given you the information?" Then he said, "Good, strip him down to his underwear and cuff him. Then put him in with the other three when they get there. Lock him up with them. Do it now."

After this, Uwe did his best to be a tour guide. He was good at it. They turned onto an old road, and the driver stopped and opened a locked gate. They arrived and were met at the doors by armed men. They let them in and closed the doors behind them. Uwe led them down one hallway and to the elevators. He took his security very seriously with armed men at every hall and level, cameras, and much more.

They arrived on the floor that Uwe had selected, and the doors opened. They stepped out, and again Uwe led them down a hallway to a set of double doors with armed men waiting for them. As they approached, one man said, "Mr. Dietrich, everything is ready."

Uwe said, "Open the door, and we do not want to be disturbed." As they went inside the room, Uwe explained, "This room is twelve meters (forty feet) wide and eighteen meters (sixty feet) long. He opened a locked door. Behind that door was a wall of steel bars and a smaller door. Inside this cell were ten men cuffed and dressed only in their underwear. Uwe continued, "As you can see, Savannah, I have done what you asked. I have taken everything except their underwear. They are being fed, and no one is beating them."

One man yelled, "Why are we here? You have no right to hold us. We are U.S. citizens and demand to speak to the U.S. consulate."

Uwe started to speak, "Shut the fuck—" Savannah cut him off by placing her hand on his arm.

Then she said in an ice cold, uncaring voice, "How dare you demand anything. You are nothing more than a fuckhead who does not deserve to live on my planet. You are here because I made a simple request of my friend." She pointed at Uwe. Then she turned her attitude and voice utterly devoid of humanity. No one, including hardened criminals, had a way this scary.

Savannah added, "I want you to think what will happen when I make a demand of my friend, like taking your head off."

Uwe said, "The men they killed. They were friends of mine. They saved my life more than once. My debt to them is now my debt to you. So, I will do as you ask. No demand is necessary."

Savannah placed her hand over Uwe's heart and said, "Thank you."

Uwe placed his hand over Savannah's and said, "Ask, and it is yours."

The man said, "Fuck you. You are nothing when the people I work for get me out. I will ensure neither of you ever see the light of day again."

Savannah waited for him to finish, then asked, "Do you mean the CIA? Now let me tell you, no one knows where you are. So, you are here for as long as I please. Now do you know who I am or why you are in here?"

The man said nothing.

Savannah turned to Uwe and asked, "Which one is he? What is his name?"

Uwe walked to a desk in the room and pulled out several IDs. He went through them one by one and then said, "Liam Smith."

Savannah said, "Liam, you and your roommates are here at my request. I had my men collect you and bring you here. The reason is simple: each one of you killed a U.S. serviceman. Twelve in all. Only three were killed outside the States. The rest of them were killed inside the States. You should know the CIA cannot operate inside the U.S. I wanted to have my men kill all of you when and where we found you. You are only alive because one person asked me not to kill you. Now what do you think?"

All the men were saying at once, "We did not kill anyone you do not know what the fuck you are talking about."

Savannah smiled and said, "Clint Haddox, Ed Johnson, Bobby Wade, John Laws, Steve Jackson, Kody Lunsford, San Hawk, Paul Martinez, Joe Metcalf, Jody Lucero, Harold Powell, and Kevin Viraman. Now, if their names don't ring a bell with you, I can tell you the one you killed and each of you killed. Now let me tell you where I got my information from: Agent Arthur Woods."

The room went silent.

Another man spoke up loud and angrily, "Fuck you. You don't have anything on us, or we would be in jail, not here."

Savannah looked at Uwe. He already had the ID. He said, "Noah Johnson."

Savannah asked, "Do you want to know how I know your real names? I will tell you I have a team of the most intelligent people in the world working for me. I have everything that you have ever done. I will keep you here until I have all the men responsible for killing U.S. S.F. soldiers. My friend here tells me he can keep you here for years. Think about this. I have the evidence to put you away for life. As for the ones who killed soldiers in Texas, I can get a death sentence."

Another man asked, "What do you want?"

Savannah smiled and said, "I want the rest of you here. When I get that, I will decide if I have you killed or not."

The man said, "You fucking bitch," and then he fell silent.

Savannah said, "I want all of you mother fuckers to know just how much I do not care if you live or die." Savannah turned to Uwe and said, "Pick one. I don't care which one. Take him outside and remove his head."

Uwe went to the entry door, opened it, and returned with the guards. He told them, "I want that one," and pointed to one man in the cell. The guards unlocked the door, went inside, and pulled the man out.

He was frantically kicking and yelling, "You cannot do this. I will do anything you want. Please stop, have mercy." Uwe hit him hard in the side of his head, and the man's body went limp.

One man said, "We play this game all the time. You are not going to kill him. All that will happen is you will put him in another room."

Uwe looked hard at him and said, "You don't know what the fuck you are talking about. She asked for his head, which is exactly what she will get."

Everyone in the cell was yelling, "Fuck you. You won't do shit."

One of the guards returned with a heavy looking bag. He gave it to Uwe. Uwe opened it and took out the head of the man he had his guards take out. Uwe looked into the cell and said, "I did as she asked."

Silence filled the room. Lee Ann was horrified and tried not to vomit.

The men in the cell were in total disbelief. Some of them were shaking uncontrollably.

At that moment, they knew their lives depended on what Savannah did next. They did not want to piss her off. Savannah, Uwe, and his men stood unmoved, staring into the cell.

Savannah looked into the cell and said, "The removal of your heads cost me nothing.

I will have one of you separated and ask him a question. I will decapitate him if I do not get the information I need. Then I will separate another and another until someone gives me what I want or until all your heads are on the floor." She pointed at the head, looked at Uwe, and said, "Leave it there. I want them to look at it every day and know what awaits them." Then she turned to look in the cell and asked, "Do you still think I am playing a game now?"

No one said a word.

Savannah told Uwe, "If one of them gives you any shit, cut all of their rations in half."

Uwe smiled and said, "Nothing will please me more."

Another man yelled out, "I want out of here. What kind of deal can I get?"

Savannah said, "Death is your only way out at this time." She turned to Uwe and said, "I am finished here. Please escort us out."

Uwe did not say a word. He closed the steel door, locked it, and they left.

When they were outside the compound, Lee Ann was pissed off and scared. Yelling, she asked Savannah, "Have you lost your fucking mind? A man was killed, and you used it as nothing more than a scare tactic. You just made me part of a murder."

Uwe spoke up, "She had nothing to do with that and did not know what I would do. I had to do this. That man was right. They knew the game we were going to play. The CIA plays the same game on other people all the time. The man that I killed was a pedophile. He killed five kids that are known, including the child of my client. I was under contract to do this. If I did not follow through with it, someone else would have, and a contract would be placed on me. Did I use his death to our benefit? Yes, I did. Now they know we are serious. We did the world a favor with his death."

Savannah said, "What is done is done. We cannot change it, and I don't think I would.

Uwe, I want you to fuck with them. Keep them up for days with spotlights and loud noise. Then spray water on them and turn the temp down to near freezing. Keep them in the dark for days. Change the times you feed them. Fuck up everything. Interrogate them individually twenty-four hours a day every day. Force them to do heavy hard work without any breaks."

Uwe said, "I know what you need, and I have done it many times before. What Information do you want?"

Savannah said, "I have all I need to have them put in prison for life. I have some evidence on Skinner. I need a smoking gun and some documentation. I want a death sentence on him."

Uwe said, "I will do what is needed to get this for you."

Savannah added, "Every day, make sure to tell them their lives are in my hands. Ask questions about who ordered the killings and why. Record everything they say. I will find someone who can use it in court against Michael Skinner."

Uwe said, "I never want to be on your bad side, and I deal with fucked up, backstabbing lowlife mother fuckers who think they are badasses."

The car ride back to Wetzlar was silent. Once Lee Ann and Savannah were out of Uwe's car at Sonia's estate, Lee Ann's knees tried to buckle. She was able to stay upright, but she was still scared and pissed off. She lashed out at Savannah and said, "Don't ever put me in a situation like that again. I want to go home now. I never want to see you again. When I get back, I am going to the police."

Savannah stood right in front of her and said, "If you do, Uwe will have you eliminated. I did not know he was going to kill a man. When he did, it made me sick."

Lee Ann replied, "No, you did *not* get sick. You stood there and gave the order to have that man's head removed."

Savannah said, "When I gave that order, I thought Uwe was going to do as we discussed on the trip and put the man in a different cell. All I wanted was to have them think he was dead."

Lee Ann was still angry, but now she understood that Savannah didn't know what Uwe was capable of. "What are we going to do?" she asked. "Uwe just did a contract killing in front of us. He has no regard for life."

Savannah asked, "What did you think would happen when we entered his world? His world is like that every day. Had I known what he would do, I would not have asked you to go with us."

"What did he mean when he said he owed his life more than once to your dad and his men?" Lee Ann asked.

Savannah said, "One night, some of the FRBs stopped a beating and took the victim to the hospital. That victim was Uwe. My dad stopped an assassination attempt on Uwe a year or so later. My dad killed five men. Uwe made all the evidence disappear. Uwe told me this story the last time we met." Then she added, "I need him and his organization. Without him, we would never be able to move the people we capture."

Lee Ann asked, "What happens if he turns on us?"

"Uwe is not a stupid man, he knows the army of men at my command, will crush him and his organization," Savannah explained.

Without thinking, Lee Ann observed, "He is afraid of you."

Savannah smiled and said, "He should be."

CHAPTER 54
Skinner's Orders

Lee Ann and Savannah started to walk inside when Savannah's phone rang. It was Uwe. She put the call on speaker. Uwe said, "Miller just gave us what you wanted. None of them were willing to follow the orders until Skinner put the orders in writing. He also said something about the orders to all the men. They have a list of the individuals to be killed and a list of the agents assigned to kill each one, and it is signed by Skinner. He said they made Skinner do this to cover their asses in case they got caught." Uwe added, "I have the bank name and address, the safe deposit box number, and where he hid the key. Savannah, you will have to pick it up. I am not allowed in the U.S. If I go, I will be arrested."

Savannah copied the information and said, "Uwe, keep up the pressure on them. This is good, but there may be more." Then she hung up.

Savannah did not move. She called Robin, put the call on speaker, and said, "Robin, I know I woke you, but I need you to make a fake ID for Morgan with the name William Miller on it." Then she gave the bank and box information to Robin. "One more thing," she added, "the key to the box is hidden here." She gave the location. "Have Morgan pick it up. Tell him he will receive resistance at that location and to go in heavy."

Robin repeated all the information back to make sure she had it right. Then she said, "I have this for you. I hope it is what they told you."

Savannah said, "If it is, copy everything in the box and then have Morgan give it to Vega."

Robin said, "I will," and hung up.

Savannah and Lee Ann went inside.

Savannah wanted to stay in Wetzlar for another week. She wanted more information and was hoping Uwe would get it. Sonia was happy to have them. Lee Ann had learned so much about her and Wetzlar, but this easygoing time ended with one call. They were eating breakfast when General Scott called. Savannah checked the caller ID and answered with the phone on speaker.

Scott said, "Please let me tell you what I know before you say or ask anything.

Skinner's Orders

Savannah said, "Okay, Lee Ann and I will listen."

Scott started, "My man in CIA Headquarters was in a meeting where an analyst informed the leadership of reports that some agents had disappeared. One man had said, 'This is not unusual. In fact, what they do sometimes requires being off the map.' The analyst said, 'You are correct when they are overseas. I am talking about three men that disappeared from Camp Peary. After they dismissed class one day and went drinking. The next morning, they did not show up to train the recruits.' Another man said, 'I talked to several people in the bar that night. We know that Miller, Garcia, and Jones were there, and no one has seen them since.' This is when Skinner started getting uneasy and said, 'We have had others taken and have not been heard from. I know all the men that have been taken. Someone is targeting us.' A man at the table said, 'Bull shit, no one is that stupid. Why do you think all of this is interlocked?' The meeting ended unexpectedly with another analyst busting in and saying, 'We have a problem.' Skinner has requested extra security at his house and more on his detail. He is scared."

Savannah said, "Thank you. I do not think we should do anything now. We still need to find Oliver Williams. Let Skinner be paranoid. We can use it. I want that fucker to think everyone is after him."

Scott said, "That is all I have for you. I will call you when I have more," then he hung up.

Lee Ann and Savannah finished eating and were cleaning up when Savannah's phone rang again. Lee Ann asked, "I wonder what he forgot to tell you?"

Savannah looked at the ID and said, "It's Robin." She answered and, again, put the speaker on.

Robin said, "I found Williams. He died a year ago."

Savannah asked, "Are you sure, or is the CIA hiding him?"

Robin said, «I know that he's dead. You have all of them now. What do you need me to do next?"

Savannah said, "Nothing yet. I need to call Morgan. Thank you, Robin. After my call, I will let you know what we will do next."

Robin said, "You know where I am," and hung up.

Savannah called Morgan. She left the speaker on. He answered, "Boss, what do you need from me?"

Skinner's Orders

Savannah told him, "Robin called and told us Williams is dead. We have everyone involved except Skinner."

Morgan said, "I have a plan. We can turn over the men that Uwe has to Vega and get Skinner simultaneously. I need you to call Uwe and have him move the men to Texas. After you know where and when they will land, call me. I will have men there to meet them. I will transport them to the ranch. If that is okay with you and Bernadette?"

Savannah said, "Yes, that will work. Morgan, Uwe told me that Liam Smith has orders in a safe that Skinner gave him."

Morgan said, "We already have the orders that Skinner gave to kill your dad and his men."

Savannah said, "I am not talking about those orders. He has orders in writing and recordings of Skinner ordering the death of others. He has done this before, and Smith has what we need to prove it."

Morgan said, "Text me the address, and I will get the safe. It will be easier to open it at my office."

Savannah did so and called Uwe. "Move them now to Texas, "she said. "Text me the landing time and location. Morgan will take it from there."

Savannah looked at Lee Ann and said, "We need to be in Texas yesterday."

She then asked Sonia for her jet. Sonia gave it without any hesitation. They were in the air four hours later.

Morgan met them at the airport. On the way home, Lee Ann slept, and they made plans.

She woke up to Morgan yelling, "I don't give a fuck. You cannot go on the raid of Skinner's house. I need you to deliver the other men to Vega simultaneously with the raid. That way, Skinner cannot find out and run."

Savannah said, "I will fucking do this your way, but I get to deliver Skinner to Vega myself. Do you fucking understand me?"

Morgan backed off and said, "You will have at least twenty men behind you, or I will not let you take him in."

Morgan's phone rang. He answered, "What?" After the call, he looked at Savannah and said, "When you take Skinner in, you will have a briefcase."

Skinner's Orders

Savannah asked, "Why?"

Morgan said, "We have opened the safe. Skinner is one sick mother fucker. Vega needs the paperwork and recordings in his hand when you give Skinner to him."

Savannah asked, "What is all of it?"

Morgan said nothing. He left the next day to meet Uwe at the coast.

A box truck and six armored SUVs arrive at the ranch. Savannah's men are driving, and more men are heavily armed in the SUVs. The truck is parked, guards are set in place, and the back is not opened.

Savannah called Morgan. All she said was, "It is here." Then Savannah walked away.

Savannah woke Lee Ann at midnight and said, "It is time we need to leave now."

All the SUVs and the truck were running when Savannah and Lee Ann walked outside. A man opened the door on the lead SUV they got in, and the group left. It was one in the morning.

Savannah called Morgan to tell him they were on the way, that she'd call again when they were in place.

The man sitting with Lee Ann handed Savannah a briefcase and said, "Make sure that fucking Skinner gets the death penalty."

Savannah said, "If he doesn't, I will kill him myself."

"I like working for you," the man said.

Savannah asked, "What's your name?"

He smiled and said, "My name is Andy."

They arrived at the Texas Ranger Headquarters at two in the morning. Savannah called Morgan to tell him that they had arrived. She then called and said, "Get your sorry ass down here now. I have a gift for you. I am at your office. Call me when you get here."

An hour later, Savannah's phone rang she answered it. She said, "I will meet you at the door."

"Showtime!" Savannah said to the man in the SUV with them.

He spoke on his headset only one word, "Move." All hell broke loose with men moving to shooting positions.

Savannah walked to the box truck and told the guard to open the door. He did so. As the men were handed over to Savannah, it was clear that they were covered in what looked like mud, slime, blood, and other

Skinner's Orders

waste. Their movements were slow, they seemed broken inside, lethargic, and lacked the will to live. The breeze changed directions, and the air around them was thick with the smell of human feces, urine, rotting flesh, and other scents one could not, nor did not, want to identify. Some of the men were trying not to gag. Savannah took the lead chain from the guard. She was holding a lead chain in her left hand, and it was hooked to a steel collar on the first man's neck. The briefcase was in her right hand. That man had a parachute cord tied to his nut sack, and it led back to the man behind him to his steel collar. This continued down the line to the last man. The last man had the parachute cord around his nut sack, which led back to Savannah's guard, holding the cord. All the men had their hands cuffed behind their backs, and their right ankle had a shackle around it and a chain going to the man's right ankle behind.

Savannah had them secured this way to prevent anyone from trying to escape. If anyone tried anything, all it would take to control them would be one yank on the chain, and all would suffer. She walked across the parking lot to the main doors of the Ranger Headquarters, where Vega was waiting. She stopped in front of Vega, handed him the chain, and said, "In this case, are the warrants you sent me for these men and new evidence I have collected about Skinner's orders to kill the FRBs. I also have orders written and signed by Skinner for other killings."

Vega started to speak, but Savannah cut him off before he got one word out. She said, "There are audio files also. I have copied everything, so if it gets lost, like the CIA takes it from you, I still have it."

Vega said, "I will go through it, copy all the documents, and record the audio files to thumb drives. I will turn the originals into the evidence room and put the copies in a safe that only I can access at the gun range."

Savannah asked, "Will they be safe there?"

Vega said, "Only the three of us know where they are."

Savannah said, "I need an arrest warrant for Michael Skinner, and I need it yesterday. Do you understand?"

Vega said, "I do not want to know what that means. I will tell you when a judge has it signed." Vega's nose wrinkled, his eyes watered, and his face lost color. He asked, "What the fuck did you put these men in to get them here, a fucking sewer?"

Lee Ann said, "I have smelled the fucking sewers of New York, and they have nothing on this stench."

Savannah smiled and said, "I don't smell anything. What are you complaining about?"

Vega said, "Something is seriously wrong with you."

Savannah looked at Lee Ann and said, "We gave him his birthday present. Let's go before he wants our help cleaning it." She turned and walked away.

Lee Ann told Vega, "I am sorry about this, but you know how she is," and then she followed Savannah to the SUV.

Vega stood there in total disbelief. He found his phone and called for more men.

CHAPTER 55
FACE TO FACE WITH SKINNER

Lee Ann and Savannah were twenty miles outside of Lubbock when Savannah's phone rang. She looked at the caller Id, answered the call, and put it on speaker.

Morgan said, "All went well. We have him and are on our way to you."

Savannah asked, "What are our losses?"

Morgan said, "None, we did not even get a scratch. I will fill you in when I get there," he hung up.

They arrived at Bernadette's ranch as the sun was coming up. She met them in the drive and asked, "Is everyone all right? Did anyone get arrested?"

Lee Ann was closest to her, so she said, "No one got hurt or arrested."

Savannah said, "We have men that need sleep. Can I put them in the bunkhouse?"

Bernadette said, "Yes, and park the trucks in the barn."

Savannah told Bernadette, "We will have more guests arriving around six or seven o'clock this evening."

Bernadette asked, "Is one of them named Skinner, I hope?"

Savannah said, "Yes, Morgan got him."

They were tired, but Savannah led the men to the bunkhouse and returned to her house. Lee Ann was waiting for her there. She said, "I need to let Malin know we are back and that I am fine."

"Let him know we will be working all night," Savannah said, "and I need you there with me." Then she asked, "Do you want to be with me, or do you need to go home and spend time with Malin?"

Lee Ann asked, "Are you going to turn Skinner over to Vega tonight?"

Savannah said, "That is the plan. Nothing can stop me now. We are so close. All I want now is to let that mother fucker know who has done this to him. To look at him and say you are going to jail, and then you will get the death penalty, and I will watch you die."

"I will be with you, but I need to go home and let Malin know that he still has a wife," Lee Ann said.

Savannah said, "Thank you. Now I need sleep." With that, she went to her bedroom.

Lee Ann borrowed a ranch pickup from Bernadette and drove home. Malin woke her at noon and said that Savannah had called to say that Morgan will arrive around six o'clock this evening. Malin was being nice to Lee Ann. He let her sleep past the time she had set the alarm clock for, and he had made breakfast of eggs, bacon, hashbrowns, and coffee.

As they enjoyed the meal, talked about her involvement. Malin said, "You are no longer writing the story. You are part of it now. Are you sure that you can remain objective?"

Lee Ann said, "When I started reporting this story, I was an outsider looking in. Now I have moved here and married you. The people here have included me in their family, and you are right. I am part of this story. It has changed me. In fact, it has consumed every aspect of my life for years. If I quit now, I will let you and everyone who has served this country down. I am unwilling to have Skinner kill soldiers and get away with it."

Malin said, "Good. Do you need my help?"

"Yes, I need you to be here for me when this is over. Now I need to go, Morgan will be here soon, and I want to see Skinner's face when Savannah tells him his future," Lee Ann said.

Malin hugged her and said, "Go get him."

She left and drove to Bernadette's ranch. More of Savannah's men had arrived when she did, and it looked like they were preparing for war. She found Bernadette and asked, "What's wrong?"

Bernadette said, "Savannah wants to be ready for anything." Lee Ann asked where she was and what she could do to help. Bernadette smiled and said, "She needs you as a friend now, not as a reporter. Ask yourself what will happen when she has that mother fucking Skinner here? I am pissed off enough to kill him. He killed my nephew. He killed her father. What will she do?"

Lee Ann stared at Bernadette and asked, "Do you think she will kill him?"

Bernadette said, "If I had her strength, fighting ability, and armed men at my back, I would kill him without a second thought." She did not

Face to Face with Skinner

let Lee Ann reply before she walked away.

Lee Ann found Savannah in her house. She asked her, "Do you want coffee or iced tea?"

"I need coffee," Lee Ann replied.

Savannah said, "I do not want to discuss this now. Can we talk about anything else?"

They drank coffee and gossiped until the phone rang. She picked it up and answered. The call lasted a few minutes. When she hung up, she said, "Everything is in place here and in Lubbock. Now we wait."

Morgan arrived an hour and a half late. He was in a group of fifteen SUVs. They were guided to a specific area prepped for security and then stopped.

Savannah, Bernadette, Will, and Lee Ann met Morgan and Robin as they stepped out of an SUV. With the men Morgan had with him, they were in the middle of fifty plus armed men ready to attack or defend against any threat.

Savannah said, "We are secure. We have overwatch and overlapping fields of fire. Where is that fucking Skinner?"

Morgan gave a hand signal, and Skinner was taken out of an SUV. He was in his underwear, and his hands cuffed behind his back.

Will stepped forward and told Skinner, "Welcome to my home, you fucking son of a bitch."

Skinner said, "Buddy I don't know who the fuck you think you are, but you just kidnapped the Deputy Executive Director of the CIA. I will make sure all of you will pay with your lives."

Savannah, standing a short distance away, said, "Buddy. Did you just call him 'Buddy'?"

Skinner said, "You're fucking right I did. I did not fucking stutter."

Savannah looked at Will and asked, "Do you want a buddy?"

Will answered, "Fuck no, I don't want a buddy, and I don't want to be a buddy."

Savannah asked Skinner, "Do you know the definition of a buddy?"

Before Skinner could speak, Savannah said, "I will tell you the definition. A buddy is a man who goes to the red-light district, gets two blow jobs, and then brings one back for you. Are you sure he is your buddy?"

Skinner yelled out, "Fuck you. You stupid fucking bitch. I will enjoy putting you in prison."

Morgan told Skinner, "I don't think you know who you are talking to." He pointed to Will and said, "He did not bring you here." Then he pointed at Savannah and said," She did."

Savannah approached Skinner and said, "I have the men you are missing, and now I have you."

She looked hard at Skinner's face and asked Morgan, "Do you know where he got that scar on his forehead from?" He had an old, ugly scar that started at his left eyebrow and went up and across his forehead and into his hairline above and behind his right eye.

Morgan said," I have no idea."

Savannah said, "The doctor gave it to him. When he was circumcised." Everyone started laughing. Savannah was now standing right in front of Skinner.

Skinner said, "Fuck you." Then he spit, and it landed on her face. Savannah slapped Skinner so hard with her right hand that his head snapped violently to the side, and his feet left the ground with the impact. His body hit the ground hard.

One of the guards that took Skinner out of the SUV bent down and checked for a pulse at his neck. He looked up and said, "He is not dead."

Savannah told the guard, "Go get the ammonia tablets out of the first aid kit." The guard was back within a few seconds with the kit. Savannah took out all the Ammonia inhalant tablets, about eight. She broke them, held Skinner's head from behind in her left arm, and placed her right hand with all the tablets over his nose. Skinner started jerking and kicking. Savannah did not let him go.

She yelled, "I want you to feel the pain, all of it, for as long as I want you to. Your fucking life is in my hands now. Can you fight or just have others do it for you?"

Morgan grabbed Savannah's arms, trying to pry them away from Skinner. He strained, his muscles bulging. Savannah did not move under his assault. He could not break her grip.

He then grabbed her around her waist and lifted her with a tremendous amount of power. Her grip did not loosen or break. The upper half of Skinner's body came off the ground with her.

Face to Face with Skinner

Morgan yelled, "You are going to kill him!"

Savannah's grip held.

Bernadette ran to Savannah's side and yelled, "Mi Hija, please let him go." Savannah released her grip. Still under the strain of lifting her, Morgan lost his footing and grip at the same time and plunged to the ground, Savannah on top of him.

Savannah hit the ground, rolled backward, and flipped back to her feet. The look of pure anger was on her. She was pissed off and had Morgan in her sight.

Morgan made it to his feet and started backing up quickly, waving his hands in front of his body and saying, "I am on your side. I could not let you kill him." Savannah did not care. She would get her pound of flesh, and Morgan was as good of a target as any.

Andy, the man who had told her that he liked working for her, stepped in front of her. He was holding a bottle of water and a four-by-four bandage from the first aid kit. He said, "You have something on your face. May I clean it off for you?" His hands were shaking as he poured water on the bandage. He held out his hand, shaking worse now, and cleaned Savannah's face.

He dropped the wet bandage and opened another package. He took the dry bandage and said, "I need to get the water off now."

Savannah tried to smile. She reached out, hugged Andy, kissed him, and said, "Thank you."

Bernadette hugged Savannah and said, "You are not angry at Morgan. He was trying to stop you from murdering that dick head."

A man ran up with a medical bag and started to look at Skinner. His left cheek was swelling. Blood and an almost clear liquid seeped through the skin. Lee Ann asked the man tending to him, "Any broken bones?"

He looked at her and said, "He should have. It looks like he was hit by a truck. She hit him so hard that his grandkids will have a handprint on their faces as a birthmark. I will know more later. He has a concussion and is in a lot of pain." He pointed at Skinner's eye and said, "She slapped him so hard that the blood vessels in his eye ruptured."

Savannah went to Morgan and said, "I have never bitch slapped anyone before. My dad only showed me how to punch with a closed fist. I am sorry. I should not have lost my cool."

Then she asked, "What would you have done if Andy hadn't stepped in and saved you?"

Morgan said, "I do not know. I had a half-werewolf, half-saber tooth tiger in a human female body coming at me with evil intentions on her mind."

Savannah smiled and asked, "Did you just call me that?" Her demeanor changed, and she walked over to Andy, put her arm around his waist, and asked, "Morgan is this man one of yours?"

Morgan said, "Yes, he is. Why?"

Savannah said, "We need to give this man a bonus. He has balls. He put himself between you and me and wiped the spit off a half-werewolf, half-saber tooth tiger's face."

Morgan, smiling, asked, "How much?"

With a devilish evil grin, Savannah said, "Five grand, but we need to take some back because he kissed his boss."

Andy said, "No, my boss kissed me."

Savannah laughed and asked, "Morgan did you kiss him?"

Morgan said, "Hell no."

Savannah said, "He just said his boss kissed him."

Andy turned red and said, "Please let me go."

Then he turned to Morgan and said, "I am sorry."

Morgan said, "Relax, she is just fucking with both of us."

While they had some downtime, Lee Ann's reporter instinct engaged, and she asked Morgan about retrieving Skinner.

He said, "We scouted his office and home. We set upon his house. Robin took out all the Wi-Fi. I had men take out all the cell towers within two hundred miles. We went in at three in the morning and silently took out his security detail. Some of them will need to see a doctor. Once inside, we cleared the house and entered his bedroom. Four of us restrained him and his wife.

I told his wife that we would call the police, so they could untie her. This is the funny part. She asked me, 'What the fuck has he done now?' So, I gave her the short story. She told me, 'Take him, and I hope he dies along the way.' We had no problems getting here."

They left the ranch at one o'clock in the morning on the way to Lubbock and arrived at 2:30 a.m. They set out overwatch and placed men around the Texas Ranger Headquarters.

Thirty minutes later, Morgan called Vega and said, "We have one more for you. Get here and pick him up." He hung up before Vega could say anything.

It took Vega about thirty minutes to arrive in the parking lot. He stopped at the door.

Savannah led Skinner to Vega. Skinner was in his underwear, hands cuffed behind his back, ankles shackled, a parachute cord tied around his nut sack. Savannah held the other end.

Vega looked at Skinner's face and asked, "What the fuck did you do to him?"

Savannah said, "He fell getting in the truck."

Vega said, "Several investigations and criminal charges are pending now because of you and your men.

Savannah said, "I kept the correct names and places for what the CIA and others did. I changed all the others."

Vega said, "Yes, you were clever with that move, and it will make investigating the FRB's life difficult. If the government tries, it will look like retribution."

"Vega, the CIA killed twelve U.S. soldiers and others. I proved it," Savannah replied.

"They did it to avenge Mr. Skinner's family, this fuck head. His brother was a traitor who the FRBs brought back to the U.S., and justice was served. He received a death sentence. You have all the evidence that we found on the CIA's illegal activity."

Vega took Skinner by the arm and said, "I will need to ask you questions later. Do not leave the state.

They returned to the ranch.

CHAPTER 56
THE GIFT

Savannah and Lee Ann returned to Wetzlar. Sonia met them at the airport and drove them to her home. Upon arrival, Monika was waiting for them. She smiled and said, "Lady Savannah, I have your apartment prepared. Christina and I will attend to your luggage. Please follow me. You must be tired from your trip."

Monika put Lee Ann in a suite next to Savannah. The three of them spoke briefly, then retired for the night. The next morning, they were served breakfast in the great hall. Savannah looked at Sonia and said," May I use a sword from the armory, the two-handed broadsword in the locked glass case?"

Sonia replied, "That sword belonged to our great grandfather five generations ago. Many swords here are in better shape and more beautiful. Can you use one of those?"

Savannah said, "I want to honor Dad and his brothers. I want to use a battle tested blade forged in the blood of war."

Sonia acknowledged, "You picked the right one. That blade was used in some of the bloodiest battles and by three kings. It is yours by right. I will disable the alarm and unlock it for you. I want to accompany you."

Savannah smiled and said, "Mom, nothing would please me more. I would love to have you there with me."

Savannah looked at Lee Ann and asked, "Lee Ann, Sis, will you please join us?"

She answered in the affirmative.

Sonia and Savannah collected the large sword. Savannah was carrying it easily in one hand. It was as if she were born to wield a weapon. She had accomplished many feats in the art of combat, but this action was still amazing. Now she leads a highly skilled and deadly army with the ability to operate worldwide. Her men respect her and call her their Queen. She is young, strong, beyond rich, and beautiful. Lee Ann looked on in amazement as she thought about the first time she met her on a ranch in Texas.

They arrived at Akita's grave. Savannah drove the point of her ancient sword into the ground, knelt on one knee, held the weapon halfway down the blade with her right hand, bowed her head, and said, "Dad, I hope you are proud of me."

Sonia and Lee Ann looked at each other in disbelief. Before they could say anything, Savannah spoke again. Sonia and Lee Ann stood in silence. Savannah raised her head to look at Akita's headstone and said, "I did not know it at the time, but your death was avenged by Blanca, a sweet girl you taught the art of shooting. On the day you died, she delivered blood for blood.

We found out your men, I'm sorry, what I meant to say is your brothers, were murdered by people working for the country you were defending. The FRBs have been avenged now as well. Sonia, the love of your life, myself, and so many others have hunted down, captured, and turned the killers over to receive justice. This is not what my men and I wanted. We wanted blood for blood. Mom was against this action and told me, 'If you do this, you will be no better than the men you hunt, and I cannot have a daughter that is a murderer.' I love her enough to listen, and she was right."

Savannah looked back at her mom with tears in her eyes and said, "Mom, I do love you."

Sonia tears flowing down her face, said, "I have always loved you."

Savannah turned her head back around to look at Akita's headstone.

Sonia grabbed Lee Ann's hand and said, "That is the first time she has told me that she loves me."

Savannah spoke again to her dad, "Now that you and your brothers have been avenged here on earth, you will sit at the right hand of the Lord as his warriors to command, not angels.

I know that all of you wanted to be warriors for eternity. The FRBs do not wish to rest in peace.

You were born for war. Now you take your orders from the highest power. How does it feel to receive this promotion? You honor the house you now represent. Dad, I miss you. My love for you will never die."

Sonia moved forward, knelt beside Savannah, wrapped her arms around her, and hugged her tightly. Lee Ann had an uneasy feeling like the one she had in Aspermont at Akita's grave. She started to shiver uncontrollably, and she could see her breath on this warm day. She looked to see if Sonia and Savannah felt the same effect. At that instant, she

THE GIFT

became scared beyond reason, and then horrified.

Savannah and Sonia were still kneeling and crying, trying to comfort each other, their faces pressed in the space between each other's shoulders and necks, and they had no idea what was standing in front of them.

Lee Ann tried to call out but could not make a sound. She was looking at twelve big men, soldiers dressed in full combat gear. Green berets adorned everyone. They were bristling with weapons and ammo, nothing out of place. She recognized one from a picture. It was Akita. He knelt and kissed the head of Savannah and then Sonia. They had no response. They did not know what was happening around them.

Lee Ann was still icy cold and could not make a sound although she was trying with all her might. Akita started walking her way and all the men followed him. One by one, they passed right through her and disappeared. When the last man stepped through her, a feeling of doom filled her. She was so scared; she felt her breakfast coming up to leave her body.

Then a female voice, sweet and comforting on her left side, said, "Don't. They mean you no harm. We have been granted this opportunity to say goodbye to the people who set us free by avenging our deaths." Lee Ann turned to see who was speaking to her. Again, her heart wanted to stop. She was looking at Blanca.

Blanca smiled and said, "Yes, I am here. I am part of the FRBs now. I was granted that title because I took blood for blood with Akita's death." Lee Ann reached out to touch her. Her hand passed through her, and it was cold.

Blanca said, "You are the only one who can see us or hear me, so, if you say anything, they will think you are losing your mind. Let me tell you what just happened to you. My brothers just gave you all their memories. You have received this gift at the request of our boss. He could have given them to you in your sleep, but he wanted you to see where they came from and how important the job you now have is."

Lee Ann thought to herself, *I am going crazy. A gift you say. If this is happening to me, it would not be a gift.*

Blanca's face hardened, and she said, "You cannot turn down what has been given. It is part of you now and always will be. Focus on one thing that happened to each man, like earning their berets. Once you can

273

do this, you will be able to separate each man's memories. I am sorry, they are your memories now, like it or not. After you can separate them, you have been assigned the task of documenting their contributions to the world. In their own words, the good and the bad. If you do not accomplish the separation, you will go insane. Remember what I have told you and remember who is watching. Another thing, up to this point, you did not have all the facts. Now you do." Blanca continued, "Please tell Savannah that you know Akita loved her and tell her that you would not be surprised if the first thing he wanted to know was, 'Will you send me into the lion's den and let me kill lions?'"

Lee Ann looked at Blanca and asked, "Did he ask that first before anything else?"

She said, "Yes he did." Then she pointed at Savannah and Sonia and said, "You need to finish the story of the lives touched by the FRBs and the loved ones left behind. Now watch this." Blanca reached out one hand and held Lee Ann's hand. She could feel it, and it was solid. She was scared all over again and tried to pull her hand away, but she could not break her grip.

Blanca smiled and said, "We have been given the ability to be seen and heard only when necessary." Blanca released her hand, and without another word, she moved and was joined by all the FRBs. They now have a sister.

All disappeared, and now Lee Ann could breathe. Her head hurt as unfamiliar visions, sounds, voices, and everything else that was foreign to her bounced around her brain. She tried to remember what Blanca told her: focus on receiving the berets. One vision popped into her head. It was a man and a woman making love, and she could feel all of it. She turned red and thought to herself, *this is not a gift.*

CHAPTER 57
Three Years Later

Lee Ann's phone rang, and she answered, "Hello." She didn't have a chance to say anything else. A voice cut her off. It was Savannah.

She said, "Do not say or ask anything. Just do what I am asking you. This phone is not secure. Go to my mom's house. I have an escort inbound. He should be there within the hour. All travel has been arranged, and an escort will accompany you for security reasons. You do not have to pack anything more than an overnight bag. I will take care of the rest. Your escort has a credit card with your name on it. Use it up to $5000.00 at a time. When you get to Mom's house, tell her I have to finish up here. It should take no more than one week. Please tell her to say nothing about our boys or the bloodline. Do this for me, and I will be in your debt. Tell Malin that I am sorry, but I need you."

Once she took a breath, Lee Ann said, "Yes, I will do as you ask." She hung up, called Malin on his cell, and told him about the call.

He said, "It sounds urgent. Go, I can take care of everything here. Be safe, love you."

Savannah is a dear friend, and Lee Ann considered her as a sister, which is why she did not hesitate to tell her "yes." Lee Ann hoped that whatever the issue was, it would not be as severe as the last time. Many people in high public offices in the government and CIA went to jail, and many more worldwide died. This was due to the actions of Savannah and her company the Phantom Warriors; two ranch owners, Will Chisum and Roy Walker; and their ranch hands. All are highly trained Army Special Forces, Navy Seals, Marine Recon, Army Rangers and other combat soldiers.

They gravitate here because they feel as if they do not belong and are not accepted in society. Once at the ranch, most fit into ranch life and feel at ease or accepted. Ranch work is hard. Some don't know one end of a cow from the other, but they learn. After a brief period of on-the-job training, they make the best employees. Their work ethic is beyond compare.

When Lee Ann first met Savannah, she was at her father's funeral. She had lived on a ranch all of her life and was finishing college. Now, she

Three Years Later

owns The Phantom Warriors, a personal protection company with 32000 hardcore SF, elite soldiers, and mercenaries from around the world in her employ. More men are seeking employment with her every week. They want to work for her company. She is by far the strongest young woman that Lee Ann had ever met. Over the last few years, she has led her battled hardened men into conflicts and uprisings on several continents. Her father always told her that he would not ask his men to do anything that he would not do himself. He led from the front (first in, last out), and now she is the living embodiment of this.

From all the accounts Lee Ann had heard from her former coworkers in New York, Savannah is in the news and completes all contracts her company takes. One coworker told Lee Ann, "Savannah's company is respected and feared." Specifically, she said, "Savannah is a combat hardened force from hell itself on her own, but when you add her men and all of the company weapons and other assets, no one can stand in her way and come out unharmed."

CHAPTER 58
The Trip to Wetzlar

Lee Ann set about packing her bags as quickly as possible.

Malin came in, hugged her, and asked, "Did Savannah tell you anything else?"

Lee Ann turned to him and said, "No, I wish I knew what has her so scared. This is not like her."

Malin smiled and said, "If she needs your help, she's scrapping the bottom of the barrel."

Lee Ann slapped him on the shoulder and said, "I am *not* the bottom of the barrel. I see she did not want you. So where does that put you?"

Malin laughed, saying, "Please be careful and call me daily."

They heard a truck pull into the drive and stop at the back deck. The horn started honking and did not stop. Lee Ann rushed outside to see a thirty-something-year-old man in a black Suburban with a scared look on his face. Yoyo, Lee Ann's "cat" or mountain lion was on the hood, showing her teeth and hissing.

Lee Ann approached the truck, reached out and took Yoyo by her collar, and said, "Leave him alone."

Malin came over, opened the door, and said, "She won't hurt you. Hop out. My name is Malin, and you are?"

The man introduced himself as Bobby. Then he explained, "Morgan sent me and told me that you don't use your front door and to pull around back. What the hell is that?" He was pointing at Yoyo.

Malin, smiling from ear to ear, said, "Her fucking pet cat that I cannot get rid of. She is fine if you don't try to play with her."

Bobby looked as if in shock and asked Lee Ann, "Why do you have that as a pet? Aren't you afraid she will eat you or someone else like me coming to your back door? I'm going to kill Morgan. He set me up. He had to know you have her."

Malin was laughing hard. It made Lee Ann laugh to the point that she almost couldn't speak. Finally, she managed to say, "You can pet her. She is like any house cat, just a little bigger."

Bobby said, "No, I think I'll keep my fingers today." Then he asked,

The Trip to Wetzlar

"Are you ready? The airplane is fueled and waiting for us. Do you need help with your bags?"

Malin said, "I will get your bags," and headed into the house.

Bobby explained, "Morgan will meet you when we arrive in Germany. Both of us are to stay with you for the duration of your stay."

Lee Ann asked, "Why do I need you and the C.E.O. of the Phantom Warriors? What's going on? Will we be in danger?"

Bobby said, "Ma'am, I do not know. I have been told you are needed and to protect you. Morgan will fill you in at the Ludwig Estate."

Malin came out of the house with Lee Ann's bags and placed them in the back of the Suburban. He looked at her and said, "You will be missed more than you know."

She hugged him tight and said, "I love you. I'll call you when I arrive."

Malin said, "I love you, too. He helped her into the truck.

Bobby started the truck and asked, "Are you ready?"

Lee Ann replied, "Yes," and waved at Malin.

Bobby and Lee Ann had some small talk on the drive to Abilene, but nothing important or memorable. When they arrived, she was expecting to board an American Eagle flight. She was wrong. Sitting on the tarmac was a Bombardier Global 7500, Savannah's private airplane.

The flight crew took their bags and ushered them inside. This very luxurious jet will seat nineteen, but Bobby and Lee Ann were the only passengers.

They were airborne within fifteen minutes. The flight was uneventful except for how well the crew cared for them. The plane landed in Munich. They didn't go through customs. Four men met them at the terminal and took their bags from the flight crew. They formed up around Lee Ann and moved her through the airport at a rapid pace. She was starting to become scared and wondered what she had landed in the middle of and why she needed all the security.

Once outside the main airport building, an armored car with the engine running was waiting. One man opened the rear door while the other four surrounded Lee Ann, forming a barrier. They were covering the backside of her entrance into the car. The car blocked the other side.

The Trip to Wetzlar

No one could get to her. Now, she appeared visibly scared. After she was seated in the middle of the rear seat, one man sat on each side of her, and Bobby was seated in the front passenger seat. The other man walked to the car in front of them and sat in the front seat. A man's voice came over a walkie talkie and said, "Move out."

When they entered the autobahn, Bobby turned in his seat, so Lee Ann could see his face and said, "Morgan arranged this security for you. We're going to the Ludwig estate. When we arrive, he will explain why he thinks we need heavy security."

"Do you know what has happened and who is involved?" Lee Ann asked.

Bobby replied, "No, not at this time. I was told to make sure you arrived safely and to tell you everything would be explained. I know that all of us, including Morgan, are under orders to get you here promptly and keep your arrival under the radar." Bobby turned back, facing the front, and told the driver, "Pick up the pace."

The driver didn't hesitate and slammed the gas pedal down. The car lurched forward, and soon, they were traveling over one hundred miles per hour. They arrived at the front gate of Sonia's house, the majestic Ludwig estate, a six-hundred room, thirteenth-century castle. Lee Ann had been there several times, and the sight still took her breath away every time.

Moments later, they arrived at the main entrance. Morgan and Sonis's staff were waiting there. Their car stopped, and they disembarked. The staff unloaded their bags and carried them inside. Morgan told Bobby, "Go get some rest. Christina will show you to your quarters." Bobby left without a word and followed Christina. Morgan asked Lee Ann, "Do you want to rest first, or do you want to find out why you are here?"

Lee Ann knew and respected Morgan, so she asked him, "What is so vital that you have dragged me halfway around the world?"

Morgan said, "Not here and not now. I have someone you need to meet. Please keep any questions or comments to yourself until we are alone. Do you understand?"

She smiled and said, "I understand. I've been through this dance before. Who do you need me to meet and why?"

The Trip to Wetzlar

Morgan said, "Please follow me," turned and went inside.

CHAPTER 59
Urbarra

Lee Ann set about packing her bags as quickly as possible.

Malin came in, hugged her, and asked, "Did Savannah tell you anything else?"

Lee Ann turned to him and said, "No, I wish I knew what has her so scared. This is not like her."

Malin smiled and said, "If she needs your help, she's scrapping the bottom of the barrel."

Lee Ann slapped him on the shoulder and said, "I am *not* the bottom of the barrel. I see she did not want you. So where does that put you?"

Malin laughed, saying, "Please be careful and call me daily."

They heard a truck pull into the drive and stop at the back deck. The horn started honking and did not stop. Lee Ann rushed outside to see a thirty-something-year-old man in a black Suburban with a scared look on his face. Yoyo, Lee Ann's "cat" or mountain lion was on the hood, showing her teeth and hissing.

Lee Ann approached the truck, reached out and took Yoyo by her collar, and said, "Leave him alone."

Malin came over, opened the door, and said, "She won't hurt you. Hop out. My name is Malin, and you are?"

The man introduced himself as Bobby. Then he explained, "Morgan sent me and told me that you don't use your front door and to pull around back. What the hell is that?" He was pointing at Yoyo.

Malin, smiling from ear to ear, said, "Her fucking pet cat that I cannot get rid of. She is fine if you don't try to play with her."

Bobby looked as if in shock and asked Lee Ann, "Why do you have that as a pet? Aren't you afraid she will eat you or someone else like me coming to your back door? I'm going to kill Morgan. He set me up. He had to know you have her."

Malin was laughing hard. It made Lee Ann laugh to the point that she almost couldn't speak. Finally, she managed to say, "You can pet her. She is like any house cat, just a little bigger."

The Trip to Wetzlar

Bobby said, "No, I think I'll keep my fingers today." Then he asked, "Are you ready? The airplane is fueled and waiting for us. Do you need help with your bags?"

Malin said, "I will get your bags," and headed into the house.

Bobby explained, "Morgan will meet you when we arrive in Germany. Both of us are to stay with you for the duration of your stay."

Lee Ann asked, "Why do I need you and the C.E.O. of the Phantom Warriors? What's going on? Will we be in danger?"

Bobby said, "Ma'am, I do not know. I have been told you are needed and to protect you. Morgan will fill you in at the Ludwig Estate."

Malin came out of the house with Lee Ann's bags and placed them in the back of the Suburban. He looked at her and said, "You will be missed more than you know."

She hugged him tight and said, "I love you. I'll call you when I arrive."

Malin said, "I love you, too. He helped her into the truck.

Bobby started the truck and asked, "Are you ready?"

Lee Ann replied, "Yes," and waved at Malin.

Bobby and Lee Ann had some small talk on the drive to Abilene, but nothing important or memorable. When they arrived, she was expecting to board an American Eagle flight. She was wrong. Sitting on the tarmac was a Bombardier Global 7500, Savannah's private airplane.

The flight crew took their bags and ushered them inside. This very luxurious jet will seat nineteen, but Bobby and Lee Ann were the only passengers.

They were airborne within fifteen minutes. The flight was uneventful except for how well the crew cared for them. The plane landed in Munich. They didn't go through customs. Four men met them at the terminal and took their bags from the flight crew. They formed up around Lee Ann and moved her through the airport at a rapid pace. She was starting to become scared and wondered what she had landed in the middle of and why she needed all the security.

Once outside the main airport building, an armored car with the engine running was waiting. One man opened the rear door while the

The Trip to Wetzlar

other four surrounded Lee Ann, forming a barrier. They were covering the backside of her entrance into the car. The car blocked the other side. No one could get to her. Now, she appeared visibly scared. After she was seated in the middle of the rear seat, one man sat on each side of her, and Bobby was seated in the front passenger seat. The other man walked to the car in front of them and sat in the front seat. A man's voice came over a walkie talkie and said, "Move out."

When they entered the autobahn, Bobby turned in his seat, so Lee Ann could see his face and said, "Morgan arranged this security for you. We're going to the Ludwig estate. When we arrive, he will explain why he thinks we need heavy security."

"Do you know what has happened and who is involved?" Lee Ann asked.

Bobby replied, "No, not at this time. I was told to make sure you arrived safely and to tell you everything would be explained. I know that all of us, including Morgan, are under orders to get you here promptly and keep your arrival under the radar." Bobby turned back, facing the front, and told the driver, "Pick up the pace."

The driver didn't hesitate and slammed the gas pedal down. The car lurched forward, and soon, they were traveling over one hundred miles per hour. They arrived at the front gate of Sonia's house, the majestic Ludwig estate, a six-hundred room, thirteenth-century castle. Lee Ann had been there several times, and the sight still took her breath away every time.

Moments later, they arrived at the main entrance. Morgan and Sonis's staff were waiting there. Their car stopped, and they disembarked. The staff unloaded their bags and carried them inside. Morgan told Bobby, "Go get some rest. Christina will show you to your quarters." Bobby left without a word and followed Christina. Morgan asked Lee Ann, "Do you want to rest first, or do you want to find out why you are here?"

Lee Ann knew and respected Morgan, so she asked him, "What is so vital that you have dragged me halfway around the world?"

Morgan said, "Not here and not now. I have someone you need to meet. Please keep any questions or comments to yourself until we are alone. Do you understand?"

She smiled and said, "I understand. I've been through this dance before. Who do you need me to meet and why?"

Morgan said, "Please follow me," turned and went inside.

CHAPTER 60
Clandestine Meeting

Sonia pushed her call button. The door opened, and Monika stepped into the room and asked, "What may I do for you, Lady Sonia?"

Sonia said, "Please take Lee Ann and Morgan to where we discussed earlier."

Monika looked at both of them and said, "This way please."

They followed her out of the main house to the staff's apartments across the side yard. She opened the door and led them to the second floor. They stopped in front of a door. She turned to them and said, "Welcome to my home." She unlocked the door and let them in. Her living room was spacious and well maintained. Lee Ann looked around and was surprised to find antiques displayed throughout the room. Monika noticed her looking and said, "My family has lived in Wetzlar and served the Ludwigs for generations. Please take your time and look. I am pleased to show them off. My family has collected all of them, and they date back to when my fifth or sixth great grandparents first started working here."

Lee Ann was amazed. She didn't know what some of the items were or their use. The ones that she did know, swords, battle axes, and ancient firearms, would raise a large sum at any auction. She caught herself walking around Monica's living room in a trance unaware that Morgan, Monika, and now Sonia were watching her.

Sonia asked Lee Ann, "Are you still with us?"

She was startled. She didn't know when she got here or how long she had been watching and looking, and then she was very embarrassed. All she could say was, "I am sorry. I love trying to figure out what old items were used for. All your antiques are beautiful.

Monika said, "Thank you." She turned to Sonia and said, "I will leave so you can talk."

Sonia said, "No, please stay. We will need your help with this problem."

Monika said, "Okay, I don't know what I can do. Please take a seat."

Sonia said, "I asked Monika if we could use her house for this meeting. I do not want any interruptions or nosey people trying to listen

285

in on us. We will find another location for meetings soon."

Sonia asked the group, "What do you think of their story?" I think it is fabricated. I think the kidnapping and recovery was set up, all to claim that Urbarra is Akita's daughter. They want something else from us, but why come to me? When I first started seeing Akita and before I called him Akita for the first time, I remember seeing Erish with him. The reason I remember her is that she had Akita's attention. Many women tried unsuccessfully to attract his attention. I also remember her accent. She was a foreigner. I will never forget her eye color. I don't know why she stopped coming around."

Morgan said, "I have a hard time with the story, also. When you told Savannah, she sent me here. She told me someone was trying to take advantage of her mom. I will not finish the rest of what she told me to do."

Sonia insisted, "Tell us I want to know."

Morgan said, "She told me to kill anyone involved."

Lee Ann changed the subject and asked, "Why would they want her blood?"

Sonia hesitated, then stated, "All the FRBs had a genetic abnormality due to an experiment that manipulated their DNA. This manipulation creates an abnormality that can be passed to the next generation. If she is Akita's child, and they test her DNA, and isolate that manipulation, they could make more FRBs or sell it to another country. If that happens, no one will be safe, and all the work Akita and General Scott have done to hide this will be for nothing."

Lee Ann felt sick. She had learned about this years ago, and Savannah has this abnormality in her DNA. She blurted out, "What about Savannah and any other FRB kids? They are at risk. Savannah is safe. She has an army at her beck and call. They will protect her. Who will protect the rest of the FRB kids? What happens to them if whoever this is gets their hands on them?"

Morgan explained, "That is why I am here and why Savannah told me to kill anyone involved. If your two guests are in this for the DNA, why not use Urbarra's blood?"

Monika spoke up and said, "I don't claim to understand any of this. What if the kidnapping was interrupted early? Maybe it was staged like you think, but Urbarra did not know. All they wanted was her blood."

Sonia said, "If you are right, Erish is sick. How could any mother do this to her child? That bitch Erish set her child up to be taken, and when that did not work. She came here."

Lee Ann's mind was on overload. She asked, "Who is she working for and why? How can you investigate her and this mess without tipping her off? How do we find the other FRB kids? If we start looking into backgrounds, we give whomever a list of people to kidnap."

Morgan said, "When Sonia told Savannah about the kidnapping. I was with her. She went through the list you just gave. It took her about fifteen seconds to conclude. We run two operations simultaneously. One that we involve your guest in. She is working out the other and will share it with us when she arrives. She is setting up as much as she can from where she is. With that said, she is in a combat zone. She did not want any phone interceptions, so she sent me. I told her I would finish what we were doing, but she would not have it. She asked me what the hell would my men think if I left now?"

Sonia said, "Morgan, we need to know where they go and who they talk to. Can you surveil them?"

Morgan said, "We will need people who speak German and English. They will need to be close enough to hear conversations, and they cannot speak English in front of Erish and Urbarra. I do not have anyone who can fill this role. Do you?"

Sonia said, "I do. I will ask them for help. I know they will say yes."

Morgan said, "This is all we will do until Savannah gets here. We don't want to damage her plan."

Sonia said, "I need to leave so I can talk to my friends. I will leave first. You need to wait and leave after me."

Morgan said, "Yes, that will be better for us."

CHAPTER 61
Mahthildis

Lee Ann asked Monika, "May I stay? I would like you to tell me what some of your prize possessions are and how they were used."

Monika smiled and said, "It would be my pleasure. We will take as long as you like."

As she looked at Monika's collection of antiques and asked too many questions, Monika was excited to tell Lee Ann the history of the item and its use. A display case with only photos was in one corner of the living room. Lee Ann noticed a photo of Monika, her husband Karl, and Akita. Lee Ann asked, "You knew Akita?"

Monika smiled and said, "Yes, when Sonia's mother, Lady Dorothea, learned about Akita. She tried to stop Lady Sonia from seeing him. When that didn't work, she sent me to watch her daughter. She told me to do anything to keep her safe and out of trouble. Basically to keep her out of his bed."

Lee Ann asked, "How did she expect you to do that?"

Monika laughed hard and, with difficulty, said, "No force on earth could have kept Lady Sonia from Akita's bed. I met Karl when I was supposed to be watching Sonia. She took this picture. I didn't feel good, and Akita was trying to comfort me. He had his arms around my shoulders. I rested my head on his chest when Karl entered the bar and saw us. Akita, being Akita, he waved him over and told him, 'She was the one that made a pass at me. This is not my fault.' Sonia heard what Akita said and almost yelled, 'That is not true. She was sick.' Akita smiled and told Karl, 'Do you see what you have done? You have gotten me in trouble.'"

Lee Ann said, "You are kidding. Akita did that to you? What did Karl do?"

Monika smiled and said, "Karl sat down next to me and told Sonia to take a picture of Monika and her two boyfriends. Karl told me later that Akita was a kind man to comfort me. He knew that Akita was the only reason I was there. Dorothea had told me to watch Sonia, and then Karl said, 'Sonia defended you. She is a good friend.'"

Lee Ann looked at Monika and said, "I want to ask you something, but I don't want to overstep our friendship."

Monika said, "Ask your question. I will let you know if you are out of line."

"I have noticed you are closer to Savannah than a business or service relationship. Savannah holds you in high regard. May I ask why?"

Monika smiled and said, "You are not overstepping. You are right. Lady Savannah and I are friends, but you're mistaken. It is me who holds her in high regard. I will tell you why. My daughter Mahthildis does not want to work here. She went to university and wants to use her education to work in IT as a programmer. After she graduated, she worked several jobs, leading to the one she has now. It is an excellent job, working for a company in the downtown area. She saved enough money to move out of here and live independently. A man who worked in her building asked her out several times and would not take no for an answer. He started following her home. He found a way to get inside her apartment. Mahthildis was ready to quit her job and move back here. I was afraid she was going to be hurt or worse. I called the authorities. They spoke to him, but he denied everything. We had made all the arrangements for her to come home. I told Lady Sonia that Mahthildis was coming home, and I told her why. Lady Sonia did not let me leave the room. She picked the phone up and called Lady Savannah. She told Lady Savannah everything. Then she handed me the phone and said, 'Savannah wants to talk to you.'"

Monika continued, "I took the phone. Lady Savannah did not let me say anything. She told me, 'Do not let Mahthildis move. I have men on the way as we speak. They will arrive tomorrow. I will text their names and information to Mom. I am also on my way. I should be there in three days. Have your girl stay with you until my men get there. I will make sure that this fucking shit ends. No one should have to live scared. Do you hear me? Now, do as I say.' Lady Savannah hung up before I could protest her actions. Lady Savannah's men took over. They walked behind Mahthildis everywhere she went. If she drove, they were there, and no one knew it."

Monika took a breath and explained, "Before Lady Savannah arrived, her men had the man's name and knew where he lived. They had his record from Polizei. I do not know how they got that, and I will never ask. Lady Savannah arrived and was madder than hell. Her men wanted to beat the fuck out of him. Lady Savannah told them if we did that, he would stop while we were here, but when we leave, he might kill her. She said, 'Let's set him up to get enough evidence and put a pretty bow on him for Polizei.' Lady Savannah moved into the apartment. Mahthildis would go to work and return as she always had. Lady Savannah's men would take her in and out of the building undetected daily."

Lee Ann cut in and asked, "Are you telling me that Savannah was using herself as bait?"

Monika replied, "Yes. That is a good way to put it."

Lee Ann asked, "What happened?"

Monika said, "Lady Savannah set the lights in the room up, so when she walked back and forth nude in front of the window curtains, her figure was on full display. It worked. Lady Savannah's men took pictures of the man breaking in and told Lady Savannah over their coms that he was on the way.

Then Polizei received a frantic call from me. I told them I had a pervert trying to get into my apartment, that I didn't want to be raped, and to please come here fast. Lady Savannah let him get to the bedroom. When he opened the door, she hit him hard enough that he hit the floor. She picked him up above her head and body-slammed him. When the authorities arrived, they saw Savannah standing nude in the center of the room with the man lifted off the floor by his throat. Later we found out that his arm was broken. He is in jail and will be there for some time."

Lee Ann said without thinking, "She did that for you."

Monika smiled and said, "That is not all. Lady Sonia moved Mahthildis into one of the empty apartments on the estate. Lady Sonia told me afterward that she had heard people say that she has a savage daughter. I agree, and I think that her savagery is justified. Lady Savannah is my friend and the savage daughter of my Lady Sonia. When Lady Savannah takes over this estate, I will proudly serve her. The Savage Lady Savannah."

Monika's phone rang. She answered and listened, then hung up. She turned to Lee Ann and said, "Lady Sonia asked if you would join her in the small library. I will accompany you."

CHAPTER 62
Memories

They left Monika's apartment and walked to the main house. Monika led Lee Ann to the library and tapped on the door. Sonia said, "Come in." They entered, and Monika closed the door as she left.

Sonia said, "I have a meeting place for us. It is away from prying eyes and ears. Will you come with me?"

Lee Ann said, "Yes, of course. Where is the meeting place?"

Sonia said, "It is the old headquarters of the FRBs. No one has been there in over twenty years. Let's go and see if it is still livable."

Lee Ann was intrigued. This is one place she had heard of but had never had the opportunity to investigate. She asked Sonia, "Why is this place abandoned? You have preserved so much of what your boys were. You have fought to have them remembered."

Sonia said regretfully, "For years, Akita wanted to remodel it but could not bring himself to take that part of their lives and change it. I tremble at the thought of opening all my feelings. We had so many good times there. That is why I needed someone with me. Someone with no ties to it or the FRBs. Does that make sense?"

"Yes, it does," Lee Ann answered. "Thank you for asking me."

Sonia's driver was waiting at the car with the door open. He helped them in and closed the door. He entered, sat behind the wheel, and asked, "Lady Sonia, are you sure you want me to take you there?"

Sonia said, "Yes, please, and hurry."

The driver started the car and left for the address of the FRB headquarters.

Lee Ann found herself wondering what awaited them. What would she find out about the lives of the warriors called the FRBs? What would she learn about Sonia and her life with them? The anticipation was killing her.

They arrived at a well-maintained five-story building. The driver pushed the button to open the gate. The hinges growled loudly from the rust buildup. The driver said, "I didn't know if the gate would open. It hasn't been used all this time."

Sonia said, "I am glad it did. I hope the door locks will work, also."

Memories

They parked. The driver got out, opened the car doors for them, and asked, "Lady Sonia, do you want me to assist you?"

Sonia said, "No, thank you. Please wait here, and do not let anyone know we are here."

The driver pushed the button and the gate closed, hiding the car and them from sight. They were at the back of the building. Sonia removed a set of keys from her handbag. She found the one she wanted, placed it in the door lock, and turned. It worked. The lock opened, and Sonia pushed the heavy door open. They went inside.

Sonia said, "I have kept the power on all this time. I could not turn it off. That would be like turning off all the memories I have."

Lee Ann replied, "I don't believe I could turn anything off either. Sonia, we don't have to do this. We can find another place. No one will fault you."

Sonia said, "It is too late now we are here. I need to do this for me, no one else."

They went up the stairs to the second floor. Sonia unlocked another door, and they walked inside. Dust covered everything, and the air was thick. Sonia walked to the nearest window and opened it.

She asked Lee Ann, "Will you open windows on your side? I will open the ones on this side." Sonia turned the lights on, and they both opened the windows.

They walked through the space. It was huge, with a wide hallway with rooms on both sides. Some had open doors, and others were closed. The hall opened into a space approximately sixty feet by sixty feet. There were two TVs, a pool table, serving tables, several recliners, and couches.

As Lee Ann made her way further inside the room, she saw another room off the side. It was a full kitchen. Sonia opened another door, and the tears started flowing. Lee Ann walked over to her, rubbed her arm, and asked, "What is wrong?"

Sonia said, "This is Akita's room. He left all his things here. I did not know he did that." Lee Ann looked in the room. The bed was made. Some clothes were laid out, boots were on the floor, and a watch and other items were on the end table. If the dust wasn't there, it looked like he had just stepped out and would return. Sonia went in and ran her fingers over the bed and clothes.

Memories

Lee Ann said, "You need to take his things home. None of this needs to be here if we use the room for meetings."

She turned and said, "I didn't know it would be this hard. I will have my staff clean this place up and take all the personal effects of Akita's and any other's home."

Lee Ann said, "Do you think Savannah would like some of her dad's stuff?"

"Yes," Sonia said. "I want to go through it with her and tell her what I remember. Let's go through the rest of the rooms."

Almost all of the rooms had items left in them. Lee Ann felt like the men always wanted to return here, a place they all called home. They finished and left. Sonia was still shaken when they arrived at the estate.

CHAPTER 63
Lazy Ass

The following day, everyone was at breakfast except Urbarra. Lee Ann mistakenly asked, "Erish, is your daughter, Okay?

Erish said, "She is fine and will join us when she is ready. Do you have any more questions? When were you put in charge of my daughter?"

Lee Ann said quickly, "I'm sorry. I didn't mean to pry into your family business. I will not do so again."

Christina entered the room, walked up to Sonia, leaned down, and whispered something into her ear. Sonia said, "Please excuse me. Erish, will you please join me?"

Sonia started to leave the room. Erish had not attempted to move. Sonia said harshly, "Erish, that was not a simple request. Do you get my meaning?" Erish slowly got up and left with Sonia.

Some male staff members rushed up the stairs a short time later. Lee Ann got up to follow them and find out what the problem was. She made it to the hallway when Christina stopped her.

She said, "Please do not interfere. We are having some issues with Urbarra and staff members. Lady Sonia will solve it, or she will ask Urbarra to leave."

Lee Ann pursued this issue no further, and she went back to finish her meal. Monika approached her and asked, "Will you come with me?" As they were walking, Monika said, "Lady Sonia wants you to speak to Urbarra. None of the staff can make Urbarra understand that we are not here to serve her. We carry out the duties that Lady Sonia assigns. No one else has any authority over the staff of this estate."

Lee Ann said, "I will try. What does Urbarra want the staff to do?"

Monika said, "Make her bed, pick up her clothes, bring her meals to her room, everything except wipe her ass. Wait, don't say anything about that. She will want me to do that."

Lee Ann replied, "What a lazy ass bitch. She's a guest here. She should appreciate Sonia's kindness. If Sonia kicks her and her mother out, they will be up shit creek."

Monika smiled wickedly, "That's why Lady Sonia wants you to deliver the news. She told me if you could not get through to her, Lady Savannah would." Lee Ann didn't want to see that. Savannah is no one to fuck with, and when it comes to her mother, she might go too far and put Urbarra in the hospital.

Monika tapped on Urbarra's door. Urbarra yelled out to go away and leave her alone.

Lee Ann stopped Monika from replying and opened the door, went inside, and closed the door behind her. Urbarra was lying in bed. Her room was a mess. Her shit was covering the bed, floor, and chest of drawers. Lee Ann ripped the covers off her, dragged her sorry ass out of bed, and let her hit the floor. Then Lee Ann went crazy: "Are you that fucking stupid? You are a fucking guest here. The house staff are not here to serve you. You do not own this estate. You cannot give them any orders. Am I making myself perfectly clear, or do I need to beat the fuck out of you?

Get your fucking ass up, clean your fucking room, make your fucking bed, apologize to the staff, and then to Sonia. If you don't do as I say, I'll kick your fucking ass out of here myself. Please think about this when Savannah arrives. She won't be as nice as I am. She will just break every fucking bone in your body." Then Lee Ann yelled out at the top of her lungs, "Get the fuck up and act like a fucking human. Do you fucking understand?" Then she stormed out and found Sonia standing in the hall.

Lee Ann said, "Sonia, I am sorry. It was not my place to."

Sonia cut her off mid-way through her apology and said, "Now I know why Savannah calls you 'sister.' That's what she needed. I wouldn't have said half of what you did, but I asked Monika to have you talk to my unwanted guest. Thank You."

Lee Ann left without another word and returned to breakfast. Monika was the only one in the room. She said, "I didn't know you would take it that far."

Lee Ann replied, "Now I wish I had not. Sonia was in the hall. I don't want to look bad in her eyes. She has been so nice to me."

Monika smiled and said, "I was also in the hall. You did what none of us could. We would lose our jobs. Not because we were wrong but because the rest of the staff would know and think they could do the same. Do you understand?"

Lee Ann said, "Yes, I don't want to lose Sonia's respect or make her

Lazy Ass

think I went too far."

Monika smiled again and said, "You have nothing to worry about. I was in the hall with her. She was impressed and told me so."

Morgan almost ran into the room. He asked Monika, "Where is Savannah's mother?"

Monika said, "I will tell her you are asking for her."

Morgan said, "Tell her a bus will be at the main gate in about an hour. Savannah will land here at the same time."

Lee Ann asked, "What do you mean *land* here?"

CHAPTER 64
Lady Savannah Arrives

Morgan said, "Savannah is going to HALO (High Altitude Low Opening parachuting) onto the grounds at the front door. This is just like her not telling me anything until the last second. Why does she do this shit to me? The bus will pick up the men she has with her. They have reservations at a Guest House in Giessen. They will be on standby for whatever she has in mind. I don't know what that is at this point, but she does not want anyone to know she is here yet.

Will you please tell Sonia? I need to get all kinds of shit lined up. Again, this is just like her to drop in like this. I am unprepared and she knows it."

As she was leaving, Monika said, "Yes. I will let Lady Sonia know, and I will let the guard at the gate know to let the bus in."

Sonia called a meeting of the estate staff, Morgan, and Lee Ann. They all met at the main entrance of the castle. Sonia said, "Morgan, please tell us what will happen and what you need us to do.

Morgan said, "Savannah and ten men will unass." He stopped and said, "Excuse me, they will exit the aircraft at forty thousand feet."

Sonia cut in and asked, "Can you tell us how high that is in meters, please?"

Morgan said, "Yes, ma'am, it is twelve thousand one hundred ninety-two meters. They will free fall until they reach one thousand five hundred feet or four hundred fifty-seven meters.

They will deploy their parachutes and steer themselves to this opening." Morgan pointed toward the grounds at the main entrance. This area was approximately two hundred and fifty feet by three hundred feet, and he said, "This area is more than we need. They can land in a twenty-foot square or six meters."

Sonia asked, "What do we need to do before they get here?"

Morgan said, "Nothing to the landing area, but the bus needs to be close. As soon as they land, the men will board the bus and unass the area. I am sorry they will leave. Only Savannah will stay. She has been in heavy combat for four months, and that environment does not allow for creature comforts."

Lady Savannah Arrives

Monika asked, "What will Lady Savannah need first?"

Morgan said," She will have been in the same uniform for the entire time. She will be covered in sweat, blood, body tissue, and shit."

Everyone acted as if they would lose their breakfast. What Morgan just described was revolting to think about. How could anyone live like that?

Monika looked at Sonia and said, "I will take care of Lady Savannah when she arrives. I will have everything she will need."

Sonia said, "Thank you. I know she will be in good hands."

Monika asked Morgan, "How long do I have to prepare?"

Morgan said, "If the aircraft is on time, under one hour." Monika said nothing. She just left in a hurry. Morgan had the bus moved and was checking the wind direction and speed. He got a call on his satellite phone. The call was under one minute. Morgan called out, "They are ahead of schedule thirty minutes out."

The main door opened, and Erish and Urbarra stepped out. Erish asked, "What is all the commotion about."

Sonia answered, "Nothing. We're preparing for my daughter's arrival. She will be here soon, and we want everything to go smoothly. You can stay and see how a Haddox makes an entrance."

Erish said in a not so friendly manner, "What do you mean a Haddox? That was Akita's last name. He is the only Haddox I have ever known."

Sonia said, "Stay and meet another one. My daughter, Savannah."

Lee Ann heard Sonia. She had thought that Erish knew Savannah was Akita's child.

Oh shit. No one told her, and Sonia just rubbed it in her face. This could get interesting.

She decided to stay outside with the short time frame since it made no sense to leave. She looked around, and everyone had come to the same conclusion.

Morgan's phone rang. He answered. It was a short call.

Morgan yelled, "They are out the door."

Sonia wrapped her arm around Lee Ann's and said, "I am scared. Why would she terrify me like this?"

Lee Ann replied, "Savannah's not trying to terrify you. She's being

Lady Savannah Arrives

clever by entering Germany without anyone knowing. She may know something we don't."

Sonia tried to smile, then said, "That does not help me feel any better. The way of life she has chosen is not what I wanted for her. The information I received from my work at the BND (Bundesnachrichtendienst Germany Federal Intelligence Service) is that she leads the world's finest, most sought-after company. Why does she insist on being in combat? Why can't she run the company and leave the fighting to others?"

Lee Ann explained, "Her company does more than combat. They also find people, retrieve stolen items, provide bodyguard services, security services, and many other services.

She is living up to her father's training and code. Lead from the front, first in, last out.

Because of the way she leads, her men would follow her into hell and know she would lead them back out. She is ferocious, violent, and savage when necessary. She is also kind and giving. She loves her family and friends. Have I just described your daughter, or did you know everything I told you? Because I also just described Akita. Did I not?"

Sonia said, "Yes. You are right on both accounts. I wanted her to make her mark on the world differently."

Lee Ann looked at Sonia and said, "Your daughter is happy, and she will lead the company from an office when the time comes."

Someone cried out, "There they are." Lee Ann looked up and saw small shapes against the sky that looked like people. Sonia's grip on her arm increased. After some time, the first chute opened, and then, one by one, eleven were opened. Each person landing took at most three steps, unhooked their harnesses, gathered their chute, and headed for the bus.

At this time, the breeze shifted, and an odor, "toxic" is its only description, hit Lee Ann. She fought back vomiting and was barely able to do so. Several of the staff were not so lucky.

Savannah handed one of the men her gear, including weapons. He was last on the bus. The bus left within a minute after the last man landed.

Sonia said, "Wow, that was quick."

Savannah walked up, smiled, and said, "Hi Mom, I got here as quickly

Lady Savannah Arrives

as possible. What have I missed?"

Sonia said, "We can talk later. Please take a shower first."

Savannah smiled and asked, "Are you calling me stinky? I am hurt. I have not seen you in over a year, and the first thing you say is I stink."

Sonia said, "I did not call you anything, but you do stink. Go in the house and clean up."

Savannah said, "No, I cannot do that to your staff. They would not be able to get the smell out of the house for a week. I'll scrub off at the stable first. I hope the horses don't get offended by the smell. If that will work for you."

Sonia said, "I don't think that will be necessary, but I think the staff will appreciate your actions."

Monika walked up with a complete shower kit.

Savannah said, "You are a lifesaver. We are headed to the stables to use the washstand for horses. Are you ready?"

With a questioning look, Monika said, "Lady Savannah, there are no walls at that washstand."

Savannah said, "Monika, I smell like a dead thing. I can put up with no walls if you can."

As Monika and Savannah were going to leave, Savannah looked over Lee Ann's shoulder and saw Erish and Urbarra. Then she asked in a low voice, "Is that the bitch claiming to be my dad's offspring?" Before anyone could answer, Monika and Savannah left.

Sonia said more to herself than anyone, "That child of mine. What am I to do with her?"

Everyone returned to their task inside the estate.

Lee Ann was in the kitchen with Sonia. Both were hungry and helping themselves. They had their plates with some of the staff at the table where the staff always eats.

Christina said, "Lady Sonia, "I can serve you in the dining hall."

Sonia started to say something when a young man burst into the room. Without looking at who was in the room. He shouted out, "Lady Sonia is naked at the stable."

Sonia stood and asked, "Are you sure it is me?"

The young man realized what he had done and who he had insulted. He turned red and lost all his words.

304

Lady Savannah Arrives

Sonia smiled and said, "Don't worry. Please go back to work." Sonia waited until he left and closed the door. Then she laughed aloud and said, "I am going to kill Savannah. My staff thinks I am the one bathing at the stable."

Christina said, "Lady Sonia, that was a compliment. He saw Lady Savannah nude and thought it was you, and you are over twenty years older than she is. Think about that. You have a rocking body. I wish mine looked that good."

Lee Ann smiled and said, "I agree with her. I wish my body was as well put together as yours."

Sonia said, "Both of you are fit and beautiful. You flatter me. Thank you."

Sonia and Lee Ann waited for Savannah in the kitchen. They were talking about Texas. Lee Ann told her about Yoyo. Sonia was going to say something when they heard Savannah and Monika laughing as they entered the kitchen. Savannah was wearing a knee-length robe, and her hair was wet. Sonia hugged her and did not want to let go.

Monika held a bag and asked, "Lady Savannah, what do you want me to do with your clothes?"

Savannah said, "Burn them. Oh shit, I don't have anything to wear."

Sonia said, "I will have my tailor bring you something tomorrow. You can use some of mine until then."

Savannah turned to Monika and said, "Thank you for helping me clean up. You didn't have to, and you got wet. How can I make it up to you?" Then she turned to Sonia and said, "Thank you, Mom. I will take you up on the clothes."

Monika said, "It is a pleasure to help someone who appreciates it. Lady Savannah, you will never owe me anything. I like that you tell me thank you. That is more than enough."

Savannah asked, "What is this about? Mom, Lee Ann, myself, and everyone I know of have always shown our appreciation for the hard work done here by the staff."

Monika said, "I am sorry, it is not my place. Please forget what I said," and she left.

Sonia asked Savannah, "May I walk you to your room? We have so much to catch up on."

Lady Savannah Arrives

Savannah said, "I would like that," and they left.

Lee Ann went to her room and started a list of questions she wanted answered. A wake-up call at 05:00 and a meeting at 06:30 were scheduled for the following day. Christina and Monika informed everyone.

CHAPTER 65
Cunning

The following day, at 05:30 a.m. Christina tapped on Lee Ann's door and said, "Miss Lee Ann, the meeting is in Lady Sonia's office in a half hour."

Lee Ann replied, "I am ready. Thank You." She arrived ten minutes early. Savannah, Sonia, and Morgan were already in Sonia's office. Good mornings were exchanged. She noticed Savannah was seated behind Sonia's desk and had four laptops opened and running.

"Good morning," a voice said over one of the laptops. Lee Ann recognized Robin's voice, "I have everything ready on my side."

Lee Ann walked around the desk. Savannah was on four separate Zoom calls. Lee Ann observed, "You've been busy. When did you start?"

Savannah said, "No rest for the wicked. I have been here since 04:00 a.m. I am still responsible for many other operations, and they demand my time."

Lee Ann said sarcastically, "Oh, you poor thing."

Savannah swatted her on the butt and said, "I expected a little more sympathy from you."

Monika tapped on the door and came in. She said, "Christina is giving the final door knocks and will be here soon."

Sonia said, "Thank you. Please take a seat." Christina tapped on the door and came in with Erish.

Savannah said, "It is time let's get started. Where is Urbarra?"

Erish said, "I told her we did not need her here."

Savannah said, "Monika, will you please go get her? We will not start the meeting until all the people I asked to be here are in attendance."

Monika said, "Yes, I will, Lady Savannah," and left the room.

Savannah turned her attention to Erish, "If I say she must be here. She will be here. If you want my help, do not ever go against me again, or I will evict you from my mother's estate and inform everyone in my world not to lift a finger to help you. Do you understand?"

Erish started protesting, but Sonia cut her off and said, "Don't say a word. Savannah will have you removed with my blessing."

A short time later, Monika tapped on the door and entered the room with Urbarra.

Savannah stood and walked in front of the desk. She was wearing a tight snakeskin skirt, displaying her powerfully built legs; a matching jacket; a silk maroon shirt with gold feathers on the collar; a wide black belt draped around her hips; and dark maroon six-inch heels.

Sonia had been described as beyond beautiful with a face that goddesses were jealous of and an hourglass figure that could stop time. Her daughter has surpassed that. No words that are adequate to describe Savannah. She exudes beauty and power. It was hard to believe that the woman standing before the group this morning, was the same woman who fell out of the sky yesterday. She had come straight from leading men in bloody close-quarters combat. She had been covered in disgusting, foul smelling who-knows-what. It was so bad that some of the staff lost their breakfast.

Savannah told Urbarra, "I am so glad you could join us. You had all of us waiting.

Now that you are here, we can start the meeting. Now take a seat."

Urbarra snapped back, "I was informed my presence was not required."

Savannah said calmly, "This is my meeting, and I will decide who needs to attend. Did I tell you not to be here?"

Urbarra said, "No, my mother did."

Savannah said, "Erish does not have the authority to release anyone. Only I can. Do you understand?"

Erish said, "She is my daughter. I know what she needs to do. You cannot."

Savannah asked, "Why are you here? Why did you run here? Why involve my mother in your fucked up shit? You have so many questions to answer. You think that your fucked up daughter is my father's offspring? If that's true, then my dad saw something in you that I cannot. So why the fuck are you here?"

Again, Robin's voice was coming from one of the laptops and said, "Savannah, the team we have in the Hindu Kush may be in for a hard time. The satellite image shows a large buildup of men about five kilometers away. We do not know if our people have been spotted. It's enough of a concern that the operations chief wanted me to interrupt you."

Savannah said, "Morgan will handle it. Let me give him this laptop. Please patch him through to the field commander and the other assets in the area."

Savannah handed the laptop to Morgan and said, "I don't care if my men have been spotted or not. I want all available assets moved to within one kilometer. If possible, have them stay unseen. If the shit goes down, I want overwhelming firepower placed on the opposing force and everything big enough to die killed. If we need to evacuate, pull everyone out."

Morgan said, "Copy that." and left the room.

Savannah asked, "Where were we?" Everyone in the room was shocked at what Savannah had just ordered Morgan to do. No one spoke. Urbarra and Erish were uneasy and sickened by Morgan's orders and his willingness to carry them out without question.

Savannah was watching their reaction. Then, the corners of her mouth turned up ever so slightly.

She had just taken advantage of her work to make them realize who she was and what she was capable of. It pleased her. She is cunning.

Savannah said, "I have a team on Zoom calls. They will assist me in this meeting and keep me informed about other items of concern. I am responsible for my men worldwide. Does anyone have a problem with this?" Again, no one spoke up.

Savannah said, "Good. Now, tell me about the supposed kidnapping."

Urbarra said in a snarky voice, "It was not supposed. They tasered me and threw me in a fucking van. I was taken, and the only reason I am here is my security."

Savannah smiled and said, "Robin oversees my IT section. I asked her to find proof of what you have told me. She has security footage from several angles of your abduction. Several of her IT team members and my investigation team have reviewed it. Do you want to know what the assessment is?"

Uabarra said, "I know what happened."

Erish Said, "My daughter was taken. Who the fuck are you to say she was not?"

Savannah said, "I have not said anything yet. Why are you so defensive? Are you hiding something from us? My investigators say your daughter was not handled roughly enough.

With all their years of experience, they have not seen that level of care in an abduction. Erish, can you explain that to us?"

Erish, almost yelling, said, "No, your fucking people are wrong. I do not have to put up with this shit. Come on, Uabarra, we are leaving."

CHAPTER 66
Cursed Savage Queen

Erish stood to leave and stopped when Savannah said, "If you leave this room, then do not stop. Leave the estate and do not return. I am not finished. Sit down now."

Erish looked at Sonia and asked, "Are you going to let her do this?" Sonia started to respond when Robin's voice stopped her.

Robin said with great urgency, Savannah, we have a problem look at the screen." Savannah made her way around the desk and looked at the screen. With a concerned look on her face, she said, "Mom, I have a problem. I need Monika and Christina to come with me." She closed two laptops, picked up the other one, looked up, and said, "Let's go."

Monika and Christina moved toward the door quickly. Savannah looked at Lee Ann and asked, "Do you need an invitation? You too, let's go. I need all of you. Mom, I do not have time to explain why, but thank you." Savannah then looked at Erish and said, "This is far from over," and they left.

They almost ran to the garage. When they arrived, Sonia's driver was waiting for them. The car's engine was running with the doors open. He hurried to get them in and headed out of the estate grounds. Once outside the main gate, he slowed the car and asked, "Lady Savannah, did I sell your story?"

Savannah said, "Yes, you did. Please go to the office."

Lee Ann looked at her and asked, "What do you mean he sold your story?"

Savannah held one finger up and opened her laptop. She said, "Robin, that went as planned. Do you have audio?"

Robin said, "Of course I do. I am plugging you in now."

Savannah looked up and said, "We are going to my dad's HQ. I wanted to leave Erish wondering what I had and what I would do next. I'm sorry that the three of you didn't know. I needed you to react as you did."

Erish's voice came over the laptop. She said, "Sonia, you know Urbarra is Akita's daughter. Don't you? If you have any doubts, we can have her DNA tested against Savannah's DNA. Or is Savannah not

311

Akita's child?"

Savannah said, "You fucking bitch. Now we know what she wants. We need to find out who is pulling her strings. I want to know if that other fucking bitch Urbarra is involved or if she is a pawn."

Robin replied, "I am already working on it."

The car stopped at the back gate of the former HQ of the FRBs. He pushed the button to open the gate. This time, the gate opened smoothly. The driver pulled in and closed the gate behind them. He got out and opened the car doors for them.

Savannah said, "I am hungry. Does anyone else want food?" They all wanted food.

Savannah asked the driver, "Will you please get yourself and us some food?"

He said, "Yes, Lady Savannah, I will," and left.

Savannah unlocked the door they entered, and she locked it behind them. She said, "We don't want anyone sniffing around. We will use the front door from now on." They made their way upstairs, where Bobby was waiting for them. The last time Lee Ann had seen him was when they arrived.

Savannah said, "From this point on, we will have guards with us."

Lee Ann asked, "Why do we need guards?"

Savannah said, "Let's get settled in, and I will tell you what we have found out so far."

They made their way down the hall and into the main room. Lee Ann could not believe the change. Everything had a fresh coat of paint, and the floors were waxed. The old TVs were replaced with four large flat screen TVs. The pool table was gone. Eight new desks and other office furniture had been moved in. The kitchen was completely redone with new appliances.

Sonia's staff had outdone themselves in a short time. Savannah had about ten of her people working here already.

A lady Lee Ann didn't know walked over and told Savannah, "We have a presentation set up for you. Let me know when you are ready."

Savannah said, "I am ready now. Let's see what we are dealing with."

The young lady led them to a table in front of a TV and said, "Please be seated." She turned the TV on, hit the play button, and said, "The IT team has found some unsettling evidence. Several months ago, Urbarra filled out a family history questionnaire." She pushed a button, and the form was displayed on the screen. "As you can see, she put the name 'Clint Haddox' as her father. We believe this is the starting point." She pushed the button again to show another form. She pointed out a section of the form and said, "This is the results. They could not link her to Mr. Haddox. No DNA sample is on record or does not exist for him."

Savannah said, "Please call Mr. Haddox 'Akita,' as all of us know him by that name. Did you have her DNA scanned for an unusual abnormality as I wanted?"

The young lady said, "Yes, and one is present. Your specialist has deleted this record and the questionnaire and will do the same with this one as soon as we are finished. They are tracking it to see who obtained the information."

Savannah said, "Thank you. Tell Robin not to delete it for now. We will need the information later." Savannah called Bobby over and asked him, "Who have Erish and Urbarra met with?"

Bobby said, "Urbarra has not met with anyone. She has not left the estate. She has tried to call her friends, but we blocked her calls. Erish has met with this man three times, always in the park. He placed a photo on the table. She has also met with another man twice at a restaurant. He placed another photo on the table. We are still working on their identities."

Savannah said, "Thank you. We need to know who they are and who they are working for."

Bobby said, "Yes, ma'am, we are working on that. We could get the information fast, but that would tip our hand."

Savannah said, "I know everyone is doing their best. Please go back to work."

Savannah turned to them and said, "This is a covert operation. No one will detect any part of it. We are also doing another one. Robin has some of her people probing. She wants this one to be intercepted. That way, we find out what they want us to know. They will try to send us in the wrong direction. We will do enough to keep them thinking we have taken the bait."

Lee Ann asked her, "What about this one? Can they find out about it and feed you incorrect information?"

Savannah said, "No, Robin and her team have infiltrated companies, countries, armies, and other things. They know what they are doing. We will have what we need. It is just a matter of time."

Lee Ann asked, "Who is following Erish and Urbarra? Who took the pictures?"

Savannah smiled and asked, "Do you remember Kirstin and Petra? They're the ones who volunteered to follow them. My men told them what to do and not to do. My mom has terrific friends. My men took the pictures from a great distance."

"Sonia was in on this, wasn't she?" Lee Ann asked.

Savannah said, "Yes, she is playing a part, and she asked Monika and Christina to help."

Sonia's driver entered and said, "I have food for everyone. May I get some help? There's a lot of food?" Monika, Christina, and Lee Ann followed him downstairs and to the car. Each of them carried two boxes up and still had to make another trip. Monika and Christina started to serve the food.

Savannah laid her hand on Christina's hand and said, "You are not here to serve us. Please let me do this."

Monika said, "Absolutely not, Lady Savannah, you will not serve. I will."

A young man stepped up. He looked like he just got out of the military. He said, "My Queen, I will serve." He began serving everyone. No one objected.

Monika asked, "Why did he call Lady Savannah 'My Queen?'"

Lee Ann explained, "When she took over the four companies and combined them into one. She broke bones of two men in front of everyone. The men in the room gave her the title "Queen of the Phantom Warriors" because of Sonia and her heritage. It is a sign of their respect."

Christina said, "With the way she leads her men in combat, she has earned that title. I may start using it. 'My Queen,' I like it."

Monika said, "I may also, but I do not want to offend her or Lady Sonia."

Lee Ann said, "I don't think either of them will be offended.

Savannah has an army larger than some countries and is richer than many others. So 'Queen' may be the only way to describe her."

Bobby overheard them and said, "Most of the men in her command address her as 'My Queen.' She has never complained, but I do not know if she likes it or not."

The three women sat down together to eat. Savannah was going to sit with them when Monika and Christina stood and said, "My Queen, please sit."

Savannah said, "Not you, too. I am going to kill Morgan. He started this."

Lee Ann didn't know if Savannah was angry or not, so she said, "This was my idea. Please don't be mad."

Before she could finish her thought, Savannah said, "I am not mad. My men have called me that for some time. It did not set well with me at first, but I have gotten used to it now. I like it coming from you two. It sounds so much better." She had difficulty getting the last part out. She was trying not to laugh.

Monika said, "I am happy to hear that, My Queen."

Now they were all laughing.

Savannah asked Monika and Christina, "Did you get the list from Mom?"

Christina said, "Yes, we did."

Savannah said, "That is a list of all the women that Kirsten, Petra, and Mom remembered dating the FRBs. Now that we know the DNA is what they are looking for. We can find each one on that list, talk to them, and find out if their kids have an FRB father."

Monika said, "We don't know who is looking for the DNA. Will they get this list?"

Savannah said, "We don't know what they know. I don't know if they are looking for FRB kids. All we can do is find the kids and keep them safe. Not just the FRB kids, but also, if the mother had other kids, they could be used against their mother. 'Give up the one and save the others' type of thing."

Lee Ann asked, "Do you think it will come to that."

Savannah said, "We don't know. We can narrow our response when we find out who wants the DNA."

"That is why you are running a soft IT intrusion. You are banging on their door to see who opens it," Lee Ann observed.

Savannah smiled and said, "Yes, and Robin has the IP address set up to trace back to Tanzania, Africa, and nowhere else. Now, back to the list. I need you to find the ladies on that list. Interview them. Tell them you are writing an article on American-German relations and how it affected them when they were young. Use my mom's name if they ask where you got their names. Tell them you interviewed her first. Lee Ann, please help here. I need your talent. Show Monika and Christina how to do this. You cannot do this, I am sorry to say. Your German needs to be better for in-depth interviews. This may be the only way to save some people who could not choose who their father was, but they are in danger anyway."

Lee Ann said, "I will help any way I can, and you are right. My German is not good enough."

Savannah called a young lady to the table. She introduced her. "This is Pam. She is a member of the IT section. She will help you locate the people on that list without any unwanted attention to the search." Monika and Christina left with Pam.

Morgan came in and told Savannah, "We are evacuating our men from the Kush. They completed their assignment. We have one minor injury."

Savannah asked, "The opposing force?"

Morgan said, "We had overwhelming firepower and placed steel on target."

"Morgan, when we find the FRB kids," Savannah said, "we need a place to hide them until we figure out what we can do with and for them."

Morgan said, "We have the stronghold in Peru. You own it, and we have tech and supplies stored there."

Savannah said, "Good. I want you to lead the recovery team. I need someone I trust. You are my first and only choice."

Morgan said, "Thank you for your vote of confidence. I am not the person to lead that team. The reason I am not—what if the FRB kids are like you?"

Savannah said, "Taser them and keep them sedated for the trip. We are not trying to be liked. We are trying to keep them alive. We don't have a choice. If their DNA gets out and into the wrong hands, they are dead. Many others will die, and you know it."

Morgan said, "What happens after that?"

Savannah said, "We will need to move their mothers and siblings to safe areas. Get them passports. Then, have them help with secure Zoom calls. Have them tell their kids to stay with us and live there until we can move them."

Lee Ann said, "If you do that, you are no better than whoever is looking for them. Can you take the whole family at one time?"

Savannah asked, "What if they do not want to be moved? What do you expect me to do then? We cannot have this curse I carry in the hands of madmen."

Lee Ann said, "It is not a curse. Look at what you have done. You have built an empire. The men you lead call you 'My Queen.' How is that a curse?"

Savannah said, "Look at what I do. Look at the way I make a living. I run a company that is paid to solve problems by using force. Can you imagine fifty thousand people like me in the world on opposite sides trying to solve problems?"

Morgan spoke up, "Before we do anything, let's find out who we are up against. We may solve this problem by eliminating the threat. Then we can hide the other people."

Savannah said, "You may be right. My way may be the last resort."

Lee Ann was stunned. She hadn't known that Savannah felt her gift was a curse. Now she knew all her hard work and training was not to be the best; it was a way she could control herself and stay human. Her dad knew this. He also must have trained himself the same way he trained her. He wanted a life for her that was not like his. He wanted her to remain human.

Lee Ann asked, "Can you do a DNA test to find the people we need to protect?"

Morgan asked, "How do we get the DNA without tipping our hand? How do we keep the test results unseen online? Every company that performs the test shares its information.

We would give them a list of the people we are trying to protect."

CURSED SAVAGE QUEEN

Savannah said, "We find the mothers and follow the family members that fit within the age category to be FRB offspring. Go through their trash and get used condoms, tampons, and anything with their body fluid on it. If we need to, we break into their homes and steal what we need."

Morgan said, "We can do that. What about the test?"

Savannah said, "We buy a test facility under the name Lee Ann Bream. We use your maiden name, and no one can link the sale back to me or my company. We can control all test results."

Morgan said, "We can limit collateral damage to other family members by only taking the people with a positive test. This is more work, but I like it better than our other options."

Savannah asked Lee Ann, "Do you want to own a test facility?" Then she said, "Of course you do."

Christina approached and said, "It's late, and I need to get home."

Savannah said, "I am going to stay a little longer. We have a company to buy. I will have Mom's driver take you home."

The next morning, Lee Ann arrived at the new office. People were packing to leave, and others like her were just getting here. Lee Ann had just found out the office was staffed 24/7.

She saw Savannah at a desk. She was still in the same clothes she was wearing yesterday.

Lee Ann asked, "Have you been here all night?"

She looked up from her work and said, "Yes, I could not find a company to buy that did DNA testing. So, I had to find a lab capable of DNA testing. I found one in Canada. I have finalized the purchase. When Robin checked in an hour ago, we started head-hunting for a small staff."

Lee Ann told her, "I know why you are doing this, but if you keep going like this, you will be unable to help anyone. Go home and get some sleep."

Savannah said, "I will, but first, I need to get the lab staffed."

Lee Ann said, "No, we are going to the estate, and you will get some sleep. Now. Yesterday, you told me you are cursed. So, My Cursed Queen Savannah, get off your ass and come with me. Or I will kick your ass."

Savannah laughed and asked, "Do you think you can kick my ass? Do you want to try right now?" Still laughing, she got up, hugged Lee Ann, and said, "You can try later if you want to. But first, will you take me home? Please."

Lee Ann said, "Yes, of course I will, My Savage Lady Savannah."

Savannah smiled and said, "I am gaining too many titles. You are my friend. Please use my name."

Lee Ann had to poke at her one more time: "I will do so, My Cursed Savage Queen of the Phantom Warriors Savannah."

Savannah laughed and said, "Keep it up, and you will suffer my wrath," and she swatted Lee Ann's butt. She had to laugh. Savannah could crush her without any effort, but all she got was a playful swat from her sister.

F. Mays was born and raised in a very poor hard-working Texas family. He joined the Army after graduating high school. He was in disbelief when he received his first paycheck of $250.00 because he had never seen that much money, and it was his. He retired from the Army after twenty-two years and moved back to Texas with his daughter. He is very proud of her; she is the first in the family to earn a college degree.

Milton Keynes UK
Ingram Content Group UK Ltd.
UKHW022123291124
451915UK00010B/499